THE UNIVERSITY OF VIRGINIA EDITION OF
THE WORKS OF STEPHEN CRANE

VOLUME VII

TALES OF WHILOMVILLE

The Bibliographer for This Edition Is
Matthew J. Bruccoli.

CENTER FOR EDITIONS OF
AMERICAN AUTHORS
AN APPROVED TEXT
MODERN LANGUAGE
ASSOCIATION OF AMERICA

®

FOREWORD

ALTHOUGH published simultaneously with Volume I, the present *Tales of Whilomville* will eventually take its place as Volume VII in the University of Virginia Edition of THE WORKS OF STEPHEN CRANE. The principles on which the editing has been based are stated in "The Text of the Virginia Edition" prefixed to Volume I, *Bowery Tales*. The Introduction by Professor J. C. Levenson in this volume offers what facts are known about the circumstances of the composition and publication of the works under discussion and places these works in the literary and historical contexts of their time and of Crane's development as a writer. The Textual Introductions detail the physical forms of the text, their authority and transmission, and examine specific problems involved in the establishment of the text in its present critical form.

The expenses of the preparation of the texts in this volume with their introductions and apparatus have been generously subsidized by a grant from the National Endowment for the Humanities administered through the Modern Language Association of America and its Center for Editions of American Authors.

The editor is much in debt for assistance and various courtesies to Professor Robert Stallman of the University of Connecticut, Professor Joseph Katz, University of South Carolina, Professor William Gibson, New York University, Commander Melvin H. Schoberlin, USN (Ret.), Mr. Alfred Prettyman of Harper and Row, Mr. C. E. Frazer Clark, Jr., of Bloomfield Hills, Michigan, and to his colleagues Professors M. J. Bruccoli of the University of South Carolina and J. C. Levenson of the University of Virginia. Mr. Kenneth A. Lohf, Librarian for Rare Books and Manuscripts of the Columbia University Libraries, has been of unfailing and particular assistance, and the editor is grateful to the late

John D. Gordan, Curator of the Berg Collection of the New York Public Library, and to the librarians of Harvard, Ohio State, Syracuse, Dartmouth, the British Museum, and the London Library for their courtesies. Mr. William Runge, Curator of Rare Books, and Miss Anne Freudenberg, Curator of Manuscripts, at the University of Virginia have been constantly helpful, and the services of Mrs. David Yalden-Thomson as research assistant have been much appreciated. The editor's debt to Mr. Clifton Waller Barrett and his magnificent collection at the University of Virginia remains constant.

For permission to utilize as copy-texts the manuscripts of the *Whilomville Stories* and to illustrate certain manuscript pages, the editor is grateful to Alfred A. Knopf, Inc.; to Commander Melvin H. Schoberlin, USN (Ret.), owner of the manuscript of "The Angel-Child"; to Mr. Clifton Waller Barrett and the University of Virginia Library, owner of "The Lover and the Tell-Tale"; and, through Mr. Kenneth A. Lohf, to Columbia University Libraries, owner of the nine other surviving Whilomville manuscripts as well as the only preserved leaf from "The Monster."

The photograph of Stephen Crane as a boy is reproduced by courtesy of the Clifton Waller Barrett Library of the University of Virginia Library. The illustrations by Peter Newell first appeared in *Harper's Magazine*.

F. B.

Charlottesville, Virginia
September 1, 1968

CONTENTS

TALES OF WHILOMVILLE

INTRODUCTION

STEPHEN CRANE'S tales of Whilomville range in form from his last great short novel "The Monster" to some of the simplest sketches he ever wrote, just as they range in texture from his uniquely mannered and sometimes apocalyptic high style to prose of the opposite kind, austere and open and plain. But as the stories began to accumulate, Crane saw them as constituting a single group. Although he wanted to bring together the separately published earlier pieces and the series from *Harper's Magazine*, which began to appear in August, 1899, and pre-empted the title *Whilomville Stories*, circumstances of publication forestalled his desire. Yet his instinct in the matter was right. There is a unity to the stories, and it is rightly suggested by the name of the town which provides a common setting to them all. Whilomville, like Thomas Bailey Aldrich's Rivermouth and Mark Twain's St. Petersburg, had its model in the author's actual experience. Port Jervis, New York, where Crane lived from the age of seven until he was twelve, was more truly the scene of his boyhood than any of the several other towns where his father's ministerial calling took him, and as the place of his father's death it marked the closing of one major chapter of boyhood. His brother William settled in Port Jervis and became a successful lawyer there. Another brother, Edmund, whom Stephen chose as guardian after his mother died, moved in the nineties to Hartwood in the hilly and wooded back country some twenty miles from Port Jervis, and eventually he too settled in the town itself. This was the area Stephen Crane thought of as home, the place he was "from." The town provided a resource of stored observation on which he found he could draw almost without limit. It was a place, on the other hand, from which he was decidedly cut off. By the time he began using Port Jervis as literary material in the latter part of 1897, he had taken up residence in England;

and by 1899, when he was writing the Whilomville series for *Harper's*, he had missed his last chance of going back. The tales in which he created his town of Once-upon-a-time, the ideal American small town of memory and imagination, appeared to be sketches from life, but they were in fact the recollections of an expatriate.

Crane had his reasons for not modeling directly from life. For one thing, he was defensive about his fellow townsmen. After his first taste of English snobbery, he was ready to stand up and declare, "The simple rustic villagers of Port Jervis have as good manners as some of the flower of England's literary set." [1] But he was also defensive *against* his fellow townsmen. When his brother William let him know that "The Monster" had prompted a certain amount of local gossip, Stephen cannily replied, "I suppose that Port Jervis entered my head while I was writing it but I particularly dont wish them to think so because people get very sensitive and I would not scold away freely if I thought the eye of your glorious public was upon me." [2] He had in fact taken care to cover his tracks. In an early note he listed names for future reference:

> Dr Edmund Trescott (M. D.) ("Ned") Lives corner of Niagrara Avenue and Ontario St. New House. Loves good horses.
> Grace, his wife. Originally from Connecticut.
> Jimmie their son. Only child. Strict obedience to father. [3]

Though the doctor bears the given name of Stephen's brother, the name does not occur in the story; and his being called "Ned" would not lead to the man in real life who was known to his intimates as "Teddy." Also, though his other brother William had, like Dr. Trescott, a substantial new house in a new part of town, Port Jervis has neither a Niagara Avenue nor an Ontario Street. It is, after all, in a region where the *Delaware* River and *Wyoming* Valley provide commonly adopted names. On another

---

[1] Thomas Beer, *Stephen Crane: A Study in American Letters* (New York, 1923), p. 168.

[2] Brede, March 2, 1899, ALS in University of Virginia Library.

[3] The list appears at the reverse end of Cora Crane's manuscript book, in the Stephen Crane Collection, Columbia University Libraries. After the family names the rest of the page is blank, but on a new leaf one more name appears, that of Judge Denning Hagenthorpe, one of Dr. Trescott's loyal friends among the solid citizens of the town.

track in search of actual models, Thomas Beer thought at one point that he had traced the origin of Henry Johnson to a "disfigured teamster in Port Jervis" by the name of Levi Hume, but he could find no one to confirm the suggestion.[4] Other particular sources, both plain and disguised, are to be noted in the sketches in the *Harper's* series, but they too contribute little to an understanding of Crane's fiction. Early and late, such items furnish evidence for a negative argument: despite his own simple ideas of art as literal representation, his work is not sufficiently accounted for in that way. Whatever else it may be, his realism is not simply a matter of direct rendering of an observed object.

Crane's realism must be defined by other exclusions, too. For one thing, even though Whilomville is important as the setting for the stories, it is not very fully realized as a place. Neither houses nor rooms nor streets nor landscapes are given a specific, independent existence. The local color which editors recommended for giving short tales and sketches a larger coherence is noticeably absent. Port Jervis was, despite Crane's affectionate joking about the "simple rustic villagers," a typical county seat and market center, with a monument to its canal builder as well as its Civil War dead. It was not very active, perhaps, but it was part of the larger world. Crane had an interest in its earlier history, but he did not feel called upon to record a real or fictitious past or any special flavor of local custom or dialect. Indeed, Whilomville is indefinite with respect to time as well as space. Although the presence of children at or near the center of the stories seems to invite the reader's nostalgia, there is no calendar by which the feeling can be measured. There is no sense of an irrevocable past and no concentration on the process of memory recapturing what is lost. There is no sense, either, of a vanishing present. Although the stories are presented as if they have just taken place, the now of the fiction seems to be unchanging. Whilomville exists outside of time, exempt from progress. But when the people, the place, and the historical moment are none of them particularized, the result is realism with a

---

[4] Beer to Edmund Crane, Yonkers, N.Y., Oct. 30, 1922, ALS in University of Virginia Library. Edmund Crane had died on September 20, 1922, and neither his widow nor his daughter could answer Beer's question. Edna Crane Sidbury said that her father, William Crane, believed a local carter, "his face eaten by cancer," to be the model, but she gave no name ("My Uncle, Stephen Crane, as I Knew Him," *Literary Digest*, IV [March, 1926], 248).

difference. There is still the illusion of actuality, enforced by the immediacy, accuracy, and vividness of Crane's writing, but the traditional categories by which realists had understood their materials are dispensed with.

Crane's representational technique is not the only reason why Whilomville bears the stamp of reality. The town is real, not because it can be photographically verified or rationally located in accordance with common-sense geography or history, but because it existed, as it still exists, in the minds of men. It is the embodiment of the tacit beliefs which Crane shared with his countrymen, real in the sense that it could palpably affect their lives and yet as intangible as any other cultural construct. It is an ideal American society, not faultless by any means, since an ideal—to be believed in—must be believable, but basically humane, equalitarian, and peaceful. It is a middle-class utopia, in which the state has virtually disappeared along with all evidence of public life. Here the concerns of men center in private interest and domestic life. Here, also, the rule of equality provides that even children and their desires and feelings are to be taken seriously. The principles by which this fictive society is organized are real enough for commentators from Tocqueville on to have noticed them at work in the actual America they were observing. Crane offered no ideological scheme by which to explain the way people conducted themselves in their business and public lives, but he did render the utopian ideal by which they seriously wished to organize their common life. And if calling Whilomville a utopia makes it sound "unreal" in this respect, it is important to remember that this model society stands in contrast to the spurious utopia of sentimentalism, in which such social aims are reduced to mere wishfulness and treated as if they explained all behavior. Thus the dream world of *Little Lord Fauntleroy,* a book which Crane thought "no kid except a sick little girl would like," [5] offered a foil for realism. It set, for popular taste, a standard according to which Thomas Bailey Aldrich and Mark Twain and Stephen Crane all wrote stories of bad boys. Obviously the word *bad,* as the opposite of *too good to live,* left plenty of room for

[5] Crane to a "Book Reviewer," [Brede, early 1900?], *Stephen Crane: Letters,* ed. R. W. Stallman and Lillian Gilkes (New York, 1960), p. 280.

Tom Bailey or Tom Sawyer or Crane's Jimmie Trescott to be fundamentally good. By allowing for mischief and a natural aptitude for minor lying, Crane and the others gave realistic plausibility to materials which sentimental perfectionists habitually falsified. By writing of "bad" boys, they could present a more convincing image of the small town as an unfallen world, a good society with real people in it. By their psychological accuracy they made it seem that such a social order was attainable or, even, attained somewhere not very far away.

In "The Monster," the first of his Whilomville tales, Crane put the town into a fuller context than in any of the later stories. The domestic certitudes are there, but they do not by any means define the boundaries of the presented world. With an accuracy of notation that extended far beyond the children of the tale, he told how Dr. Trescott, firmly set in the established order and prompted only by motives of which his society approved, acted to bring on himself a relentless process of exclusion and alienation. At this level of generalization, one can even say that the story is taken from life: not that the incidents of the story actually occurred, but that Crane analogized from his own experience. Just as he claimed to have learned the emotions of *The Red Badge of Courage* on the football field, he could be said to have learned the emotions of "The Monster" in the events which cut him off from Port Jervis, from New York, and from the United States. What his experience taught was that in order to remain in the comfortable safety of the domestic order, it was not enough to have the prescribed virtues of honesty, good intentions, and a sense of obligation. Even in the realm of imagination, these virtues proved dangerous. Honesty, for example, the main tenet of Howellsian realism, led him early into dark areas which it took Howells many years to reach. The distinctive note of his writing was the perception of a world beyond the accepted order he had been brought up to cherish. His special subjects, war and poverty, were beyond the pale of gentility, but subject matter alone did not account for his alienation. Howells himself proved that the motive of informing the educated public of scenes, situations, and social classes beyond their everyday awareness was by and large compatible with American middle-class values. For Crane, however, seeing "with his own pair of

The other girl, Dora Clark by name, was not so easily got off. But at that juncture Crane's friend the chorus girl wailed, "If you don't go to court and speak for that girl, you are no man!" Crane's first response to this further demand on his gallantry was one of common sense: "By George! I cannot. . . . I can't afford to do that sort of thing." [9] Unfortunately he did not hold to his refusal. He testified for Dora Clark not only in magistrate's court, where she was cleared of the particular charge, but also in her suit against the arresting officer, which, given her record, she could not possibly have won. And Crane, despite the friendship initially of Police Commissioner Theodore Roosevelt and of other commissioners as well, found that he had helped in an attempt to "get" a policeman and thereby made himself persona non grata to the force. The result was surveillance, threatened arrests, and general harassment by the police—enough so that he came to think that he could no longer live in New York. As he reflected in a note written at the time of the Dora Clark trial, "There is such a thing as a moral obligation arriving inopportunely. The inopportune arrival of a moral obligation can bring just as much personal humiliation as can a sudden impulse to steal or any of the other mental suggestions which we account calamitous." [10]

Another adventure beyond the bounds of American normalcy had still greater effect on Crane's being able freely to go home. After the Dora Clark affair had occupied Crane—and the newspapers—during much of September and October, Crane headed south in November, 1896, to cover the Cuban revolution. In Jacksonville he struck up with Cora Howorth Stewart, the keeper of a flashy nightclub-hotel and the toast of visiting newsmen. She could talk like one of the boys, she could keep herself distinct from the girls who frequented her establishment, she was intellectually responsive to Crane's writing as well as a sympathetic listener to his talk. After the sinking of the *Commodore* on January 1 and the ordeal which he was to make the subject of

[9] "Adventures of a Novelist. By Stephen Crane. The Distinguished Author's Narrative of How He Sought 'Material' in Real Life in the 'Tenderloin' and Found More than He Bargained For," New York *Journal*, Sept. 20, 1896; reprinted in *The New York City Sketches of Stephen Crane and Related Pieces*, ed. R. W. Stallman and E. R. Hagemann (New York, 1966), pp. 228–229.

[10] *New York City Sketches*, p. 260.

"The Open Boat," it was she who cared for him. Crane had been in love with other women, but they had always been too prudent to become involved in the unstable life of a writer. Now Cora, on the other hand, after their "honeymoon" in the Indian River swamp country, declined to become uninvolved. Although she stood 100 per cent for female emancipation, she was five years older than Stephen and made wiser by the unhappy experience of two failed marriages. So she took thought not only for the liberation of women, but also for a new morality. "I've no claim upon you," she told him. "But I know now—though I did not always think so—that the obligations we have incurred in the past are chains forged whether we will or no, to bind the future." [11] So they were. When Crane went off to report the Greek-Turkish War, she followed him across the Atlantic, made the grand tour with him, became the "first woman war correspondent" and otherwise shared his life, and after the brief campaign returned to England and set up housekeeping with him. The irregular arrangement (Cora's second husband had never given her a divorce) seemed to work out well, except that Cora shared two of Stephen's great weaknesses: she was ever hospitable to friends who descended for meals or weekends, uninvited and in incredible numbers, and she had a fateful compulsion to spend more and more lavishly as the unpaid bills mounted. As for Crane, though he was willing to work very, very hard to try and pay for the indulgence and the gaiety, he had a romantic incapacity for thrift in any sense. He was also too gallant ever to think of his destiny as chains. Yet he had reason once more to consider the meaning of obligation, however casually or untimely incurred.

The theme of "The Monster" is adapted from Crane's experience of obligation and its consequences, but the details of the story which express that theme are a matter of his invention. The story opens with Dr. Trescott mowing his lawn and little Jimmie playing nearby. When the boy accidentally tramples a peony bed, we have occasion to glimpse an idealized all-male domestic scene: the seven-year-old who tells only the truth to his father and the father who dispenses a justice that is regular but

[11] Lillian Gilkes, *Cora Crane: A Biography of Mrs. Stephen Crane* (Bloomington, Ind., 1960), p. 65.

mild discuss the accident, and when they agree that the proper penalty should be temporary banishment from the garden, the boy meekly withdraws to his favorite refuge, the stable. What the opening scene establishes is that in the circle of private life, fathers have a place as well as mothers—and reasonability as well as sentiment. The complications arise when violence invades the tranquil world of domesticity. On a warm Saturday night when the doctor is away on a late call, fire breaks out in his house. Mrs. Trescott, "waving her arms as if they were two reeds," screams at the Negro stableman Henry Johnson to save her child, and he plunges through the smoke to rescue the sleeping boy. Johnson, trapped and almost submitting to the terrors of the fire, remembers a passage through the doctor's laboratory, but he is just too late: "The room was like a garden in the region where might be burning flowers. Flames of violet, crimson, green, blue, orange, and purple were blooming everywhere." Here, in this surrealist inversion of the peaceful domestic garden, in this otherworld where violence weirdly triumphs over order, the rescuer collapses. And at this juncture, among men who experience the two worlds of Stephen Crane, a special bond is forged. The now-returned doctor, met by his wife's screaming, goes into "the garden of burning flowers" and succeeds in bringing out the blanket-wrapped child, while a nameless bystander from "one of the rear streets near the Trescotts" brings out the apparently lifeless Johnson. Thereafter the doctor commits himself to saving the man who tried to save his son, even though he stands warned that he may be committing "one of the blunders of virtue." In restoring life to one whom Nature had given up, he is told, he would be creating a monster. In Crane's domestication of the Frankenstein theme, Johnson recovers life, but with his face burned away and his mind destroyed; and Dr. Trescott must confront the power he has evoked, not in the harmless Negro swathed in bandages, but in public opinion. For the townspeople quickly tire of heroism and want the strange survivor of the fire put away where he cannot frighten the squeamish. As the victim of horrible experience gradually becomes a horror to others, the doctor keeps his loyalty to Henry Johnson at the expense of alienating his prissy friends and neighbors and a great many of his patients. Neither the economic pressure of a rapidly shrinking practice nor the prudent advice of well-meaning friends can bring the doctor around, but the story ends as the last turn of the screw is applied: the doctor counts the unused Wednesday-afternoon teacups of his socially boycotted and sobbing wife. Loyalty to Henry Johnson, the highest value in the plot and the ground of a possibly tragic commitment, has evidently come to a dead end. That a woman's tears can end what a woman's screams began suggests where the ultimate power lies in domestic fiction; but before Crane arrived at that point, he went far to prove that he could conceive a private world that included men as well as women and children. Within that world, an ideal model realistically examined, he explored the ways of moral obligation and found the point beyond which commitment meant a final and absolute exclusion from the happy arrangement of things-as-they-are. At that point he stopped.

To say that experience gave Crane his theme and invention, his plot, is not the whole story, for though the details of "The Monster" are not literally taken from life, they have an imaginative history—a set of sources to be traced at deeper levels of the writer's consciousness. The fire, for example, seems to have had its origin in a sketch which Crane did for the New York *Press* of November 25, 1894, headlined "When Every One Is Panic Stricken" but simply called "Fire!" in the typescript which the author preserved.[12] In this newspaper story, the smoke "writhed out from the tops of the second story windows, and from the basement there glared a deep and terrible hue of red, the color of satanic wrath," prefiguring the serpentine flames that twisted in the weird garden of fire where Henry Johnson fell. There is also a frenzied mother, screaming for her baby and tossing her arms "in maniacal gestures," and a man who reacts instantaneously by plunging into the inferno to attempt a rescue. Moreover, the horror of nature gone wild is matched by a horror of human helplessness that is scarcely distinguishable from indifference:

> "Say, did a copper go in there?"
> "Yeh! He come out again, though."
> "He did not! He's in there yet!"

[12] Stephen Crane Collection, Columbia University Libraries; reprinted in *New York City Sketches*, pp. 97–102.

"Well, didn't I see 'im?"
"How long ago was the alarm sent in?"
" 'Bout a minute."

Like the watchers in the crowd, the sketch writer lost track of both rescuer and child, but though he turned his attention elsewhere, the raveled threads of the story stayed in his mind as a symbolic problem which he had not worked out. That it was genuinely a symbolic problem is borne out by curious circumstance: search of other newspapers around that date, according to John S. Mayfield, discloses "nothing at all about any fire having taken place, much less about any policeman rescuing a child from a burning building." [13] The scholarly search for rescuer and child testifies, like the admiration of Howells and the editor of the *Press*, Edward Marshall, to the vividness of Crane's writing. But the fact that policeman and child drop out of the sketch halfway along is itself evidence of a made-up story; there seems to have been no rescue, even in the fictive realm, because the situation and its possible meanings had not yet been worked out.

The problem of fire and rescue crossed with another problem, and a less conscious one, namely, Crane's affinity for naming characters Jimmie. His first Jimmie is "the little champion of Rum Alley," in *Maggie*, the fierce street urchin with a brutal father and drunken mother, whose situation is a nightmare parody of conventional domestic tranquillity. Jimmie Johnson was a frightful *alter ego* of the novelist; his last name, John Berryman points out, became the intended first name of Crane's pseudonym for the 1893 *Maggie*.[14] The "Johnson" connection to "The Monster" is evident, though it is not so clear what to make of it. A more intricate history lies behind "Jimmie," which has a second and quite different starting point in that exemplar of true courage Jim Conklin, who, in *The Red Badge*, seems to die in order that Henry Fleming may live. In a short sequel to that novel, "The Veteran" (1896), old Henry Fleming scandalizes his

---

[13] *American Book Collector*, January, 1957; quoted in *New York City Sketches*, p. 97 n., by the editors, Professors Stallman and Hagemann, who strongly concur in the view that the story is a hoax.

[14] *Stephen Crane* (New York, 1950), p. 194. A printer's error changed the name to "Johnston Smith."

grandson, called variously "little Jim" and "Jimmie," by telling how he had run at Chancellorsville. The old veteran explains that standing up to fire depends on getting used to it, unless one is like "young Jim Conklin, Old Si Conklin's son—that used to keep the tannery—you none of you recollect him—well, he went into it from the start just as if he was born to it." The veteran almost immediately gets the chance to demonstrate his point, for fire breaks out in his barn. He goes unhesitatingly into the barn, rescues horses, cattle, and panic-stricken farmhand, and at the end goes back into the fiery barn for the almost forgotten colts —" 'The poor little things,' he said." Perishing in that last attempt, he undergoes apotheosis:

> When the roof fell in, a great funnel of smoke swarmed toward the sky, as if the old man's mighty spirit, released from its body—a little bottle—had swelled like the genie of the fable. The smoke was tinted rose-hue from the flames, and perhaps the unutterable midnights of the universe will have no power to daunt the color of this soul.

The debt to Jim Conklin, which gives meaning to the name of Henry Fleming's grandson, is redeemed in the spontaneous act of courage and sacrifice. But the solution to the problem is so neat as to require more mythic belief than a reader may be willing to lend.

"The Monster," too, depends on an antirealistic symbolic moment, an ordeal of fire that changes everything, but that visionary moment is set in a realistic context and presented in a tone that is wholly unsentimental. The story is told at first from a boy's point of view. Then the narrative moves to the townspeople who, in the banality of barbership conversation or the easy leisure of a Saturday night band concert, establish the social setting. Not until after the fire breaks out do the principals of the action take control of what the readers see. But when first Henry Johnson and then the doctor brave panic and go in to rescue little Jimmie, the reader sees the ordeal as they do and shares the experience of the irrational which binds them together. After that climax, the stableman and the doctor share the bond of being outsiders. Henry Johnson is outside the perceptual range of the townspeople at first merely because he is a Negro and later because his facelessness has become a literal fact, while Trescott becomes an outsider because he holds to an obligation of love and honor and thus isolates himself from men of changeable opinion and short memory. As John Berryman has argued, the characters may be conceived as expressions of Crane's response to authority, suffering, and redemption in the unconscious depths of his mind. Given the pressure from within, Crane was able to organize recurrent figures of his imagination in a fable which also measured the possibilities and limitations of the ideal American small town. At its widest reach of suggestion, it is a fable of relations between the races, which begins in utopian pleasantness with little Jimmie's visit to his friend at the stable and ends with Dr. Trescott facing a characteristically American dilemma. For handling this dilemma between loyalty to friend and prudence for family, the ideological resources of Whilom-ville—as of Mark Twain's St. Petersburg—are inadequate. If, as Beer says, Crane thought the ending of *Huckleberry Finn* to be poor,[15] he now learned something of the difficulty involved. Having shifted the focus of his own boy's story to the world of adults, he invited his readers to compare the doctor's counting of empty teacups and Huck Finn's final view of Widow Douglas' "siviliza-tion," two symbolic judgments on a social ideal that could not cope with the exigencies of American life.

Crane's ability to fuse such a variety of materials, social, psychological, and literary, in "The Monster" is ample evidence that in 1897 he was at the height of his powers as well as the crest of his career. On their return to England, he and Cora had taken a house in Oxted, Surrey, where he settled down to hard work. At first the financial pressures to which he was responding seemed only moderate. He owed McClure's five hundred dollars on old advances, and payment from other publishers was barely trickling in; but his work went well, and gaiety seemed to go with productivity. One of his most convivial friends was Harold Frederic, the newspaperman and novelist who had sent home the first dispatches of Crane's British fame and thus helped to make the American success of *The Red Badge*. Frederic had his own unusual establishment—with his mistress and children—in Kenley, not far from the Cranes. One August afternoon, while they were driving over to see the Frederics, the Cranes' horse ran away,

---

[15] *Crane*, p. 113.

their carriage overturned, and they sustained serious injuries. The Frederics took them in and nursed them back to health. Although Crane was later to reckon the economic loss heavy which kept him from his desk for several weeks, the recuperation merged into a happy jaunt to Ireland as the Frederics' guests. There, as far as conceivable from the social and moral environment of Port Jervis, he wrote "The Monster." On September 9, in a letter from Schull, County Cork, he wrote his brother Edmund that he had "finished a novelette of 20,000 words—'The Monster.'" [16] The same tide of energy which produced this story led in quick succession to "The Bride Comes to Yellow Sky," "The Blue Hotel," and "Death and the Child," as well as lesser work. Yet the flood of imagination was not the only interesting part of Crane's history during these months, for the same period is marked by his not mentioning his private life in his letters home except in the vaguest terms. Specifically, neither his September letter to Edmund nor a letter of October 29 to William Crane mentioned marriage. To William he declared that he was settling down in temperament, but he omitted to mention the one fact which had most to do with his settling down and most to do with his not going home. As if he were making a general reference to the New York newspaper scandals after the Dora Clark affair—a year before—he told his brother that he was worried about the gossip that must have found its way to Port Jervis: "I have managed my success like a fool and a child but then it is difficult to succeed gracefully at 23. However I am learning every day. I am slowly becoming a man. My idea is to come finally to live at Port Jervis or Hartwood. I am a wanderer now and I must see enough but—afterwards—I think of P. J. & Hartwood." [17] Toughening himself against malicious talk, postponing nostalgia till the discipline of the writer be mastered, even recollecting how he used to borrow but explicitly not asking for a loan "in my present financial extremity," [18] Crane was still keeping his nerve in a time of strain. But the strain was there, nevertheless, in the deferred confrontation of facts as well as creditors.

Although the facts of his private life had much to do with the

[16] Berryman, *Crane*, p. 189.
[17] London, Oct. 29, [1897], *Letters*, p. 147. Crane gave his return address in the letter, not as Oxted, but care of his London publisher, William Heinemann.
[18] *Letters*, p. 148.

writing of "The Monster," it was his relation to creditors that had most to do with its publication. Among these was McClure's, which evidently took Crane manuscripts as security for loans even when it had no intention of publishing the work. In October he wrote to his American agent, Paul Revere Reynolds, and gave him complete charge of all his writings:

Now one of the reasons of this thing is to get me out of the ardent grasp of the S. S. McClure Co. I owe them about $500, I think, and they seem to calculate on controlling my entire out-put. They have in their possession "The Monster" (21,000 words) and "The Bride Comes to Yellow Sky" (4500) both for the American rights alone. The American rights alone of "The Monster" ought to pay them easily, minus your commission. No; perhaps it wouldn't pay them fully but it would pay them a decent amount of it. . . .

Robert McClure here in London told me he thought you had "The Monster" in New York but I judge, if that were so, that you would have mentioned it in your letter this morning. I will write to Phillips [John Phillips of McClure's New York office] and ask him to let you have it under the agreement that the money minus your commission shall be paid to them. Then *if* the money for "The Monster" goes far toward paying my debt, you can ask them about "The Bride." [19]

In the letter to William, written later in that same month of October, 1897, he gave roughly the same view of his affairs, claiming to have earned some two thousand dollars since his coming to England but to have received in cash not even $120. And the mortgaged manuscripts were the center of the problem: "McClures, with security of over 1000 dollars against my liability of four hundred, refuse to advance me any money." [20] By December he was instructing Reynolds to try McClure's for an advance on his "Greek novel" (*Active Service*) and offering to mortgage "Death and the Child" as he had the earlier stories. He thought he was clear of the earlier debts when he pleaded: "For heaven's sake raise me all the money you can and *cable* it, *cable* it sure between Xmas and New Year's. Sell 'The Monster'! Don't forget that—cable me some money this month." [21] Reynolds was able to act promptly on this plea, and on December 20 Crane responded

---

[19] [Oxted, Oct., 1897], *Letters*, pp. 144–145.
[20] London, Oct. 29, 1897, *Letters*, p. 146.
[21] [Oxted, Dec., 1897], *Letters*, p. 157.

favorably to an offer from Harper's to pay $450 for the serial rights and $250 as an advance toward book publication. His answer indicated that, while McClure's was still being difficult, his English publisher Heinemann was most co-operative:

The Harpers terms I perfectly understand and agree to them. I will send over soon, proofs of a lot of stuff of mine which is to appear in the English edition of The Open Boat, but not in the American edition. These stories added to the Monster would make about 40000 or 45000 words. If Harpers does not like this plan, it would be necessary to wait until I had finished more stories. I will soon forward my plan of the book as it could be made from existing stories unpublished and published. Heineman by the way promptly and politely released me from an agreement which would have prevented us from selling the international book rights to Harper's. . . .

Why McClure is monkeying around about The Monster I dont quite understand. It might make me come a cropper if I dont get that money directly.[22]

Christmas and New Year's came and went with the business still unsettled. On January 14, 1898, however, it seemed as if an end had been reached. Crane wrote to Reynolds:

I received your letter yesterday and promptly cabled you that McClure was not concerned in the matter. When I sent him "The Monster" I owed him a lot of money but when I paid him up, I went to see Robert McClure here and he agreed that "The Monster" was released. He said he would inform the N.Y. office to that effect or even write the same to you, if I liked. I said I did like but it seems the affair was bungled. McClure's claim on the story was one which I gave him through courtesy and honor—no other. Your final manipulation of the novelette I consider very brilliant and I am sorry to see it handicapped by that Scotch ass.

In all the months I have been in England I have never received a

---

[22] Oxted, Dec. 20, [1897], typed copy in Syracuse University Library. The financial details, not given in this letter, are taken from Harper and Brothers Contract Book 10, p. 322, contract of March 8, 1899. The $450 was not paid until the legal obstacles put in the way by McClure's were cleared in January, 1898.

The typed correspondence in the Syracuse University Library collection of Stephen Crane material consists of copies made by Ames W. Williams from ALS originals sold as item no. 32 in the Parrish sale by Parke-Bernet on March 3, 1938, some sections from which were also quoted in the catalogue. Ownership of these letters seems to have passed to Commander Melvin H. Schoberlin, USN (Ret.), but they are at the moment of writing in storage and unavailable for inspection and identification.

cent from America which has not been borrowed. Just read that over twice! The consequences of this have lately been that I have been obliged to make arrangements here with English agents of American houses but in all cases your commission will be protected. This is the best I could do. My English expenses have chased me to the wall. Even now I am waiting for you to cable me my share of the Monster money and if there is a fluke I am lost.[23]

But of course the episode was not over. On January 31 he noted that McClure's had taken the last $71.09 of his debt out of a payment for other, later work. At the same time he had had a chance to understand that McClure's did not represent his only complication. International copyright arrangements meant that he did not have for Harper's a ready-made book of stories: "Of course I see my mistake about their taking some of the stories that Heineman is to use here."[24] It was finally March 31 when Reynolds settled the agreement with Harper's for "The Monster" and "another story" and drew half the advance ($125).[25] Crane had extricated himself from having anticipated his literary productivity with one publisher only to get into very much the same sort of position with another.

"The Monster" was involved in Crane's life in ways other than economic, for it brought out more sharply the difference between an old easygoing friendship like that with Harold Frederic and the special intimacy of fellow artists that existed between Crane and Conrad. Impressed by *The Nigger of the "Narcissus"* as he was reading it in a serial version, Crane arranged to meet Conrad in October, 1897. They became friends at once. It turned out that Conrad was at least as much Crane's admirer as the other way around and that they shared aims so closely that each of them overcame his usual reticence for literary talk. But they saw each other rarely that autumn since Conrad's wife was about to give birth to their first child and could hardly travel to Oxted, and Conrad himself, apart from his being occupied with his work and with the depressions that kept him from work, did not fit easily into the informality of the Crane household. Crane did visit the

[23] [Oxted], *Letters*, p. 168.

[24] Crane to Reynolds, Oxted, Jan. 31, [1898], typed copy in Syracuse University Library.

[25] Harper and Brothers Contract Book 11, p. 18.

Conrads at Stanford-le-Hope on Sunday, November 28, and it seems to have been on this occasion that he told Conrad about "The Monster" in some detail. The two were out of touch during the next few weeks when there was so much business activity about the story, but on January 16, just when the *Harper's Magazine* sale was completed, Conrad wrote to announce the birth of his son and added the postscript: "Say—what about *The Monster*. The damned story has been haunting me ever since. I think it must be fine. It's a subject for you." [26] Such sympathy and encouragement were typical of Conrad's relation with Crane, and they stood in contrast to the hearty insensitivity of Harold Frederic. Frederic was one of the "Comanche braves," as Crane called them, who "seem to think I am running a free lunch counter." [27] It was a run on the free lunch counter by Frederic and five of his friends that forced Crane at one point to flee his own house in order to have quiet for his work. It was in character, however, that he should soon have had Frederic as his guest again and, mindful of Conrad's responsiveness, that he tried reading "The Monster" to him. Frederic, according to another listener on that occasion, found the story offensive and told Crane to throw it away, and Crane reacted strongly. This was a story, he told his friend, "with some sense in it," and as for the shock to public taste, why "men of sense" would not care that the victim should have been made faceless.[28] The defense became more and more heated, and when Frederic went on to include Conrad in his literary condemnation, Crane exploded, pounded the table for emphasis, and smashed a luncheon plate. The shattered decorum of that moment provides a measure of the strain under which he was laboring, for Crane was known for his consistently even temper: Mrs. Edmund Crane reported that she "never saw him angry nor excited," [29] and Cora, protesting too much perhaps, recorded in a notebook "To use in Stephen's Life," "He never got in childish rages with people because they did not

---

[26] [Stanford-le-Hope], Jan. 16, 1898, *Letters*, p. 169.

[27] Crane to Acton Davies, [Oxted, Dec. 5? 1897], *Letters*, p. 155.

[28] Beer, *Crane*, p. 165. The other listener was Sanford Bennett, who was deeply affected by the story.

[29] Edith F. Crane to Thomas Beer, Port Jervis, Nov. 19, 1922, ALS in University of Virginia Library.

consider his work as good as he, himself considered it." [30] Moreover, the strain must have been made greater by an intuition that
the mixed response of his friends might represent the larger
world. The incident with Frederic occurred at almost the same
time that Richard Watson Gilder of the *Century* promptly returned "The Monster" manuscript to Reynolds, supposedly saying, "We couldn't publish that thing with half the expectant
mothers in America on our subscription list." [31] Luckily, however,
the world included Conrad as well as Frederic, *Harper's* as well
as *Century*. Two letters of February 8, 1898, underscore the
point: Frederic wrote to Cora Crane acknowledging that his invitation to renew the Irish holiday of the previous summer could
not work since "so much had changed since then," [32] and Crane
wrote to Reynolds, "Please say to Harpers that it will be very
necessary for me to have early proofs of The Monster as I note
now, from the original ms, many crudities of style." [33] Amidst the
welter of complications, he still could turn his mind to essentials.

The reworking that Crane did for the final version of "The
Monster" can be estimated from the single leaf of surviving
manuscript, the last page (page 68) of the story. As is often the
case with his work for which fair copy exists, the changes are
few and involve relatively unimportant niceties. That "the wind
was whining round the house," instead of *around* it as the manuscript has it, may well have been a change made by printers; but
that the doctor, with his unhappy wife in his arms, "found himself occasionally trying to count the cups" instead of *beginning* to
count them is typical of Crane's logical fussiness, since the doctor
not only began his count but reached the number fifteen by which
to reckon the desertion by Whilomville of his cause and his
family. In the final draft itself Crane had added the word "new"
in describing the sudden crimson of the stove, underscoring thus
the reminder of fire which was literally a part of the final domestic scene. More suggestive than this evidence of Crane's last
retouchings is the other side of the surviving manuscript leaf.
This is a canceled earlier draft of the beginning of "Chapter

[30] MS in Columbia University Libraries.
[31] Beer, *Crane*, p. 164.
[32] Kenley, Feb. 8, 1898, *Letters*, p. 174.
[33] Oxted, Feb. 8, [1898], typed copy in Syracuse University Library.

XXXIII," actually Chapter XXIII, the next to last chapter of the tale. The story must have been nearly in final shape, for the page number 64 indicates the same numeration as the final 68-page manuscript. The scratched-out draft shows that Crane thoroughly rewrote the chapter opening after having worked out a clearer conception of changing seasons and of foreshortened time between the disasters of the early-summer Saturday night and the beating snow of winter on that final Wednesday of the story. The changes are principally additions by which he made over the realistic and almost plain setting into an expression of enveloping sadness:

Early Draft: The autumn smote all the leaves and the trees of Whilomville were in crimson and yellow. The little boys dreamed of the [prospective time *deleted*] near time when they could heap bushels of brown leaves in the [dusk *deleted*] streets and burn them during the abrupt evenings.[34]

Final Text: The autumn smote the leaves, and the trees of Whilomville were panoplied in crimson and yellow. The winds grew stronger, and in the melancholy purple of the nights the home shine of a window became a finer thing. The little boys, watching the sear and sorrowful leaves drifting down from the maples, dreamed of the near time when they could heap bushels in the streets and burn them during the abrupt evenings.

As the winds mount about Whilomville, the cadences of "The Open Boat" seem to echo. In that story, which offers a paradigm for Crane's tragic imagination, the ordeal of the irrational occurs at sea rather than in fire; when the narrator's sensibility has been awakened by suffering, it is the mawkish poem "A soldier of the Legion lay dying in Algiers" which changes from something meaningless into "an actuality—stern, mournful, and fine"; and balancing the waste of disaster and death, there is "the subtle brotherhood of men that was here established on the seas" and which the narrator "knew even at the time was the best experience of his life." In "The Monster," instead of abrupt waves, there are abrupt evenings; instead of the banal "soldier of the Legion," now "the home shine of a window became a finer thing"; but instead of the subtle brotherhood of the sea, there is nothing. The sense of that nothingness is the other meaning of the empty

[34] MS in Columbia University Libraries.

teacups, a meaning which transcended the symbolism of small-town social life and thereby made it clear what Whilomville left out.

II

Because Harper and Brothers wanted to publish "The Monster" in book form in both New York and London, they declined to fill out the volume with previously published stories that would compromise their international rights. Consequently, Crane kept back "The Blue Hotel" from British publication so that it could meet the Harper stipulation. He sent the story to Reynolds on February 7, 1898, at the same time that he was juggling "Death and the Child" in McClure's direction. The instructions he sent suggested that he had been making private promises to his old creditor McClure's, but he added a literary rationale:

> Besides it would be absurd to conjoin "Death and The Child" with "The Monster." They don't fit. It would be rotten. Now, "The Blue Hotel" goes in very neatly with "The Monster" and together they make 32,000. Very little more is needed for a respectably sized $1.00 book, and that can be readily submitted within the next six weeks.[35]

Commenting that his settling in England had put him $2,000 in debt, he promised to "bombard" Reynolds with material until he should have worked himself into the clear. The agent, however much faith he may have put in that promise, could not persuade Harper's to share it. On March 3 he settled for $125, that is, for half the advance agreed on for the volume, because Harper's would pay only for completed manuscript in hand. On March 13 Crane renewed his plea to him to "try to get the book right £50—from Harper." [36] But matters remained at a standstill until "His New Mittens" eventually completed the volume.

A great deal happened in the year before the matter was settled. At the end of March, 1898, a financial crisis was expected in the Crane household, but it seems to have been put off by more borrowing. In April, Crane decided suddenly to go to Cuba to cover the Spanish-American War, a war that would have

---

[35] [Oxted], Feb. 7, [1898], *Letters*, p. 172.
[36] Oxted, typed copy in Syracuse University Library.

the advantage, from his point of view, of being fought in English rather than Greek. His scheme must have been more or less a practical one, for Joseph Conrad was ready to help his friend by borrowing £50 from Blackwood's with his own future work pledged as security. Pulitzer's *World* wanted Crane to report the war for them, but before he accepted, he tried to enlist in the navy, according to Beer, and had the shock of learning that he did not qualify physically. His depression at that news and later the effects of hardship and Cuban fever partly explain the long lapses of his letters in the next few months. At the beginning there was another explanation, too. Pulitzer had chartered the seagoing tug *The Three Friends* as a press boat, and Crane found himself on a Caribbean jaunt with some of his newspaper cronies from the Greek war. No letters of his from this period got through to Cora, as none of hers reached him, but the few surviving letters sound cheerful enough. On the other hand, John Berryman reports that beyond the circle of his old friends Crane was not at all popular with correspondents on the press boat: "There was his fame, and his incongruity with it—slovenly in a wretched outfit, taciturn, ironic, unwilling to talk about his books or pass gossip about his celebrated friends." Instead of shining as a famous star ought, he set himself apart as the man who wore pajamas all day and worked at his writing table. The origin of "His New Mittens," Berryman tells us, was "an incident, not altogether humorous, of the casual persecution he enjoyed" aboard the tug, an incident apparently focused on his singular dress.[37] In any event, Crane was able to work at his fiction as well as his dispatches—Pulitzer was later to question whether he worked hard enough at the latter. On May 30 he wrote to Reynolds from "Off Havana": "I enclose you a short story of boy life in Whilomville—the town of The Monster. I think Harpers ought to take it for about £40 and also cough up that other $125."[38]

Apart from the incident on *The Three Friends*, "His New Mittens" depended on Crane's biography in a more general way. It is the story of a boy who runs away, written by a man who had

---

[37] *Crane*, pp. 218, 220. Berryman, when he uses sources which he is not permitted to cite, has been consistently corroborated by the results of later research.

[38] Typed copy in Syracuse University Library.

put three thousand miles between himself and his urgent respon-sibilities. Such analogies to the writer's experience, however, only become interesting because the *literary* biography behind the story helps account for the excellence of the telling. To find his way back to the Whilomville material, Crane had invented a new set of characters—characters that did not compel him to deal with recurrent motifs from his deepest imagination but did permit him to adhere more closely to the child's point of view and to say some original things about a boy's psychology. For rendering this special subject, the sustained metaphor he used was the game of war. The correspondent on active duty, what-ever the burden of smarting injury or escapist fantasy that he may have been expressing, had control enough of his actual situation to play with it in imagination.

The leading characters of "His New Mittens" comprise a group which, better than that of "The Monster," fits the canons of domestic fiction: they are a seven-year-old boy, his widowed mother, and the maiden aunt who lives with them. The boy is set apart from other children, who can enjoy their after-school snow fight, because he has been strictly enjoined not to soak his new red mittens. The other boys, instinctively detecting the cause of his holding back, taunt him with being "A-fray-ed of his mit-tens!" and chase him away. Describing the boy's flight, Crane revealed what was early and late the first principle of his work-ing psychology: "He had, of course, the dismal conviction that they were going to dog him to his grave. But near the corner of the field they suddenly seemed to forget all about it. Indeed, they possessed only the malevolence of so many flitter-headed spar-rows. The interest had swung capriciously to some other matter." The lesson of the child was not very different from that of Henry Fleming in *The Red Badge*: men who were reduced by extraordi-nary stress to their natural state, and boys in their normal cir-cumstances, were subject to the capricious flux of consciousness; the emotions of the playing field and the emotions of red battle could be mutually enlightening. Despite the fall in intensity from the rock-throwing street fight of Rum Alley to the safe snowball-ing of Whilomville, Crane in his later work was showing a more seasoned skill and achieving something original in his psycholog-ical realism. The novelty of "His New Mittens" was not a matter of the code which makes boys cruel to an outsider—in the country of Hawthorne, Crane could hardly claim originality for that! —but the speed with which they forget their jeering once little Horace has joined the embattled play-soldiers and Indians. In the boys' war game Crane applied his conception of the stream of consciousness to both the group and the individual with equal sureness. The changeable flow of inner emotion and outer event sets the condition in which boys, or soldiers, or men under the pressure of crisis must act.

Crane's other innovation in this story was to suggest that for Americans, in Whilomville at least, the war between the sexes had become a war of mothers and their boy-children. Little Horace, marched home with his wet mittens, is put in isolation to contemplate his guilt, but stern punishment is confused by the plate of food that is brought to him in his confinement. The child recognizes in his way that in a maternally centered family, nurture is transformed into an instrument of domination. At any rate, he knows that if he rejects the solicitation of love and refuses to eat, he can usually bring his mother round to softer sentiments and get her to forget her sternness. The play of self-pity and anger, even "hatred," in his mind becomes more and more intense, since each time he feels tempted to eat, he resolves anew to hurt his mother by depriving himself. The outcome is that the rejection of food grows into a decision to run away. And when Horace slips out into the snowy, windy night, he seems suddenly to have reason for his self-pity: "Panting, stung, half-blinded with the driving flakes, he was now a waif, exiled, friendless, and poor. With a bursting heart, he thought of his home and his mother." Then he switches easily to renewed anger at his mother's "merciless ferocity. . . . It was she who had thrust him into this wild storm." Despite the swift and erratic changes of emotion, intelligence of a sort does function, and the boy quickly realizes that he cannot make good his running away. Aware that he is "conquered" but concerned not to "surrender" before the most advantageous moment, he spots the ideal refuge in the Niagara Avenue butcher shop that belongs to a friend of his father. Seen through the window, the chunks of beef, the strung-up pigs, the hanging turkeys, are not to be thought of as food to beguile a child and rule him; rather, they are the fine solid realities of a manly and workmanly world. At the center of all and presiding over this masculine scene is the friendly Mr. Stickney, "whistling cheerily and assorting his knives." Once the boy has entered this man's world, emotions no longer get in the way of facts and he easily assents to the idea of being taken home. And his friend the butcher, who understands the whole situation at a glance, gives him believable reassurance: "It'll be all right. I'll fix it." Moreover, properly timed surrender proves to be a conquest of sorts. After the tearful reunion in which both mother and boy are at once contrite and joyous, the stern maiden-aunt gets the last word, using women's weapons to the very end: "Aunt Martha turned defiantly upon the butcher because her face betrayed her. She was crying. She made a gesture half military, half feminine. "Won't you have a glass of our root-beer, Mr. Stickney? We make it ourselves.' " The conclusion of this war game, as is usual in such literary battles, seems happily to fit with the order of nature and the renewal of society. But the society being reconfirmed in this case is a rather special one, even for domestic-sentimental fiction. The comedy ends with the sound, not of wedding bells as under the older convention, but of suppressed maternal sobs. But the tears signify a kind of pleasure, and the ending—so ambiguous as to be win, lose, and draw all at once—is doubtless to be taken as happy.

"His New Mittens" did not portend an imminent capitulation to domesticity on the part of Crane. A rather different turn of events was in store for him, for shortly after he sent the story to Reynolds on May 30 his luck and his health began to run out. After this date there is less and less evidence of his literary work, like correcting proofs and sending them off to Reynolds. Rather, he became more and more deeply engaged in the observation of combat, and word began to spread of his hardships, gallantry, and even reckless self-exposure before enemy fire.[39] On July 8, when he had been delirious for two or three days, he was sent back to Old Point Comfort, Virginia, as a suspected victim of yellow fever.[40] His problem was not yellow fever, however, and

---

[39] See, for example, Ralph Paine, *Roads of Adventure* (Boston and New York, 1922), pp. 244 ff.

[40] Ames W. Williams and Berryman suggest that hardship and the onset of his fatal tuberculosis brought on the physical breakdown at this time (Williams, "Stephen Crane, War Correspondent," *New Colophon*, I [April, 1948], 119; Berryman, *Crane*, p. 225). In this they follow Beer (*Crane*, p. 194).

insofar as it was exhaustion, rest helped him considerably. It was at this time that he may have made a trip to the Trudeau Sanitarium at Lake Saranac, New York, in order to be checked by the great tuberculosis specialist.[41] Although he did not get a good report from Dr. Trudeau, he went doggedly back to the war zone, this time for Hearst's *Journal.* By late August, when the Porto Rican campaign was over, he managed to get into Havana despite a general ban on American reporters. There he re-enacted halfway round the world his earlier flight from Oxted to London, when he had to escape from "Indians" in order to work and set himself up from his labors in no less an establishment than Brown's Hotel in Albemarle Street. Now, he took rooms at the Hotel Pasaje—the reporters' dream, according to Ralph Paine [42] —and began writing furiously in the attempt to get himself out of debt. Crane's detractors suggest that the undocumented period of his stay in Havana was a time of escape into dissipation,[43] but the flow of stories and dispatches is evidence that he was working hard. His letters to Reynolds indicate awareness that his English creditors were closing in on Cora (for example, in early October he wrote, "If I dont receive a rather fat sum from you before the last of the month, I am *ruined*" [44]) and that his own situation in Havana was precarious. He had to move into cheap quarters, for Hearst cut off his expense money and left him with the big hotel bill he had run up, plus the need to work off his advance at twenty dollars a column, a figure calculated originally on the basis of his expenses being paid.[45] He had got into literary peonage worse than ever, and there was every reason to believe his declaration in a letter to Reynolds: "I am working like a dog. When—oh, when,—am I to have some money? If you could only witness my poverty!" [46] His long-standing scheme to write syndicated features was frustrated by his owing copy to Hearst, and he came to the end of his ideas for becoming solvent

[41] Dr. Edward Livingston Trudeau to Cora Crane, Paul Smith's, N.Y., Sept. 16, [1898], *Letters,* p. 184.

[42] *Roads of Adventure,* p. 281. For good reason, according to old Baedekers.

[43] They are followed by Frederick Lewis Allen, *Paul Revere Reynolds* (New York, 1944), p. 62. Allen carelessly speaks of Crane's being "enamored" of Havana as if he were a runaway on a spree.

[44] [Havana, Oct., 1898], typed copy in Syracuse University Library.

[45] Crane to Reynolds, Havana, Oct. 24, [1898], typed copy in Syracuse University Library.

[46] Havana, Nov. 1, [1898], typed copy in Syracuse University Library.

again. In November, just as "His New Mittens" was coming out simultaneously in *McClure's* and *Cornhill*, he called an end to his withdrawal from the world and cabled his brother William for money.

Actuality did not have so neat an ending as fiction. It seems unlikely that William Crane sent the money which enabled Crane to leave Havana, and when Crane got to New York he made no attempt to see his brother. Cora, who had endured long lapses in which she heard nothing from him and who must have wondered if she had been deserted, did not jump at his suggestion that she leave their British creditors and the place in the world she had made for herself and join him in New York. Crane for his part learned that a fresh start in New York would hardly be easy for anyone with his fine set of enemies, but he stayed on in the city for almost six weeks. When he finally determined to go back to England, he left without having once gone home to Port Jervis. He did not know that Cora had made herself known to William by cable in one of her anguished inquiries after her missing and silent husband, and he had no idea of how to break the news of his marital state. His brother, however, did know how to break the ice, and Stephen's first letter home after his return to England was a warm, though scarcely candid, response:

My dear William: So I have run by you in the dark again but really my position in England was near to going smash and I rushed to save it as soon as I could get enough money to leave Havana. Appleton's cable me that for the past 12 months my royalties amount to *thirty-five dollars*. Do you know what they mean?

Yes, it is true I am married to an English lady and through her connections we have this beautiful old manor but we are beastly short on ready money owing to my long illness and that is why I want to propose the five hundred loan. Otherwise I may go bankrupt here in February. If you can do it, cable me "Crane, care Sunlocks, London." You need merely say "Sending." Love to all from the wayward brother.[47]

Cordiality was in order all around. The older brother, who became "My dear Will" in later letters, eventually provided the

[47] Letterhead of Brede Place, Northiam, Sussex, [probably Oxted, January, 1899], ALS in University of Virginia Library.

cash,[48] and there followed an active and friendly correspondence.

Once the family relation was re-established, Stephen sent his brother a historical account of Brede Place, the manor where he and Cora were about to start economizing on a still grander scale, and he even began talking about a family visit to Port Jervis that he and Cora might make "as soon as I am out of this hole." [49] And he hoped William and his wife would visit Brede in the spring. But wishful thinking did not do much to alter the essential difficulty that he was trying to climb out of quicksand. Among the facts he could not wish away was the slowness of concluding literary business. Thirteen months after "The Monster" had been sold as part of a book and more than six months after he had sent in "His New Mittens," the book had not yet taken shape. Pressing need for what he now regarded as Harper's "miserly £25"—the sum still payable as an advance whenever the book should be completed—led at last to the making of a table of contents. Crane's process of thought was manifest in the letter he sent Reynolds on January 19, 1899:

I am all fuzzy with money troubles and last night a writ was served on my by a leading creditor. I must raise heaven and earth between now and the middle of February. I must have every pennie that you can wrest from the enemy. Go to Harpers and beg them for that £25. It is only fair that they shoud pay it because it was *they* who proposed buying the book rights of the "Monster", for a £50.— advance. We didn't make any such suggestion. Indeed we were rather reluctant. Then they discover that they don't think the book is long enough and hold out £25.— —. Who on our side said anything about the length of the "Monster"? Ask them why they don't print "The Blue Hotel" and "His New Mittens" in one volumn with the "Monster" and then pay up like little men. That would make 36000 words. I fail to see where they get such a hell of a right to decide as to what stories shall be published in a book that bears my name in a damn sight bigger type than it bears their imprint.[50]

48 W. H. Crane to Cora Crane, Port Jervis, April 30, 1900, refers to the £100 sent to his younger brother in March, 1899 (*Letters*, p. 279).

49 Two letters on Brede Place letterhead, one dated Feb. 6 and therefore written at Oxted, the other undated but written before the loan of $500 had arrived, ALS in University of Virginia Library.

50 Typed copy in Syracuse University Library.

As Crane progressed in this letter from a tone of complaint to one of authority, he revealed how little he had been in control of his own affairs during the long period of his absence and illness. "I find," he wrote, "that 'His New Mittens' has been published over here in 'Cornhill'—where did they get it? And who reaped the money?" But it was only one short step from seeming to take matters in hand to *merely* seeming to do so. As he contemplated his situation, a note of overconfidence crept in, followed by a switch to self-pity: "I can make lots of money this year if I can only get started fair. If I can't raise some money at once I'm going bankrupt. You know what that means. It won't do. I am going to borrow money from pretty near every body in the world and you must give me all the assistance you are able. I had just got things arranged in England so that I could live for half what I've been usually spending and taking that in conjunction with my increased power of making money, the cruelity of any smash now is beyond language." The flux of thought and emotion, for Crane, was rapid, and in particular he moved very quickly from his conception of a project to his counting of the reward. But the realities of his world had a pace of their own. On March 6, 1899, not quite a year after he received the first half of his advance, the payment was completed, and Harper's proceeded to draw up the final contract (dated March 8).[51] Crane's instinct had been right, nine months before, when he suggested that "His New Mittens" would round out the volume, but his sense of timing had been very wrong. Copyright for the finished volume was applied for on November 2 and copyright deposit made on December 2, 1899, with the official announcement of publication made in the *Publishers' Weekly* for December 9. By that time more changes had occurred in his life, adding up to more of the same frenzied finance, weakened health, and driven talent. It was not long after the volume finally came out that the final change and the last ordeal of character began.

III

Crane's failure to get letters or money through to Cora during his time at the wars, followed by his virtual disappearance in Cuba

---

[51] Harper & Brothers Contract Book 11, p. 18; Contract Book 10, pp. 321–22.

and his lingering in New York, made it seem as if he was running away. Yet he could at no time have had a very strong illusion of escape. In the man's world of war reporters there had been mean jealousy as well as comradeship and courage, and along with adventure had come hardship that broke the body and sapped the will to live. On the supposed holiday in Havana, expense-account living gave way suddenly to poverty such as he had not known since apprentice days. In the Bohemia of New York, where he struck up exciting new friendships with men like Huneker and Ryder, he also found that old grudges among the police lasted undiminished. Besides, wherever he went, he had his unfulfilled contracts with publishers on his mind and tried to do something about them. His habits of hard work were as astonishing as his knack for inopportune commitments and his apparent irresponsibility. Just as absence had not been the same as escape, return was not simply surrender. In England he had a place in the world that had been enhanced by Cora's rise in the Society of American Women in London; it was through her new connections that she arranged to rent the grand, if dilapidated, manor house at Brede for them. In England, even during absence, old ties of friendship strengthened: Joseph Conrad, Henry James, and Edward Garnett looked forward solicitously to his return. In England, most of all, he was taken seriously as an artist. Garnett, at the end of 1898, published his important essay in praise of Crane's work, and Crane was delighted to have the essay greet him almost literally as he got off the boat.[52] But such public recognition happened also to indicate how very much Crane's professional career was tied up with his domestic. Garnett had naturally sent a copy of the essay to Cora, who acknowledged it gratefully but went on to take wifely exception to its one note of stricture. When Garnett suggested that Crane's talent depended on a fund of experience that might soon run out, she reacted at once; and in her reply, with a dignity which was both real and affected, she disclosed her view of the artist as family man:

[52] "Stephen Crane: An Appreciation," *Academy*, LV (Dec. 17, 1898), 483–484. Crane landed at Gravesend on January 10 or 11, 1899, and on January 13 he received from Conrad a letter thanking him for the return of the £50 loan and commenting on what must have been a jubilant note: "You haven't lost time in looking up the old Academy. I only heard of it today" (Stanford-le-Hope, *Letters*, p. 205). Clearly he had lost no time.

Dear Mr. Garnet: Thank you so much for sending me the clipping. I like it very much indeed—one must value a true opinion: but I disagree with you when you say that he may fail when the "picturesque phases of the environment that nurtured him give out." The beautiful thoughts in Stephen's mind are simply endless! His great difficulty is the lack of that machine-like application which makes a man work steadily. I hope that the perfect quiet of Brede Place and the freedom from a lot of dear good people, who take his mind from his work, will let him show the world a book that will live.[53]

Crane returned to a domesticity such as he had never known, for while he was away Cora had worked to provide him with a ready-made family. When Harold Frederic died in October, 1898, she took in Kate Lyon and her children, Frederic's second household. After a while Kate Lyon went up to London with her seven-year-old daughter Helen Frederic, but Héloise and Barry, at ages five and four, stayed on with their nursemaid at the Cranes'. Cora, with unusual practicality, worked to establish a fund for the Frederic orphans so that Stephen would not be burdened with their support, and she also saw to it that the children went up to stay with their mother during the January of Crane's return.[54] He for his part liked the idea of the enlarged family circle, and they arranged for the two younger children to join them as soon as they should be able to move to Brede. The prospect led his mind back to Whilomville, and he began to write children's stories again. The new beginning was sudden and decisive: on January 19, when he wrote Reynolds that he was taking his affairs in hand, he gave no hint that "The Monster" and "His New Mittens" might lead to other stories about the same town, and indeed neither of those tales implied further development of the subject. To get to Whilomville, Crane had to go back of the parable of the runaway child and, still more important, back of the realistic story which related the child's world of once-upon-a-time so forcefully to the world of anarchic

[53] Oxted, [Jan., 1899], *Letters*, p. 203.

[54] John Scott-Stokes, co-chairman with Cora of the Frederic children's fund, responded to her plan by writing: "This—your idea—is excellent and generous. No, Stephen must *not* be saddled with the burden of supporting this young family" (Purley, Surrey, Jan. 3, 1899, ALS in Columbia University Libraries). Also in the Stephen Crane Collection at Columbia are the receipts for the support money forwarded to Kate (Lyon Frederic) Forman during January.

violence. Domesticity took him in precisely this direction, and by the end of January he had completed the first two of the new series of *Whilomville Stories*.

"Lynx-Hunting," the earliest story to be composed in this new series, depended for its anecdote on an incident of Stephen Crane's childhood which he referred to laconically in an autobiographical letter some months after he had written the story: "Will, one of my brothers gave me a toy gun and I tried to shoot a cow with it over at Middletown when father was preaching there." [55] It also depended on his recollection of what the Port Jervis landscape had been like for boys, especially "that freeland of hills and woods in which they lived in some part their romance of the moment—whether it was of Indians, miners, smugglers, soldiers or outlaws. The paths were their paths and much was known to them of the secrets of the dark-green hemlock thickets, the wastes of sweet-fern and huckleberry, the cliffs of gaunt blue-stone with the sumach burning red at their feet." The boys' fancies put them in touch with something their elders missed: "The grown folk seemed to regard these wastes merely as so much distance between one place and another place or as rabbit cover, or as a district to be judged according to the value of the timber." In contrast to the utilitarian calculations of adults, the play of children evoked a mystery of being that enhanced their lives. The realities they touched were not necessarily benign, and their acts did not invite sentimentalizing. When the boys, armed with Willie Dalzel's gun, encountered "an innocent bird who happened to be looking another way at the time," one shot "blew this poor thing into a mere rag of wet feathers." Such antisentimental toughness suggests that there is a great deal of observation as well as reminiscence in this sketch. Crane's delight in the fact that boys may lie "as naturally as most animals swim" and his sympathetic notation of the flux of fear and guilt that children as much as soldiers may feel testify that the mature realist had found a fresh subject. And yet it took a leap of childlike fancy to put him in touch with this special world, a fancy that ruled out of consideration some of his most important themes. Crane, for his leading character, revived Jim-

[55] Crane to Willis B. Clarke, [Brede, Nov. 1899], *Letters*, p. 243.

mie Trescott: the child who had once been burned so badly now reappeared without a scar. And when Jimmie shoots at a chipmunk, with at least one eye squeezed shut, and sets "bellowing and bucking" the poor cow that had been grazing in his line of fire, the outraged farmer who comes upon the scene is a similarly unscathed Henry Fleming. Considering these two remarkable recoveries, the truthfulness of the child's world in this story seems less than the whole truth of human experience that Crane had once insisted on. The only ordeal of fire in this tale is in the imaginary "agonies of the fire-regions" suffered by the boys when they see the farmer coming. But the grim figure who approaches, fortuitously, with whip in hand does not administer hellish punishment to the guilty. Instead, when he hears the boy's panicky claim that he thought the cow was a lynx, the old farmer laughs himself helpless. The terrors of authority, like those of nature, seem more fabulous than real when the fiction of children evokes them.

Once Crane left the realm of the ordeal for that of domestic accommodation, he took up the role of family man with enthusiasm. The woman he had left behind had been the World's First Woman War Correspondent. The vigorous and well-established matron to whom he came back turned his mind to home thoughts, and in those first days of their reunion Stephen and Cora came to know each other more intimately than either would have guessed possible in their more adventurous youth. The prospect of children in the household aided the spirit of reminiscence, and in the exchange of recollections the young couple gradually forged common memories. Out of such memories Crane made "The Angel-Child," combining an incident out of his own past with characters out of Cora's. The child called "Cora" in the story has plenty of what is called cuteness but little character; apart from the name, however, there is Cora Crane's explicit testimony to identify her as the Angel-Child.[56] More to the point, the parents of the fictional Cora are an ineffectual artist and a proud and dominating woman who resemble John and Elizabeth Howorth, the parents of the actual Cora.[57] The anecdote of the

[56] Edith Crane to Beer, Poughkeepsie, N.Y., Jan. 14, 1934, ALS in University of Virginia Library.

[57] Gilkes, *Cora Crane*, pp. 30–36, offers the evidence for taking Crane's characterization as modeled on them. Supporting testimony comes from Edith

money carelessly given to the spoiled child may have belonged to Cora's past, but using the money to cut off Fauntleroy curls and thus to break the hearts of foolish parents comes from Stephen's. Since it is a twice-told tale, however, once told of brother Edmund rescuing Stephen from the onus of his golden tresses and once told of Stephen rescuing some anonymous young sufferers in Albany, New York,[58] it is fair to wonder if the incident may not have been made up. Reminiscence and invention are woven together by literary means that were to serve for this story and a number to follow. In the telling of the tale, Crane established what were to be his Whilomville conventions: the children act spontaneously and see things as they happen; the women, who set the tone of the town, cry after illusion, sentiment, and rank; Dr. Trescott, and by implication a few other men of his sort, stand at the calm center of things and offer a norm of the good and reasonable. In retrospect, "Lynx-Hunting" was a farewell to themes of man and nature that run through Crane's work, whereas "The Angel-Child" opened a new line of development. "Lynx-Hunting" was a boy's story, but "The Angel-Child" was a children's story which involved the family and town—children in society rather than boys in the woods. Because it pointed forward thus, it rightly came first when the editors of *Harper's Magazine* began publishing the series in August, 1899. But Crane, in his enthusiasm for the story, seemed to be prompted less by the opening of new material than by the origins of the story in his household circle. In sending it to Reynolds, he subsumed his own opinion of it in the family view: "We all think that this is the best story that I have done for many a moon." [59]

The aura of shared reminiscence also hovers over the third story of the new group, "The Lover and the Tell-Tale." This time the memory concerned the Crane household during Stephen's absence. While little Helen Frederic was still staying with Cora in the house in Oxted, Michael Pease, the eleven-year-old son of the Cranes' good friends from nearby Limpsfield, fell very much

---

Richie Jones, the Crane's guest at Brede from July, 1899, to January, 1900: "One day Stephen was talking about his *Whilomville Stories.* He said most of them were founded on stories Cora had told him of her childhood" ("Stephen Crane at Brede," *Atlantic Monthly,* CXCIV [July, 1954], 60).

[58] Beer, *Crane,* p. 111; Berryman, *Crane,* p. 13.

[59] Oxted, Jan. 31, 1899, typed copy in Syracuse University Library.

in love with her. The letter of Jimmie Trescott to the departed Angel-Child may well be a word-for-word transcription of a letter of Michael Pease, or at least Michael Pease thought it possible fifty years after the event.[60] But the incident of the telltale, as Mr. Pease affirmed, belongs entirely to Crane's invention. The schoolgirl who spies out Jimmie's letter is a study on a small scale of the backbiting female gossip who occupied so special a place among Crane's dislikes; but despite his animus, he gave a circumstantial and sympathetic account of the way she came by her priggery and viciousness. Once again, he redeemed a slight story that seemed to play on sentiment by the shrewdness of his telling.

Sorting out the chronology of the *Whilomville Stories* makes it clear that economic pressure constantly made itself felt in the midst of Crane's domestic felicity. As to "Lynx-Hunting," there is no way to date it more precisely than after January 19, 1899, and before "The Angel-Child." The latter story Crane sent to Reynolds on January 31 (the word count confirms the identification) with comment on the making of the *Monster* volume and on the prices he could get for serial publication. He wrote: "Here is another story (3500 words) which belongs to the Whilomville series. I am annoyed with the Harpers and I dont care whether they get their bookful or not. I would rather you would treat this as a boost on the McClure loan, if your keen eye discovers that this loan is certain. For my second reason I would again point out to you that my English magazine rights are now going for a sure nine guineas a thousand words, and so it does not behoove me to sell many stories to the three all-over-the-places. Indeed, you might point out to some of these people that I can no longer afford to write for either Century, Harper's or Scribners." [61] Determined to get separate fees totaling more than the single payment that the international magazines might offer, he sent a second copy of "The Angel-Child" the next day to James B. Pinker, his London agent, and this time he made it clear that "Lynx-Hunting" had been previously submitted: "I enclose you a short story (3500 words) which is in the same series with 'Lynx Hunting,'

[60] Michael Pease to Melvin Schoberlin, Cambridge, Eng., Nov. 27, 1948, ALS in University of Virginia Library.

[61] Letter already cited of Jan. 31, 1899.

'The Monster,' and 'His New Mittens.' We like it a little—Harper's, in one sense has the bookrights to this series but this right is mainly based upon an artistic reason—the fact that I do not think it correct to separate the stories. (Harper's have the rights to the Monster.)" [62] In adding that he had sent a copy of "The Angel-Child" to Reynolds on the previous day, he made clear the history up to that date both of his manuscripts and of his emergent intention to develop the Whilomville material into a single book.

After February 1, 1899, the chronology becomes more obscure. Early in the month, in an exchange of presents preceding the Cranes' move to Brede, Cora Crane sent Mrs. Edward Pease a manuscript of "The Angel-Child" to go with what she called Michael's story: "I thought you would like them both. You can see that Michael for the moment is 'Jimmie,' and he writes to 'The Angel Child.' " [63] Yet Crane did nothing about sending "The Lover and the Tell-Tale" to an agent until March 2. In the meantime, while forwarding another story on February 13, he once more brought up the question of the Whilomville series with Reynolds:

I suppose I have not yet had time to hear from you in regard to "Lynx Hunting" and "The Angel Child"? Of course Harpers should have the whole collection but they dodged first on "His New Mittens" and now

[62] Oxted, Feb. 1, 1899, *Letters*, p. 206.

[63] It is likely that this letter refers to an earlier gift of the manuscript of "The Lover and the Tell-Tale" presented in person, for the Pease family kept the two manuscripts with but this one letter of transmittal. Even so, Crane's giving away a manuscript before selling the story is hard to explain. Because of the problems of chronology, it is worth recording the letter in full. It is on letterhead stationery of Brede Place and is undated:

My dear Mrs. Pease: We are so very pleased with the warming-pan, and we shall use it, too. It's really very kind of you to give it to us but believe me, we appreciate it very, very much.

I was going to send you by tonights post the enclosed ms. of a little story that comes before Michael's "story." I thought you would like them both. You can see that Michael for the moment is "Jimmie," and he writes to "The Angel Child." Tell him, I shall ask him to bring the pigeons down to Brede.

This is to be our P. O. address—but you must run in as you are going by—and give us a chance of seeing you once again before we go.

Very Sincerel Ever
Cora Crane

ALS in University of Virginia Library.

with you in the U.S. getting quite ten pounds a thousand for the American serial rights alone and Pinker over here getting quite seven pounds a thousand for English serial rights alone, it seems that the International Magazines are mainly a source of pain and they will jolly well have to wait until my present difficulties are over. Anyhow the book could'nt come out until next year. Because I'm going to have two big novels this year.[64]

Apparently Crane had misunderstood just how much he was being paid, for he was later content with ten pounds a thousand words for international rights.[65] What helped him settle for the lower figure was Pinker's failure to sell the new Whilomville stories in England, combined with Reynolds' arrangement for *Harper's Magazine* to have first refusal of all such stories Crane might write. On March 2, when he finally sent "The Lover and the Tell-Tale" to New York as "a third story to follow 'The Angel Child,' " he commented to his agent: "I will not offer it for sale over here until I hear from you that Harpers have refused it. . . . Your last two sales with Harpers pleased me immensely and I was delighted to withdraw them without sacrifice from Pinker who was ass enough to think them not good enough." [66] Four days later, when it turned out that another story was to be withdrawn from the English market, Cora took up correspondence with Pinker on Stephen's behalf. Playing the role of wife and partner with a truly Dickensian haughtiness, she told him:

I cannot understand what can be the reason for the English publishers refusing such stuff as those children stories and "God Rest Ye." They seem to fancy themselves as judges of literature but to me they appear to be a good set of idiots to refuse really clever and artistic stuff and to print the rot they do. Mr. Reynolds has pleased us very much by his prompt placing of these stories. We hope that you will be equally successful in placing the serial rights of "Active Service" and in also, perhaps by pointing out to London publishers that Harpers have not only thought "Lynx Hunting" and "The Angel Child" good

---

[64] Brede, Feb. 13, 1899, typed copy in Syracuse University Library.

[65] When, the following October, Pinker tried to sell some Crane stories to *Scribner's*, and referred to the *Harper's* rate as ten guineas per thousand words, he was—very likely on instructions—trying to raise the rate ([London], Oct. 26, 1899, *Letters*, p. 237 n.).

[66] Brede, March 2, 1899, typed copy in Syracuse University Library.

enough but have asked for *all* the "Whilomville" stories that Mr. Crane may write, that they have a lot to learn and that the firm of Pinker are the people to teach them. It is a good opportunity for you to let them know that there are others, as we say in America.[67]

By March, then, three of the *Whilomville Stories* were written and a sure cash market was set up at *Harper's Magazine* for further stories to come. This tally, confirmed by Crane's letter to his brother (and prospective creditor) William, also written on March 2,[68] requires that several letters published under conjectural dating as of February be reassigned. The letters to Pinker, nos. 274, 277, and 278 on pages 212 and 214 of *Stephen Crane: Letters*, edited by R. W. Stallman and Lillian Gilkes, must be dated after August 4, when the London agent began handling Crane's stories for the American market; the *Harper's* arrangement had at first edged out Pinker so that, when Crane acknowledged sale of "The Lover and the Tell-Tale" on March 31, he congratulated Reynolds invidiously: "I may say for your edification that you have one bitter enemy in England, Pinker by name." [69] Also, the word count mentioned in those letters indicates that they refer to "The Carriage-Lamps," "The Knife," and "The Stove," the first two of which were paid for, under the immediate cash system, in September.[70] Moreover, there is evidence of only one more Whilomville tale sent to Reynolds in March, and the covering letter of March 30 mentions neither title nor word count.[71] The reason for the falling off was hardly Crane's desertion of a lucrative arrangement; it was simply that in March and April he was working desperately to finish his novel *Active Service*. While he was giving the novel priority, he had time to give to the business but not to the production of stories. March thus became the month of final negotiations concerning the *Monster* volume. On March 8, a little more than a year after they had paid the first half of the advance on *The Monster and Other Stories*, Harper's drew a check for the remaining half and turned over to Reynolds a contract for publica-

[67] Brede, March 6, 1899, *Letters*, pp. 216–217.
[68] Brede, March 2, 1899, ALS in University of Virginia Library.
[69] Brede, March 31, 1899, typed copy in Syracuse University Library.
[70] Crane to Pinker, Brede, Sept. 22, 1899, *Letters*, p. 231.
[71] Brede, March 30, 1899, typed copy in Syracuse University Library.

tion.[72] Discussion presumably followed, for it was not until March 15 that Reynolds forwarded the contract to Crane along with his queries about giving up dramatization rights and about a proposed four-month lag between royalty statements and actual payment.[73] Crane returned the contract on March 31 with the objections which Reynolds had prompted and with some unsettling suggestions of his own concerning the table of contents. He wanted to withdraw "The Blue Hotel" from the collection since its inclusion had been proposed "before any other stories of Jimmie Trescott had been written" and as "an expedient to fill up space":

I suggest now that the phrase in the contract should read: "The said work is to include stories by the author entitled "The Monster, His New Mittens, Lynx Hunting, The Angel Child, The Lover and the Tell-Tale and is also to include other stories of Whilomville which have not yet been named." This to my mind would make a grand book. For my part I would consider it the best book which has yet come from my pen. However I recognize the right of Harper & Bro's. to have the phrase read as it now reads in the contract if they chose because it was originally our proposal.[74]

How much longer the dickering continued after the last surviving document of the affair cannot be guessed. But luckily Crane had, out of recognition of Harper's legal rights in the matter, hedged the suggestion that might have delayed publication indefinitely. Harper's was able to proceed to manufacture the book, applying for copyright on November 2, 1899, and making copyright deposit on December 2, sixteen months after the magazine appearance of the title work. Reynolds patently had consulted his client's interest in sticking to the original selection of stories and getting the book published at last.

Reynolds continued to work during the spring of 1899 to secure book publication of the new series. The result was a new advance payment for Crane and eventually a second book from the group of stories which the writer counted on for only a single volume. But Harper's was wary of advances to Crane and stipulated conditions by which the advance would be forfeited and the

---

[72] Harper and Brothers Contract Book 10, pp. 321–322, cited above.
[73] New York, March 15, 1899, ALS in Columbia University Libraries.
[74] Brede, March 31, 1899, typed copy in Syracuse University Library.

stories combined with those in the *Monster* volume, if the equivalent of a dozen more stories totaling 40,000 words were not supplied by the end of 1899. The proposal, which also renewed the exclusive option of *Harper's Magazine* to serial rights, went out on May 31, and on the next day there was a flurry of cables. Immediately on receiving the offer, Reynolds sent word to Crane; then, as soon as he got the acceptance, he wrote Harper's for an immediate check for the advance of $250, collected the payment, and cabled the funds to Crane.[75] The reward of such effort is obscure, for the Crane-Reynolds correspondence survives incom-

[75] The proposal was made by letter, Harper & Brothers (Per J. F. P.) to Reynolds, New York, May 31, 1899, Harper and Brothers Contract Book 11, pp. 64–65.

Dear Sir:

Your letter of the 23rd inst. is at hand.

We have purchased the serial rights of Mr. Stephen Crane's four Whilomville Stories, viz:

"Making an Oracle",

"The Lover and the Tell Tale",

"Lynx Hunting",

"The Angel Child",

for which we paid $481.75—the stories making 9600 words. They have been handsomely illustrated by Mr. Newell. In order to make a volume of convenient size for publication, the equivalent of at least twelve more stories should be supplied, so as to bring the entire matter up to about 40,000 words. If Mr. Crane will agree to supply before November next say twelve available stories to fill out the volume, as explained, we will make the advance of $250. asked for, upon the following understanding:

1. That we shall have the option of the exclusive use of the stories in HARPER'S MAGAZINE.

2. The stories to be subject, however, to the acceptance of the editor of HARPER'S MAGAZINE.

3. The stories in all to make not less than 40,000 words.

4. Mr. Crane to give us the book rights of the said stories upon the basis of a royalty of fifteen per cent. of the trade-list retail price of all copies sold, subject to the same terms and conditions as those for the publication of "The Monster" —the payment of $250. to be treated as an advance of such royalty.

5. If Mr. Crane fails to supply the available stories, as required, on or before Jan. 1, 1900, we shall be at liberty to include the four Whilomville stories now in our hands in the same volume with "The Monster", "His New Mittens", and "The Blue Hotel", and in that case, the $250. which we proposed to advance, together with the $250. which we have already advanced to Mr. Crane on account of royalty upon the volume containing "The Monster", that is to say $500. in all, is to be full payment for the American copyright in this one volume of short stories.

The relaying of Crane's acceptance and the forwarding of the check are documented in Reynolds to Harper and Brothers, New York, June 1, 1899, Harper and Brothers Contract Book 11, p. 64, and Harper and Brothers to Reynolds, New York, June 1, 1899, Harper and Brothers Contract Book 11, p. 66.

pletely and the record lapses after that fateful day. But Pinker in London evidently became sole agent for Crane's new work during the summer. The change must have occurred very near August 4, when Crane wrote to Pinker: "I enclose a statement concerning the best American buyers. I shall write to some of the editors who lately [have] been asking me for stories." [76] If, as Crane earlier suggested, there was rivalry between Reynolds and Pinker, it is hard to say who benefited most from this reversal of fortunes. By October 24 Pinker was explaining to the importunate Cranes that he had already advanced them some £230 [$1150] for stories on which he had not yet received payment.[77] The pressure mounted still higher until, at the first of the year, it seemed to reach a snapping point. When Cora tried to mollify Pinker's resentment, the hard-used agent replied on January 9:

I am sure it is not necessary for me to tell you that you and Mr. Crane may always count on all the help I can give, but as you know, the demands on my help have been greater in extent and persistency than was ever contemplated, and I was therefore very much surprised to receive Mr. Crane's letter of the 5th. As you and he think I misinterpreted it, let me repeat what he said: —

"I must have the money. I cannot get on without it. If you cannot send £50 by the next mail, I will have to find a man who can. I know this is abrupt and unfair, but self-preservation forces my game with you precisely as it did with Reynolds."

If this did not mean what I took it to mean, I am at a loss to understand it. However, I am glad to have your assurance that Mr. Crane did not threaten any breach of our Agreement.[78]

The crisis with Pinker suggests rather forcibly what must have happened between Crane and Reynolds in the summer of 1899.

The evidence of Crane's relations with publishers and agents, together with pertinent letters and fragmentary records that have survived in manuscript, sheds some light on when the *Whilomville Stories* were composed. Except for the reversal of order

[76] Brede, Aug. 4, 1899, *Letters*, p. 223.
[77] London, Oct. 24, 1899, *Letters*, p. 236.
[78] Pinker to Cora Crane, London, Jan. 9, 1900, *Letters*, p. 260. Reynolds continued to handle materials received earlier and was agent for the American literary interests of Crane's estate.

between "Lynx-Hunting" and "The Angel-Child," the order of appearance in *Harper's Magazine* and of the book is probably the order of writing. A minor discrepancy arises in that the Harper's proposal of May 31 refers to having bought the serial rights of the first three stories plus "Making an Orator." (The Harper letter, signed "J.F.P.," speaks of "Making an Oracle." "J.F.P." was obviously not very well informed about Crane's work and may have made a mistake of omission as well.) But whether or not "Making an Orator" was the story Crane submitted on March 30, " 'Showin' Off,' " the fourth sketch to be published, was written before it. Supporting this order is the evidence of two story lists of March, 1899, written in Crane's hand. Both lists antedate the final settlement of the *Monster* volume since they bear the title "Harper's Book" and include "The Monster" and "His New Mittens" as well as later Whilomville tales. In the first such list, "Lynx-Hunting" and "The Angel-Child" are recorded not only with word length but also with the notation that they were sold to *Harper's Magazine* and with a blank in the column which noted actual publication. In this list "The Lover and the Tell-Tale" appears with a word count but without notation of sale, and it is followed by two other entries:

"Showin' Off." (Jim Trescott.)
Death of the Faceless Man   Never written [*In a larger script, evidently added later*]

The second of these lists still records "The Lover and the Tell-Tale" without notation of a sale, and it is therefore earlier than March 31; but in this case " 'Showin' Off' " not only has the note "(Jimmie Trescott)" which indicates a story still in Crane's mind, but also has the figure *1835* written into the word-count column. It may thus be concluded that " 'Showin' Off' " was completed in March before "Making an Orator" had yet been conceived. On the same sheet with this second list is another category "*War Stories*, etc.," and "The Death of the Faceless Man. (Henry Johnson)" has fallen into this miscellaneous group. Crane never did find a way to bring together his earliest Whilomville subject with his later work in domestic fiction, and this projected story got no further.[79]

[79] MSS in Columbia University Libraries.

There is one other relevant story list, which omits "The Monster" and "His New Mittens" and is therefore considerably later than the first or second Whilomville tallies. It includes in random order the first eight titles of *Whilomville Stories*, that is, the five which existed by May, 1899, plus "Shame," "The Carriage-Lamps," and "The Knife." [80] Now one of the few firmly dated letters to Pinker is Cora's note of August 31 promising a Whilomville story of 4000 words "in three or four days" and begging for an immediate check in order to keep the wine merchant from serving papers; [81] "The Knife," 4095 words long, would fit that description. On September 22 Crane wrote Pinker to complain that he had been underpaid by Harper's for either "The Carriage-Lamps" or "The Knife"; he seems to have been right about "The Carriage-Lamps," but, more important, he set a date by which an accounting from New York had been received. Also, he reported that he was about to finish still another one of the series, possibly "The Stove." [82] The undated letter sent with a Whilomville story of 3230 words—this would be "The Trial, Execution, and Burial of Homer Phelps"—might well follow this.[83] Later, on October 24, Pinker acknowledged what must have been "The Fight": "The Whilomville tale that you sent me today is the eleventh, so that one more will complete that series, unless Harpers think of extending it. Why do you not do the battle articles for Lippincotts?" [84] Cora replied on October 26 by *begging* (the word was hers) cash for the story Pinker had just received, which by a mechanical slip she called "The Light," and she promised yet another Whilomville tale for the next day. The production of cash stories was evidently quickening as more creditors began closing in, and, under the circumstances, she felt called upon to chide Pinker for cautioning Crane "not to dump too many short stories upon the market for fear of spoiling it." As for Lippincott's, she promised nothing before November 10, but with respect to the children's tales, she wrote: "Will you see from Harpers if they want eighteen 'Whilomville' stories. I believe this was the number named at one time. At present they

[80] MS in Columbia University Libraries.
[81] Brede, *Letters*, p. 226.
[82] Brede, *Letters*, p. 231.
[83] Crane to Pinker, Brede, [conjecturally dated Sept. 14? 1899], *Letters*, p. 230.
[84] London, *Letters*, p. 236.

will not make a very large book and Mr. Crane wants to make it larger than it now is." [85] It is after this that she must have written the undated "Monday" letter for which October 30 is a possible date:

Dear Mr. Pinker: I send you another Whilomville Story.

Please send to Oxted Bank £30—more than story is worth and Mr. Crane will be glad if you can send it at once.

There will be another Whilomville story for you in four days.

One of the Lippincott's articles is almost finished, also, but Mr. Crane finds difficulty in getting at it. However you will get it soon. [86]

Unless the Cranes were reckoning on the agent's commission, to which they did not characteristically give much thought, a Whilomville story worth less than £30 would have had to be shorter than 3000 words. After "Making an Orator," which dated from the time when Reynolds had charge of the Harper stories, the next sketch of fewer than 3000 words was the twelfth, "The City Urchin and the Chaste Villagers." Then the other story referred to would be "A Little Pilgrim," presumably completed in early November, 1899, before Crane turned to Lippincott's and *Great Battles of the World* as his chief source of quick cash. He thus made his contractual deadline; and Harper's had stories enough to fill out the magazine series, which had been running since August, and the book. That seemed to end it.

The literary pattern of *Whilomville Stories* also suggests that, though he thought he might go on and on with the subject, Crane had approached the limit of what he could do along a domestic-utopian line. The early tales catch the foibles of the town and especially of the women who dominate its manners, but the ironies are gentle. The great evils, whether of character or of the cosmos, never come into question, and the lesser evils of sentimentality and foolishness can be corrected by a simple realism. The storyteller's accuracy in rendering the way children

---

[85] *Letters*, pp. 237–238.

[86] Cora Crane to Pinker, Brede, [conjecturally dated Oct. 9? 1899, by Stallman and Gilkes], *Letters*, p. 234.

Letter no. 308, Crane to Pinker, Brede, [conjecturally dated Oct. 24? 1899], *Letters*, p. 236, is mistakenly identified as a Whilomville covering letter. Whilomville stories, however, were not "appropriate to the times" and, not being marketed separately in the United States and England, were not submitted in two copies.

react sets a norm for judging the reactions of those who live by illusion, and, in the narrative, adult common sense exerts control of events on the rare occasions when control is needed. The world is obviously well ordered in which unwanted haircuts can seem to be "disasters." And Crane makes clear the social basis of that order: his special concern is with the children of the leading families, "born in whatever purple there was to be had in the vicinity of Whilomville." In using the adjective "middle-class"—a rare word in American fiction—for the social group he was satirizing, he did not categorically separate himself from his subject. When something like alienation occurs in the story called "Shame," it is a matter of the inner workings of the material, not the prejudgment of the author. Little Jimmie, left in the charge of the family cook, will miss a picnic unless she fixes him a lunch, but her hurriedly making crude sandwiches and jamming them in a pail proves to be worse than giving him nothing at all. The lunch pail (badge of the working class) sets the boy apart, and "Got his picnic in a pail!" becomes a cry of torment much like "A-fray-ed of his mittens!" in the earlier story. An unnamed young woman, sister of one of the hostess-mothers and a visitor from New York, sees through the "prigs" and comforts the "exile." Adult intervention can in this instance turn aside the terrible power of exclusion which Crane knew to be an instrument of middle-class stability, but "shame" almost cracks the happy conformity and general freedom from pain on which the social order of Whilomville rests.

"Shame" ends with a brief scene involving Jimmie and Dr. Trescott's stableman Peter Washington, and the Negro servant reappears in the next three stories. In his relations with the boy Washington is gentle, friendly, and firm, but he is very close to the stereotype of the simple, jocular Negro servant. Only in "The Knife," the one story that takes him out of the middle-class master-servant context, does he move into a more interesting role. Walking out of town one summer afternoon, he passes a few minutes in good-natured conversation with Si Bryant on the subject of Bryant's superb melon patch: "The effete joke in regard to an American negro's fondness for water-melons was still an admirable pleasantry to them and this was not the first time they had engaged in badinage over it." Role and actuality get mixed up later in the story when, in special circumstances, Washington really is tempted and is almost caught in the act. The next day the old joke is acted out in earnest when Bryant tries to identify the knife which has been dropped on the scene of the unperformed crime. The stableman's crony, under cross-examination by the farmer, ignores his motive, realistically speaking, for getting Washington in trouble. Instead, he plays his role Brer-Rabbit style and evades the white man's foxy questions with his quick wits. Appropriately, in "The Knife," the one story where the name of Henry Johnson is mentioned, Crane used more complex social and narrative conventions than elsewhere in the series.

After "The Knife" Crane wrote two characteristic Whilomville tales, slight realistic sketches of middle-class life as seen from the inside. Then he once more began to waver from the premises on which he had been working. In "The Fight" and "The City Urchin and the Chaste Villagers," he returned to the theme of the outsider. The initiation of the new boy, who has no known place in the pecking order, was a subject that he could not treat unequivocally from the insider's point of view. The new boy, taunted for his name when no other cause for taunting can be found, is made to feel that "his name was the most disgraceful thing which had ever been attached to a human being." Shame is the wound that exclusion makes, and "absolute strangeness" is the bewilderment of sense with which the boy must cope: "he was a foreigner. The village school was like a nation." It takes several fights to settle the matter, and yet it seems as if the boy's world will work out its problems perfectly happily. Crane assures his readers that "the long-drawn animosities of men have no place in the life of a boy." And yet the changeable fortunes of the new boy do not stay within the boundaries of such assurances. When a wild and bitter sequel to the initial fight takes place in the Trescott garden, Peter Washington comes forward to part the boys and send them away and to scold Jimmie for encouraging them to scrap. The new boy and his little brother walk away, and when they are at a safe distance, the little brother suddenly turns and shouts, "Nig-ger-r-r! Nig-ger-r-r!" The shocking breach of decorum was important enough to warrant one of the most graphic illustrations of the whole series, and the breach of tone in Crane's narrative is so sharp as to stay in the mind even though the incident gets little space. The very meaning of the title of "The City Urchin and the Chaste Villagers" depends on the revelation of that one vicious moment, and yet Crane quickly passes by the incident and makes no comment from the author's point of view. What is clear, however, is that the otherworld which the middle-class utopia excludes must not be sentimentalized. The new boys from the city test the openness of the old society and, as the victims of exclusion, are pitiable, but they also bring intimations of other cruelties and more anarchic realms of being. But in this situation, the small town prevails. When the boys' fighting resumes once more, the new boy's mother pulls them apart and, boxing their ears, proves for once and for all where the ordering authority lies in this special fictive world.

In "A Little Pilgrim" Crane follows Jimmie Trescott's passage from Sunday School to Sunday School in search of one which may not be so unspeakably pious as to spend its Christmas tree money on more distant, but somehow holier good works. Despite his move, the boy gets no tree. And despite his disappointment, he scarcely begins to measure the ironies through which he moves. In satirizing the fatuous schoolmarm who runs Jimmie's class and the unctuous superintendent who runs the school, Crane referred to norms outside the experience of Whilomville boys—or even grownups. The trouble with the superintendent, for instance, may be summed up in his being "one who had never felt hunger or thirst or the wound of the challenge of dishonor." The things he did not know were precisely the things that Stephen Crane knew all too well as the result of having left Whilomville for a greater world. From the worldly outsider's view, the spiritual geography of the small town might seem curiously undifferentiated: the little pilgrim's shift to the Big Progressive Church gets him no closer to a celebration of Christmas. Traced on the map of Port Jervis, the pilgrim's progress from the Presbyterian Church to the Dutch Reformed Church, named rather too obviously in Crane's original version, took him from the town square where Stephen Crane's Methodist father also had his pulpit up to the more fashionable part of town where Stephen Crane's successful brother had his residence, a portentous journey that did not really get him anywhere. The changelessness of

Whilomville, which in moments of reminiscence seemed the very essence of security, was equivocal when looked at from the outside. When the freshness and naïveté of the earlier stories had gone, it was well that Crane called a halt to the series.

When Crane shifted from Whilomville to his other, more modern subject, war, he did not renew his imaginative energy. *Great Battles of the World* only confirmed that he had become a machine for writing, but it is hard to say how much he understood of what was happening to him. Of all his friends, only Conrad had guessed—from his own first hand knowledge of what it was like to fight against depression and flagging energy—that Crane's troubles might be the signs of a painful mental crisis. And even Conrad did not guess that Crane was also fighting a physical battle. Indeed, it was almost two months after the *Whilomville Stories* were completed when, on New Year's Day, 1900, Crane had the hemorrhage which revealed his serious condition. He went on as gallantly as he could, doing his work without complaint. Although he had bolted once, he had no thought now for escape. Everyone behaved according to role. Crane worked at his Irish romance *The O'Ruddy*, and when he saw that he could not finish it, he tried to arrange for others who could. Cora tended him faithfully and managed to find, thanks to the well-meant help of Henry James, the most expensive specialist in London, who came to Brede and did nothing. And his brother William, once a partial model for Dr. Trescott, turned out to be very careful about untimely commitments. During the spring he took back Stephen's share of Hartwood Club as partial payment on his debt, he constantly pleaded that he could not help with money just now, and he recommended a book on how to get well called *A Consumptive's Struggle for Life*. But this representative of small-town purple was neither a villain nor a hypocrite, but an ambiguous character such as Stephen Crane might have understood. When he was being most tight-fisted about money, he also suggested—and repeated the suggestion with a tone of conviction—that Stephen and Cora leave the English climate and stay indefinitely with the William Cranes in Port Jervis.[87] His own financial situation was in fact somewhat tight, for at the time of

[87] W. H. Crane to Stephen and Cora Crane, Port Jervis, April 7, 13, 21, 30, and May 10, 1900, *Letters*, pp. 268, 271, 274–275, 278–279, 281.

Stephen's death, June 5, 1900, he borrowed $500 in order to pay Cora's expenses as she brought Stephen home for burial. And he saw to it that Cora came on to Port Jervis for a month's visit before she went back to England. He consulted her before signing a new Whilomville contract as executor of Stephen's estate,[88] and evidently he considered the widow as well as the creditors as he conducted his administrative duties. He saw no conflict in that dual responsibility. On November 6, 1900, he wrote: "The $500 that I sent last spring I should not like to consider a gift, as I borrowed it and owe it yet. But, you may rest assured, my dear sister, that your interests will be more than safe in my hands." [89]

The momentum of publication continued at its own rate after Crane's death as before. Although William Crane worried about the *Whilomville* contract in his letter of August 21, he had had to apply for copyright as executor on August 15, with copyright deposit made the next day. In the autumn Cora Crane wrote worriedly to Pinker about what additional stories to include in a London edition of *The Monster*, and on October 3 she told him the final contents in a decisive tone—without a hint as to how the list was arrived at.[90] And she tried valiantly to sell her own Whilomville story, "The Lavender Trousers," preferably to Harper's, but publishers saw nothing in it of the collaboration in reminiscence which had once been so vital.[91] The British Museum deposit of *Whilomville Stories* was made on February 19, 1901, and of *The Monster*, on February 25, 1901. By the time of those English editions, the close bond between William and Cora was loosening rapidly. It had been created by family feeling in a moment when other considerations did not seem to matter. Such a simple, affectionate world proved to be more durable in fiction than in life.

J. C. L.

---

[88] W. H. Crane to Cora Crane, Port Jervis, Aug., 21, 1900, ALS in Columbia University Libraries.

[89] Same, Port Jervis, ALS in Columbia University Libraries.

[90] Three letters addressed from London, two undated, one Oct. 3, [1900], ALS in Dartmouth College Library.

[91] Cora Crane to G. H. Perris, London, Nov. 2, 1900, ALS in Columbia University Libraries.

"The Monster"

TEXTUAL INTRODUCTION

THE first appearance of "The Monster" was in *Harper's New Monthly Magazine* for August, 1898 (XCVII, 343–376), illustrated by Peter Newell (H). The text in *The Monster and Other Stories*, a book collection published by Harper in New York in 1899 (A1), is a straight reprint from the magazine version with only a handful of minor substantive changes that can have no authority.

The book was announced in the *Publishers' Weekly* of December 9, 1899. Copyright had been applied for on November 2, and the copyright deposit was made in the Library of Congress on December 2. The price was $1.25.

The first book edition collates π^4 A^8 B-M^8, pp. [2] *i–iv* v *vi*, *1–2* 3–38 *39* 40–105 *106–108* 109–160 *161–164* 165–188 *189–192*. The title-page reads: '[within rules] THE MONSTER | AND | *OTHER STORIES* ‖ BY | STEPHEN CRANE | ILLUSTRATED ‖ [Harper device] ‖ NEW YORK AND LONDON | HARPER & BROTHERS PUBLISHERS | 1899'. After two blank pages the title comes on p. i, the copyright notice by Harper on p. ii, the Contents on p. iii with p. iv blank, the list of Illustrations on pp. v–vi, the half-title 'THE MONSTER' on p. 1 with blank verso, and the text on p. 3. "The Blue Hotel" and "His New Mittens" with their half-titles follow on pp. 107 and 163 respectively, the text ending on p. 189 followed by blank p. 190 and publisher's advertisements on pp. 191–192. "The Monster" occupies sigs. A1–G5^v, pp. 1–106; the frontispiece and eleven of the tipped-in illustrations, the same as in the *Magazine*, belong to it; the other stories are illustrated within the text.

The University of Virginia Barrett copy (551436) retains the dust jacket, mustard colored and printed in black. The front reads: 'THE | MONSTER | & Other Stories | By Stephen Crane | Illustrated | M^R. CRANE has given no more striking evidence of

marked with the Britannia seal and written in black ink. Its verso is foliated 68 and contains the conclusion, as follows:

"There—there," he said. "Dont cry, Grace. Dont cry."

The wind was whining around the house and the snow beat aslant upon the windows. Sometimes the coal in the stove settled with a crumbling sound and the four panes of mica flushed [a] a sudden new [b] crimson. As [c] he sat [d] holding his [e] head on his shoulder Trescott found himself occasionally beginning to count the cups. There were fifteen of them.

#
The End.

[a] flushed] 'f' *altered from* 'b'
[b] new] *interlined with a caret*
[c] As] *preceded by deleted* 'Tres'
[d] sat] *followed by deleted* 'there'
[e] his] *sic*

On the recto of this leaf is the foliation 64 and the following crossed-out material:

XXXIII [a]

The autumn smote the leaves and the trees of Whilomville were panoplied in crimson and yellow. The little boys dreamed of the near time [b] when they could heap up bushels of brown leaves in the streets [c] and burn them during the abrupt evenings.

[a] XXXIII] *sic for* XXIII
[b] near time] *preceded by deleted* 'prospective time'
[c] streets] *preceded by deleted* 'dusk'

Parallel with the long side of the paper and written in black ink is the number 70, circled, and below this the number 400 with a short rule beneath it. These appear to be in Crane's hand. About halfway down the page and parallel with the short side of the paper, double circled, is the pencil figure 102, also probably in Crane's hand. To the right of this is the pencil word 'Monster' in a strange hand, and below, to the left, in another hand, penciled, 'Last page of *The Monster*'.

The paper of this leaf resembles that used in the manuscript of the Whilomville story " 'Showin' Off.' "

Since only the *Harper's Magazine* version has authority, it has been chosen as the copy-text for this edition, although a few changes have been made on the authority of the manuscript leaf, most notably the manuscript reading *flushed* at 65.8 for the misreading *flashed* found in all printed texts. Only a few silent alterations have been made in the copy-text form: one of the *Harper's Magazine* compositors set the uncharacteristic form *'ain't*, and this has been silently changed to the more usual form of the other compositor, *ain't*, which coincides—usually in the form *aint*—with Crane's manuscripts; also, a scattering of the abbreviation *Dr.* has been expanded silently to *Doctor*.

The *Harper's Magazine* text in xeroxes from the University of Virginia Library has been used as printer's copy, sight-collated against the text in the 1899 Harper's edition (A1) in the Barrett Collection PS1449.C85M6, 1899 (89571). This Barrett copy 1 has been machined against Barrett copy 2 (452272) and copy 3 (551436) without discovery of any textual variation in the plates. Finally, the control copy 1 has been machined against the text of the 1901 London edition (E1) in Barrett 554137, again without evidence for variation, even in the misprint 'the marrogant' on p. 69, line 6, of the 1899 and 1901 editions (45.8 in the present text), although missing pagination on text pages has been supplied in the London plates.

F. B.

TEXT OF "THE MONSTER"

LITTLE JIM was, for the time, engine Number 36, and he was making the run between Syracuse and Rochester. He was fourteen minutes behind time, and the throttle was wide open. In consequence, when he swung around the curve at the flower-bed, a wheel of his cart destroyed a peony. Number 36 slowed down at once and looked guiltily at his father, who was mowing the lawn. The doctor had his back to this accident, and he continued to pace slowly to and fro, pushing the mower.

Jim dropped the tongue of the cart. He looked at his father and at the broken flower. Finally he went to the peony and tried to stand it on its pins, resuscitated, but the spine of it was hurt, and it would only hang limply from his hand. Jim could do no reparation. He looked again toward his father.

He went on to the lawn, very slowly, and kicking wretchedly at the turf. Presently his father came along with the whirring machine, while the sweet new grass blades spun from the knives. In a low voice, Jim said, "Pa!"

The doctor was shaving this lawn as if it were a priest's chin. All during the season he had worked at it in the coolness and peace of the evenings after supper. Even in the shadow of the cherry-trees the grass was strong and healthy. Jim raised his voice a trifle. "Pa!"

The doctor paused, and with the howl of the machine no longer occupying the sense, one could hear the robins in the cherry-trees arranging their affairs. Jim's hands were behind his back, and sometimes his fingers clasped and unclasped. Again he said, "Pa!" The child's fresh and rosy lip was lowered.

The doctor stared down at his son, thrusting his head forward and frowning attentively. "What is it, Jimmie?"

"Pa!" repeated the child at length. Then he raised his finger and pointed at the flower-bed. "There!"

"What?" said the doctor, frowning more. "What is it, Jim?"

After a period of silence, during which the child may have undergone a severe mental tumult, he raised his finger and repeated his former word—"There!" The father had respected this silence with perfect courtesy. Afterward his glance carefully followed the direction indicated by the child's finger, but he could see nothing which explained to him. "I don't understand what you mean, Jimmie," he said.

It seemed that the importance of the whole thing had taken away the boy's vocabulary. He could only reiterate, "There!"

The doctor mused upon the situation, but he could make nothing of it. At last he said, "Come, show me."

Together they crossed the lawn toward the flower-bed. At some yards from the broken peony Jimmie began to lag. "There!" The word came almost breathlessly.

"Where?" said the doctor.

Jimmie kicked at the grass. "There!" he replied.

The doctor was obliged to go forward alone. After some trouble he found the subject of the incident, the broken flower. Turning then, he saw the child lurking at the rear and scanning his countenance.

The father reflected. After a time he said, "Jimmie, come here." With an infinite modesty of demeanor the child came forward. "Jimmie, how did this happen?"

The child answered, "Now—I was playin' train—and—now —I runned over it."

"You were doing what?"

"I was playin' train."

The father reflected again. "Well, Jimmie," he said, slowly, "I guess you had better not play train any more to-day. Do you think you had better?"

"No, sir," said Jimmie.

During the delivery of the judgment the child had not faced his father, and afterward he went away, with his head lowered, shuffling his feet.

II

It was apparent from Jimmie's manner that he felt some kind of desire to efface himself. He went down to the stable. Henry Johnson, the negro who cared for the doctor's horses, was sponging the buggy. He grinned fraternally when he saw Jimmie coming. These two were pals. In regard to almost everything in life they seemed to have minds precisely alike. Of course there were points of emphatic divergence. For instance, it was plain from Henry's talk that he was a very handsome negro, and he was known to be a light, a weight, and an eminence in the suburb of the town, where lived the larger number of the negroes, and obviously this glory was over Jimmie's horizon; but he vaguely appreciated it and paid deference to Henry for it mainly because Henry appreciated it and deferred to himself. However, on all points of conduct as related to the doctor, who was the moon, they were in complete but unexpressed understanding. Whenever Jimmie became the victim of an eclipse he went to the stable to solace himself with Henry's crimes. Henry, with the elasticity of his race, could usually provide a sin to place himself on a footing with the disgraced one. Perhaps he would remember that he had forgotten to put the hitching-strap in the back of the buggy on some recent occasion, and had been reprimanded by the doctor. Then these two would commune subtly and without words concerning their moon, holding themselves sympathetically as people who had committed similar treasons. On the other hand, Henry would sometimes choose to absolutely repudiate this idea, and when Jimmie appeared in his shame would bully him most virtuously, preaching with assurance the precepts of the doctor's creed, and pointing out to Jimmie all his abominations. Jimmie did not discover that this was odious in his comrade. He accepted it and lived in its shadow with humility, merely trying to conciliate the saintly Henry with acts of deference. Won by this attitude, Henry would sometimes allow the child to enjoy the felicity of squeezing the sponge over a buggy-wheel, even when Jimmie was still gory from unspeakable deeds.

Whenever Henry dwelt for a time in sackcloth, Jimmie did not patronize him at all. This was a justice of his age, his condition. He did not know. Besides, Henry could drive a horse, and Jimmie had a full sense of this sublimity. Henry personally conducted the moon during the splendid journeys through the country roads, where farms spread on all sides, with sheep, cows, and other marvels abounding.

"Hello, Jim!" said Henry, poising his sponge. Water was dripping from the buggy. Sometimes the horses in the stalls stamped thunderingly on the pine floor. There was an atmosphere of hay and of harness.

For a minute Jimmie refused to take an interest in anything. He was very downcast. He could not even feel the wonders of wagon-washing. Henry, while at his work, narrowly observed him.

"Your pop done wallop yer, didn't he?" he said at last.

"No," said Jimmie, defensively; "he didn't."

After this casual remark Henry continued his labor, with a scowl of occupation. Presently he said: "I done tol' yer many's th' time not to go a-foolin' an' a-projjeckin' with them flowers. Yer pop don' like it nohow." As a matter of fact, Henry had never mentioned flowers to the boy.

Jimmie preserved a gloomy silence, so Henry began to use seductive wiles in this affair of washing a wagon. It was not until he began to spin a wheel on the tree, and the sprinkling water flew everywhere, that the boy was visibly moved. He had been seated on the sill of the carriage-house door, but at the beginning of this ceremony he arose and circled toward the buggy, with an interest that slowly consumed the remembrance of a late disgrace.

Johnson could then display all the dignity of a man whose duty it was to protect Jimmie from a splashing. "Look out, boy! look out! You done gwi' spile yer pants. I raikon your mommer don't 'low this foolishness, she know it. I ain't gwi' have you round yere spilin' yer pants, an' have Mis' Trescott light on me pressen'ly. 'Deed I ain't."

He spoke with an air of great irritation, but he was not annoyed at all. This tone was merely a part of his importance. In reality he was always delighted to have the child there to witness the business of the stable. For one thing, Jimmie was invariably

overcome with reverence when he was told how beautifully a
harness was polished or a horse groomed. Henry explained each
detail of this kind with unction, procuring great joy from the
child's admiration.

III

After Johnson had taken his supper in the kitchen, he went to his
loft in the carriage-house and dressed himself with much care.
No belle of a court circle could bestow more mind on a toilet
than did Johnson. On second thought, he was more like a priest
arraying himself for some parade of the church. As he emerged
from his room and sauntered down the carriage drive, no one
would have suspected him of ever having washed a buggy.

It was not altogether a matter of the lavender trousers, nor yet
the straw hat with its bright silk band. The change was somewhere far in the interior of Henry. But there was no cake-walk
hyperbole in it. He was simply a quiet, well-bred gentleman of
position, wealth, and other necessary achievements out for an
evening stroll, and he had never washed a wagon in his life.

In the morning, when in his working-clothes, he had met a
friend—"Hello, Pete!" "Hello, Henry!" Now, in his effulgence, he
encountered this same friend. His bow was not at all haughty. If
it expressed anything, it expressed consummate generosity—
"Good-evenin', Misteh Washington." Pete, who was very dirty,
being at work in a potato-patch, responded in a mixture of
abasement and appreciation—"Good-evenin', Misteh Johnsing."

The shimmering blue of the electric arc-lamps was strong in
the main street of the town. At numerous points it was conquered by the orange glare of the outnumbering gas-lights in the
windows of shops. Through this radiant lane moved a crowd,
which culminated in a throng before the post-office, awaiting the
distribution of the evening mails. Occasionally there came into it
a shrill electric street-car, the motor singing like a cageful of
grasshoppers, and possessing a great gong that clanged forth
both warnings and simple noise. At the little theatre, which was
a varnish and red-plush miniature of one of the famous New
York theatres, a company of strollers was to play *East Lynne*.
The young men of the town were mainly gathered at the corners,

in distinctive groups, which expressed various shades and lines of chumship, and had little to do with any social gradations. There they discussed everything with critical insight, passing the whole town in review as it swarmed in the street. When the gongs of the electric cars ceased for a moment to harry the ears, there could be heard the sound of the feet of the leisurely crowd on the blue-stone pavement, and it was like the peaceful evening lashing at the shore of a lake. At the foot of the hill, where two lines of maples sentinelled the way, an electric lamp glowed high among the embowering branches, and made most wonderful shadow-etchings on the road below it.

When Johnson appeared amid the throng a member of one of the profane groups at a corner instantly telegraphed news of this extraordinary arrival to his companions. They hailed him. "Hello, Henry! Going to walk for a cake to-night?"

"Ain't he smooth?"

"Why, you've got that cake right in your pocket, Henry!"

"Throw out your chest a little more."

Henry was not ruffled in any way by these quiet admonitions and compliments. In reply he laughed a supremely good-natured, chuckling laugh, which nevertheless expressed an underground complacency of superior metal.

Young Griscom, the lawyer, was just emerging from Reifsnyder's barber shop, rubbing his chin contentedly. On the steps he dropped his hand and looked with wide eyes into the crowd. Suddenly he bolted back into the shop. "Wow!" he cried to the parliament; "you ought to see the coon that's coming!"

Reifsnyder and his assistant instantly poised their razors high and turned toward the window. Two belathered heads reared from the chairs. The electric shine in the street caused an effect like water to them who looked through the glass from the yellow glamour of Reifsnyder's shop. In fact, the people without resembled the inhabitants of a great aquarium that here had a square pane in it. Presently into this frame swam the graceful form of Henry Johnson.

"Chee!" said Reifsnyder. He and his assistant with one accord threw their obligations to the winds, and leaving their lathered victims helpless, advanced to the window. "Ain't he a taisy?" said Reifsnyder, marvelling.

But the man in the first chair, with a grievance in his mind, had found a weapon. "Why, that's only Henry Johnson, you blamed idiots! Come on now, Reif, and shave me. What do you think I am—a mummy?"

Reifsnyder turned, in a great excitement. "I bait you any money that vas not Henry Johnson! Henry Johnson! Rats!" The scorn put into this last word made it an explosion. "That man vas a Pullman-car porter or someding. How could that be Henry Johnson?" he demanded, turbulently. "You vas crazy."

The man in the first chair faced the barber in a storm of indignation. "Didn't I give him those lavender trousers?" he roared.

And young Griscom, who had remained attentively at the window, said: "Yes, I guess that was Henry. It looked like him."

"Oh, vell," said Reifsnyder, returning to his business, "if you think so! Oh, vell!" He implied that he was submitting for the sake of amiability.

Finally the man in the second chair, mumbling from a mouth made timid by adjacent lather, said: "That was Henry Johnson all right. Why, he always dresses like that when he wants to make a front! He's the biggest dude in town—anybody knows that."

"Chinger!" said Reifsnyder.

Henry was not at all oblivious of the wake of wondering ejaculation that streamed out behind him. On other occasions he had reaped this same joy, and he always had an eye for the demonstration. With a face beaming with happiness he turned away from the scene of his victories into a narrow side street, where the electric light still hung high, but only to exhibit a row of tumble-down houses leaning together like paralytics.

The saffron Miss Bella Farragut, in a calico frock, had been crouched on the front stoop, gossiping at long range, but she espied her approaching caller at a distance. She dashed around the corner of the house, galloping like a horse. Henry saw it all, but he preserved the polite demeanor of a guest when a waiter spills claret down his cuff. In this awkward situation he was simply perfect.

The duty of receiving Mr. Johnson fell upon Mrs. Farragut, because Bella, in another room, was scrambling wildly into her best gown. The fat old woman met him with a great ivory smile, sweeping back with the door, and bowing low. "Walk in, Misteh Johnson, walk in. How is you dis ebenin', Misteh Johnson—how is you?"

Henry's face showed like a reflector as he bowed and bowed, bending almost from his head to his ankles. "Good-evenin', Mis' Fa'gut; good-evenin'. How is you dis evenin'? Is all you' folks well, Mis' Fa'gut?"

After a great deal of kowtow, they were planted in two chairs opposite each other in the living-room. Here they exchanged the most tremendous civilities, until Miss Bella swept into the room, when there was more kowtow on all sides, and a smiling show of teeth that was like an illumination.

The cooking-stove was of course in this drawing-room, and on the fire was some kind of a long-winded stew. Mrs. Farragut was obliged to arise and attend to it from time to time. Also young Sim came in and went to bed on his pallet in the corner. But to all these domesticities the three maintained an absolute dumbness. They bowed and smiled and ignored and imitated until a late hour, and if they had been the occupants of the most gorgeous salon in the world they could not have been more like three monkeys.

After Henry had gone, Bella, who encouraged herself in the appropriation of phrases, said, "Oh, ma, isn't he divine?"

IV

A Saturday evening was a sign always for a larger crowd to parade the thoroughfare. In summer the band played until ten o'clock in the little park. Most of the young men of the town affected to be superior to this band, even to despise it; but in the still and fragrant evenings they invariably turned out in force, because the girls were sure to attend this concert, strolling slowly over the grass, linked closely in pairs, or preferably in threes, in the curious public dependence upon one another which was their inheritance. There was no particular social aspect to this gathering, save that group regarded group with interest, but mainly in silence. Perhaps one girl would nudge another girl and suddenly say, "Look! there goes Gertie Hodgson and her sister!" And they would appear to regard this as an event of importance.

On a particular evening a rather large company of young men were gathered on the sidewalk that edged the park. They remained thus beyond the borders of the festivities because of their dignity, which would not exactly allow them to appear in anything which was so much fun for the younger lads. These latter were careering madly through the crowd, precipitating minor accidents from time to time, but usually fleeing like mist swept by the wind before retribution could lay its hands upon them.

The band played a waltz which involved a gift of prominence to the bass horn, and one of the young men on the sidewalk said that the music reminded him of the new engines on the hill pumping water into the reservoir. A similarity of this kind was not inconceivable, but the young man did not say it because he disliked the band's playing. He said it because it was fashionable to say that manner of thing concerning the band. However, over in the stand, Billie Harris, who played the snare-drum, was always surrounded by a throng of boys, who adored his every whack.

After the mails from New York and Rochester had been finally distributed, the crowd from the post-office added to the mass already in the park. The wind waved the leaves of the maples, and, high in the air, the blue-burning globes of the arc lamps caused the wonderful traceries of leaf shadows on the ground. When the light fell upon the upturned face of a girl, it caused it to glow with a wonderful pallor. A policeman came suddenly from the darkness and chased a gang of obstreperous little boys. They hooted him from a distance. The leader of the band had some of the mannerisms of the great musicians, and during a period of silence the crowd smiled when they saw him raise his hand to his brow, stroke it sentimentally, and glance upward with a look of poetic anguish. In the shivering light, which gave to the park an effect like a great vaulted hall, the throng swarmed, with a gentle murmur of dresses switching the turf, and with a steady hum of voices.

Suddenly, without preliminary bars, there arose from afar the great hoarse roar of a factory whistle. It raised and swelled to a sinister note, and then it sang on the night wind one long call that held the crowd in the park immovable, speechless. The band-master had been about to vehemently let fall his hand to start the band on a thundering career through a popular march, but, smitten by this giant voice from the night, his hand dropped slowly to his knee, and, his mouth agape, he looked at his men in silence. The cry died away to a wail, and then to stillness. It released the muscles of the company of young men on the sidewalk, who had been like statues, posed eagerly, lithely, their ears turned. And then they wheeled upon each other simultaneously, and, in a single explosion, they shouted, "One!"

Again the sound swelled in the night and roared its long ominous cry, and as it died away the crowd of young men wheeled upon each other and, in chorus, yelled, "Two!"

There was a moment of breathless waiting. Then they bawled, "Second district!" In a flash the company of indolent and cynical young men had vanished like a snowball disrupted by dynamite.

V

Jake Rogers was the first man to reach the home of Tuscarora Hose Company Number Six. He had wrenched his key from his pocket as he tore down the street, and he jumped at the spring-lock like a demon. As the doors flew back before his hands he leaped and kicked the wedges from a pair of wheels, loosened a tongue from its clasp, and in the glare of the electric light which the town placed before each of its hose-houses the next comers beheld the spectacle of Jake Rogers bent like hickory in the manfulness of his pulling, and the heavy cart was moving slowly toward the doors. Four men joined him at the time, and as they swung with the cart out into the street, dark figures sped toward them from the ponderous shadows back of the electric lamps. Some set up the inevitable question, "What district?"

"Second," was replied to them in a compact howl. Tuscarora Hose Company Number Six swept on a perilous wheel into Niagara Avenue, and as the men, attached to the cart by the rope which had been paid out from the windlass under the tongue, pulled madly in their fervor and abandon, the gong under the axle clanged incitingly. And sometimes the same cry was heard, "What district?"

"Second."

On a grade Johnnie Thorpe fell, and exercising a singular muscular ability, rolled out in time from the track of the on-coming wheel, and arose, dishevelled and aggrieved, casting a look of mournful disenchantment upon the black crowd that poured after the machine. The cart seemed to be the apex of a dark wave that was whirling as if it had been a broken dam. Back of the lad were stretches of lawn, and in that direction front doors were banged by men who hoarsely shouted out into the clamorous avenue, "What district?"

At one of these houses a woman came to the door bearing a lamp, shielding her face from its rays with her hands. Across the cropped grass the avenue represented to her a kind of black torrent, upon which, nevertheless, fled numerous miraculous figures upon bicycles. She did not know that the towering light at the corner was continuing its nightly whine.

Suddenly a little boy somersaulted around the corner of the house as if he had been projected down a flight of stairs by a catapultian boot. He halted himself in front of the house by dint of a rather extraordinary evolution with his legs. "Oh, ma," he gasped, "can I go? Can I, ma?"

She straightened with the coldness of the exterior mother-judgment, although the hand that held the lamp trembled slightly. "No, Willie; you had better come to bed."

Instantly he began to buck and fume like a mustang. "Oh, ma," he cried, contorting himself—"oh, ma, can't I go? Please, ma, can't I go? Can't I go, ma?"

"It's half past nine now, Willie."

He ended by wailing out a compromise: "Well, just down to the corner, ma? Just down to the corner?"

From the avenue came the sound of rushing men who wildly shouted. Somebody had grappled the bell-rope in the Methodist church, and now over the town rang this solemn and terrible voice, speaking from the clouds. Moved from its peaceful business, this bell gained a new spirit in the portentous night, and it swung the heart to and fro, up and down, with each peal of it.

"Just down to the corner, ma?"

"Willie, it's half past nine now."

VI

The outlines of the house of Doctor Trescott had faded quietly into the evening, hiding a shape such as we call Queen Anne against the pall of the blackened sky. The neighborhood was at this time so quiet, and seemed so devoid of obstructions, that Hannigan's dog thought it a good opportunity to prowl in forbidden precincts, and so came and pawed Trescott's lawn, growling, and considering himself a formidable beast. Later, Peter Washington strolled past the house and whistled, but there was no dim light shining from Henry's loft, and presently Peter went his way. The rays from the street, creeping in silvery waves over the grass, caused the row of shrubs along the drive to throw a clear, bold shade.

A wisp of smoke came from one of the windows at the end of the house and drifted quietly into the branches of a cherry-tree. Its companions followed it in slowly increasing numbers, and finally there was a current controlled by invisible banks which poured into the fruit-laden boughs of the cherry-tree. It was no more to be noted than if a troop of dim and silent gray monkeys had been climbing a grape-vine into the clouds.

After a moment the window brightened as if the four panes of it had been stained with blood, and a quick ear might have been led to imagine the fire-imps calling and calling, clan joining clan, gathering to the colors. From the street, however, the house maintained its dark quiet, insisting to a passer-by that it was the safe dwelling of people who chose to retire early to tranquil dreams. No one could have heard this low droning of the gathering clans.

Suddenly the panes of the red window tinkled and crashed to the ground, and at other windows there suddenly reared other flames, like bloody spectres at the apertures of a haunted house. This outbreak had been well planned, as if by professional revolutionists.

A man's voice suddenly shouted: "Fire! Fire! Fire!" Hannigan had flung his pipe frenziedly from him because his lungs demanded room. He tumbled down from his perch, swung over the fence, and ran shouting toward the front door of the Trescotts'. Then he hammered on the door, using his fists as if they were mallets. Mrs. Trescott instantly came to one of the windows on the second floor. Afterward she knew she had been about to say, "The doctor is not at home, but if you will leave your name, I will let him know as soon as he comes."

Hannigan's bawling was for a minute incoherent, but she understood that it was not about croup.

"What?" she said, raising the window swiftly.

"Your house is on fire! You're all ablaze! Move quick if—" His cries were resounding in the street as if it were a cave of echoes. Many feet pattered swiftly on the stones. There was one man who ran with an almost fabulous speed. He wore lavender trousers. A straw hat with a bright silk band was held half crumpled in his hand.

As Henry reached the front door, Hannigan had just broken the lock with a kick. A thick cloud of smoke poured over them, and Henry, ducking his head, rushed into it. From Hannigan's clamor he knew only one thing, but it turned him blue with horror. In the hall a lick of flame had found the cord that supported "Signing the Declaration." The engraving slumped suddenly down at one end, and then dropped to the floor, where it burst with the sound of a bomb. The fire was already roaring like a winter wind among the pines.

At the head of the stairs Mrs. Trescott was waving her arms as if they were two reeds. "Jimmie! Save Jimmie!" she screamed in Henry's face. He plunged past her and disappeared, taking the long-familiar routes among these upper chambers, where he had once held office as a sort of second assistant house-maid.

Hannigan had followed him up the stairs, and grappled the arm of the maniacal woman there. His face was black with rage. "You must come down," he bellowed.

She would only scream at him in reply: "Jimmie! Jimmie! Save Jimmie!" But he dragged her forth while she babbled at him.

As they swung out into the open air a man ran across the

lawn, and seizing a shutter, pulled it from its hinges and flung it far out upon the grass. Then he frantically attacked the other shutters one by one. It was a kind of temporary insanity.

"Here, you," howled Hannigan, "hold Mrs. Trescott— And stop—"

The news had been telegraphed by a twist of the wrist of a neighbor who had gone to the fire-box at the corner, and the time when Hannigan and his charge struggled out of the house was the time when the whistle roared its hoarse night call, smiting the crowd in the park, causing the leader of the band, who was about to order the first triumphal clang of a military march, to let his hand drop slowly to his knee.

VII

Henry pawed awkwardly through the smoke in the upper halls. He had attempted to guide himself by the walls, but they were too hot. The paper was crimpling, and he expected at any moment to have a flame burst from under his hands.

"Jimmie!"

He did not call very loud, as if in fear that the humming flames below would overhear him.

"Jimmie! Oh, Jimmie!"

Stumbling and panting, he speedily reached the entrance to Jimmie's room and flung open the door. The little chamber had no smoke in it at all. It was faintly illumined by a beautiful rosy light reflected circuitously from the flames that were consuming the house. The boy had apparently just been aroused by the noise. He sat in his bed, his lips apart, his eyes wide, while upon his little white-robed figure played caressingly the light from the fire. As the door flew open he had before him this apparition of his pal, a terror-stricken negro, all tousled and with wool scorching, who leaped upon him and bore him up in a blanket as if the whole affair were a case of kidnapping by a dreadful robber chief. Without waiting to go through the usual short but complete process of wrinkling up his face, Jimmie let out a gorgeous bawl, which resembled the expression of a calf's deepest terror. As Johnson, bearing him, reeled into the smoke of the hall, he flung his arms about his neck and buried his face in the blanket. He called twice in muffled tones: "Mam-ma! Mam-ma!"

When Johnson came to the top of the stairs with his burden, he took a quick step backward. Through the smoke that rolled to him he could see that the lower hall was all ablaze. He cried out then in a howl that resembled Jimmie's former achievement. His legs gained a frightful faculty of bending sideways. Swinging about precariously on these reedy legs, he made his way back slowly, back along the upper hall. From the way of him then, he had given up almost all idea of escaping from the burning house, and with it the desire. He was submitting, submitting because of his fathers, bending his mind in a most perfect slavery to this conflagration.

He now clutched Jimmie as unconsciously as when, running toward the house, he had clutched the hat with the bright silk band.

Suddenly he remembered a little private staircase which led from a bedroom to an apartment which the doctor had fitted up as a laboratory and work-house, where he used some of his leisure, and also hours when he might have been sleeping, in devoting himself to experiments which came in the way of his study and interest.

When Johnson recalled this stairway the submission to the blaze departed instantly. He had been perfectly familiar with it, but his confusion had destroyed the memory of it.

In his sudden momentary apathy there had been little that resembled fear, but now, as a way of safety came to him, the old frantic terror caught him. He was no longer creature to the flames, and he was afraid of the battle with them. It was a singular and swift set of alternations in which he feared twice without submission, and submitted once without fear.

"Jimmie!" he wailed, as he staggered on his way. He wished this little inanimate body at his breast to participate in his tremblings. But the child had lain limp and still during these headlong charges and countercharges, and no sign came from him.

Johnson passed through two rooms and came to the head of the stairs. As he opened the door great billows of smoke poured out, but gripping Jimmie closer, he plunged down through them.

All manner of odors assailed him during this flight. They seemed to be alive with envy, hatred, and malice. At the entrance to the laboratory he confronted a strange spectacle. The room was like a garden in the region where might be burning flowers. Flames of violet, crimson, green, blue, orange, and purple were blooming everywhere. There was one blaze that was precisely the hue of a delicate coral. In another place was a mass that lay merely in phosphorescent inaction like a pile of emeralds. But all these marvels were to be seen dimly through clouds of heaving, turning, deadly smoke.

Johnson halted for a moment on the threshold. He cried out again in the negro wail that had in it the sadness of the swamps. Then he rushed across the room. An orange-colored flame leaped like a panther at the lavender trousers. This animal bit deeply into Johnson. There was an explosion at one side, and suddenly before him there reared a delicate, trembling sapphire shape like a fairy lady. With a quiet smile she blocked his path and doomed him and Jimmie. Johnson shrieked, and then ducked in the manner of his race in fights. He aimed to pass under the left guard of the sapphire lady. But she was swifter than eagles, and her talons caught in him as he plunged past her. Bowing his head as if his neck had been struck, Johnson lurched forward, twisting this way and that way. He fell on his back. The still form in the blanket flung from his arms, rolled to the edge of the floor and beneath the window.

Johnson had fallen with his head at the base of an old-fashioned desk. There was a row of jars upon the top of this desk. For the most part, they were silent amid this rioting, but there was one which seemed to hold a scintillant and writhing serpent.

Suddenly the glass splintered, and a ruby-red snakelike thing poured its thick length out upon the top of the old desk. It coiled and hesitated, and then began to swim a languorous way down the mahogany slant. At the angle it waved its sizzling molten head to and fro over the closed eyes of the man beneath it. Then, in a moment, with mystic impulse, it moved again, and the red snake flowed directly down into Johnson's upturned face.

Afterward the trail of this creature seemed to reek, and amid flames and low explosions drops like red-hot jewels pattered softly down it at leisurely intervals.

VIII

Suddenly all roads led to Doctor Trescott's. The whole town flowed toward one point. Chippeway Hose Company Number One toiled desperately up Bridge Street Hill even as the Tuscaroras came in an impetuous sweep down Niagara Avenue. Meanwhile the machine of the hook-and-ladder experts from across the creek was spinning on its way. The chief of the fire department had been playing poker in the rear room of Whiteley's cigar-store, but at the first breath of the alarm he sprang through the door like a man escaping with the kitty.

In Whilomville, on these occasions, there was always a number of people who instantly turned their attention to the bells in the churches and school-houses. The bells not only emphasized the alarm, but it was the habit to send these sounds rolling across the sky in a stirring brazen uproar until the flames were practically vanquished. There was also a kind of rivalry as to which bell should be made to produce the greatest din. Even the Valley Church, four miles away among the farms, had heard the voices of its brethren, and immediately added a quaint little yelp.

Doctor Trescott had been driving homeward, slowly smoking a cigar, and feeling glad that this last case was now in complete obedience to him, like a wild animal that he had subdued, when he heard the long whistle, and chirped to his horse under the unlicensed but perfectly distinct impression that a fire had broken out in Oakhurst, a new and rather high-flying suburb of the town which was at least two miles from his own home. But in the second blast and in the ensuing silence he read the designation of his own district. He was then only a few blocks from his house. He took out the whip and laid it lightly on the mare. Surprised and frightened at this extraordinary action, she leaped forward, and as the reins straightened like steel bands, the doctor leaned backward a trifle. When the mare whirled him up to the closed gate he was wondering whose house could be afire. The man who had rung the signal-box yelled something at him, but he already knew. He left the mare to her will.

In front of his door was a maniacal woman in a wrapper. "Ned!" she screamed at sight of him. "Jimmie! Save Jimmie!"

Trescott had grown hard and chill. "Where?" he said. "Where?"

Mrs. Trescott's voice began to bubble. "Up—up—up—" She pointed at the second-story windows.

Hannigan was already shouting: "Don't go in that way! You can't go in that way!"

Trescott ran around the corner of the house and disappeared from them. He knew from the view he had taken of the main hall that it would be impossible to ascend from there. His hopes were fastened now to the stairway which led from the laboratory. The door which opened from this room out upon the lawn was fastened with a bolt and lock, but he kicked close to the lock and then close to the bolt. The door with a loud crash flew back. The doctor recoiled from the roll of smoke, and then bending low, he stepped into the garden of burning flowers. On the floor his stinging eyes could make out a form in a smouldering blanket near the window. Then, as he carried his son toward the door, he saw that the whole lawn seemed now alive with men and boys, the leaders in the great charge that the whole town was making. They seized him and his burden, and overpowered him in wet blankets and water.

But Hannigan was howling: "Johnson is in there yet! Henry Johnson is in there yet! He went in after the kid! Johnson is in there yet!"

These cries penetrated to the sleepy senses of Trescott, and he struggled with his captors, swearing, unknown to him and to them, all the deep blasphemies of his medical-student days. He arose to his feet and went again toward the door of the laboratory. They endeavored to restrain him, although they were much affrighted at him.

But a young man who was a brakeman on the railway, and lived in one of the rear streets near the Trescotts, had gone into the laboratory and brought forth a thing which he laid on the grass.

IX

There were hoarse commands from in front of the house. "Turn on your water, Five!" "Let 'er go, One!" The gathering crowd swayed this way and that way. The flames, towering high, cast a wild red light on their faces. There came the clangor of a gong from along some adjacent street. The crowd exclaimed at it. "Here comes Number Three!" "That's Three a-comin'!" A panting and irregular mob dashed into view, dragging a hose-cart. A cry of exultation arose from the little boys. "Here's Three!" The lads welcomed Never-Die Hose Company Number Three as if it was composed of a chariot dragged by a band of gods. The perspiring citizens flung themselves into the fray. The boys danced in impish joy at the displays of prowess. They acclaimed the approach of Number Two. They welcomed Number Four with cheers. They were so deeply moved by this whole affair that they bitterly guyed the late appearance of the hook and ladder company, whose heavy apparatus had almost stalled them on the Bridge Street hill. The lads hated and feared a fire, of course. They did not particularly want to have anybody's house burn, but still it was fine to see the gathering of the companies, and amid a great noise to watch their heroes perform all manner of prodigies.

They were divided into parties over the worth of different companies, and supported their creeds with no small violence. For instance, in that part of the little city where Number Four had its home it would be most daring for a boy to contend the superiority of any other company. Likewise, in another quarter, when a strange boy was asked which fire company was the best in Whilomville, he was expected to answer "Number One." Feuds, which the boys forgot and remembered according to chance or the importance of some recent event, existed all through the town.

They did not care much for John Shipley, the chief of the department. It was true that he went to a fire with the speed of a falling angel, but when there he invariably lapsed into a certain still mood, which was almost a preoccupation, moving leisurely around the burning structure and surveying it, puffing meanwhile at a cigar. This quiet man, who even when life was in danger seldom raised his voice, was not much to their fancy. Now old Sykes Huntington, when he was chief, used to bellow continually like a bull and gesticulate in a sort of delirium. He was much finer as a spectacle than this Shipley, who viewed a fire with the same steadiness that he viewed a raise in a large jack-pot. The greater number of the boys could never understand why the members of these companies persisted in re-electing Shipley, although they often pretended to understand it, because "My father says" was a very formidable phrase in argument, and the fathers seemed almost unanimous in advocating Shipley.

At this time there was considerable discussion as to which company had gotten the first stream of water on the fire. Most of the boys claimed that Number Five owned that distinction, but there was a determined minority who contended for Number One. Boys who were the blood adherents of other companies were obliged to choose between the two on this occasion, and the talk waxed warm.

But a great rumor went among the crowds. It was told with hushed voices. Afterward a reverent silence fell even upon the boys. Jimmie Trescott and Henry Johnson had been burned to death, and Doctor Trescott himself had been most savagely hurt. The crowd did not even feel the police pushing at them. They raised their eyes, shining now with awe, toward the high flames.

The man who had information was at his best. In low tones he described the whole affair. "That was the kid's room—in the corner there. He had measles or somethin', and this coon—Johnson—was a-settin' up with 'im, and Johnson got sleepy or somethin' and upset the lamp, and the doctor he was down in his office, and he came running up, and they all got burned together till they dragged 'em out."

Another man, always preserved for the deliverance of the final judgment, was saying: "Oh, they'll die sure. Burned to flinders. No chance. Hull lot of 'em. Anybody can see." The crowd concentrated its gaze still more closely upon these flags of fire which waved joyfully against the black sky. The bells of the town were clashing unceasingly.

A little procession moved across the lawn and toward the street. There were three cots, borne by twelve of the firemen. The police moved sternly, but it needed no effort of theirs to open a lane for this slow cortége. The men who bore the cots were well known to the crowd, but in this solemn parade during the ringing of the bells and the shouting, and with the red glare upon the sky, they seemed utterly foreign, and Whilomville paid them a deep respect. Each man in this stretcher party had gained a reflected majesty. They were footmen to death, and the crowd made subtle obeisance to this august dignity derived from three prospective graves. One woman turned away with a shriek at sight of the covered body on the first stretcher, and people faced her suddenly in silent and mournful indignation. Otherwise there was barely a sound as these twelve important men with measured tread carried their burdens through the throng.

The little boys no longer discussed the merits of the different fire companies. For the greater part they had been routed. Only the more courageous viewed closely the three figures veiled in yellow blankets.

X

Old Judge Denning Hagenthorpe, who lived nearly opposite the Trescotts, had thrown his door wide open to receive the afflicted family. When it was publicly learned that the doctor and his son and the negro were still alive, it required a specially detailed policeman to prevent people from scaling the front porch and interviewing these sorely wounded. One old lady appeared with a miraculous poultice, and she quoted most damning scripture to the officer when he said that she could not pass him. Throughout the night some lads old enough to be given privileges or to compel them from their mothers remained vigilantly upon the kerb in anticipation of a death or some such event. The reporter of the *Morning Tribune* rode thither on his bicycle every hour until three o'clock.

Six of the ten doctors in Whilomville attended at Judge Hagenthorpe's house.

Almost at once they were able to know that Trescott's burns were not vitally important. The child would possibly be scarred badly, but his life was undoubtedly safe. As for the negro Henry Johnson, he could not live. His body was frightfully seared, but more than that, he now had no face. His face had simply been burned away.

Trescott was always asking news of the two other patients. In the morning he seemed fresh and strong, so they told him that Johnson was doomed. They then saw him stir on the bed, and sprang quickly to see if the bandages needed readjusting. In the sudden glance he threw from one to another he impressed them as being both leonine and impracticable.

The morning paper announced the death of Henry Johnson. It contained a long interview with Edward J. Hannigan, in which the latter described in full the performance of Johnson at the fire. There was also an editorial built from all the best words in the vocabulary of the staff. The town halted in its accustomed road of thought, and turned a reverent attention to the memory of this hostler. In the breasts of many people was the regret that they had not known enough to give him a hand and a lift when he was alive, and they judged themselves stupid and ungenerous for this failure.

The name of Henry Johnson became suddenly the title of a saint to the little boys. The one who thought of it first could, by quoting it in an argument, at once overthrow his antagonist, whether it applied to the subject or whether it did not.

> Nigger, nigger, never die,
> Black face and shiny eye.

Boys who had called this odious couplet in the rear of Johnson's march buried the fact at the bottom of their hearts.

Later in the day Miss Bella Farragut, of No. 7 Watermelon Alley, announced that she had been engaged to marry Mr. Henry Johnson.

XI

The old judge had a cane with an ivory head. He could never think at his best until he was leaning slightly on this stick and smoothing the white top with slow movements of his hands. It was also to him a kind of narcotic. If by any chance he mislaid it, he grew at once very irritable, and was likely to speak sharply to his sister, whose mental incapacity he had patiently endured for thirty years in the old mansion on Ontario Street. She was not at all aware of her brother's opinion of her endowments, and so it might be said that the judge had successfully dissembled for more than a quarter of a century, only risking the truth at the times when his cane was lost.

On a particular day the judge sat in his arm-chair on the porch. The sunshine sprinkled through the lilac-bushes and poured great coins on the boards. The sparrows disputed in the trees that lined the pavements. The judge mused deeply, while his hands gently caressed the ivory head of his cane.

Finally he arose and entered the house, his brow still furrowed in a thoughtful frown. His stick thumped solemnly in regular beats. On the second floor he entered a room where Doctor Trescott was working about the bedside of Henry Johnson. The bandages on the negro's head allowed only one thing to appear, an eye, which unwinkingly stared at the judge. The latter spoke to Trescott on the condition of the patient. Afterward he evidently had something further to say, but he seemed to be kept from it by the scrutiny of the unwinking eye, at which he furtively glanced from time to time.

When Jimmie Trescott was sufficiently recovered, his mother had taken him to pay a visit to his grandparents in Connecticut. The doctor had remained to take care of his patients, but as a matter of truth he spent most of his time at Judge Hagenthorpe's house, where lay Henry Johnson. Here he slept and ate almost every meal in the long nights and days of his vigil.

At dinner, and away from the magic of the unwinking eye, the judge said, suddenly, "Trescott, do you think it is—" As Trescott paused expectantly, the judge fingered his knife. He said, thoughtfully, "No one wants to advance such ideas, but somehow I think that that poor fellow ought to die."

There was in Trescott's face at once a look of recognition, as if in this tangent of the judge he saw an old problem. He merely sighed and answered, "Who knows?" The words were spoken in a deep tone that gave them an elusive kind of significance.

The judge retreated to the cold manner of the bench. "Perhaps we may not talk with propriety of this kind of action, but I am induced to say that you are performing a questionable charity in preserving this negro's life. As near as I can understand, he will hereafter be a monster, a perfect monster, and probably with an affected brain. No man can observe you as I have observed you and not know that it was a matter of conscience with you, but I am afraid, my friend, that it is one of the blunders of virtue." The judge had delivered his views with his habitual oratory. The last three words he spoke with a particular emphasis, as if the phrase was his discovery.

The doctor made a weary gesture. "He saved my boy's life."

"Yes," said the judge, swiftly—"yes, I know!"

"And what am I to do?" said Trescott, his eyes suddenly lighting like an outburst from smouldering peat. "What am I to do? He gave himself for—for Jimmie. What am I to do for him?"

The judge abased himself completely before these words. He lowered his eyes for a moment. He picked at his cucumbers.

Presently he braced himself straightly in his chair. "He will be your creation, you understand. He is purely your creation. Nature has very evidently given him up. He is dead. You are restoring him to life. You are making him, and he will be a monster, and with no mind."

"He will be what you like, judge," cried Trescott, in sudden, polite fury. "He will be anything, but, by God! he saved my boy."

The judge interrupted in a voice trembling with emotion: "Trescott! Trescott! Don't I know?"

Trescott had subsided to a sullen mood. "Yes, you know," he answered, acidly; "but you don't know all about your own boy being saved from death." This was a perfectly childish allusion to the judge's bachelorhood. Trescott knew that the remark was infantile, but he seemed to take desperate delight in it.

But it passed the judge completely. It was not his spot.

"I am puzzled," said he, in profound thought. "I don't know what to say."

Trescott had become repentant. "Don't think I don't appreciate what you say, judge. But—"

"Of course!" responded the judge, quickly. "Of course."

"It—" began Trescott.

"Of course," said the judge.

In silence they resumed their dinner.

"Well," said the judge, ultimately, "it is hard for a man to know what to do."

"It is," said the doctor, fervidly.

There was another silence. It was broken by the judge:

"Look here, Trescott; I don't want you to think—"

"No, certainly not," answered the doctor, earnestly.

"Well, I don't want you to think I would say anything to— It was only that I thought that I might be able to suggest to you that—perhaps—the affair was a little dubious."

With an appearance of suddenly disclosing his real mental perturbation, the doctor said: "Well, what would you do? Would you kill him?" he asked, abruptly and sternly.

"Trescott, you fool," said the old man, gently.

"Oh, well, I know, judge, but then—" He turned red, and spoke with new violence: "Say, he saved my boy—do you see? He saved my boy."

"You bet he did," cried the judge, with enthusiasm. "You bet he did." And they remained for a time gazing at each other, their faces illuminated with memories of a certain deed.

After another silence, the judge said, "It is hard for a man to know what to do."

XII

Late one evening Trescott, returning from a professional call, paused his buggy at the Hagenthorpe gate. He tied the mare to the old tin-covered post, and entered the house. Ultimately he appeared with a companion—a man who walked slowly and carefully, as if he were learning. He was wrapped to the heels in an old-fashioned ulster. They entered the buggy and drove away.

After a silence only broken by the swift and musical humming of the wheels on the smooth road, Trescott spoke. "Henry," he said, "I've got you a home here with old Alek Williams. You will have everything you want to eat and a good place to sleep, and I hope you will get along there all right. I will pay all your expenses, and come to see you as often as I can. If you don't get along, I want you to let me know as soon as possible, and then we will do what we can to make it better."

The dark figure at the doctor's side answered with a cheerful laugh. "These buggy wheels don' look like I washed 'em yestehday, docteh," he said.

Trescott hesitated for a moment, and then went on insistently, "I am taking you to Alek Williams, Henry, and I—"

The figure chuckled again. "No, 'deed! No seh! Alek Williams don' know a hoss! 'Deed he don't. He don' know a hoss from a pig." The laugh that followed was like the rattle of pebbles.

Trescott turned and looked sternly and coldly at the dim form in the gloom from the buggy-top. "Henry," he said, "I didn't say anything about horses. I was saying—"

"Hoss? Hoss?" said the quavering voice from these near shadows. "Hoss? 'Deed I don't know all erbout a hoss! 'Deed I don't." There was a satirical chuckle.

At the end of three miles the mare slackened and the doctor leaned forward, peering, while holding tight reins. The wheels of the buggy bumped often over out-cropping bowlders. A window shone forth, a simple square of topaz on a great black hill-side. Four dogs charged the buggy with ferocity, and when it did not promptly retreat, they circled courageously around the flanks, baying. A door opened near the window in the hill-side, and a man came and stood on a beach of yellow light.

"Yah! yah! You Roveh! You Susie! Come yah! Come yah this minit!"

Trescott called across the dark sea of grass, "Hello, Alek!"

"Hello!"

"Come down here and show me where to drive."

The man plunged from the beach into the surf, and Trescott could then only trace his course by the fervid and polite ejaculations of a host who was somewhere approaching. Presently Williams took the mare by the head, and uttering cries of welcome and scolding the swarming dogs, led the equipage toward the lights. When they halted at the door and Trescott was climbing out, Williams cried, "Will she stand, docteh?"

"She'll stand all right, but you better hold her for a minute. Now, Henry." The doctor turned and held both arms to the dark figure. It crawled to him painfully like a man going down a ladder. Williams took the mare away to be tied to a little tree, and when he returned he found them awaiting him in the gloom beyond the rays from the door.

He burst out then like a siphon pressed by a nervous thumb. "Hennery! Hennery, ma ol' frien'. Well, if I ain' glade. If I ain' glade!"

Trescott had taken the silent shape by the arm and led it forward into the full revelation of the light. "Well, now, Alek, you can take Henry and put him to bed, and in the morning I will—"

Near the end of this sentence old Williams had come front to front with Johnson. He gasped for a second, and then yelled the yell of a man stabbed in the heart.

For a fraction of a moment Trescott seemed to be looking for epithets. Then he roared: "You old black chump! You old black —Shut up! Shut up! Do you hear?"

Williams obeyed instantly in the matter of his screams, but he continued in a lowered voice: "Ma Lode amassy! Who'd ever think? Ma Lode amassy!"

Trescott spoke again in the manner of a commander of a battalion. "Alek!"

The old negro again surrendered, but to himself he repeated in a whisper, "Ma Lode!" He was aghast and trembling.

As these three points of widening shadows approached the golden doorway a hale old negress appeared there, bowing. "Good-evenin', docteh! Good-evenin'! Come in! come in!" She had evidently just retired from a tempestuous struggle to place the room in order, but she was now bowing rapidly. She made the effort of a person swimming.

"Don't trouble yourself, Mary," said Trescott, entering. "I've brought Henry for you to take care of, and all you've got to do is to carry out what I tell you." Learning that he was not followed, he faced the door, and said, "Come in, Henry."

Johnson entered. "Whee!" shrieked Mrs. Williams. She almost achieved a back somersault. Six young members of the tribe of Williams made simultaneous plunge for a position behind the stove, and formed a wailing heap.

XIII

"You know very well that you and your family lived usually on less than three dollars a week, and now that Doctor Trescott pays you five dollars a week for Johnson's board, you live like millionaires. You haven't done a stroke of work since Johnson began to board with you—everybody knows that—and so what are you kicking about?"

The judge sat in his chair on the porch, fondling his cane, and gazing down at old Williams, who stood under the lilac-bushes. "Yes, I know, jedge," said the negro, wagging his head in a puzzled manner. " 'Tain't like as if I didn't 'preciate what the docteh done, but—but—well, yeh see, jedge," he added, gaining a new impetus, "it's—it's hard wuk. This ol' man nev' did wuk so hard. Lode, no."

"Don't talk such nonsense, Alek," spoke the judge, sharply. "You have never really worked in your life—anyhow enough to support a family of sparrows, and now when you are in a more prosperous condition than ever before, you come around talking like an old fool."

The negro began to scratch his head. "Yeh see, jedge," he said at last, "my ol' 'ooman she cain't 'ceive no lady callahs, nohow."

"Hang lady callers!" said the judge, irascibly. "If you have flour in the barrel and meat in the pot, your wife can get along without receiving lady callers, can't she?"

"But they won't come ainyhow, jedge," replied Williams, with an air of still deeper stupefaction. "Noner ma wife's frien's ner noner ma frien's'll come near ma res'dence."

"Well, let them stay home if they are such silly people."

The old negro seemed to be seeking a way to elude this argument, but evidently finding none, he was about to shuffle meekly off. He halted, however. "Jedge," said he, "ma ol' 'ooman's near driv' abstracted."

"Your old woman is an idiot," responded the judge.

Williams came very close and peered solemnly through a branch of lilac. "Jedge," he whispered, "the chillens."

"What about them?"

Dropping his voice to funereal depths, Williams said, "They— they cain't eat."

"Can't eat!" scoffed the judge, loudly. "Can't eat! You must think I am as big an old fool as you are. Can't eat—the little rascals! What's to prevent them from eating?"

In answer, Williams said, with mournful emphasis, "Hennery." Moved with a kind of satisfaction at his tragic use of the name, he remained staring at the judge for a sign of its effect.

The judge made a gesture of irritation. "Come, now, you old scoundrel, don't beat around the bush any more. What are you up to? What do you want? Speak out like a man, and don't give me any more of this tiresome rigamarole."

"I ain't er-beatin' round 'bout nuffin, jedge," replied Williams, indignantly. "No, seh; I say whatter got to say right out. 'Deed I do."

"Well, say it, then."

"Jedge," began the negro, taking off his hat and switching his knee with it, "Lode knows I'd do jes 'bout as much fer five dollehs er week as ainy cul'd man, but—but this yere business is awful, jedge. I raikon ain't been no sleep in—in my house sence docteh done fetch 'im."

"Well, what do you propose to do about it?"

Williams lifted his eyes from the ground and gazed off through the trees. "Raikon I got good appetite, an' sleep jes like er dog, but he—he's done broke me all up. 'Tain't no good, nohow. I wake up in the night; I hear 'im, mebbe, er-whimperin' an' er-whimperin', an' I sneak an' I sneak until I try th' do' to see if he locked in. An' he keep me er-puzzlin' an' er-quakin' all night long. Don't know how 'll do in th' winter. Can't let 'im out where th' chillen is. He'll done freeze where he is now." Williams spoke these sentences as if he were talking to himself. After a silence of deep reflection he continued: "Folks go round sayin' he ain't Hennery Johnson at all. They say he's er devil!"

"What?" cried the judge.

"Yesseh," repeated Williams in tones of injury, as if his veracity had been challenged. "Yesseh. I'm er-tellin' it to yeh straight, jedge. Plenty cul'd people folks up my way say it is a devil."

"Well, you don't think so yourself, do you?"

"No. 'Tain't no devil. It's Hennery Johnson."

"Well, then, what is the matter with you? You don't care what a lot of foolish people say. Go on 'tending to your business, and pay no attention to such idle nonsense."

" 'Tis nonsense, jedge; but he *looks* like er devil."

"What do you care what he looks like?" demanded the judge.

"Ma rent is two dollehs and er half er month," said Williams, slowly.

"It might just as well be ten thousand dollars a month," responded the judge. "You never pay it, anyhow."

"Then, anoth' thing," continued Williams, in his reflective tone. "If he was all right in his haid I could stan' it; but, jedge, he's crazier 'n er loon. Then when he looks like er devil, an' done skears all ma frien's away, an' ma chillens cain't eat, an' ma ole 'ooman jes raisin' Cain all the time, an' ma rent two dollehs an' er half er month, an' him not right in his haid, it seems like five dollehs er week—"

The judge's stick came down sharply and suddenly upon the floor of the porch. "There," he said, "I thought that was what you were driving at."

Williams began swinging his head from side to side in the strange racial mannerism. "Now hol' on a minit, jedge," he said, defensively. " 'Tain't like as if I didn't 'preciate what the docteh done. 'Tain't that. Docteh Trescott is er kind man, an' 'tain't like as if I didn't 'preciate what he done; but—but—"

"But what? You are getting painful, Alek. Now tell me this: did you ever have five dollars a week regularly before in your life?"

Williams at once drew himself up with great dignity, but in the pause after that question he drooped gradually to another atti-tude. In the end he answered, heroically: "No, jedge, I ain't. An' 'tain't like as if I was er-saying' five dollehs wasn't er lot er money fer a man like me. But, jedge, what er man oughter git fer this kinder wuk is er salary. Yesseh, jedge," he repeated, with a great impressive gesture; "fer this kinder wuk er man oughter git er Salary." He laid a terrible emphasis upon the final word.

The judge laughed. "I know Doctor Trescott's mind concerning this affair, Alek; and if you are dissatisfied with your boarder, he is quite ready to move him to some other place; so, if you care to leave word with me that you are tired of the arrangement and wish it changed, he will come and take Johnson away."

Williams scratched his head again in deep perplexity. "Five dollehs is er big price fer bo'd, but 'tain't no big price fer the bo'd of er crazy man," he said, finally.

"What do you think you ought to get?" asked the judge.

"Well," answered Alek, in the manner of one deep in a balanc-ing of the scales, "he looks like er devil, an' done skears e'rybody, an' ma chillens cain't eat, an' I cain't sleep, an' he ain't right in his haid, an'—"

"You told me all those things."

After scratching his wool, and beating his knee with his hat, and gazing off through the trees and down at the ground, Williams said, as he kicked nervously at the gravel, "Well, jedge, I think it is wuth—" He stuttered.

"Worth what?"

"Six dollehs," answered Williams, in a desperate outburst.

The judge lay back in his great arm-chair and went through all the motions of a man laughing heartily, but he made no sound save a slight cough. Williams had been watching him with apprehension.

"Well," said the judge, "do you call six dollars a salary?"

"No, seh," promptly responded Williams. " 'Tain't a salary. No, 'deed! 'Tain't a salary." He looked with some anger upon the man who questioned his intelligence in this way.

"Well, supposing your children can't eat?"

"I—"

"And supposing he looks like a devil? And supposing all those things continue? Would you be satisfied with six dollars a week?"

Recollections seemed to throng in Williams's mind at these interrogations, and he answered dubiously. "Of co'se a man who ain't right in his haid, an' looks like er devil— But six dollehs—" After these two attempts at a sentence Williams suddenly appeared as an orator, with a great shiny palm waving in the air. "I tell yeh, jedge, six dollehs is six dollehs, but if I git six dollehs for bo'ding Hennery Johnson, I uhns it! I uhns it!"

"I don't doubt that you earn six dollars for every week's work you do," said the judge.

"Well, if I bo'd Hennery Johnson fer six dollehs er week, I uhns it! I uhns it!" cried Williams, wildly.

XIV

Reifsnyder's assistant had gone to his supper, and the owner of the shop was trying to placate four men who wished to be shaved at once. Reifsnyder was very garrulous—a fact which made him rather remarkable among barbers, who, as a class, are austerely speechless, having been taught silence by the hammering reiteration of a tradition. It is the customers who talk in the ordinary event.

As Reifsnyder waved his razor down the cheek of a man in the chair, he turned often to cool the impatience of the others with pleasant talk, which they did not particularly heed.

"Oh, he should have let him die," said Bainbridge, a railway engineer, finally replying to one of the barber's orations. "Shut up, Reif, and go on with your business!"

Instead, Reifsnyder paused shaving entirely, and turned to front the speaker. "Let him die?" he demanded. "How vas that? How can you let a man die?"

"By letting him die, you chump," said the engineer. The others laughed a little, and Reifsnyder turned at once to his work, sullenly, as a man overwhelmed by the derision of numbers.

"How vas that?" he grumbled later. "How can you let a man die when he vas done so much for you?"

" 'When he vas done so much for you?' " repeated Bainbridge. "You better shave some people. How vas that? Maybe this ain't a barber shop?"

A man hitherto silent now said, "If I had been the doctor, I would have done the same thing."

"Of course," said Reifsnyder. "Any man vould do it. Any man that vas not like you, you—old—flint-hearted—fish." He had sought the final words with painful care, and he delivered the collection triumphantly at Bainbridge. The engineer laughed.

The man in the chair now lifted himself higher, while Reifsnyder began an elaborate ceremony of anointing and combing his hair. Now free to join comfortably in the talk, the man said: "They say he is the most terrible thing in the world. Young Johnnie Bernard—that drives the grocery wagon—saw him up at Alek Williams's shanty, and he says he couldn't eat anything for two days."

"Chee!" said Reifsnyder.

"Well, what makes him so terrible?" asked another.

"Because he hasn't got any face," replied the barber and the engineer in duet.

"Hasn't got any face?" repeated the man. "How can he do without any face!"

> "He has no face in the front of his head,
> In the place where his face ought to grow."

Bainbridge sang these lines pathetically as he arose and hung his hat on a hook. The man in the chair was about to abdicate in his favor. "Get a gait on you now," he said to Reifsnyder. "I go out at 7.31."

As the barber foamed the lather on the cheeks of the engineer he seemed to be thinking heavily. Then suddenly he burst out. "How would you like to be with no face?" he cried to the assemblage.

"Oh, if I had to have a face like yours—" answered one customer.

Bainbridge's voice came from a sea of lather. "You're kicking because if losing faces became popular, you'd have to go out of business."

"I don't think it will become so much popular," said Reifsnyder.

"Not if it's got to be taken off in the way his was taken off," said another man. "I'd rather keep mine, if you don't mind."

"I guess so!" cried the barber. "Just think!"

The shaving of Bainbridge had arrived at a time of comparative liberty for him. "I wonder what the doctor says to himself?" he observed. "He may be sorry he made him live."

"It was the only thing he could do," replied a man. The others seemed to agree with him.

"Supposing you were in his place," said one, "and Johnson had saved your kid. What would you do?"

"Certainly!"

"Of course! You would do anything on earth for him. You'd take all the trouble in the world for him. And spend your last dollar on him. Well, then?"

"I wonder how it feels to be without any face?" said Reifsnyder, musingly.

The man who had previously spoken, feeling that he had expressed himself well, repeated the whole thing. "You would do anything on earth for him. You'd take all the trouble in the world for him. And spend your last dollar on him. Well, then?"

"No, but look," said Reifsnyder; "supposing you don't got a face!"

XV

As soon as Williams was hidden from the view of the old judge he began to gesture and talk to himself. An elation had evidently penetrated to his vitals, and caused him to dilate as if he had been filled with gas. He snapped his fingers in the air, and whistled fragments of triumphal music. At times, in his progress toward his shanty, he indulged in a shuffling movement that was really a dance. It was to be learned from the intermediate monologue that he had emerged from his trials laurelled and proud. He was the unconquerable Alexander Williams. Nothing could exceed the bold self-reliance of his manner. His kingly stride, his heroic song, the derisive flourish of his hands—all betokened a man who had successfully defied the world.

On his way he saw Zeke Paterson coming to town. They hailed each other at a distance of fifty yards.

"How do, Broth' Paterson?"

"How do, Broth' Williams?"

They were both deacons.

"Is you' folks well, Broth' Paterson?"

"Middlin', middlin'. How's you' folks, Broth' Williams?"

Neither of them had slowed his pace in the smallest degree. They had simply begun this talk when a considerable space separated them, continued it as they passed, and added polite questions as they drifted steadily apart. Williams's mind seemed to be a balloon. He had been so inflated that he had not noticed that Paterson had definitely shied into the dry ditch as they came to the point of ordinary contact.

Afterward, as he went a lonely way, he burst out again in song and pantomimic celebration of his estate. His feet moved in prancing steps.

When he came in sight of his cabin, the fields were bathed in a blue dusk, and the light in the window was pale. Cavorting and gesticulating, he gazed joyfully for some moments upon this light. Then suddenly another idea seemed to attack his mind, and he stopped, with an air of being suddenly dampened. In the end he approached his home as if it were the fortress of an enemy.

Some dogs disputed his advance for a loud moment, and then discovering their lord, slunk away embarrassed. His reproaches were addressed to them in muffled tones.

Arriving at the door, he pushed it open with the timidity of a new thief. He thrust his head cautiously sideways, and his eyes met the eyes of his wife, who sat by the table, the lamp-light defining a half of her face. " 'Sh!" he said, uselessly. His glance travelled swiftly to the inner door which shielded the one bed-chamber. The pickaninnies, strewn upon the floor of the living-room, were softly snoring. After a hearty meal they had promptly dispersed themselves about the place and gone to sleep. " 'Sh!" said Williams again to his motionless and silent wife. He had allowed only his head to appear. His wife, with one hand upon the edge of the table and the other at her knee, was regarding him with wide eyes and parted lips as if he were a spectre. She looked to be one who was living in terror, and even the familiar face at the door had thrilled her because it had come suddenly.

Williams broke the tense silence. "Is he all right?" he whispered, waving his eyes toward the inner door. Following his glance timorously, his wife nodded, and in a low tone answered,

"I raikon he's done gone t' sleep."

Williams then slunk noiselessly across his threshold.

He lifted a chair, and with infinite care placed it so that it faced the dreaded inner door. His wife moved slightly, so as to also squarely face it. A silence came upon them in which they seemed to be waiting for a calamity, pealing and deadly.

Williams finally coughed behind his hand. His wife started, and looked upon him in alarm. " 'Pears like he done gwine keep quiet ter-night," he breathed. They continually pointed their speech and their looks at the inner door, paying it the homage due to a corpse or a phantom. Another long stillness followed this sentence. Their eyes shone white and wide. A wagon rattled down the distant road. From their chairs they looked at the window, and the effect of the light in the cabin was a presentation of an intensely black and solemn night. The old woman adopted the attitude used always in church at funerals. At times she seemed to be upon the point of breaking out in prayer.

"He mighty quiet ter-night," whispered Williams. "Was he good ter-day?" For answer his wife raised her eyes to the ceiling in the supplication of Job. Williams moved restlessly. Finally he tiptoed to the door. He knelt slowly and without a sound, and placed his ear near the key-hole. Hearing a noise behind him, he turned quickly. His wife was staring at him aghast. She stood in front of the stove, and her arms were spread out in the natural movement to protect all her sleeping ducklings.

But Williams arose without having touched the door. "I raikon he er-sleep," he said, fingering his wool. He debated with himself for some time. During this interval his wife remained, a great fat statue of a mother shielding her children.

It was plain that his mind was swept suddenly by a wave of temerity. With a sounding step he moved toward the door. His fingers were almost upon the knob when he swiftly ducked and dodged away, clapping his hands to the back of his head. It was as if the portal had threatened him. There was a little tumult near the stove, where Mrs. Williams's desperate retreat had involved her feet with the prostrate children.

After the panic Williams bore traces of a feeling of shame. He returned to the charge. He firmly grasped the knob with his left hand, and with his other hand turned the key in the lock. He pushed the door, and as it swung portentously open he sprang nimbly to one side like the fearful slave liberating the lion. Near the stove a group had formed, the terror-stricken mother with her arms stretched, and the aroused children clinging frenziedly to her skirts.

The light streamed after the swinging door, and disclosed a room six feet one way and six feet the other way. It was small enough to enable the radiance to lay it plain. Williams peered warily around the corner made by the door-post.

Suddenly he advanced, retired, and advanced again with a howl. His palsied family had expected him to spring backward, and at his howl they heaped themselves wondrously. But Williams simply stood in the little room emitting his howls before an open window. "He's gone! He's gone! He's gone!" His eye and his hand had speedily proved the fact. He had even thrown open a little cupboard.

Presently he came flying out. He grabbed his hat, and hurled the outer door back upon its hinges. Then he tumbled headlong into the night. He was yelling: "Docteh Trescott! Docteh Trescott!" He ran wildly through the fields, and galloped in the direction of town. He continued to call to Trescott, as if the latter was within easy hearing. It was as if Trescott was poised in the contemplative sky over the running negro, and could heed this reaching voice—"Docteh Trescott!"

In the cabin, Mrs. Williams, supported by relays from the battalion of children, stood quaking watch until the truth of daylight came as a re-enforcement and made them arrogant, strutting, swashbuckler children, and a mother who proclaimed her illimitable courage.

XVI

Theresa Page was giving a party. It was the outcome of a long series of arguments addressed to her mother, which had been overheard in part by her father. He had at last said five words, "Oh, let her have it." The mother had then gladly capitulated.

Theresa had written nineteen invitations, and distributed them at recess to her schoolmates. Later her mother had composed five large cakes, and still later a vast amount of lemonade.

So the nine little girls and the ten little boys sat quite primly in the dining-room, while Theresa and her mother plied them with cake and lemonade, and also with ice-cream. This primness sat now quite strangely upon them. It was owing to the presence of Mrs. Page. Previously in the parlor alone with their games they had overturned a chair; the boys had let more or less of their hoodlum spirit shine forth. But when circumstances could be possibly magnified to warrant it, the girls made the boys victims of an insufferable pride, snubbing them mercilessly. So in the dining-room they resembled a class at Sunday-school, if it were not for the subterranean smiles, gestures, rebuffs, and poutings which stamped the affair as a children's party.

Two little girls of this subdued gathering were planted in a settle with their backs to the broad window. They were beaming lovingly upon each other with an effect of scorning the boys.

Hearing a noise behind her at the window, one little girl turned to face it. Instantly she screamed and sprang away, covering her face with her hands. "What was it? What was it?" cried every one in a roar. Some slight movement of the eyes of the weeping and shuddering child informed the company that she had been frightened by an appearance at the window. At once they all faced the imperturbable window, and for a moment there was a silence. An astute lad made an immediate census of the other lads. The prank of slipping out and looming spectrally at a window was too venerable. But the little boys were all present and astonished.

As they recovered their minds they uttered warlike cries, and through a side door sallied rapidly out against the terror. They vied with each other in daring.

None wished particularly to encounter a dragon in the darkness of the garden, but there could be no faltering when the fair ones in the dining-room were present. Calling to each other in stern voices, they went dragooning over the lawn, attacking the shadows with ferocity, but still with the caution of reasonable beings. They found, however, nothing new to the peace of the night. Of course there was a lad who told a great lie. He described a grim figure, bending low and slinking off along the fence. He gave a number of details, rendering his lie more splendid by a repetition of certain forms which he recalled from romances. For instance, he insisted that he had heard the creature emit a hollow laugh.

Inside the house the little girl who had raised the alarm was still shuddering and weeping. With the utmost difficulty was she brought to a state approximating calmness by Mrs. Page. Then she wanted to go home at once.

Page entered the house at this time. He had exiled himself until he concluded that this children's party was finished and gone. He was obliged to escort the little girl home because she screamed again when they opened the door and she saw the night.

She was not coherent even to her mother. Was it a man? She didn't know. It was simply a thing, a dreadful thing.

XVII

In Watermelon Alley the Farraguts were spending their evening as usual on the little rickety porch. Sometimes they howled gossip to other people on other rickety porches. The thin wail of a baby arose from a near house. A man had a terrific altercation with his wife, to which the alley paid no attention at all.

There appeared suddenly before the Farraguts a monster making a low and sweeping bow. There was an instant's pause, and then occurred something that resembled the effect of an upheaval of the earth's surface. The old woman hurled herself backward with a dreadful cry. Young Sim had been perched gracefully on a railing. At sight of the monster he simply fell over it to the ground. He made no sound, his eyes stuck out, his nerveless hands tried to grapple the rail to prevent a tumble, and then he vanished. Bella, blubbering, and with her hair suddenly and mysteriously dishevelled, was crawling on her hands and knees fearsomely up the steps.

Standing before this wreck of a family gathering, the monster continued to bow. It even raised a deprecatory claw. "Don' make no botheration 'bout me, Miss Fa'gut," it said, politely. "No, 'deed. I jes drap in ter ax if yer well this evenin', Miss Fa'gut. Don' make no botheration. No, 'deed. I gwine ax you to go to er daince with me, Miss Fa'gut. I ax you if I can have the magnifercent gratitude of you' company on that 'casion, Miss Fa'gut."

The girl cast a miserable glance behind her. She was still crawling away. On the ground beside the porch young Sim raised a strange bleat, which expressed both his fright and his lack of wind. Presently the monster, with a fashionable amble, ascended the steps after the girl.

She grovelled in a corner of the room as the creature took a chair. It seated itself very elegantly on the edge. It held an old cap in both hands. "Don' make no botheration, Miss Fa'gut. Don' make no botherations. No, 'deed. I jes drap in ter ax you if you won' do me the proud of acceptin' ma humble invitation to er daince, Miss Fa'gut."

She shielded her eyes with her arms and tried to crawl past it, but the genial monster blocked the way. "I jes drap in ter ax you 'bout er daince, Miss Fa'gut. I ax you if I kin have the magnifercent gratitude of you' company on that 'casion, Miss Fa'gut."

In a last outbreak of despair, the girl, shuddering and wailing, threw herself face downward on the floor, while the monster sat on the edge of the chair gabbling courteous invitations, and holding the old hat daintily to its stomach.

At the back of the house, Mrs. Farragut, who was of enormous weight, and who for eight years had done little more than sit in an arm-chair and describe her various ailments, had with speed and agility scaled a high board fence.

XVIII

The black mass in the middle of Trescott's property was hardly allowed to cool before the builders were at work on another house. It had sprung upward at a fabulous rate. It was like a magical composition born of the ashes. The doctor's office was the first part to be completed, and he had already moved in his new books and instruments and medicines.

Trescott sat before his desk when the chief of police arrived. "Well, we found him," said the latter.

"Did you?" cried the doctor. "Where?"

"Shambling around the streets at daylight this morning. I'll be blamed if I can figure on where he passed the night."

"Where is he now?"

"Oh, we jugged him. I didn't know what else to do with him. That's what I want you to tell me. Of course we can't keep him. No charge could be made, you know."

"I'll come down and get him."

The official grinned retrospectively. "Must say he had a fine career while he was out. First thing he did was to break up a children's party at Page's. Then he went to Watermelon Alley. Whoo! He stampeded the whole outfit. Men, women, and children running pell-mell, and yelling. They say one old woman broke her leg, or something, shinning over a fence. Then he went right out on the main street, and an Irish girl threw a fit, and there was a sort of a riot. He began to run, and a big crowd chased him, firing rocks. But he gave them the slip somehow down there by the foundry and in the railroad yard. We looked for him all night, but couldn't find him."

"Was he hurt any? Did anybody hit him with a stone?"

"Guess there isn't much of him to hurt any more, is there? Guess he's been hurt up to the limit. No. They never touched him. Of course nobody really wanted to hit him, but you know how a crowd gets. It's like—it's like—"

"Yes, I know."

For a moment the chief of the police looked reflectively at the floor. Then he spoke hesitatingly. "You know Jake Winter's little girl was the one that he scared at the party. She is pretty sick, they say."

"Is she? Why, they didn't call me. I always attend the Winter family."

"No? Didn't they?" asked the chief, slowly. "Well—you know —Winter is—well, Winter has gone clean crazy over this business. He wanted—he wanted to have you arrested."

"Have me arrested? The idiot! What in the name of wonder could he have me arrested for?"

"Of course. He is a fool. I told him to keep his trap shut. But then you know how he'll go all over town yapping about the thing. I thought I'd better tip you."

"Oh, he is of no consequence; but then, of course, I'm obliged to you, Sam."

"That's all right. Well, you'll be down to-night and take him out, eh? You'll get a good welcome from the jailer. He don't like his job for a cent. He says you can have your man whenever you want him. He's got no use for him."

"But what is this business of Winter's about having me arrested?"

"Oh, it's a lot of chin about your having no right to allow this —this—this man to be at large. But I told him to tend to his own business. Only I thought I'd better let you know. And I might as well say right now, doctor, that there is a good deal of talk about this thing. If I were you, I'd come to the jail pretty late at night, because there is likely to be a crowd around the door, and I'd bring a—er—mask, or some kind of a veil, anyhow."

XIX

Martha Goodwin was single, and well along into the thin years. She lived with her married sister in Whilomville. She performed nearly all the house-work in exchange for the privilege of existence. Every one tacitly recognized her labor as a form of penance for the early end of her betrothed, who had died of small-pox, which he had not caught from her.

But despite the strenuous and unceasing workaday of her life, she was a woman of great mind. She had adamantine opinions upon the situation in Armenia, the condition of women in China, the flirtation between Mrs. Minster of Niagara Avenue and young Griscom, the conflict in the Bible class of the Baptist Sunday-school, the duty of the United States toward the Cuban insurgents, and many other colossal matters. Her fullest experience of violence was gained on an occasion when she had seen a hound clubbed, but in the plan which she had made for the reform of the world she advocated drastic measures. For instance, she contended that all the Turks should be pushed into the sea and drowned, and that Mrs. Minster and young Griscom should be hanged side by side on twin gallows. In fact, this woman of peace, who had seen only peace, argued constantly for a creed of illimitable ferocity. She was invulnerable on these questions, because eventually she overrode all opponents with a sniff. This sniff was an active force. It was to her antagonists like a bang over the head, and none was known to recover from this expression of exalted contempt. It left them windless and conquered. They never again came forward as candidates for suppression. And Martha walked her kitchen with a stern brow, an invincible being like Napoleon.

Nevertheless her acquaintances, from the pain of their defeats, had been long in secret revolt. It was in no wise a conspiracy, because they did not care to state their open rebellion, but nevertheless it was understood that any woman who could not coincide with one of Martha's contentions was entitled to the support of others in the small circle. It amounted to an arrangement by which all were required to disbelieve any theory for which Martha fought. This, however, did not prevent them from speaking of her mind with profound respect.

Two people bore the brunt of her ability. Her sister Kate was visibly afraid of her, while Carrie Dungen sailed across from her kitchen to sit respectfully at Martha's feet and learn the business of the world. To be sure, afterward, under another sun, she always laughed at Martha and pretended to deride her ideas, but in the presence of the sovereign she always remained silent or admiring. Kate, the sister, was of no consequence at all. Her principal delusion was that she did all the work in the upstairs rooms of the house, while Martha did it downstairs. The truth was seen only by the husband, who treated Martha with a kindness that was half banter, half deference. Martha herself had no suspicion that she was the only pillar of the domestic edifice. The situation was without definitions. Martha made definitions, but she devoted them entirely to the Armenians and Griscom and the Chinese and other subjects. Her dreams, which in early days had been of love of meadows and the shade of trees, of the face of a man, were now involved otherwise, and they were companioned in the kitchen curiously, Cuba, the hot-water kettle, Armenia, the washing of the dishes, and the whole thing being jumbled. In regard to social misdemeanors, she who was simply the mausoleum of a dead passion was probably the most savage critic in town. This unknown woman, hidden in a kitchen as in a well, was sure to have a considerable effect of the one kind or the other in the life of the town. Every time it moved a yard, she had personally contributed an inch. She could hammer so stoutly upon the door of a proposition that it would break from its hinges and fall upon her, but at any rate it moved. She was an engine, and the fact that she did not know that she was an engine contributed largely to the effect. One reason that she was formidable was that she did not even imagine that she was formidable. She remained a weak, innocent, and pig-headed creature, who alone would defy the universe if she thought the universe merited this proceeding.

One day Carrie Dungen came across from her kitchen with speed. She had a great deal of grist. "Oh," she cried, "Henry Johnson got away from where they was keeping him, and came to town last night, and scared everybody almost to death."

Martha was shining a dish-pan, polishing madly. No reasonable person could see cause for this operation, because the pan already glistened like silver. "Well!" she ejaculated. She imparted to the word a deep meaning. "This, my prophecy, has come to pass." It was a habit.

The overplus of information was choking Carrie. Before she could go on she was obliged to struggle for a moment. "And, oh, little Sadie Winter is awful sick, and they say Jake Winter was around this morning trying to get Doctor Trescott arrested. And poor old Mrs. Farragut sprained her ankle in trying to climb a fence. And there's a crowd around the jail all the time. They put Henry in jail because they didn't know what else to do with him, I guess. They say he is perfectly terrible."

Martha finally released the dish-pan and confronted the head-long speaker. "Well!" she said again, poising a great brown rag. Kate had heard the excited new-comer, and drifted down from the novel in her room. She was a shivery little woman. Her shoulder-blades seemed to be two panes of ice, for she was constantly shrugging and shrugging. "Serves him right if he was to lose all his patients," she said suddenly, in blood-thirsty tones. She snipped her words out as if her lips were scissors.

"Well, he's likely to," shouted Carrie Dungen. "Don't a lot of people say that they won't have him any more? If you're sick and nervous, Doctor Trescott would scare the life out of you, wouldn't he? He would me. I'd keep thinking."

Martha, stalking to and fro, sometimes surveyed the two other women with a contemplative frown.

XX

After the return from Connecticut, little Jimmie was at first much afraid of the monster who lived in the room over the carriage-house. He could not identify it in any way. Gradually, however, his fear dwindled under the influence of a weird fasci-nation. He sidled into closer and closer relations with it.

One time the monster was seated on a box behind the stable basking in the rays of the afternoon sun. A heavy crêpe veil was swathed about its head.

Little Jimmie and many companions came around the corner of the stable. They were all in what was popularly known as the baby class, and consequently escaped from school a half-hour before the other children. They halted abruptly at sight of the figure on the box. Jimmie waved his hand with the air of a proprietor.

"There he is," he said.

"O-o-o!" murmured all the little boys—"o-o-o!" They shrank back, and grouped according to courage or experience, as at the sound the monster slowly turned its head. Jimmie had remained in the van alone. "Don't be afraid! I won't let him hurt you," he said, delighted.

"Huh!" they replied, contemptuously. "We ain't afraid."

Jimmie seemed to reap all the joys of the owner and exhibitor of one of the world's marvels, while his audience remained at a distance—awed and entranced, fearful and envious.

One of them addressed Jimmie gloomily. "Bet you dassent walk right up to him." He was an older boy than Jimmie, and habitually oppressed him to a small degree. This new social elevation of the smaller lad probably seemed revolutionary to him.

"Huh!" said Jimmie, with deep scorn. "Dassent I? Dassent I, hey? Dassent I?"

The group was immensely excited. It turned its eyes upon the boy that Jimmie addressed. "No, you dassent," he said, stolidly, facing a moral defeat. He could see that Jimmie was resolved. "No, you dassent," he repeated, doggedly.

"Ho!" cried Jimmie. "You just watch!—you just watch!"

Amid a silence he turned and marched toward the monster. But possibly the palpable wariness of his companions had an effect upon him that weighed more than his previous experience, for suddenly, when near to the monster, he halted dubiously. But his playmates immediately uttered a derisive shout, and it seemed to force him forward. He went to the monster and laid his hand delicately on its shoulder. "Hello, Henry," he said, in a voice that trembled a trifle. The monster was crooning a weird line of negro melody that was scarcely more than a thread of sound, and it paid no heed to the boy.

Jimmie strutted back to his companions. They acclaimed him and hooted his opponent. Amidst this clamor the larger boy with difficulty preserved a dignified attitude.

"I dassent, dassent I?" said Jimmie to him. "Now, you're so smart, let's see you do it!"

This challenge brought forth renewed taunts from the others. The larger boy puffed out his cheeks. "Well, I ain't afraid," he explained, sullenly. He had made a mistake in diplomacy, and now his small enemies were tumbling his prestige all about his ears. They crowed like roosters and bleated like lambs, and made many other noises which were supposed to bury him in ridicule and dishonor. "Well, I ain't afraid," he continued to explain through the din.

Jimmie, the hero of the mob, was pitiless. "You ain't afraid, hey?" he sneered. "If you ain't afraid, go do it, then."

"Well, I would if I wanted to," the other retorted. His eyes wore an expression of profound misery, but he preserved steadily other portions of a pot-valiant air. He suddenly faced one of his persecutors. "If you're so smart, why don't you go do it?" This persecutor sank promptly through the group to the rear. The incident gave the badgered one a breathing-spell, and for a moment even turned the derision in another direction. He took advantage of his interval. "I'll do it if anybody else will," he announced, swaggering to and fro.

Candidates for the adventure did not come forward. To defend themselves from this counter-charge, the other boys again set up their crowing and bleating. For a while they would hear nothing from him. Each time he opened his lips their chorus of noises made oratory impossible. But at last he was able to repeat that he would volunteer to dare as much in the affair as any other boy.

"Well, you go first," they shouted.

But Jimmie intervened to once more lead the populace against the large boy. "You're mighty brave, ain't you?" he said to him. "You dared me to do it, and I did—didn't I? Now who's afraid?" The others cheered this view loudly, and they instantly resumed the baiting of the large boy.

He shamefacedly scratched his left shin with his right foot. "Well, I ain't afraid." He cast an eye at the monster. "Well, I ain't afraid." With a glare of hatred at his squalling tormentors, he finally announced a grim intention. "Well, I'll do it, then, since you're so fresh. Now!"

The mob subsided as with a formidable countenance he turned toward the impassive figure on the box. The advance was also a regular progression from high daring to craven hesitation. At last, when some yards from the monster, the lad came to a full halt, as if he had encountered a stone wall. The observant little boys in the distance promptly hooted. Stung again by these cries, the lad sneaked two yards forward. He was crouched like a young cat ready for a backward spring. The crowd at the rear, beginning to respect this display, uttered some encouraging cries. Suddenly the lad gathered himself together, made a white and desperate rush forward, touched the monster's shoulder with a far-outstretched finger, and sped away, while his laughter rang out wild, shrill, and exultant.

The crowd of boys reverenced him at once, and began to throng into his camp, and look at him, and be his admirers. Jimmie was discomfited for a moment, but he and the larger boy, without agreement or word of any kind, seemed to recognize a truce, and they swiftly combined and began to parade before the others.

"Why, it's just as easy as nothing," puffed the larger boy. "Ain't it, Jim?"

"Course," blew Jimmie. "Why, it's as e-e-easy."

They were people of another class. If they had been decorated for courage on twelve battle-fields, they could not have made the other boys more ashamed of the situation.

Meanwhile they condescended to explain the emotions of the excursion, expressing unqualified contempt for any one who could hang back. "Why, it ain't nothin'. He won't do nothin' to you," they told the others, in tones of exasperation.

One of the very smallest boys in the party showed signs of a wistful desire to distinguish himself, and they turned their attention to him, pushing at his shoulders while he swung away from them, and hesitated dreamily. He was eventually induced to make furtive expedition, but it was only for a few yards. Then he paused, motionless, gazing with open mouth. The vociferous entreaties of Jimmie and the large boy had no power over him.

Mrs. Hannigan had come out on her back porch with a pail of water. From this coign she had a view of the secluded portion of the Trescott grounds that was behind the stable. She perceived the group of boys, and the monster on the box. She shaded her eyes with her hand to benefit her vision. She screeched then as if she was being murdered. "Eddie! Eddie! You come home this minute!"

Her son querulously demanded, "Aw, what for?"

"You come home this minute. Do you hear?"

The other boys seemed to think this visitation upon one of their number required them to preserve for a time the hang-dog air of a collection of culprits, and they remained in guilty silence until the little Hannigan, wrathfully protesting, was pushed through the door of his home. Mrs. Hannigan cast a piercing glance over the group, stared with a bitter face at the Trescott house, as if this new and handsome edifice was insulting her, and then followed her son.

There was wavering in the party. An inroad by one mother always caused them to carefully sweep the horizon to see if there were more coming. "This is my yard," said Jimmie, proudly. "We don't have to go home."

The monster on the box had turned its black crêpe countenance toward the sky, and was waving its arms in time to a religious chant. "Look at him now," cried a little boy. They turned, and were transfixed by the solemnity and mystery of the indefinable gestures. The wail of the melody was mournful and slow. They drew back. It seemed to spellbind them with the power of a funeral. They were so absorbed that they did not hear the doctor's buggy drive up to the stable. Trescott got out, tied his horse, and approached the group. Jimmie saw him first, and at his look of dismay the others wheeled.

"What's all this, Jimmie?" asked Trescott, in surprise.

The lad advanced to the front of his companions, halted, and said nothing. Trescott's face gloomed slightly as he scanned the scene.

"What were you doing, Jimmie?"

"We was playin'," answered Jimmie, huskily.

"Playing at what?"

"Just playin'."

Trescott looked gravely at the other boys, and asked them to please go home. They proceeded to the street much in the manner of frustrated and revealed assassins. The crime of trespass on another boy's place was still a crime when they had only accepted the other boy's cordial invitation, and they were used to being sent out of all manner of gardens upon the sudden appearance of a father or a mother. Jimmie had wretchedly watched the departure of his companions. It involved the loss of his position as a lad who controlled the privileges of his father's grounds, but then he knew that in the beginning he had no right to ask so many boys to be his guests.

Once on the sidewalk, however, they speedily forgot their shame as trespassers, and the large boy launched forth in a description of his success in the late trial of courage. As they went rapidly up the street, the little boy who had made the furtive expedition cried out confidently from the rear, "Yes, and I went almost up to him, didn't I, Willie?"

The large boy crushed him in a few words. "Huh!" he scoffed. "You only went a little way. I went clear up to him."

The pace of the other boys was so manly that the tiny thing had to trot, and he remained at the rear, getting entangled in their legs in his attempts to reach the front rank and become of some importance, dodging this way and that way, and always piping out his little claim to glory.

XXI

"By-the-way, Grace," said Trescott, looking into the dining-room from his office door, "I wish you would send Jimmie to me before school-time."

When Jimmie came, he advanced so quietly that Trescott did not at first note him. "Oh," he said, wheeling from a cabinet, "here you are, young man."

"Yes, sir."

Trescott dropped into his chair and tapped the desk with a thoughtful finger. "Jimmie, what were you doing in the back garden yesterday—you and the other boys—to Henry?"

"We weren't doing anything, pa."

Trescott looked sternly into the raised eyes of his son. "Are you sure you were not annoying him in any way? Now what were you doing, exactly?"

"Why, we—why, we—now—Willie Dalzel said I dassent go right up to him, and I did; and then he did; and then—the other boys were 'fraid; and then—you comed."

Trescott groaned deeply. His countenance was so clouded in sorrow that the lad, bewildered by the mystery of it, burst suddenly forth in dismal lamentations. "There, there. Don't cry, Jim." said Trescott, going round the desk. "Only—" He sat in a great leather reading-chair, and took the boy on his knee. "Only I want to explain to you—"

After Jimmie had gone to school, and as Trescott was about to start on his round of morning calls, a message arrived from

Doctor Moser. It set forth that the latter's sister was dying in the old homestead, twenty miles away up the valley, and asked Trescott to care for his patients for the day at least. There was also in the envelope a little history of each case and of what had already been done. Trescott replied to the messenger that he would gladly assent to the arrangement.

He noted that the first name on Moser's list was Winter, but this did not seem to strike him as an important fact. When its turn came, he rang the Winter bell. "Good-morning, Mrs. Winter," he said, cheerfully, as the door was opened. "Doctor Moser has been obliged to leave town to-day, and he has asked me to come in his stead. How is the little girl this morning?"

Mrs. Winter had regarded him in stony surprise. At last she said: "Come in! I'll see my husband." She bolted into the house. Trescott entered the hall, and turned to the left into the sitting-room.

Presently Winter shuffled through the door. His eyes flashed toward Trescott. He did not betray any desire to advance far into the room. "What do you want?" he said.

"What do I want? What do I want?" repeated Trescott, lifting his head suddenly. He had heard an utterly new challenge in the night of the jungle.

"Yes, that's what I want to know," snapped Winter. "What do you want?"

Trescott was silent for a moment. He consulted Moser's memoranda. "I see that your little girl's case is a trifle serious," he remarked. "I would advise you to call a physician soon. I will leave you a copy of Doctor Moser's record to give to any one you may call." He paused to transcribe the record on a page of his note-book. Tearing out the leaf, he extended it to Winter as he moved toward the door. The latter shrunk against the wall. His head was hanging as he reached for the paper. This caused him to grasp air, and so Trescott simply let the paper flutter to the feet of the other man.

"Good-morning," said Trescott from the hall. This placid retreat seemed to suddenly arouse Winter to ferocity. It was as if he had then recalled all the truths which he had formulated to hurl at Trescott. So he followed him into the hall, and down the hall to the door, and through the door to the porch, barking in fiery rage from a respectful distance. As Trescott imperturbably turned the mare's head down the road, Winter stood on the porch, still yelping. He was like a little dog.

XXII

"Have you heard the news?" cried Carrie Dungen, as she sped toward Martha's kitchen. "Have you heard the news?" Her eyes were shining with delight.

"No," answered Martha's sister Kate, bending forward eagerly. "What was it? What was it?"

Carrie appeared triumphantly in the open door. "Oh, there's been an awful scene between Doctor Trescott and Jake Winter. I never thought that Jake Winter had any pluck at all, but this morning he told the doctor just what he thought of him."

"Well, what did he think of him?" asked Martha.

"Oh, he called him everything. Mrs. Howarth heard it through her front blinds. It was terrible, she says. It's all over town now. Everybody knows it."

"Didn't the doctor answer back?"

"No! Mrs. Howarth—she says he never said a word. He just walked down to his buggy and got in, and drove off as co-o-o-l. But Jake gave him jinks, by all accounts."

"But what did he say?" cried Kate, shrill and excited. She was evidently at some kind of a feast.

"Oh, he told him that Sadie had never been well since that night Henry Johnson frightened her at Theresa Page's party, and he held him responsible, and how dared he cross his threshold—and—and—and—"

"And what?" said Martha.

"Did he swear at him?" said Kate, in fearsome glee.

"No—not much. He did swear at him a little, but not more than a man does anyhow when he is real mad, Mrs. Howarth says."

"O-oh!" breathed Kate. "And did he call him any names?"

Martha, at her work, had been for a time in deep thought. She now interrupted the others. "It don't seem as if Sadie Winter had been sick since that time Henry Johnson got loose. She's been to school almost the whole time since then, hasn't she?"

They combined upon her in immediate indignation. "School? School? I should say not. Don't think for a moment. School!"

Martha wheeled from the sink. She held an iron spoon, and it seemed as if she was going to attack them. "Sadie Winter has passed here many a morning since then carrying her school-bag. Where was she going? To a wedding?"

The others, long accustomed to a mental tyranny, speedily surrendered.

"Did she?" stammered Kate. "I never saw her."

Carrie Dungen made a weak gesture.

"If I had been Doctor Trescott," exclaimed Martha, loudly, "I'd have knocked that miserable Jake Winter's head off."

Kate and Carrie, exchanging glances, made an alliance in the air. "I don't see why you say that, Martha," replied Carrie, with considerable boldness, gaining support and sympathy from Kate's smile. "I don't see how anybody can be blamed for getting angry when their little girl gets almost scared to death and gets sick from it, and all that. Besides, everybody says—"

"Oh, I don't care what everybody says," said Martha.

"Well, you can't go against the whole town," answered Carrie, in sudden sharp defiance.

"No, Martha, you can't go against the whole town," piped Kate, following her leader rapidly.

" 'The whole town,' " cried Martha. "I'd like to know what you call 'the whole town.' Do you call these silly people who are scared of Henry Johnson 'the whole town'?"

"Why, Martha," said Carrie, in a reasoning tone, "you talk as if you wouldn't be scared of him!"

"No more would I," retorted Martha.

"O-oh, Martha, how you talk!" said Kate. "Why, the idea! Everybody's afraid of him."

Carrie was grinning. "You've never seen him, have you?" she asked, seductively.

"No," admitted Martha.

"Well, then, how do you know that you wouldn't be scared?"

Martha confronted her. "Have you ever seen him? No? Well, then, how do you know you *would* be scared?"

The allied forces broke out in chorus: "But, Martha, everybody says so. Everybody says so."

"Everybody says what?"

"Everybody that's seen him say they were frightened almost to death. 'Tisn't only women, but it's men too. It's awful."

Martha wagged her head solemnly. "I'd try not to be afraid of him."

"But supposing you could not help it?" said Kate.

"Yes, and look here," cried Carrie. "I'll tell you another thing. The Hannigans are going to move out of the house next door."

"On account of him?" demanded Martha.

Carrie nodded. "Mrs. Hannigan says so herself."

"Well, of all things!" ejaculated Martha. "Going to move, eh? You don't say so! Where they going to move to?"

"Down on Orchard Avenue."

"Well, of all things! Nice house?"

"I don't know about that. I haven't heard. But there's lots of nice houses on Orchard."

"Yes, but they're all taken," said Kate. "There isn't a vacant house on Orchard Avenue."

"Oh yes, there is," said Martha. "The old Hampstead house is vacant."

"Oh, of course," said Kate. "But then I don't believe Mrs. Hannigan would like it there. I wonder where they can be going to move to?"

"I'm sure I don't know," sighed Martha. "It must be to some place we don't know about."

"Well," said Carrie Dungen, after a general reflective silence, "it's easy enough to find out, anyhow."

"Who knows—around here?" asked Kate.

"Why, Mrs. Smith, and there she is in her garden," said Carrie, jumping to her feet. As she dashed out of the door, Kate and Martha crowded at the window. Carrie's voice rang out from near the steps. "Mrs. Smith! Mrs. Smith! Do you know where the Hannigans are going to move to?"

XXIII

The autumn smote the leaves and the trees of Whilomville were panoplied in crimson and yellow. The winds grew stronger, and in the melancholy purple of the nights the home shine of a window became a finer thing. The little boys, watching the sear and sorrowful leaves drifting down from the maples, dreamed of the near time when they could heap bushels in the streets and burn them during the abrupt evenings.

Three men walked down Niagara Avenue. As they approached Judge Hagenthorpe's house he came down his walk to meet them in the manner of one who has been waiting.

"Are you ready, judge?" one said.

"All ready," he answered.

The four then walked to Trescott's house. He received them in his office, where he had been reading. He seemed surprised at this visit of four very active and influential citizens, but he had nothing to say of it.

After they were all seated, Trescott looked expectantly from one face to another. There was a little silence. It was broken by John Twelve, the wholesale grocer, who was worth $400,000, and reported to be worth over a million.

"Well, doctor," he said, with a short laugh, "I suppose we might as well admit at once that we've come to interfere in something which is none of our business."

"Why, what is it?" asked Trescott, again looking from one face to another. He seemed to appeal particularly to Judge Hagenthorpe, but the old man had his chin lowered musingly to his cane, and would not look at him.

"It's about what nobody talks of—much," said Twelve. "It's about Henry Johnson."

Trescott squared himself in his chair. "Yes?" he said.

Having delivered himself of the title, Twelve seemed to become more easy. "Yes," he answered, blandly, "we wanted to talk to you about it."

"Yes?" said Trescott.

Twelve abruptly advanced on the main attack. "Now see here, Trescott, we like you, and we have come to talk right out about this business. It may be none of our affairs and all that, and as for me, I don't mind if you tell me so; but I am not going to keep quiet and see you ruin yourself. And that's how we all feel."

"I am not ruining myself," answered Trescott.

"No, maybe you are not exactly ruining yourself," said Twelve, slowly, "but you are doing yourself a great deal of harm. You have changed from being the leading doctor in town to about the last one. It is mainly because there are always a large number of people who are very thoughtless fools, of course, but then that doesn't change the condition."

A man who had not heretofore spoken said, solemnly, "It's the women."

"Well, what I want to say is this," resumed Twelve. "Even if there are a lot of fools in the world, we can't see any reason why you should ruin yourself by opposing them. You can't teach them anything, you know."

"I am not trying to teach them anything." Trescott smiled wearily. "I—It is a matter of—well—"

"And there are a good many of us that admire you for it immensely," interrupted Twelve; "but that isn't going to change the minds of all those ninnies."

"It's the women," stated the advocate of this view again.

"Well, what I want to say is this," said Twelve. "We want you to get out of this trouble and strike your old gait again. You are simply killing your practice through your infernal pig-headedness. Now this thing is out of the ordinary, but there must be ways to—to beat the game somehow, you see. So we've talked it over—about a dozen of us—and, as I say, if you want to tell us to mind our own business, why, go ahead; but we've talked it over, and we've come to the conclusion that the only way to do is to get Johnson a place somewhere off up the valley, and—"

Trescott wearily gestured. "You don't know, my friend. Everybody is so afraid of him, they can't even give him good care. Nobody can attend to him as I do myself."

"But I have a little no-good farm up beyond Clarence Mountain that I was going to give to Henry," cried Twelve, aggrieved. "And if you—and if you—if you—through your house burning down, or anything—why, all the boys were prepared to take him right off your hands, and—and—"

Trescott arose and went to the window. He turned his back upon them. They sat waiting in silence. When he returned he kept his face in the shadow. "No, John Twelve," he said, "it can't be done."

There was another stillness. Suddenly a man stirred on his chair.

"Well, then, a public institution—" he began.

"No," said Trescott; "public institutions are all very good, but he is not going to one."

In the background of the group old Judge Hagenthorpe was thoughtfully smoothing the polished ivory head of his cane.

XXIV

Trescott loudly stamped the snow from his feet and shook the flakes from his shoulders. When he entered the house he went at once to the dining-room, and then to the sitting-room. Jimmie was there, reading painfully in a large book concerning giraffes and tigers and crocodiles.

"Where is your mother, Jimmie?" asked Trescott.

"I don't know, pa," answered the boy. "I think she is upstairs."

Trescott went to the foot of the stairs and called, but there came no answer. Seeing that the door of the little drawing-room was open, he entered. The room was bathed in the half-light that came from the four dull panes of mica in the front of the great stove. As his eyes grew used to the shadows he saw his wife curled in an arm-chair. He went to her. "Why, Grace," he said, "didn't you hear me calling you?"

She made no answer, and as he bent over the chair he heard her trying to smother a sob in the cushion.

"Grace!" he cried. "You're crying!"

She raised her face. "I've got a headache, a dreadful headache, Ned."

"A headache?" he repeated, in surprise and incredulity.

He pulled a chair close to hers. Later, as he cast his eye over the zone of light shed by the dull red panes, he saw that a low table had been drawn close to the stove, and that it was burdened with many small cups and plates of uncut tea-cake. He remembered that the day was Wednesday, and that his wife received on Wednesdays.

"Who was here to-day, Gracie?" he asked.

From his shoulder there came a mumble, "Mrs. Twelve."

"Was she—um," he said. "Why—didn't Anna Hagenthorpe come over?"

The mumble from his shoulder continued, "She wasn't well enough."

Glancing down at the cups, Trescott mechanically counted them. There were fifteen of them. "There, there," he said. "Don't cry, Grace. Don't cry."

The wind was whining around the house and the snow beat aslant upon the windows. Sometimes the coal in the stove settled with a crumbling sound and the four panes of mica flushed a sudden new crimson. As he sat holding her head on his shoulder, Trescott found himself occasionally trying to count the cups. There were fifteen of them.

APPENDIXES

TEXTUAL NOTES

21.3 perch] Although a strong temptation may exist to alter H, A1 *perch* to the more natural *porch,* the original reading is not so demonstrably in error as positively to require emendation. As used in "The Pace of Youth" a perch is some high spot from which one can keep track of affairs. Later in "The Monster" when Mrs. Hannigan calls back her son, she 'had come out on her back porch with a pail of water. From this coign she had a view of the secluded portion of the Trescott grounds that was behind the stable' (55.25–28). The fire that Hannigan discovers is specified as being on the side of the Trescott house. Hence the position of the two houses as beside each other in "The Fight" and in "The City Urchin and the Chaste Villagers" can be confirmed. The Hannigan back porch, thus, was high enough to see into the Trescott grounds at the level of the first floor where the fire was showing through the side window. Hannigan, normally, might not be permitted to smoke his pipe indoors, and his back porch would be the logical place for this exercise. Finally, the description of his tumbling down from his perch, swinging across the fence, and rushing to the Trescott front door suggests a progress through continuous territory, not, for example, a tumbling down the stairs from an upstairs room and then a swinging across the fence. Hannigan, then, must be on his porch, and it is from his porch that he frenziedly flings his pipe and tumbles down the steps. Yet this pinpointing does not demonstrate the need for emendation. *Perch* is an unusual enough word not to be confused with the common *porch;* moreover, in Crane's hand the two do not look alike, and they are at opposite sides of the typewriter keyboard. Given the suggestion of height in the use of *coign* for the porch describing Mrs. Hannigan's line of sight, it may not be too much to accept Crane's word for it as a *perch;* and, of course, for all we know Hannigan may have been perched on its railing, although that is not necessary for an acceptance of the meaning. In short, Hannigan tumbled down from his perch on the porch.

22.12 knee] H, A1 *knees* is unnatural; the fact of error is revealed by the account of the original action in 18.6–7: *his hand dropped slowly to his knee.* . . . See also, 43.14: *His wife, with one hand upon the edge of the table and the other at her knee.* . . .

22.23 illumined] That the A1 form *illuminated* is a sophistication may be suggested by the use of *illumed* in "His New Mittens" 90.15, even though both H and A1 have *illuminated* at 33.12 of the present text.

30.2 impracticable] For a similar use of this word, see "The Stove," in *Whilomville Stories,* 197.20.

38.8 minit] This emendation of H, A1 *minnet* is justified by the spelling *minit* at 34.16, which, in turn, is confirmed by *minit* in *Maggie* at 59.22,37 and 60.3; on the other hand, for *minnet* see *George's Mother* 173.26; 177.22,23; and 178.20.

EDITORIAL EMENDATIONS IN THE COPY-TEXT

[NOTE: Except for such silent typographical alterations as are remarked in "The Text of the Virginia Edition" that prefaces Vol. I, every editorial change made from the *Harper's Magazine* copy-text of "The Monster" is listed here. Only the direct source of the emendation, with its antecedents, is noticed; the Historical Collation may be consulted for the complete history, within the editions collated, of any substantive readings that qualify for inclusion in that listing. An alteration assigned to the Virginia Edition (V) is made for the first time in the present text, if 'by the first time' is understood 'the first time in respect to the editions chosen for collation.' Asterisked readings are discussed in the Textual Notes. The following editions are referred to: H (*Harper's New Monthly Magazine*, XCVII [August, 1898], 343–376); A1 (Harper's, New York, 1899); MS (manuscript leaf in Columbia University Libraries). The 1901 Harper's edition in London (E1) is not noticed here since it was printed from the same plates, without variation, as A1.]

18.28,29; 21.4   toward] V; towards H, A1
*21.3   perch] *stet* H, A1
21.7   Afterward] V; Afterwards H, A1
*22.12   knee] V; knees H, A1
*22.23   illumined] *stet* H
23.4   backward] A1; backwards H
24.37   Afterward] V; Afterwards H, A1
*30.2   impracticable] *stet* H
33.30–31   yestehday] V; yesterday H, A1

*38.8   minit] V; minnet H, A1
38.19   fer] V; for H, A1
39.4   Williams,] A1; ~ ; H
46.9   side door] A1; ~ - | ~ H
50.35   afterward] V; afterwards H, A1
61.34   leaves,] MS; ~ , H, A1
62.5   Niagara] V; the Niagara H, A1
65.6   around] MS; round H, A1
65.6   house,] MS; ~ , H, A1
65.8   sound,] MS; ~ , H, A1
65.8   flushed] MS; flashed H, A1

WORD-DIVISION

1. *End-of-the-Line Hyphenation in the Virginia Edition*

[NOTE: No hyphenation of a possible compound at the end of a line in the Virginia text is presented in the copy-text except for the following readings, which are hyphenated within the line in H. Hyphenated compounds in which both elements are capitalized are not included.]

18.21   spring-|lock
19.26   mother-|judgment
58.15   sitting-|room

2. *End-of-the-Line Hyphenation in the Copy-Text*

[NOTE: The following compounds, or possible compounds, are hyphenated at the end of the line in the copy-text. The form in which they have been transcribed in the Virginia text, as listed below, represents the practice of H as ascertained by other appearances or by parallels.]

10.32	to-day	38.20	Yesseh
11.34	buggy-wheel	39.5	arm-chair
14.7	blue-stone	44.2	tiptoed
14.15	to-night	44.8	er-sleep
22.29	terror-stricken	44.23	terror-stricken
25.24	high-flying	50.6	Sunday-school
27.39	jack-pot	52.10	blood-thirsty
28.33	firemen	54.6	breathing-spell
31.2	sunshine	64.14	drawing-room
37.15	er-quakin'	64.29	tea-cake

3. *Special Cases*

[NOTE: In the following the compound, or possible compound, is hyphenated at the end of the line in H and in the Virginia text.]

43.8   bed-|chamber (i.e. bed-chamber)
43.9   living-|room (i.e. living-room)

HISTORICAL COLLATION

[NOTE: The Historical Collation records substantive variants between the text of the Virginia Edition and the editions collated; viz. H (*Harper's Monthly*, 1898), A1 (Harper's 1899), and MS (the single leaf in the Columbia University Libraries Special Collections). The substantive reading to the left of the bracket is that of the Virginia text; the reading to the right is the variant in the editions thereupon specified. Any collated edition not noticed agrees with the Virginia text. The 1901 Heinemann edition (E1) is not collated since it was printed without change from the plates of A1.]

9.13; 10.15   toward] towards A1
10.7   Afterward] Afterwards A1
10.36   afterward] afterwards A1
12.75; 14.29   toward] towards A1
15.7   vas] was A1
17.11   its] *omit* A1
18.28,29; 21.4   toward] towards H, A1
21.7   Afterward] Afterwards H, A1
22.12   knee] knees H, A1
22.23   illumined] illuminated A1
23.4   backward] backwards H
24.35   mystic] a mystic A1
24.37   Afterward] Afterwards H, A1
25.2; 26.16,27   toward] towards A1
26.27   arose] rose A1
27.23   when] where A1
28.13   Afterward] Afterwards A1
28.17,32   toward] towards A1
29.18   scripture] Scripture A1
31.1   latter] later A1
34.24   toward] towards A1
35.26   made] made a A1
38.8   minit] minnet H, A1

38.19   fer] for H, A1
42.6   toward] towards A1
42.27   Afterward] Afterwards A1
43.19; 44.12   toward] towards A1
45.8   them   arrogant]   the   mar-rogant A1
47.39   its] his A1
50.6; 53.17; 54.28; 56.8; 58.18,31; 59.5   toward] towards A1
50.35   afterward]   afterwards   H, A1
53.28   amidst] amid A1
61.34   the leaves] all the leaves MS
61.35–62.1   The winds . . . thing.] *omit* MS
62.1–2,   watching   . . .   maples,] *omit* MS
62.3   heap] heap up MS
62.3   bushels] bushels of brown leaves MS
62.5   Niagara] the Niagara H, A1
65.6   around] round H, A1
65.8   flushed] flashed H, A1
65.9   her] his MS
65.10   trying] beginning MS

72

"His New Mittens"

TEXTUAL INTRODUCTION

"HIS NEW MITTENS" first appeared in *McClure's Magazine* for November, 1898 (XII, 54–61), with unsigned illustrations. In the same month it was also printed in England in the *Cornhill Magazine* (n.s. XXIX, 630–639) without illustrations and with the footnote 'Copyright, 1898, by Stephen Crane in the United States of America.'

The relationship of these two texts is not entirely demonstrable. That Crane mailed the manuscript on May 30, 1898, from 'off Havana' to his agent Paul Reynolds in New York is definite, and it is also definite that at a later time he did not recall the appearance of the story in the *Cornhill*. From the occurrence in *McClure's* of such a characteristic Crane spelling as *marvelous* (C *marvellous*) at 86.3 or the characteristic use of a period to introduce dialogue as with 'him.' at 83.3 (C 'him:'), and especially the characteristic use at 85.23 of *Now.* as a sentence (C prefaced by a comma as concluding the sentence), it is impossible to derive McC from a proof of C, a hypothesis implausible on its face, anyway.

On the other hand, although in general the accidentals of McC are closer to Crane's characteristics than those of C, yet the lighter punctuation system frequently though not invariably found in C in respect to commas about parenthetical phrases, and commas separating the clauses of compound or complex sentences or separating a phrase inverted before the subject at the start of a sentence, suggests the influence of Crane copy. If this is so, it is unlikely that C was set from a proof of McC. Indeed, the various substantive errors and variants in C would necessitate the hypothesis—if a proof of McC were the copy—that a raw, uncorrected proof from *McClure's* was sent across the ocean. This possibility cannot be ignored, but the simultaneous publication of the two texts of the story may militate against such a theory since it leaves very little time for a *Cornhill* schedule of publication. Moreover, if Reynolds were to sell the story to England, he would ordinarily be expected to proceed without waiting for proof, even provided he were ever delegated to receive the proof. This theory, then, can be substantially ignored.[1]

It would seem either that (a) C derives from the printer's copy used by McC, as from a carbon of the typescript that Reynolds would have had made from the Crane holograph,[2] or that (b) both McC and C radiate in some manner from the Crane holograph.

The first hypothesis is not at all impossible but it does not conveniently explain the number and the nature of the *Cornhill* errors. Such C misprints as *On* for *In* at 84.20 or *tone* for *tune* at 87.6 seem to represent the faithful reproduction of literal errors in the copy, and *agreement* for *argument* at 85.10 may represent the same, as may *sniffles* for *snuffles* at 91.29 or *turkey* for *turkeys* at 92.7. On the other hand, it is more likely that such a variant as C *bickering* for McC *dickering* at 92.9 results from the unfamiliarity of an English compositor with an American expression, and it may be that such variants as the addition of *he* at 84.33 and of *to* at 91.29, and even the recasting of *form, manner,* at 91.30 to *form and manner,* are the English compositor's 'improvements.' Nevertheless, the total impression gained from a comparison of the two texts is that the *Cornhill* version is on the whole a text that has been set with considerable fidelity to a corrupt copy save where idiom is concerned. If so, the twenty substantive variants cannot be allocated exclusively as English errors from the same essential copy set by *McClure's,* like a carbon of the original typescript, unless we are to suppose, first, that the typescript Reynolds had made originally was very cor-

[1] Even allowing for a certain amount of English error, and adding to that variants in McC caused by Crane's theoretical proof alterations, the amount of error prevailing in a typescript intended for McClure's printer's copy, with a carbon for England, would seem to be excessive. The case might be different if a second typescript were hurriedly made up for English sale (see below).

[2] The editor of *Collier's Weekly* writing to Reynolds about "The Blue Hotel" (New York, Sept. 20, 1898, *Letters,* p. 185) inquires: "Do you remember the date on which you left the shortened version here? It was in manuscript, not typewriting; was it not?" But since the question of a shortened version had arisen, perhaps this was a special case in which a marked-up manuscript was submitted for initial approval, thus saving the original typescript if an agreement were not reached. We can only guess.

rupt indeed and, second, that the corrections, as well as what may perhaps be revisions in the text, were made in proof by Crane in an original typesetting for *McClure's* that had not differed substantially in the wording from what we now read in *Cornhill*. Otherwise, one is driven to the second alternative, that *Cornhill* was set from a form of copy that was itself variant in some details from that which served the *McClure's* compositor.

Crane was in the United States, though ill at first, from early July into August, and it would have been a physical possibility for him to have read proof for *McClure's* if the copy had been set that far ahead; indeed, about a three-month spread between proof and publication would not have been unusual, as seems to be evidenced in the *Whilomville* stories. (Reading proof in Havana later would seem to be an almost impossible hypothesis.) It may be that such variants as the presence in McC of *on a chair* at 85.15 or of *even* at 89.30, and perhaps of *colors* at 85.31 (absent in C) are best accounted for as evidences of Crane's attentions in proof rather than errors in the English copy or typesetting.

On the other hand, one may accept the possibility that certain variants resulted from Crane's proofreading but reject the hypothesis that the original Reynolds typescript was so full of errors (most of them reproduced in C) that only this authorial proofreading prevented the *McClure's* text from closely approximating what is now found in *Cornhill*.

Variant printer's copy for the *Cornhill* text, then, is a possibility not to be ignored, whether or not accompanied by authorial proofreading of the *McClure's* version. Here one may only speculate. Yet the nature of the *Cornhill* errors agrees best with the hypothesis that Reynolds either had a fresh typescript made from the holograph manuscript, or else sent the manuscript itself abroad where an English typescript was made from it. Whichever it may have been, the second typescript was a careless job that had a number of misreadings not weeded out by checking back against copy. It would seem that this hypothesis is the simpler and accords best with the evidence. According to it, then, the *Cornhill* copy radiated directly from the manuscript through the medium of a new typescript made from it for English sale following, perhaps at an interval, the sale of the original typescript to *McClure's*. Whether all the variants in the *Cornhill* copy came about from this careless typescript compounded by English printer's errors or whether some of the variants derive from Crane's correction and revision of *McClure's* proof is not to be demonstrated.

Hence, whether there were a form of derivation or—what may be more probable—a form of radiation from the holograph, the *McClure's* version seems firmly established as the copy-text both in respect to its accidentals and to its substantives. However, the relation of the *Cornhill* version is such, in either case, as to encourage the belief that it preserves certain features of the holograph accidentals that have been lost as a result of the *McClure's* editing and styling; and thus in the formation of the present eclectic text some of the *Cornhill* accidentals have been accepted as conjecturally representing with greater purity the lost holograph than does the edited form of the *McClure's* text.

The real question centers on the authority of the twenty substantive variants. Eight of these are almost demonstrably *Cornhill* errors.[3] One, the plural *hands* at 87.35 for McC *hand*, seems correct (see the same confusion at 69.36 between *Maggie* in 1893 and 1896; a second, *illumed* at 90.15 for *illumined*, is right on the evidence of "Marines Signaling Under Fire." The remaining ten are relatively neutral. Possibly the typist who, theoretically, made up the English printer's copy consciously or unconsciously edited the text; and to this natural variation may be added the English compositor's tendency to edit his American copy, especially if it were in the form of typescript and not proof. The combination of these forces might well add to the mechanical error of such readings as *agreement* for *argument* and *tone* for *tune* to produce the added or subtracted words at 84.33, 85.31, 87.7, 87.19, 88.15, 89.30, 91.6, 91.30, 91.31, and even 92.28. In short, if one were determined to believe that there was no suitable opportunity for Crane to read proof during the parts of July and August that he was available, authorial revision in the *McClure's* version is not positively required in order to account for the neutral variants in the *Cornhill* text if we may suppose

---

[3] These are *On* for *In* at 84:20, *agreement* for *argument* at 85.10, *'em* for *'im* at 86.28, *tone* for *tune* at 87.6, *for* for *fer* at 88.28, *sniffles* for *snuffles* at 91.29, *turkey* for *turkeys* at 92.7, and *bickering* for *dickering* at 92.9. Various of these may have originated in the *Cornhill* copy.

that the *McClure's* and *Cornhill* printers' copy radiated independently from the original Crane holograph. On the other hand, despite Crane's poor health, he could have gone through *McClure's* proofs while he was in the United States. The possibility that certain of the *Cornhill* variants may represent the readings in the holograph cannot therefore be utterly denied.

Under the textual hypothesis which has governed the editing of the present text, then, the accidentals of the *McClure's* print are taken as in general the more authoritative, but a number of the *Cornhill* accidentals, chiefly in the punctuation, are assumed to represent a purer derivation from the holograph than the house-styled *McClure's* text. On the other hand, the textual hypothesis does not encourage the belief that, in general, the substantive variants of the *Cornhill* print hold divided authority as do the accidentals. It would be chaotic to pick and choose according to one's personal predilections. The hypothesized derivation of the text requires one to accept the *McClure's* substantive readings as of greater authority except in such a case of positive error as seems to be corrected in the *Cornhill* plural *hands* at 87.35, which—though correct—may be no less a sophistication than the added *it* at 91.6 or the repetitive *from* at 92.28. The *Cornhill* reading *illumed* at 90.15 is quite definitely Crane's. It may be that the typescript made for *McClure's* omitted *he* at 84.33, *there* at 87.7, or *even* at 89.30, and—if an independent typescript for *Cornhill* were made from the holograph—the second typist correctly copied these words from the manuscript. But the case cannot be demonstrated, and thus the *McClure's* substantives must be accepted *en bloc* except in the case of such positive error as seems to be represented in 87.35 and 90.15.

When Harper came to include "His New Mittens" in the 1899 New York collected volume of *The Monster and Other Stories* (A1), the *McClure's* text and illustrations were chosen for a faithful reprint that shows no sign of authorial correction or revision. In the *Monster* volume (for which see its Textual Introduction), "His New Mittens" occupied sigs. L2-M8, pp. 163–189 plus blank 190. The first English edition in 1901 of the collection (E1) utilized for "His New Mittens" the New York 1899 plates without textual alteration.

F. B.

TEXT OF "HIS NEW MITTENS"

I

LITTLE Horace was walking home from school, brilliantly decorated by a pair of new red mittens. A number of boys were snow-balling gleefully in a field. They hailed him. "Come on, Horace. We're having a battle."

Horace was sad. "No," he said, "I can't. I've got to go home." At noon his mother had admonished him. "Now, Horace, you come straight home as soon as school is out. Do you hear? And don't you get them nice new mittens all wet, either. Do you hear?" Also his aunt had said: "I declare, Emily, it's a shame the way you allow that child to ruin his things." She had meant mittens. To his mother, Horace had dutifully replied: "Yes'm." But he now loitered in the vicinity of the group of uproarious boys, who were yelling like hawks as the white balls flew.

Some of them immediately analyzed this extraordinary hesitancy. "Hah!" they paused to scoff, "afraid of your new mittens, ain't you?" Some smaller boys, who were not yet so wise in discerning motives, applauded this attack with unreasonable vehemence. "A-fray-ed of his mit-tens! A-fray-ed of his mit-tens!" They sang these lines to cruel and monotonous music which is as old perhaps as American childhood and which it is the privilege of the emancipated adult to completely forget. "A-fray-ed of his mit-tens!"

Horace cast a tortured glance toward his playmates, and then dropped his eyes to the snow at his feet. Presently he turned to the trunk of one of the great maple trees that lined the kerb. He made a pretense of closely examining the rough and virile bark. To his mind this familiar street of Whilomville seemed to grow dark in the thick shadow of shame. The trees and the houses were now palled in purple.

"A-fray-ed of his mit-tens!" The terrible music had in it a meaning from the moonlit war-drums of chanting cannibals.

At last Horace, with supreme effort, raised his head. " 'Tain't them I care about," he said gruffly. "I've got to go home. That's all."

Whereupon each boy held his left forefinger as if it were a pencil and began to sharpen it derisively with his right forefinger. They came closer, and sang like a trained chorus, "A-fray-ed of his mittens!"

When he raised his voice to deny the charge it was simply lost in the screams of the mob. He was alone fronting all the traditions of boyhood held before him by inexorable representatives. To such a low state had he fallen that one lad, a mere baby, outflanked him and then struck him in the cheek with a heavy snow-ball. The act was acclaimed with loud jeers. Horace turned to dart at his assailant, but there was an immediate demonstration on the other flank, and he found himself obliged to keep his face toward the hilarious crew of tormentors. The baby retreated in safety to the rear of the crowd, where he was received with fulsome compliments upon his daring. Horace retreated slowly up the walk. He continually tried to make them heed him, but the only sound was the chant, "A-fray-ed of his mit-tens!" In this desperate withdrawal the beset and haggard boy suffered more than is the common lot of man.

Being a boy himself, he did not understand boys at all. He had of course the dismal conviction that they were going to dog him to his grave. But near the corner of the field they suddenly seemed to forget all about it. Indeed, they possessed only the malevolence of so many flitter-headed sparrows. The interest had swung capriciously to some other matter. In a moment they were off in the field again, carousing amid the snow. Some authoritative boy had probably said, "Aw, come on."

As the pursuit ceased, Horace ceased his retreat. He spent some time in what was evidently an attempt to adjust his self-respect, and then began to wander furtively down toward the group. He, too, had undergone an important change. Perhaps his sharp agony was only as durable as the malevolence of the others. In this boyish life obedience to some unformulated creed of manners was enforced with capricious but merciless rigor. However, they were, after all, his comrades, his friends.

They did not heed his return. They were engaged in an altercation. It had evidently been planned that this battle was between Indians and soldiers. The smaller and weaker boys had been induced to appear as Indians in the initial skirmish, but they were now very sick of it, and were reluctantly but steadfastly affirming their desire for a change of caste. The larger boys had all won great distinction, devastating Indians materially, and they wished the war to go on as planned. They explained vociferously that it was proper for the soldiers always to thrash the Indians. The little boys did not pretend to deny the truth of this argument; they confined themselves to the simple statement that, in that case, they wished to be soldiers. Each little boy willingly appealed to the others to remain Indians, but as for himself he reiterated his desire to enlist as a soldier. The larger boys were in despair over this dearth of enthusiasm in the small Indians. They alternately wheedled and bullied, but they could not persuade the little boys, who were really suffering dreadful humiliation rather than submit to another onslaught of soldiers. They were called all the baby names that had the power of stinging deep into their pride, but they remained firm.

Then a formidable lad, a leader of reputation, one who could whip many boys that wore long trousers, suddenly blew out his cheeks and shouted, "Well, all right then. I'll be an Indian myself. Now." The little boys greeted with cheers this addition to their wearied ranks, and seemed then content. But matters were not mended in the least, because all of the personal following of the formidable lad, with the addition of every outsider, spontaneously forsook the flag and declared themselves Indians. There were now no soldiers. The Indians had carried everything unanimously. The formidable lad used his influence, but his influence could not shake the loyalty of his friends, who refused to fight under any colors but his colors.

Plainly there was nothing for it but to coerce the little ones. The formidable lad again became a soldier, and then graciously permitted to join him all the real fighting strength of the crowd, leaving behind a most forlorn band of little Indians. Then the soldiers attacked the Indians, exhorting them to opposition at the same time.

The Indians at first adopted a policy of hurried surrender, but this had no success as none of the surrenders were accepted.

They then turned to flee, bawling out protests. The ferocious soldiers pursued them amid shouts. The battle widened, developing all manner of marvelous detail.

Horace had turned toward home several times, but as a matter of fact this scene held him in a spell. It was fascinating beyond anything which the grown man understands. He had always in the back of his head a sense of guilt, even a sense of impending punishment for disobedience, but they could not weigh with the delirium of this snow battle.

II

One of the raiding soldiers, espying Horace, called out in passing, "A-fray-ed of his mit-tens!" Horace flinched at this renewal, and the other lad paused to taunt him again. Horace scooped some snow, molded it into a ball, and flung it at the other. "Ho," cried the boy, "you're an Indian, are you? Hey, fellers, here's an Indian that ain't been killed yet." He and Horace engaged in a duel in which both were in such haste to mold snow-balls that they had little time for aiming.

Horace once struck his opponent squarely in the chest. "Hey," he shouted, "you're dead. You can't fight any more, Pete. I killed you. You're dead."

The other boy flushed red, but he continued frantically to make ammunition. "You never touched me," he retorted glowering. "You never touched me. Where, now?" he added defiantly. "Where'd you hit me?"

"On the coat! Right on your breast. You can't fight any more. You're dead."

"You never!"

"I did, too. Hey, fellers, ain't he dead? I hit 'im square."

"He never!"

Nobody had seen the affair, but some of the boys took sides in absolute accordance with their friendship for one of the concerned parties. Horace's opponent went about contending, "He never touched me. He never came near me. He never came near me."

The formidable leader now came forward and accosted Horace. "What was you? An Indian? Well, then, you're dead—that's all. He hit you. I saw him."

"Me?" shrieked Horace. "He never came within a mile of me——"

At that moment he heard his name called in a certain familiar tune of two notes, with the last note shrill and prolonged. He looked toward the sidewalk and saw his mother standing there in her widow's weeds, with two brown paper parcels under her arm. A silence had fallen upon all the boys. Horace moved slowly toward his mother. She did not seem to note his approach; she was gazing austerely off through the naked branches of the maples where two crimson sunset bars lay on the deep blue sky.

At a distance of ten paces Horace made a desperate venture. "Oh, ma," he whined, "can't I stay out for a while?"

"No," she answered solemnly, "you come with me." Horace knew that profile; it was the inexorable profile. But he continued to plead, because it was not beyond his mind that a great show of suffering now might diminish his suffering later.

He did not dare to look back at his playmates. It was already a public scandal that he could not stay out as late as other boys and he could imagine his standing now that he had been again dragged off by his mother in sight of the whole world. He was a profoundly miserable human being.

Aunt Martha opened the door for them. Light streamed about her straight skirt. "Oh," she said, "so you found him on the road, eh? Well, I declare! It was about time!"

Horace slunk into the kitchen. The stove, spraddling out on its four iron legs, was gently humming. Aunt Martha had evidently just lighted the lamp, for she went to it and began to twist the wick experimentally.

"Now," said the mother, "let's see them mittens."

Horace's chin sank. The aspiration of the criminal, the passionate desire for an asylum from retribution, from justice, was aflame in his heart. "I—I—don't—don't know where they are," he gasped finally as he passed his hands over his pockets.

"Horace," intoned his mother, "you are telling me a story!"

" 'Tain't a story," he answered just above his breath. He looked like a sheep-stealer.

His mother held him by the arm, and began to search his pockets. Almost at once she was able to bring forth a pair of very wet mittens. "Well, I declare!" cried Aunt Martha. The two women went close to the lamp and minutely examined the mittens, turning them over and over. Afterward, when Horace looked up, his mother's sad-lined, homely face was turned toward him. He burst into tears.

His mother drew a chair near the stove. "Just you sit there now, until I tell you to git off." He sidled meekly into the chair. His mother and his aunt went briskly about the business of preparing supper. They did not display a knowledge of his existence; they carried an effect of oblivion so far that they even did not speak to each other. Presently, they went into the dining and living room; Horace could hear the dishes rattling. His Aunt Martha brought a plate of food, placed it on a chair near him, and went away without a word.

Horace instantly decided that he would not touch a morsel of the food. He had often used this ruse in dealing with his mother. He did not know why it brought her to terms, but certainly it sometimes did.

The mother looked up when the aunt returned to the other room. "Is he eatin' his supper?" she asked.

The maiden aunt, fortified in ignorance, gazed with pity and contempt upon this interest. "Well, now, Emily, how do I know?" she queried. "Was I goin' to stand over 'im? Of all the worryin' you do about that child! It's a shame the way you're bringing up that child."

"Well, he ought to eat something. It won't do fer him to go without eatin'," the mother retorted weakly.

Aunt Martha, profoundly scorning the policy of concession which these words meant, uttered a long contemptuous sigh.

III

Alone in the kitchen, Horace stared with sombre eyes at the plate of food. For a long time he betrayed no sign of yielding. His mood was adamantine. He was resolved not to sell his vengeance for bread, cold ham, and a pickle, and yet it must be known that

the sight of them affected him powerfully. The pickle in particular was notable for its seductive charm. He surveyed it darkly.

But at last unable to longer endure his state, his attitude in the
presence of the pickle, he put out an inquisitive finger and
touched it, and it was cool and green and plump. Then a full
conception of the cruel woe of his situation swept upon him
suddenly and his eyes filled with tears which began to move
down his cheeks. He sniffled. His heart was black with hatred.
He painted in his mind scenes of deadly retribution. His mother
would be taught that he was not one to endure persecution
meekly, without raising an arm in his defense. And so his
dreams were of a slaughter of feelings, and near the end of them
his mother was pictured as coming, bowed with pain, to his feet.
Weeping, she implored his charity. Would he forgive her? No;
his once tender heart had been turned to stone by her injustice.
He could not forgive her. She must pay the inexorable penalty.

The first item in this horrible plan was the refusal of the food.
This he knew by experience would work havoc in his mother's
heart. And so he grimly waited.

But suddenly it occurred to him that the first part of his
revenge was in danger of failing. The thought struck him that
his mother might not capitulate in the usual way. According to
his recollection, the time was more than due when she should
come in, worried, sadly affectionate, and ask him if he was ill. It
had then been his custom to hint in a resigned voice that he was
the victim of secret disease, but that he preferred to suffer in
silence and alone. If she was obdurate in her anxiety, he always
asked her in a gloomy, low voice to go away and leave him to
suffer in silence and alone in the darkness without food. He had
known this manœuvering to result even in pie.

But what was the meaning of the long pause and the stillness?
Had his old and valued ruse betrayed him? As the truth sank into
his mind, he supremely loathed life, the world, his mother. Her
heart was beating back the besiegers; he was a defeated child.

He wept for a time before deciding upon the final stroke. He
would run away. In a remote corner of the world he would
become some sort of bloody-handed person driven to a life of
crime by the barbarity of his mother. She should never know his

fate. He would torture her for years with doubts and doubts and drive her implacably to a repentant grave. Nor would his Aunt Martha escape. Some day, a century hence, when his mother was dead, he would write to his Aunt Martha and point out her part in the blighting of his life. For one blow against him now he would in time deal back a thousand; aye, ten thousand.

He arose and took his coat and cap. As he moved stealthily toward the door he cast a glance backward at the pickle. He was tempted to take it, but he knew if he left the plate inviolate his mother would feel even worse.

A blue snow was falling. People bowed forward were moving briskly along the walks. The electric lamps hummed amid showers of flakes. As Horace emerged from the kitchen a shrill squall drove the flakes around the corner of the house. He cowered away from it, and its violence illumed his mind vaguely in new directions. He deliberated upon a choice of remote corners of the globe. He found that he had no plans which were definite enough in a geographical way, but without much loss of time he decided upon California. He moved briskly as far as his mother's front gate on the road to California. He was off at last. His success was a trifle dreadful; his throat choked.

But at the gate he paused. He did not know if his journey to California would be shorter if he went down Niagara Avenue or off through Hogan Street. As the storm was very cold and the point was very important, he decided to withdraw for reflection to the wood-shed. He entered the dark shanty and took seat upon the old chopping-block upon which he was supposed to perform for a few minutes every afternoon when he returned from school. The wind screamed and shouted at the loose boards, and there was a rift of snow on the floor to leeward of a crack.

Here the idea of starting for California on such a night departed from his mind, leaving him ruminating miserably upon his martyrdom. He saw nothing for it but to sleep all night in the wood-shed and start for California in the morning bright and early. Thinking of his bed, he kicked over the floor and found that the innumerable chips were all frozen tightly, bedded in ice.

Later he viewed with joy some signs of excitement in the house. The flare of a lamp moved rapidly from window to window. Then the kitchen door slammed loudly and a shawled figure sped toward the gate. At last he was making them feel his power. The shivering child's face was lit with saturnine glee as in the darkness of the wood-shed he gloated over the evidences of consternation in his home. The shawled figure had been his Aunt Martha dashing with the alarm to the neighbors.

The cold of the wood-shed was tormenting him. He endured only because of the terror he was causing. But then it occurred to him that, if they instituted a search for him they would probably examine the wood-shed. He knew that it would not be manful to be caught so soon. He was not positive now that he was going to remain away forever, but at any rate he was bound to inflict some more damage before allowing himself to be captured. If he merely succeeded in making his mother angry, she would thrash him on sight. He must prolong the time in order to be safe. If he held out properly, he was sure of a welcome of love, even though he should drip with crimes.

Evidently the storm had increased, for when he went out it swung him violently with its rough and merciless strength. Panting, stung, half-blinded with the driving flakes, he was now a waif, exiled, friendless, and poor. With a bursting heart, he thought of his home and his mother. To his forlorn vision they were as far away as Heaven.

IV

Horace was undergoing changes of feeling so rapidly that he was merely moved hither and then thither like a kite. He was now aghast at the merciless ferocity of his mother. It was she who had thrust him into this wild storm, and she was perfectly indifferent to his fate, perfectly indifferent. The forlorn wanderer could no longer weep. The strong sobs caught at his throat, making his breath come in short quick snuffles. All in him was conquered save the enigmatical childish ideal of form, manner. This principle still held out, and it was the only thing between him and submission. When he surrendered, he must surrender in a way that deferred to the undefined code. He longed simply to go to the kitchen and stumble in, but his unfathomable sense of fitness forbade him.

Presently he found himself at the head of Niagara Avenue,

staring through the snow into the blazing windows of Stickney's butcher-shop. Stickney was the family butcher, not so much because of a superiority to other Whilomville butchers as because he lived next door and had been an intimate friend of the father of Horace. Rows of glowing pigs hung head downward back of the tables which bore huge pieces of red beef. Clumps of attenuated turkeys were suspended here and there. Stickney, hale and smiling, was bantering with a woman in a cloak, who, with a monster basket on her arm, was dickering for eight cents' worth of something. Horace watched them through a crusted pane. When the woman came out and passed him, he went toward the door. He touched the latch with his finger, but withdrew again suddenly to the sidewalk. Inside Stickney was whistling cheerily and assorting his knives.

Finally Horace went desperately forward, opened the door, and entered the shop. His head hung low. Stickney stopped whistling. "Hello, young man," he cried, "what brings you here?"

Horace halted, but said nothing. He swung one foot to and fro over the saw-dust floor.

Stickney had placed his two fat hands palms downward and wide apart on the table, in the attitude of a butcher facing a customer, but now he straightened.

"Here," he said, "what's wrong? What's wrong, kid?"

"Nothin'," answered Horace huskily. He labored for a moment with something in his throat, and afterward added, "O'ny—I've —I've run away, and——"

"Run away!" shouted Stickney. "Run away from what? Who?"

"From—home," answered Horace. "I don't like it there any more. I—" He had arranged an oration to win the sympathy of the butcher; he had prepared a table setting forth the merits of his case in the most logical fashion, but it was as if the wind had been knocked out of his mind. "I've run away. I——"

Stickney reached an enormous hand over the array of beef and firmly grappled the emigrant. Then he swung himself to Horace's side. His face was stretched with laughter, and he playfully shook his prisoner. "Come—come—come. What dashed nonsense is this? Run away, hey? Run away?" Whereupon the child's long-tried spirit found vent in howls.

"Come, come," said Stickney busily. "Never mind, now, never

mind. You just come along with me. It'll be all right. I'll fix it. Never you mind."

Five minutes later the butcher, with a great ulster over his apron, was leading the boy homeward.

At the very threshold Horace raised his last flag of pride. "No —no," he sobbed. "I don't want to. I don't want to go in there." He braced his foot against the step, and made a very respectable resistance.

"Now, Horace," cried the butcher. He thrust open the door with a bang. "Hello there!" Across the dark kitchen the door to the living room opened and Aunt Martha appeared. "You've found him!" she screamed.

"We've come to make a call," roared the butcher.

At the entrance to the living room a silence fell upon them all. Upon a couch Horace saw his mother lying limp, pale as death, her eyes gleaming with pain. There was an electric pause before she swung a waxen hand toward Horace. "My child," she murmured tremulously. Whereupon the sinister person addressed, with a prolonged wail of grief and joy, ran to her with speed. "Ma —ma! Ma—ma! Oh, ma—ma!" She was not able to speak in a known tongue as she folded him in her weak arms.

Aunt Martha turned defiantly upon the butcher because her face betrayed her. She was crying. She made a gesture half military, half feminine. "Won't you have a glass of our root-beer, Mr. Stickney? We make it ourselves."

Appendixes

83.0   I] C; omit McC
83.18   mit-tens!"] C; ~ ." McC
83.25   kerb] C; curb McC
83.27   mind$_\wedge$] C; ~ , McC
84.37   capricious$_\wedge$ . . . merciless$_\wedge$]
    C; ~ , . . . ~ , McC
85.4   reluctantly$_\wedge$ . . . steadfast-
    ly$_\wedge$] C; ~ , . . . ~ , McC
85.39   success$_\wedge$] C; ~ , McC
86.4–5   but$_\wedge$ . . . fact$_\wedge$] C; ~ , . . .
    ~ , McC
87.7   sidewalk$_\wedge$] C; ~ , McC
87.13   paces$_\wedge$] C; ~ , McC
87.20   boys$_\wedge$] C; ~ , McC
87.35   hands] C; hand McC
87.37   answered$_\wedge$] C; ~ , McC
88.4   lamp$_\wedge$] C; ~ , McC
88.5   Afterward] C; Afterwards
    McC
88.31   long$_\wedge$] C; ~ , McC
88.32   sombre] C; somber McC
89.3   last$_\wedge$] C; ~ , McC
89.7   suddenly$_\wedge$] C; ~ , McC
89.7   tears$_\wedge$] C; ~ , McC

90.1   and doubts$_\wedge$] C; ~ , McC
90.4   Martha$_\wedge$] C; ~ , McC
90.6   would$_\wedge$ . . . time$_\wedge$] C; ~ ,
    . . . ~ , McC
90.13   kitchen$_\wedge$] C; ~ , McC
90.15   illumed] C; illumined McC
90.26   shanty$_\wedge$] C; ~ , McC
91.8   him$_\wedge$] C; ~ , McC
91.22   Heaven] C; heaven McC
91.29   short$_\wedge$] C; ~ , McC
92.2   butcher-shop] C; ~ $_\wedge$ ~ McC
92.6   tables$_\wedge$] C; ~ , McC
92.24   Horace$_\wedge$] C; ~ , McC
92.25   afterward] V; afterwards
    McC, C, A1
92.33   beef$_\wedge$] C; ~ , McC
92.39   Stickney$_\wedge$] C; ~ , McC
92.39   mind,] C; ~ $_\wedge$ McC
93.3   later$_\wedge$] C; ~ , McC
93.5   threshold$_\wedge$] C; ~ , McC
93.11,14   living room] C; ~ - ~
    McC
93.14   ⟨ At] C; no ⟨ McC
93.15   couch$_\wedge$] C; ~ , McC

WORD-DIVISION

End-of-the-Line Hyphenation in the McClure's *Copy-Text*

83.24	playmates	90.27	chopping-block
84.4,5	forefinger	91.3,6	wood-shed
87.19	playmates	92.38	long-tried

HISTORICAL COLLATION

[NOTE: Since the 1899 New York Harper's edition of *The Monster and Other Stories* (A1) is identical with the 1901 London edition (E1), only the A1 readings are recorded here.]

83.23;84.16　toward] towards A1
84.20　In] On C
84.33　began] he began C
84.33　toward] towards A1
85.10　argument] agreement C
85.31　his colors.] his. C
86.4　toward] towards A1
86.24　Where'd] Where did A1
86.28　'im] 'em C
87.6　tune] tone C
87.7,10　toward] towards A1
87.7　there] *omit* C
87.19　to] *omit* C
87.27　spraddling] straddling A1
87.35　hands] hand McC, A1
87.36　telling] tellin' A1
88.5　Afterward] Afterwards McC, A1
88.6–7　toward] towards A1
88.15　on a chair] *omit* C

88.28　something] somethin' A1
88.28　fer] for C
89.30　even] *omit* C
90.8　toward] towards A1
90.9　knew if] knew that if A1
90.15　illumed] illumined McC, A1
91.1　toward] towards A1
91.6　endured] endured it C
91.29　come] to come C
91.29　snuffles] sniffles C
91.30　form, manner] form and manner C
92.7　turkeys] turkey C
92.9　dickering] bickering C
92.12　toward] towards A1
92.25　afterward] afterwards McC, C, A1
92.28　From—] From—from C
93.17　toward] towards A1
93.24　root-beer] roo-beer C

99

Whilomville Stories

TEXTUAL INTRODUCTION

EGINNING in August, 1899, and ending posthumously in August, 1900, *Harper's New Monthly Magazine* in successive numbers published the thirteen *Whilomville Stories* illustrated by Peter Newell. Except for the first two, the order of publication seems to be that of composition. The magazine appearances are as follows: The Angel-Child, XCIX (August, 1899), 358–364; Lynx-Hunting, XCIX (September, 1899), 552–557; The Lover and the Tell-Tale, XCIX (October, 1899), 759–763; "Showin' Off," XCIX (November, 1899), 855–860; Making an Orator, C (December, 1899), 25–28; Shame, C (January, 1900), 321–325; The Carriage-Lamps, C (February, 1900), 366–372; The Knife, C (March, 1900), 591–598; The Stove, C (April, 1900), 798–804; The Trial, Execution, and Burial of Homer Phelps, C (May, 1900), 963–968; The Fight, CI (June, 1900), 56–63; The City Urchin and the Chaste Villagers, CI (July, 1900), 216–221; A Little Pilgrim, CI (August, 1900), 401–404.

With the exception of "Shame" and "The Carriage-Lamps," the manuscripts for the stories are preserved. "The Angel-Child" is owned by Commander Melvin H. Schoberlin, USN (Ret.), and "The Lover and the Tell-Tale" is in the Barrett Collection at the University of Virginia. The rest are preserved in the Columbia University Crane Collection, which came from Brede Place. Both "The Angel-Child" and "The Lover and the Tell-Tale" manuscripts were tracked down in England by Commander Schoberlin and bought from Michael Pease in 1948. "The Angel-Child" was sent by Cora Crane to Mrs. Pease on February 7, 1899 (the date is not original and is noted on the letter); the gift of the manuscript of "The Lover and the Tell-Tale" had been made earlier.

The early part of "Making an Orator" is in Cora Crane's hand, and the early part of "The City Urchin and the Chaste Villagers" is in the hand of Edith Richie (in the latter story Crane's hand enters when dialect begins). Otherwise, the manuscripts are holograph.

The thirteen stories were collected in book form by Harper in 1900 and published in New York. Announcement was made in the *Publishers' Weekly* for August 25, 1900; copyright had been applied for by William Crane on August 15, with deposit in the Library of Congress on August 16. One of the two deposit copies has the usual copyright notice on p. ii in the name of William Howe Crane, who was his brother's executor (Stephen had died on June 5). The other copy, however, is unique in being copyrighted in the name of Stephen Crane. The explanation given by Williams and Starrett is almost certainly right in its general premise; i.e., that the original plate held the name of Stephen Crane and that the usual π^4 preliminary gathering with the name of William is a cancellans.[1] It is also probable, as they suggest, that the book was being printed near the time of Stephen's death. However, their remaining conjectures are less certain. That is, the suggestion is without evidence that news of the author's death interrupted the printing of this gathering so that the state with William's name is in part a true press variant during the original impression and in part a cancellans substitution for the already printed sheets with Stephen's name. Indeed, this attempted pinpointing is almost certainly wrong, since William Crane was appointed executor only on July 27, 1900; and though he had been acting in that capacity before the end of July, anything approaching this late date for the original printing of the last gathering of the book is almost impossible given the evidence for the typesetting of "A Little Pilgrim," with its proofing before Crane's death in the magazine version issued in the August *Harper's*. Thus the half-sheet preliminaries with the William Crane copyright notice must be a complete later reprinting of the original gathering just before binding.

It is also doubtful that the only copy known with Stephen's

[1] Ames W. Williams and Vincent Starrett, *Stephen Crane: A Bibliography* (Glendale, Calif., 1948), pp. 48–49.

copyright was an error deposited by pure chance: the publishers may deliberately have deposited both versions as a form of protection. That the book was very likely printed in May or early June seems probable from the peculiar facts about the text of "A Little Pilgrim," detailed below. But the discovery that the copyright would need to be transferred to Stephen's literary executor and that a cancel half-sheet would be required would not necessarily have been simultaneous with the news of Stephen's death.

This book collection (A1) collates π^4 A–M^8 N^4, pp. *i–iv* v–vi *vii–viii* 1–198 *199–200*. Its title reads: '[within a frame of type-ornaments] Whilomville | Stories | by | *Stephen Crane* | *Illustrated by* | *Peter Newell* | [Harper's device] | *New York and London* | *Harper & Brothers* | *Publishers* | *1900*'. This title is on p. i, the copyright notice on p. ii, contents on p. iii, p. iv blank, list of illustrations on pp. v–vi, half-title on p. vii, p. viii blank, with the text beginning on p. 1, ending on p. 199, p. 200 blank. A frontispiece portrait faces p. i. Thirty-three full-page tipped-in illustrations are present. The price was $1.50.

One of the Barrett copies (551468) retains the original mustard dust jacket. The front reads 'Whilomville | Stories | By Stephen Crane | Illustrated by Peter Newell | T³HE scenes of these tales are laid in a country town. | The doings of the children, and their many amusing peculi-|arities, are related with a power of depiction which in-|sures the late Mr. Crane's high rank amongst short-story | writers. The incidental sketches of negro character are | remarkably well done.' The spine reads 'WHILOM=|VILLE | STORIES | Stephen Crane | HARPERS'. The back has a notice of nine books by Mary E. Wilkins and the imprint 'NEW YORK AND LONDON | HARPER & BROTHERS, Publishers' all within a frame of type-ornaments. The printing is in black.

With only a change in the final digit in the imprint date on the title-plate, a 1902 printing (A2) from the same plates, and with the same illustrations, came from Harper, followed at some unknown time by an undated printing (A3), the date removed from the plate, with only fifteen illustrations. Machine collation of these two impressions back against the 1900 control copy reveals no textual variation except for the one-page list of fifteen illustrations in the undated printing versus the two-page list of thirty-three. Not all thirty-three illustrations, in fact, are always present in the 1902 printing since copies may exhibit different patterns of omission from one to several of the tipped-in plates. The undated volume may or may not have a foliage decoration on the spine and cover. The order of the 1902 and the undated printings cannot be established by the type batter but is assigned on general probability.

In 1900 Harper put out an English issue (E1) which consisted of the American sheets (the same unwatermarked laid paper, vertical chainlines) with a variant imprint '*London and New York*' in an English blue-cloth binding. The frontispiece and the thirty-three illustrations are present as in the New York issue. Although publication was announced in the *Publishers' Circular* for November 17, 1900, sale of the English issue may have been delayed since the British Museum deposit copy (shelf mark 012707.ee.42) is stamped February 19, 1901. Possible corroboration of a gap between publication announcement and actual sale may be found in the fact that the London Library copy purchased for its membership on December 29, 1900, is the New York issue. The publication price was five shillings. Three royalty statements from Harper's to Pinker, Crane's agent, are preserved in the Berg Collection of the New York Public Library; they suggest that the book's popularity was not long-lived. On September 30, 1905, nine shillings were paid, and on March 31, 1906, and March 28, 1907, one shilling sixpence each.

Except for part of "A Little Pilgrim," the *Harper's Magazine* texts derive from the manuscripts probably through the intermediary of lost typescripts, and the book collection (A1) was set up from clippings (but probably for stories X–XII from corrected proofs) of the magazine prints. The book is a relatively close reprint of the magazine texts; the few variants appear to be compositorial and without authority. On the contrary, the later pages of "A Little Pilgrim" [2] were set up in the book (A1) from copy directly deriving from the manuscript, presumably a type-

---

[2] This is the presumably authoritative revised form of the title as it appears in *Harper's Magazine*, substituting for the manuscript and A1 title, "A Little Pilgrimage."

script; and the corresponding *Harper's Magazine* text was type-set from the book proofs, and *vice versa*.

No external evidence seems to bear on this anomaly. Professor Levenson has suggested the strong probability that "A Little Pilgrim" was written and presumably sent to Crane's new agent, Pinker, in November, 1899. He has also shown that about this time Pinker, who cared little for the series and had not executed the original contracts, was inquiring of Harper whether more than twelve stories would be welcome. It may be that the story lingered in Pinker's office and was not sent to the United States until April or May, 1900. It may be that the story was in Harper's hands by the first of the year but some lack of communication between the book and the magazine editors revealed to one or other of them its existence only at the last moment. It may be, however, that no irregularity at all existed. Stories X–XII were almost certainly set in the book from magazine proof, not clip-pings, since these were stories that were published in May, June, and July, 1900, respectively. Thus it is by no means impossible to imagine that having exhausted the stories in proof the book printer called for the thirteenth only to find that it had not yet been set for the magazine. His demand might well have decided the magazine editor to set the type at the same time in order to preserve what seems to have been about a three months' interval between the pulling of the first proof and the appearance in print of a Whilomville story.

Speculation is idle in the absence of all information. What we do know, from the evidence of the text itself, is that the book printer required the copy before the magazine printer had set it, and hence on a time schedule that made it impossible to send the book proofs of this story to Crane. The necessity to complete the book from copy that had not yet been set up for the magazine and proofread by the author, as had been the procedure for the other twelve stories, accounts for the hurried production and for the differences in the text of the book and the author-revised magazine version. Hence the date would seem to be fairly firm that it was set in type simultaneously in April–May 1900, that the book was thereupon printed, but that magazine proof was sent to Crane and read and returned by him before his death on June 5.

Given this textual situation, especially for the book as a whole, the preserved manuscripts of the *Whilomville Stories* must be chosen as the copy-texts since they alone represent Crane's accidentals unaffected by house styling, even when as in "Making an Orator" and "The City Urchin" the early parts are in other hands. (For "Shame" and "The Carriage-Lamps" not known to exist in manuscript form, the *Harper's Magazine* version is the closest to the lost holograph and must be selected as copy-text.) However, in each case the magazine version shows signs of authoritative variation from the manuscript as the result of changes conjecturally made in the lost typescript, or in the lost proofs, or in both. Hence the substantives of the magazine texts have a general authority superior to those of the manuscripts and are ordinarily adopted except in specific cases where editorial or compositorial intervention is suspected. The book collection, being a simple reprint of the magazine texts except for "A Little Pilgrim," has no authority for the first twelve stories in any of its forms as A1, A2, A3, or E1.

The fact that the manuscripts were not themselves the printer's copy but were made into typescripts that became this copy complicates the textual procedures by the introduction of a lost stage of transmission. It seems to be fairly well established that Crane himself could not or did not type. We have no means of knowing whether he had his Whilomville manuscripts typed locally or through his agent, but the available evidence strongly indicates that the manuscripts were typewritten by Cora or Edith Richie and worked over before being sent to his agent in New York or London. That he retained these manuscripts may suggest not so much that they were returned separately as that typed copy was available to him for revision before being released as printer's copy; moreover, it is established that he and Cora had given the manuscripts of "The Lover and the Tell-Tale" and then "The Angel-Child" to Mrs. Pease several months before the sale of the stories. Although once while Cora was away Crane sent Pinker two chapters of a book in holograph (see *Letters*, pp. 266, 272, 277), a number of letters remark on typed copy being mailed (for example, see pp. 241, 247, 248, 261, 264, 266, 267, 270, 272). Finally, "A Little Pilgrim" has at least one authoritative alteration that must have been made in typescript.

The law of simplicity suggests that the authoritative nature of a revised reading is not modified whether Crane made the

change in the typescript or in the proof. Clear-cut literary alterations present no problem, therefore. On the other hand, any
extra stage of transmission between manuscript and print intro-
duces the expectation of more than normal corruption, especially
in relatively neutral readings, by the typist in addition to the
compositor; and these transmissional variants may be compounded if the original typescript was revised and thereupon
retyped in order to provide clean printer's copy. Hence the variants between manuscript and print encourage a perilous bal-
ance in editorial judgment, for the probability that an author will
make more relatively minor changes when going over his work in
two or more different stages than in the single stage of proof
must be matched against the probability that both typist and
compositor will consciously or unconsciously alter copy in a
manner that will not always be noticed by an author reading over
their transcripts. On the whole, however, the present editor has
come to feel that this lost intermediate stage of transmission
does not detract significantly from the reliability of those substantive magazine variants from the manuscripts that are rather
clearly not the kind of house styling and correction to which
Crane's idiosyncratic prose was usually subjected.

As for the accidentals, the evidence of "A Little Pilgrim" suggests something of a stand-off. Unquestionably, in some cases
unauthoritative modification of Crane's texture of accidentals
must have been created in the typescript. On the other hand, the
typescript itself and its revision offered an opportunity for correcting anomalies and for improving authoritatively the significant presentation of the accidentals more freely than in proof.
As an example, it appears to the editor to be probable that in
considerable part the extension of Crane's characteristic use of
the dash in the magazine prints as against the manuscripts may
have resulted from his alterations of the punctuation in the
typescript copy. But balancing such optimistic interpretation are
examples such as those in "The Little Pilgrim" in which some
capitalization variants between manuscript and print may have
been created unauthoritatively in the typescript and not by the
compositors.

Because of its unusual textual history, "A Little Pilgrim" offers
the only evidence available in the Whilomville series to estab-

lish with fair certainty (a) the substantive (and in some small part the accidentals) differences between the preserved manuscript and the lost typescript, and (b) the actual changes made in proof for the magazine text. An attempt to extrapolate all of the evidence procurable from "A Little Pilgrim" to the other Whilomville material runs into two difficulties. First, the evidence may perhaps be distorted by the unique circumstance that as late as the proof stage someone (conjectured to be Crane himself) decided to tone down the religious satire present in the manuscript and book form of the story. Second, "A Little Pilgrim" is a very short story and therefore does not constitute a large enough sample from which to expand the evidence statistically except with considerable caution. Even in these circumstances, however, the textual history of this text, and what can be learned from it, is important enough to deserve analysis.

"A Little Pilgrim" in A1, the book collection, starts on p. 191, sig. M7, and ends on p. 199, sig. N4. This constitutes nine pages of text, but if the sixteen lines on p. 199 are balanced against the six lines occupied by the drop heading on p. 191, the start of p. 195 marks the halfway point of the text minus five lines. In pp. 191–194 eleven substantive and accidentals readings differ between A1 and H, and of these eight agree in MS and H. Of the eight, all are substantives or semisubstantives: MS, H *in a* versus A1 *in* (235.10), three agreements of MS and H in *Presperterian* versus *Presbyterian* (235.21, 236.10, 236.24–25), *victims* versus *victim* (235.23), *denominations* versus *denomimation* (235.24), *ever you* versus *you ever* (235.25), and *friend* versus *friends* (237.7). The agreements of MS and A1 as against H are confined to the single substantive *pain* versus *distress* (235.12) and the two accidentals *tree* with no comma versus a comma (235.10) and *December* with a comma versus no comma (236.1).

These readings make it certain that in these pages the MS (through a lost typescript) was the direct copy for H, the magazine text. To reverse the hypothesis would require one to believe that the three MS and A1 agreements were all operative and that the eight MS and H agreements resulted from a scrupulous proof correction in H of eight errors originally transmitted to H from A1. That these are errors in A1 that would not automatically have been corrected by the compositors of H is clear enough when one considers the odds against the H compositors altering consistent *Presbyterian* readings to coincide by pure chance with the MS dialect readings *Presperterian,* or the perfectly satisfactory A1 *that you ever saw in the world* to coincide by chance with MS *that ever you saw in the world.* The two accidentals agreements between MS and A1 are not of a nature on which to build a theory of textual transmission; and the concurrence of MS and A1 in *pain* (235.12) as against H *distress* can be explained by an overall hypothesis of proof correction in H detailed below.

On the other hand, the alternative hypothesis that H and A1 were set independently either from identical copy or from roughly similar (as of a typescript and its carbon) may be discarded on the evidence of the thirty-nine agreements in accidentals between H and A1 versus MS in these four pages, as against the two instances in which MS and A1 agree against H and the lack of any example of an accidentals agreement of MS and H against A1. Some of these H and A1 agreements, like the conventional compositorial spelling *manœuvred* versus MS *manoevred* are unquestionably due to house styling; others might be the result of both prints following common features in the similar printer's copy; but that this overwhelming statistical concurrence could arise from the faithful representation of MS copy by two independent compositors is unbelievable, and the qualitative analysis appears to bear out this contention. That is, when compositors set from typescript they are obliged to impose house style and as much uniformity as possible on the variable characteristics of the copy. That two such compositors would automatically agree in adding exclamation points after *Huh* (235.20, 24) for MS semicolon and comma, respectively, may be doubtful; that an exclamation is required as in H and A1 at 236.32 after *Hello, Homer* instead of MS comma is also doubtful; that both would retain MS colon at 236.13 after *said* introducing dialogue but alter MS colons to commas at 236.29 and 237.9 is more doubtful.

But one absolute piece of evidence exists that demonstrates that H and A1 derive one from another and not independently from MS. Throughout the Whilomville series one of the H compositors has consistently inserted an apostrophe before *ain't* whereas his fellow(s) did not. In the text of "The Little Pilgrim" *ain't* is found in H and in A1 without the apostrophe at 235.21, 23, and 236.11 but with the apostrophe as *'ain't* in both at 236.35 and 37. In each case the MS reads *aint* but A1 agrees with the variation here that is characteristic of H in other stories where A1 also usually agrees. The coincidence constitutes true demonstration. This being so, the evidence of the readings can lead to only one conclusion: in the four pages 191–194 of A1 the printer's copy must have been proofs of H.

On the other hand, the pattern alters in the latter half of the text, the four and a half A1 pages 195–199. Here of the twelve variants between A1 and H, the six substantives show MS and A1 invariably agreeing against H, and of the six accidentals (counting such a sequence of caps as in the hymn title at 237.9–10 as a single unit) four show agreement between MS and A1 against H, whereas only two have MS and H in agreement against A1. The substantive agreements of MS and A1 are *fat* versus its H omission (237.11), *a man . . . children* versus H omission (237.14), *oily and* versus H omission (237.20), omission versus H addition *at the story* (238.1–2), *knew* versus *know* (238.14, a misprint in H), and *fat hand of the* versus H omission (239.8). Of the accidentals, the four agreements of MS and A1 are in the caps in the hymn title versus lower case (237.9–10), *melody* with no comma versus a comma (237.11), no paragraph versus a paragraph indentation (237.21), and *The* versus *the* (238.25). The two accidentals in which H and MS agree against A1 are in hyphenating *fairy-tales* versus no hyphen in A1 (238.14), and in a comma after *saying* versus no comma (237.31), although the spacing in A1 suggests a plate defect and the possible existence of a comma in proof. In this group the evidence of the agreement in no paragraphing versus a paragraph at 237.21 is especially significant. All the evidence points to the hypothesis that in these pages A1 was set from MS through its intermediary typescript and that a proof of A1 was the printer's copy for H.

An anomaly like this must have a physical explanation that conforms to normal printing practice if we are to believe that for pp. 191–194 of the book a proof of H (which had derived from MS) served as printer's copy for A1, but for pp. 195–199 the

printer's copy for A1 was MS (through its typescript) and H **was**
set from a proof of A1.

The pattern of the printer's copy changes abruptly between
the text on p. 194 and p. 195. For example, the highly significant
agreement of H and A1 in *'ain't* appears twice on p. 194, and
only four lines from its foot we have the MS and H agreement in
friend as against A1 *friends*. Yet in the hymn title that appears
in the first line of p. 195 the shift begins to the agreement of MS
and of A1 against H, maintained in the five other variants on p.
195, including three substantives and the significant paragraphing difference. The point is, that the change in printer's copy
coincides with the physical division of A1 between pages 194 and
195, and not with anything observable in the physical characteristics of H, where the difference starts with the fourteenth line
from the bottom of the first column on p. 402.

This clue leads to the answer. Both A1 and H were set simultaneously from typescript copy cast off on the basis of A1's pages.
Copy for the first four pages of A1 was given to the H printer,
and copy for the final four and a half pages of A1 was given to
the A1 printer. Each set his copy from the cast-off typescript and
then pulled a proof, which was exchanged. Thus pp. 191–194 of
A1 were set from an unrevised proof of H, and pp. 195–199
were set from typescript. Correspondingly, the text contained in
the first four pages of A1 was set by H from typescript, and the
text of the remainder of the story from a proof of A1. The virtue
of this exchange lay first in its speed and second in the conven-
ience of setting a half of each text from styled proof instead of
unstyled typescript, a procedure that also increased the speed.

This explanation, also, agrees with the evidence of the cancel-
landum preliminary gathering with the Stephen Crane copyright
that printing of the book (possibly though not necessarily with
π^4 imposed with N^4) was completed before news of Crane's
death on June 5, 1900, reached the publisher. A date in April or
May for the typesetting of book and of magazine text also agrees
with the previous scheduling of the stories for magazine appearance, in which "The Angel-Child" in the first set purchased in
May, 1899, was published in *Harper's Monthly* for August.

The application of this hypothesis enables us to reconstruct
certain features of the textual transmission of this story. Logic

suggests that any substantive reading shared by H and A1 against a MS variant must represent either an alteration in the typescript or else a printer's error in H repeated in A1 if in pp. 191–194 (235.1–237.9 'Number 33—' |); or a printer's error in A1 repeated in H if in pp. 195–199. In pp. 191–194 these shared substantives in H–A1 are *Big Progressive* at 236.3, 5, 16, 19, 28 for *Dutch Reformed Church* in MS; *Trescott* at 236.12 for *Again Trescott* in MS; and *once more* at 236.12 wanting in MS. In pp. 195–199 this variation is confined to *her work* at 237.36 for MS *the work*. The latter is conjectured to be a typescript or an A1 compositorial sophistication passed on to H, but the others are clearly authorial. For this story, at least, Crane made few changes when he read over the typescript. It is interesting to see him at this early stage tinkering with the religious satire by removing a too precise reference. Otherwise, at 236.12 he made one trifling stylistic change, and just possibly one at 237.36 if this latter is not instead a typescript or printer's error.

The case seems to be different with a few of the accidentals. Given conventional house styling from both printers, most of the punctuation variants in H and A1 from MS cannot be isolated as due to the typescript or typesetting as in such matters as the invariable hyphenation in both H and A1 of *Sunday-school* as against *Sunday School* of MS irregularly mixed with dominant *Sunday-School*. On the other hand, the consistent lower case adopted by both printers in *school* and *church* for MS dominant *School* and invariable *Church* may be a reflection of the type-script form as readily as coincidental house styling. If the latter, the typescript would appear to be unauthoritative, as remarked in the Textual Note to 237.12. It is interesting to see all of the MS dashes reproduced in the prints, but no new ones added. The differences between MS capitals and the lower case of the prints as in *Tree* (235.4, 10), *Fairy-Tales* (238.14), *Eve* (235.4), and *Martyrdom* (239.5) are perhaps not to be distinguished: it would be idle speculation that a compositor would be less likely than a typist to reduce copy *Martyrdom* to *martyrdom*. The variant paragraphings may well be compositorial, on the evidence of the independent action of H from its A1 proof at 237.21 (provided this is not a proof revision).

In the A1 text set from H (pp. 191–194) substantive variants in which A1 and MS agree against H would theoretically be

either the A1 correction of obvious H errors, a careful proofreading by the printer against copy, or else proof corrections or
revisions in H following the use of its proof as printer's copy for
A1. No clear-cut examples of the first two classes appear, but in
the H change of title from MS–A1 *PILGRIMAGE* to *PILGRIM*
and in the alteration of *pain* to the more accurate *distress*
(235.12) we seem to see the operations of proof alteration.

Correspondingly, when in pp. 195–199 A1 proof served as
printer's copy for H, H variants from MS and A1 agreement
would result either from printer's errors, a faithful rendition of
an A1 proof error later corrected before printing, editorial
changes in the A1 printer's copy before H typesetting, or else
revision in H proof whether editorial or authorial. The H misprint *know* for MS–A1 *knew* (238.14) appears to belong to
either one of the first two classes. To either one of the latter two
classes would belong the stylistic addition of *at the story* at
238.1–2 and the series of omissions to soften the religious satire
at 237.11, 14, 20, and 238.8.

Here the overall view favors the hypothesis that the substantive variants in H in these pages (the misprint at 238.14 ex-
cepted) represent authorial changes in the H proof sent Crane,
this being the only proof for the story that he ever saw because of
the speed with which the book was set and printed. The evidence
is of two kinds. First, the stylistic alteration of *pain* to *distress*
(235.12) in the early pages set from MS, as well as the change
of title, shows when MS and A1 agree that H must originally
have read with them and thus that the H variants must represent
alteration in proof, not editorial intervention in the typescript. If,
then, stylistic changes in proof appear in pp. 191–194, a similar
variant at 238.1–2 from pp. 195–199 can be inferred to come
from the same process. These stylistic changes are so relatively
neutral and unnecessary as to offer little evidence whether they
were editorial or authorial. But since type was set for H in time
to be sent to Crane before his death, and since the total evidence
of the other stories suggests that he regularly read proof before
their magazine appearance, it may appear to be more natural to
assign these to the author than to a hypothetical editor.

The question then arises whether any evidence separates the
stylistic alterations in H that may be imputed to Crane's reading
proof from the cuts in pp. 195–199 that remove what might be

thought of as excesses in the tone of the satire on the Sunday school. If we take it that the change in pp. 191–194 of the typescript to *Big Progressive* from MS *Dutch Reformed* was Crane's work before he sent off the copy, then no particular reason exists to invent editorial intervention for the cuts in the proof of H. Of course, if one were determined to saddle an editor with censorship throughout, one might argue that this editor altered *Dutch Reformed* in the typescript and continued his censorship in proof. But the fatal split in logic is apparent, for it is difficult to imagine the circumstances that would lead such a censor to alter the typescript for pp. 192–194 but not for pp. 195–196 if he were searching for ways to avoid giving offense to his readers.[3] Moreover, the hypothetical offense these cut passages would give is not wholly of a piece, for considerable difference exists between the implications of *greasy victorious beneficence* and *an oily and deeply religious voice* and the three deleted references to the fat hands of the superintendent. Given this complex of circumstances, the simplest and most natural agent for the revisions was the very author already identified as a reader of his proofs, tinkering a few times with his style and changing his mind about the literary effect of ostentatious pejorative detail in the otherwise light good humor of the satire. One may also compare even deeper cuts in such stories as "The Trial" and "The Stove."

On the contrary, when in pp. 191–194 substantive variants appear in which H and MS agree against A1, the A1 variants must represent printer's errors or unauthoritative A1 proof correction. The simplest example of error is no doubt the omission of *a* at 235.10 and the obtuse alterations of dialect *Presperterian* to *Presbyterian*. Whether such sophistications as appear in 235.23–24, or 235.10, or 237.7 are compositorial or due to the proofreader can scarcely be determined, although simplicity would suggest the compositor(s). Since none of the variants in this area can possibly be authoritative, the only purpose in an attempted distinction would be to extrapolate compositorial error

---

[3] Of course, untrammeled speculation can assign a reason to anything. For example, one could argue that two editors with differing ideas of censorship went over the story, the one in typescript but the other in proof. Or that the same editor, who had been at first intent only on avoiding a specific offense, at a later time decided that for magazine publication more generally offensive passages should be canceled.

from this sample to the rest of the volume. As remarked, such a procedure would be statistically dangerous. On the other hand, the demonstration that in four book pages the compositor setting from proof might have made as many as eight significant changes does not altogether jibe with the evidence for few and venial alterations in A1 set from H in the other stories, and it may be that because of the peculiar circumstances of the A1 typesetting a proofreader did indeed intervene in part.[4]

In the latter half of the story, pp. 195–199, substantive variants in which H and MS agree against A1 are wanting.

The editorial method for "A Little Pilgrim" will vary, therefore, according to the section that was set from manuscript-derived copy. The copy-text for both sections must, of course, be the manuscript, which preserves more faithfully than either print the general texture of Crane's accidentals. When changes are to be made in the accidentals of the MS, only variants in H that appear in the text of pp. 191–194 or variants in A1 that appear in pp. 195–199 can be selected as having any possible authority and as other than advisable editorial changes.

The procedures for incorporating into the copy-text the authoritative substantive variants present in the prints will differ from the treatment of the accidentals. In pp. 191–194 no substantive variant in A1 from MS–H concurrence can possibly have any authority. Variants in which H and A1 agree against MS may represent typescript changes from MS or unauthoritative variants in the setting of H passed on to A1. Finally, if the hypothesis governing this edition's editorial procedure be accepted, i.e., that the H substantive variants from MS–A1 agreement are authorial proof revisions, then all H substantive readings in these pages have overriding authority and are to be accepted. Within pp. 195–199 H substantive variation from MS–A1 agreement is also accepted as authoritative proof revision. On the other hand, A1–H agreement in pp. 195–199 against MS may derive either from typescript readings differing from MS or from an A1 compositorial error transmitted to H and not caught in proof.

---

[4] An added source of error in A1, not present in other stories which would have been set from corrected H proof or the actual clippings of the print, could be mistakes in the uncorrected H proof from which A1 may have been set in pp. 191–194.

The theory of copy-text governing the editing of the first twelve stories, and the exception represented by the thirteenth, has already been remarked. Some specifics applicable to the whole of the *Whilomville* text remain. The possibility that Crane in working over the typescripts may have altered a few of the accidentals of the manuscript has led to a somewhat freer acceptance of certain features of these accidentals in H, like the more frequent use of the dash, than would have been plausible on any theory of proof correction. The differences in paragraphing between H and MS have usually been accepted from the H version, less on the theory that they are authoritative than that they constitute normalizing detail of the sort ordinarily undertaken by the present editor, such as the attempt to make uniform the variable MS word-division and spelling practices.

In three stories greater than usual freedom in normalizing emendation has been adopted. In "Making an Orator" and in "The City Urchin" the parts of the manuscripts copied by Cora Crane and by Edith Richie, respectively, are brought into general conformity in their accidentals with the parts that Crane himself wrote out in order to avoid a distracting and unauthoritative division of the texture that would have resulted from a pedantic adherence to the forms of the manuscripts. Similarly, when in "The Trial, Execution, and Burial of Homer Phelps" the manuscript is wanting for the latter part and H must become the copy-text, the accidentals of H are freely altered to bring them into conformity with the characteristics of the preceding MS copy-text for the story.

On the other hand, when as with "Shame" and "The Carriage-Lamps" no manuscript at all is preserved and the entire copy-text must be H, pure textual theory applicable to larger works would suggest that each should be treated as a unit according to its copy-text since no evidence is available (except by analogy) as to the exact forms of the accidentals in its manuscript. This theory has been adhered to in general, and no attempt has been made to reconstruct the lost manuscripts of these two stories such as appears in the continuation of the preserved part of the manuscript of "The Trial." On the other hand, a distinction is made here between reconstruction by independent emendation and that form of regular editorial normalizing that constitutes a usual procedure in a critical edition. Thus the punctuation system of these two stories is accepted in its H form except for such correction as would ordinarily be made in MS anomalies. On the other hand, just such normalizing of word-division to coincide with Crane's usual manuscript practice has been undertaken as would be performed in order to make a manuscript copy-text consistent with itself and with Crane's other Whilomville stories.

A number of silent alterations of manuscript characteristics unsuitable for print and burdensome to list have been made. MS forms like *dont, cant, aint,* and *em* have been given the conventional apostrophes; and in H copy-texts the compositorial *'ain't* has been silently reduced to *ain't. Mrs* and *Mr* have had periods added; and *Dr* has been silently expanded to *Doctor.* Spacing variants are silently normalized. Thus the erratic placement of punctuation in relation to quotation marks has been adjusted to agree with standard American usage, and contractions like *'ll* have been uniformly spaced. Although Crane's misspellings are recorded, his characteristic error *it's* for the possessive pronoun *its* is so common as to be included among the silent corrections.

The manuscripts at Columbia University and the University of Virginia have all been personally collated and checked by the editor. "The Angel-Child" manuscript was collated from Xerox prints, but its owner, Commander Melvin Schoberlin, very kindly checked doubtful readings on several occasions. The *Harper's New Monthly Magazine* texts were collated from copies at the University of Virginia. The three copies of the 1900 New York Harper edition (A1) in the Barrett Collection at the University of Virginia have been collated on the Hinman Machine without sign of textual variation: these are PS1449.C85W4 1900 with acquisition numbers 241357, 433597, and 551468. The first of these has also been machine-collated against the 1900 London issue (E1) in the Barrett copy PS1449.C85W4 1900a (551469).[5] The Ohio State University Libraries copy of A1 has been machine-collated against the Harvard copy of 1902 (A2) and the copy of the undated printing (A3) owned by Professor M. J. Bruccoli. No textual variation in the plates was observed except

---

[5] The endpapers of A1 are described by Williams and Starrett as white wove, and this is their form in the Columbia University copy of E1; however, the Barrett copy is an unrecorded variant with white laid-paper endpapers.

for the differences in the illustrations list of the undated impression reducing the noted illustrations to fifteen.

The manuscripts are mostly written on the same cheap thin ruled wove quarto paper, the rules 9 mm. apart, on the recto only. The few times that foolscap paper is used may, thus, be significant. Only a few have titles; certain of these by differences in pen or in ink indicate that they were added later. Numbered parts always begin on a fresh page. On the verso of each leaf in Crane's hand appears the word count for the recto and then, by addition, the cumulative word count. The two items were sometimes written at different times. The first two leaves of "A Little Pilgrim" and fol. 8 of "The Fight" are unique in having vertical pencil strokes in the text at each hundred words and a single digit in the margin for the count by hundreds for each leaf as well as the verso word count. The manuscripts have been folded for mailing in an envelope, and each one, written vertically in what appears to be the same unidentified hand, has on the verso of the final leaf the title of the story and sometimes the notation 'Whilomville'. Since this notation appears on the verso of the last leaf of the incomplete manuscript of "The Trial . . . of Homer Phelps" and does not occur in the gift manuscripts to Mrs. Pease, it is likely that the notation was made by some owner of the manuscripts. However, Crane himself on the verso of the last leaf of "The Stove" wrote 'The Stove   Whilomville Series'.

THE ANGEL-CHILD: Ten numbered leaves of the ruled quarto paper 263 × 212 mm., titled 'The Angel-Child | By Stephen Crane | Part I'. The manuscript is written in blue ink and altered in the same ink except for six pencil changes in Cora's hand (rejected, and listed in the emendations list). The symbol # appears below the last line of text on fol. 10. To the left of the title, circled, is the count '3485 words'. On the verso of fol. 1 is the circled word count 430 in blue ink below deleted 425. On the verso of fol. 2, all in ink, is the circled figure 400, and beneath the total 830. On the lower part of the leaf, aslant, various sums are worked out in ink. Reading from left to right we have 60 added to 120 for a total of 180 and 100 added to that for a total of 280. Then 343 is subtracted from 500 for a result of 157. Then 273 is subtracted from 500 for a result of 329. Finally, below these, the figure 280 is written and immediately beneath it is 220 divided by 15 for a partial result of 12. On the versos of fols. 3–10 the word count for each leaf is written and then added to the cumulative total, all in ink, except that a circled word count for the leaf in pencil appears on fol. 8ᵛ, and on fol. 9ᵛ the total to date, 2980, was written in ink, but below it the leaf word count in pencil is added for a cumulative total in pencil of 3315. On fol. 8ᵛ, in addition, the word count 430 of fol. 7 is added in ink to the word count 390 of fol. 8 for a total of 820, and this 820 is also written in ink on the verso of fol. 9. *Owned by Commander Melvin H. Schober-lin, USN (Ret.).*

LYNX-HUNTING: Nine numbered leaves of quarto paper 263 × 212 mm., untitled. The first paragraph starts in black ink but by the end of the first paragraph changes slowly to blue ink as if the pen had initially been dipped in black and thereafter in blue. The rest of the manuscript is written in the blue ink and is corrected in this ink save for a pencil alteration on fol. 3 and another on fol. 5 in Cora's hand. On the verso of fol. 1 the circled word count 235 is written in pencil; thereafter the count is in blue ink up to the total 2355 on the verso of the final leaf. In pencil in the unidentified hand on this leaf appears the notation 'Lynx | Hunting'. *Columbia University.*

THE LOVER AND THE TELL-TALE: Four leaves of quarto paper 263 × 212 mm., titled 'The Lover and the Tell-Tale | By Stephen Crane'. To the left of the title is inscribed 'For Mrs Edward Pease | S. C.' Written in blue ink. The first leaf seems to show the sign of perforations at the top, as from a pad, and is shorter than the others (without these perforations), measuring 237 × 212 mm. On the verso of each leaf are the circled word counts in ink and the added cumulative totals up to 2030 on fol. 4ᵛ. *University of Virginia (Barrett Collection).*

"SHOWIN' OFF": Four numbered leaves of thick unruled laid foolscap, watermarked Britannia within an oval, measuring 330 × 203 mm., entitled ' "Showin' Off." | By Stephen Crane'. To the left of the title is the notation '2465 words', the figure altered from 2455. Just possibly the title and name were added later, but the matter is not certain. The manuscript is written in blue ink with alterations in the same ink except for a single pencil altera-tion by Cora at the foot of fol. 1. Crane's word count on the versos is written in blue ink. On the final verso the cumulative addition is 2455 but then he wrote '10' under this and added to make a new total of 2465. Vertically in pencil the unidentified hand has inscribed 'Whilomville | Showin' off'. *Columbia University.*

MAKING AN ORATOR: Eight numbered leaves of quarto paper, 265 × 212 mm., untitled. The first three leaves and the first six lines of fol. 4 were written by Cora in blue ink. When Stephen took over, with the new paragraph at 160.17, he used a finer pen but started out by dipping it in blue ink. Towards the end of the page he began to use a black ink which for a line or two is mixed with the blue. Crane's revisions both to Cora's part and to his own are written in blue ink with the fine pen, and a double slant that concludes the story on fol. 8 is also in the blue ink following the black-ink text. The word count on the versos is in pencil through the total 1835 on the verso of fol. 8. Curiously, on the verso of fol. 7, written vertically in pencil in an unidentified hand is the notation 'Making | an Orator'; and in a hand that seems to be unique in these notations on fol. 8ᵛ appears, vertically in pencil, 'Making a Public | Speaker | Whilomville'. Crane's revisions seem to have been made in both parts at the same time. Whether Cora was copying a rough worked-over draft or was writing at dictation cannot be demonstrated. One small piece of evidence, the deletion at 118 of *take* before writing *recognize* might suggest dictation, but the evidence is insufficient for a decision. The amount of alteration that Crane made in the part of the manuscript written by Cora is considerably greater than that in his own inscription. The use of blue ink at the moment of transition from Cora's section to his own, followed within a few lines by his change to black may suggest that he took over from her without delay. *Columbia University.*

THE KNIFE: Eight numbered leaves of quarto paper but of a slightly different size from that preceding, this being 263 × 208 mm. The manuscript is written and revised in blue ink but the title 'The Knife | Part I' and the other part numbers, also in blue, were added later. The word count on the verso of the first leaf is in pencil, but the remaining counts through the cumulative total on fol. 8ᵛ of 4095 are in blue ink. Written vertically in pencil in the unidentified hand on this verso is 'The Knife'. On fol. 6ᵛ the paragraphs represented by 191.18–21 have a blue-ink rule drawn across the page above and below. The significance of this marking is not to be determined, and it would be mere speculation that a deletion had been considered, for this marking is unique in the Whilomville manuscripts. On fol. 8 a blue-ink # concludes the text. *Columbia University.*

THE STOVE: Nine numbered leaves, untitled. The first leaf is thick laid-paper foolscap, 326 × 201 mm., watermarked with Britannia in an oval, the rules 9 mm. apart. The remaining leaves are the quarto paper 263 × 208. The first leaf, the foolscap, is written in black ink and the quarto leaves in blue ink, but the ink at the top of fol. 2 is black becoming blue as the pen is freshly dipped, and thus it is probable that the first leaf is not a later copying-out and revision. No evidence for compression or expansion appears in the size of the writing on this leaf. The few alterations on this leaf appear to have been made *currente calamo* and are thus in black ink. The changes in the remaining pages are in blue, and the part number 'I' that heads fol. 1 is also in blue as a sign that it was added later. On the verso of fol. 1 the word count is in black ink; on fol. 2ᵛ the count 575 is in pencil but the cumulative addition 1335 is in blue ink, which is used on the versos of the remaining leaves up to the final total of 4250. On the verso of the ninth leaf Crane himself has written, aslant, 'The Stove | Whilomville Series' and the notation of the strange hand is missing. *Columbia University.*

THE TRIAL, EXECUTION, AND BURIAL OF HOMER PHELPS: Three leaves are preserved of quarto paper, 263 × 208 mm., untitled. The inscription and alterations are in blue ink. On fol. 3ᵛ appears the blue-ink cumulative word count 1770, and the unidentified hand has written vertically in pencil, 'Whilomville | The Trial, Execution & Burial | of Homer Phelps'. *Columbia University.*

THE FIGHT: Eight numbered leaves of quarto paper 263 × 208 mm., entitled 'Whilomville Stories | By Stephen Crane | [rule] | The Fight.' This title and the part number II on fol. 4 may have been written at the same time as the text. The inscription throughout is in blue ink with changes also in blue. The circled word count on the versos of fols. 1, 2, 5, 7, and 8 is in pencil and in large figures. Fols. 5ᵛ, 7ᵛ, and 8ᵛ also contain the cumulative added totals in pencil, and in the same large figures, although on fol. 7ᵛ the count 725 is repeated, below, in small figures and blue ink. Fols. 3ᵛ, 4ᵛ, and 6ᵛ have the count and total in blue-ink small figures. These differences may reflect recopying of the leaves with the pencil counts, and indeed the text on fol. 5, though normally written at the start and the end of the leaf, is much smaller and cramped in the mid-section. The final leaf, 8, has the pencil strokes in the text and the marginal figures to count off the text by hundreds such as are found in "A Little Pilgrim." Each part begins a fresh page and # is marked at the end of the text of the first and third parts. *Columbia University.*

THE CITY URCHIN AND THE CHASTE VILLAGERS: Five leaves of quarto paper, 263 × 208 mm., the first two leaves and the first thirteen lines of the third written in a hand identified as that of Edith Richie. The manuscript was originally untitled, but the unknown hand that seems to be the usual one that notes the titles on the final versos has inserted the title in pencil at the head of fol. 1 and has repeated it in blue-black ink on fol. 5ᵛ. Edith Richie's inscription is in black ink, and Crane's alterations in her part are in black. Edith Richie stops her inscription with the sentences beginning a paragraph, "Peter Washington came out of the stable and observed this tragedy of the back garden. He stood transfixed for a moment and then ran toward it, shouting." Crane continues on the same line with the dialect speech " 'Hi! What's all dish yere? . . .' " and in black ink. The fourth leaf is a smaller piece of the quarto paper measuring 132 × 208 mm. It is numbered 4 in pencil, deleting the original identification 'a' in blue ink. Crane's inscription starts with black ink but about halfway down changes to blue ink. Fol. 5 is in blue ink but numbered 5 in pencil, replacing the original heading 'B' in blue ink. The word count on fols. 1ᵛ and 2ᵛ is in Edith Richie's hand in black ink. On fol. 3ᵛ Crane's hand inscribes the word count in black ink, noting his own and Edith Richie's shares separately before adding them. The circled word count 240 on fol. 4ᵛ is in large figures and in pencil but the cumulative totals are in smaller figures and in blue ink as is the total on fol. 5ᵛ. The original identification of fols. 4 and 5 (the first to be inscribed wholly by Crane) as 'a' and 'B' respectively suggests that he may have broken the original draft manuscript in two for simultaneous copying and thus did not know what numbers the leaves would be. If this is so, his continuation on fol. 3 of Edith Richie's inscription could be regarded as having followed on his writing out what were to become fols. 4–5 were it not that the evidence of the change on fol. 4 from the black ink characteristic of fol. 4 to the blue ink characteristic of fol. 5 might appear to negate this hypothesis and to suggest *seriatim* inscription from fol. 3 to 4. Yet if this is so, the original notation of fols. 4 and 5 can scarcely be explained, even though the blue ink of the 'a' at the top of fol. 4 demonstrates that this identification was written not at the start but at the end of the inscription of this leaf. Also difficult to explain is the use of a half-sheet of quarto paper for fol. 4. One very tentative hypothesis suggests itself. That is, perhaps Crane did indeed write in blue ink a now lost fol. 4, heading it 'a' or more likely 'A', and the present fol. 5 originally headed B, while Edith Richie was busy copying out the earlier part of the manuscript. Possibly it was agreed that when Peter Washington entered and dialect speech began, difficult to copy exactly, Crane would take over. This he did, and it could be guessed that to finish fol. 3 he copied out some of the material he had already written on fol. 4, perhaps revising it as he proceeded. The half-sheet fol. 4 might, then, represent either a recopying of the remaining part of the original fol. 4, or else (since it is the lower part of a sheet) the left-over original with the duplicated material cut away. However, the amount of white space above the first line is considerably more than would be found if text above had been cut off, and hence only the first alternative seems to be physically possible. In either case, the heading 'a' would represent an inadvertent reproduction of the 'a' or 'A' present at the top of the original sheet. There are so many difficulties in this hypothesis that it can be held, if at all, only very speculatively. The evidence of this manuscript does indeed appear to be quite contradictory. In a letter of April 26, 1942, from Edith Richie Jones to her brother preserved in the Berg Collection of the New York Public Library, she remarks of the accompanying manuscript of the Crane story "Kim Up the Kickers," which is entirely in her hand, that as she recalls Crane had dictated it to her: "Why I wrote it in that tiny script I know not. I must have typed it later. Sometimes in a train or out-doors or in a room he'd say:

'Anyone got a pencil & paper? I've just thought of something.' Then Cora or I wd write it down & afterwards type it. He rarely altered any of it but seemed to have it all straight in his mind when he began." [6] On the other hand, the evidence does not suggest dictation here, especially since the dictation of dialect speech with the spelling precisely as Crane wanted it would be difficult, although the possibility cannot be entirely discounted. *Columbia University.*

A LITTLE PILGRIM: Three leaves, titled 'Whilomville Stories | By Stephen Crane | [rule] | A Little Pilgrimage.' This title was added later since it is in black ink whereas the text starts in blue and changes to black ink about one-third down the page. The second and third leaves are written in black, and all changes are in black ink. The first two leaves are ruled laid-paper foolscap with the Britannia watermark in an oval, the left margin irregularly reduced and thus the measurements 326 × 201 mm. The third leaf is the quarto paper, 263 × 208 mm. On the first two leaves, but not on the third, pencil strokes mark each hundred words and single digits in the margin count by hundreds. The circled word count for each leaf on the versos of the first two folios is in pencil and does not seem to be in Crane's hand, nor is there a cumulative added total on the verso of fol. 2. On the verso of the third leaf in dark ink Crane has multiplied 36 by 2.0 for a result of 7.20. What seem to be curved division lines are on the left of this 7.20 and also on the right. On the left is the deleted figure 25 and on the right a deleted figure starting with a 2 that may be 26. Below the 7.20 is written 1.30. Apparently without relation to these figures, which are of unknown import, on this verso also appear a 3 above a 2, and elsewhere a 3. Vertically inscribed in light-brown ink in the unknown hand is 'A Little Pilgrimage' and under it, in black ink, 'Whilomville Stories'. Whether the inscription was continuous and the change of paper for only fourteen lines on fol. 3 an economy measure, or whether the difference in paper marks revised inscription of one or other part cannot be determined. *Columbia University.*

F. B.

TEXT OF THE
Whilomville Stories

I

THE ANGEL-CHILD

I

ALTHOUGH Whilomville was in no sense a summer resort, the advent of the warm season meant much to it for then came visitors from the city—people of considerable confidence—alighting upon their country cousins. Moreover, many citizens who could afford to do so escaped at this time to the seaside. The town, with the commercial life quite taken out of it, drawled and drowsed through long months during which nothing was worse than the white dust which arose behind every vehicle at blinding noon and nothing was finer than the cool sheen of the hose-sprays over the cropped lawns under the many maples in the twilight.

One summer, the Trescotts had a visitation. Mrs. Trescott owned a cousin who was a painter of high degree. I had almost said that he was of national reputation but—come to think of it —it is better to say that almost everybody in the United States who knew about art and its travail, knew about him. He had picked out a wife and naturally, looking at him, one wondered how he had done it. She was quick, beautiful, imperious while he was quiet, slow and misty. She was a veritable queen of health while he apparently was of a most brittle constitution. When he played tennis—particularly—he looked every minute as if he were going to break.

They lived in New York in awesome apartments wherein Japan and Persia and, indeed, all the world, confounded the observer. At the end, was a cathedral-like studio. They had one child. Perhaps it would be better to say that they had one CHILD. It was a girl. When she came to Whilomville with her parents it was patent that she had an inexhaustible store of white frocks and that her voice was high and commanding. These things the town knew quickly. Other things it was doomed to discover by a process.

Her effect upon the children of the Trescott neighborhood was singular. They at first feared, then admired, then embraced; in two days she was a Begum. All day long her voice could be heard directing, drilling, and compelling those free-born children, and to say that they felt oppression would be wrong, for they really fought for records of loyal obedience.

All went well until one day was her birthday.

On the morning of this day she walked out into the Trescott garden and said to her father confidently: "Papa, give me some money because this is my birthday."

He looked dreamily up from his easel. "Your birthday?" he murmured. Her envisioned father was never energetic enough to be irritable unless some one broke through into that place where he lived with the desires of his life. But neither wife nor child ever heeded or even understood the temperamental values and so some part of him had grown hardened to their inroads. "Money?" he said. "Here." He handed her a five-dollar bill. It was that he did not at all understand the nature of a five-dollar bill. He was deaf to it. He had it; he gave it; that was all.

She sallied forth to a waiting people—Jimmie Trescott, Dan Earl, Ella Earl, the Margate twins, the three Phelps children and others. "I've got some pennies now," she cried waving the bill, "and I am going to buy some candy." They were deeply stirred by this announcement. Most children are penniless three hundred days in the year and to another possessing five pennies they pay deference. To little Cora, waving a bright green note, these children paid heathenish homage. In some disorder they thronged after her to a small shop on Bridge Street hill. First of all, came ice-cream. Seated in the comic little back parlor, they clamored shrilly over plates of various flavors and the shop-keeper marveled that cream could vanish so quickly down throats that seemed wide open, always, for the making of excited screams.

These children represented the families of most excellent people. They were all born in whatever purple there was to be had in the vicinity of Whilomville. The Margate twins, for example, were out-and-out prize-winners. With their long golden curls and their countenances of similar vacuity, they shone upon the front bench of all Sunday-School functions, hand in hand, while their uplifted mother felt about her the envy of a hundred other parents, and less heavenly children scoffed from near the door.

Then there was little Dan Earl, probably the nicest boy in the world, gentle, fine-grained, obedient to the point where he obeyed anybody. Jimmie Trescott himself was indeed the only child who was at all versed in villainy, but in these particular days he was on his very good behavior. As a matter of fact, he was in love. The beauty of his regal little cousin had stolen his manly heart.

Yes, they were all most excellent children, but loosened upon this candy-shop with five dollars, they resembled, in a tiny way, drunken revelling soldiers within the walls of a stormed city. Upon the heels of ice-cream and cake came chocolate mice, butter-scotch, "ever-lastings," chocolate cigars, taffy-on-a-stick, taffy-on-a-slate-pencil, and many semi-transparent devices resembling lions, tigers, elephants, horses, cats, dogs, cows, sheep, tables, chairs, engines (both railway and for the fighting of fire), soldiers, fine ladies, odd-looking men, clocks, watches, revolvers, rabbits and bedsteads. A cent was the price of a single wonder.

Some of the children, going quite daft, soon had thought to make fight over the spoils but their queen ruled with an iron grip. Her first inspiration was to satisfy her own fancies but as soon as that was done, she mingled prodigality with a fine justice, dividing, balancing, bestowing and sometimes taking away from somebody even that which he had.

It was an orgy. In thirty-five minutes those respectable children looked as if they had been dragged at the tail of a chariot. The sacred Margate twins, blinking and grunting, wished to take seat upon the floor and even the most durable Jimmie Trescott found occasion to lean against the counter, wearing at the time a solemn and abstracted air as if he expected something to happen to him shortly.

Of course, their belief had been in an unlimited capacity but they found there was an end. The shop-keeper handed the queen her change.

"Two-seventy-three from five leaves two-twenty-seven, Miss Cora," he said looking upon her with admiration.

She turned swiftly to her clan. "O-oh," she cried in amazement. "Look how much I have left!" They gazed at the coins in her palm. They knew then that it was not their capacities which were endless; it was the five dollars.

The queen led the way to the street. "We must think up some way of spending more money," she said frowning. They stood in silence awaiting her further speech.

Suddenly she clapped her hands and screamed with delight. "Come on," she cried, "I know what let's do!" Now, behold, she had discovered the red and white pole in front of the shop of one William Neeltje, a barber by trade.

It becomes necessary to say a few words concerning Neeltje. He was new to the town. He had come and opened a dusty little shop on dusty Bridge Street hill and although the neighborhood knew from the courier winds that his diet was mainly cabbage, they were satisfied with that meagre data. Of course, Reifsnyder came to investigate him for the local Barbers' Union, but he found in him only sweetness and light, with a willingness to charge any price at all for a shave or a hair-cut. In fact the advent of Neeltje would have made barely a ripple upon the placid bosom of Whilomville if it were not that his name was Neeltje.

At first the people looked at his signboard out of the eye-corner and wondered lazily why anyone should bear the name of Neeltje, but as time went on, men spoke to other men saying, "How do you pronounce the name of that barber up there on Bridge Street hill?" And, then, before anyone could prevent it, the best minds of the town were splintering their lances against William Neeltje's signboard. If a man had a mental superior, he guided him seductively to this name and watched with glee his wrecking. The clergy of the town even entered the lists. There was one among them who had taken a collegiate prize in Syriac, as well as in several less opaque languages, and the other clergymen—at one of their weekly meetings—sought to betray him into this ambush. He pronounced the name correctly but that mattered little since none of them knew whether he did or did not; and so they took triumph according to their ignorance. Under these arduous circumstances it was certain that the town should look for a nickname and at this time the nickname was in process of formation. So William Neeltje lived on with his secret, smiling foolishly toward the world.

"Come on," cried little Cora. "Let's all get our hair cut! That's what let's do. Let's all get our hair cut! Come on! Come on! Come

"AROUND THE CORNER OF THE HOUSE CAME THE TWINS"

One of Peter Newell's illustrations for the *Whilomville Stories*

For Mrs Edward Pease!
S.C.

The Lover and the Tell-Tale
By Stephen Crane

First page of the manuscript of "The Lover and the Tell-Tale"

on!" The others were carried off their feet by the fury of this assault. To get their hair cut! What joy! Little did they know if this were fun; they only knew that their small leader said it was fun. Chocolate-stained but confident, the band marched into William Neeltje's barber-shop.

"We want to get our hair cut," said little Cora haughtily.

Neeltje, in his shirt sleeves, stood looking at them with his half-idiot smile.

"Hurry, now," commanded the queen. A dray horse toiled step by step, step by step, up Bridge Street hill; a far woman's voice arose; there could be heard the ceaseless hammers of shingling carpenters; all was summer peace. "Come on, now! Who's goin' first? Come on, Ella, you go first. Gettin' our hair cut! Oh, what fun!"

Little Ella Earl would not however be first in the chair. She was drawn toward it by a singular fascination but at the same time she was afraid of it and so she hung back, saying: "No! You go first! No! You go first!" The question was precipitated by the twins and one of the Phelps children. They made simultaneous rush for the chair and screamed and kicked, each pair preventing the third child. The queen entered this melee and decided in favor of the Phelps boy. He ascended the chair; thereat an awed silence fell upon the band. And always William Neeltje smiled fatuously.

He tucked a cloth in the neck of the Phelps boy and taking scissors began to cut his hair. The group of children came closer and closer. Even the queen was deeply moved. "Does it hurt any?" she asked in a wee voice.

"Naw," said the Phelps boy with dignity. "Anyhow, I've had m' hair cut afore."

When he appeared to them looking very soldierly with his cropped little head, there was a tumult over the chair. The Margate twins howled; Jimmie Trescott was kicking them on the shins. It was a fight.

But the twins could not prevail, being the smallest of all the children. The queen herself took the chair and ordered Neeltje as if he were a lady's-maid. To the floor there fell proud ringlets blazing even there in their humiliation with a full fine bronze light. Then Jimmie Trescott; then Ella Earl (two long ash-colored plaits); then a Phelps girl; then another Phelps girl; and so on from head to head. The ceremony received unexpected check when the turn came to Dan Earl. This lad, usually docile to any rein, had suddenly grown mulishly obstinate. No, he would not; he would not. He himself did not seem to know why he refused to have his hair cut, but despite the shrill derision of the company, he remained obdurate. Anyhow the twins, long held in check and now feverishly eager, were already struggling for the chair.

And so to the floor at last came the golden Margate curls, the heart-treasure and glory of a mother, three aunts and some feminine cousins.

All having been finished, the children, highly elate, thronged out into the street. They crowed and cackled with pride and joy, anon turning to scorn the cowardly Dan Earl.

Ella Earl was an exception. She had been pensive for some time and now the shorn little maiden began vaguely to weep. In the door of his shop William Neeltje stood watching them, upon his face a grin of almost inhuman idiocy.

II

It now becomes the duty of the unfortunate writer to exhibit these children to their fond parents. "Come on, Jimmie," cried little Cora, "let's go show mamma." And they hurried off, these happy children, to show mamma.

The Trescotts and their guests were assembled, indolently awaiting the luncheon bell. Jimmie and the angel-child burst in upon them. "Oh, mamma," shrieked little Cora, "see how fine I am! I've had my hair cut! Isn't it splendid! And Jimmie too."

The wretched mother took one sight, emitted one yell and fell into a chair. Mrs. Trescott let fall a large lady's-journal and made a nerveless mechanical clutch at it. The painter gripped the arms of his chair and leaned forward staring until his eyes were like two little clock-faces. Doctor Trescott did not move or speak.

To the children the next moments were chaotic. There was a loudly wailing mother and a pale-faced aghast mother; a stammering father and a grim and terrible father. The angel-child did not understand anything of it save the voice of calamity and in a moment all her little imperialism went to the winds. She ran sobbing to her mother. "Oh, ma-ma! Ma-ma! Ma-ma!"

The desolate Jimmie heard out of this inexplicable situation a voice which he knew well, a sort of a colonel's voice, and he obeyed like any good soldier. "Jimmie!"

He stepped three paces to the front. "Yessir."

"How did this—how did this happen?" said Trescott.

Now Jimmie could have explained how had happened anything which had happened but he did not know what had happened, so he said: "I—I—nothin'."

"And, oh, look at her frock," said Mrs. Trescott brokenly.

The words turned the mind of the mother of the angel-child. She looked up, her eyes blazing. " 'Frock'!" she repeated. " 'Frock'! What do I care for her 'frock'? 'Frock'!" she choked out again from the depths of her bitterness. Then she arose suddenly and whirled tragically upon her husband. "Look!" she declaimed. "All —her lovely—hair—all her lovely hair—gone—gone!" The painter was apparently in a fit; his jaw was set, his eyes were glazed, his body was stiff and straight. "All gone—all—her lovely hair—all gone—my poor little darlin'—my—poor—little—darlin'!" And the angel-child added her heart-broken voice to her mother's wail as they fled into each other's arms.

In the meantime, Trescott was patiently unravelling some skeins of Jimmie's tangled intellect. "And then you went to this barber's on the hill. Yes. And where did you get the money? Yes. I see. And who besides you and Cora had their hair cut? The Margate twi— Oh, lord!"

Over at the Margate place, old Eldridge Margate, the grandfather of the twins, was in the back garden picking peas and smoking ruminatively to himself. Suddenly he heard from the house great noises. Doors slammed; women rushed up stairs and down stairs calling to each other in voices of agony. And full and mellow upon the still air arose the roar of the twins in pain.

Old Eldridge stepped out of the pea patch and moved toward the house, puzzled, staring, not yet having decided that it was his duty to rush forward. Then, around the corner of the house shot his daughter Mollie, her face pale with excitement.

"What's the matter?" he cried.

"Oh, father," she gasped, "the children! They—"

Then around the corner of the house came the twins, howling at the top of their power, their faces flowing with tears. They were still hand in hand, the ruling passion being strong even in this suffering. At sight of them old Eldridge took his pipe hastily out of his mouth. "Good god!" he said.

And now what befell one William Neeltje, a barber by trade? And what was said by angry parents of the mother of such an angel-child? And what was the fate of the angel-child herself?

There was surely a tempest. With the exception of the Margate twins, the boys could well be eliminated from the affair. Of course it didn't matter if their hair was cut. Also the two little Phelps girls had had very short hair anyhow and their parents were not too greatly incensed. In the case of Ella Earl it was mainly the pathos of the little girl's own grieving, but her mother played a most generous part and called upon Mrs. Trescott and condoled with the mother of the angel-child over their equivalent losses. But the Margate contingent! They simply screeched.

Trescott, composed and cool-blooded, was in the middle of a giddy whirl. He was not going to allow the mobbing of his wife's cousins nor was he going to pretend that the spoliation of the Margate twins was a virtuous and beautiful act. He was elected, gratuitously, to the position of buffer.

But, curiously enough, the one who achieved the bulk of the misery was old Eldridge Margate who had been picking peas at the time. The feminine Margates stormed his position as individuals, in pairs, in teams and en masse. In two days they may have aged him seven years. He must destroy the utter Neeltje. He must midnightly massacre the angel-child and her mother. He must dip his arms in blood to the elbows.

Trescott took the first opportunity to express to him his concern over the affair but when the subject of the disaster was mentioned, old Eldridge, to the doctor's great surprise, actually chuckled long and deeply. "Oh, well, lookahere," said he. "I never was so much in love with them there damn curls. The curls was purty—yes—but then I'd a darn sight rather see boys look more like boys than like two little wax figgers. An', ye know, the little cusses like it 'emselves. *They* never took no stock in all this washin' an' combin' an' fixin' an' goin' to church an' paradin' an' showin' off. They stood it because they was told to. That's all. Of course this here Neel-te-gee, er-whatever-his-name-is, is a plumb dumb ijit but I don't see what's to be done, now that the kids is full-well cropped. I might go and burn his shop over his head but that wouldn't bring no hair back onto the kids. They're even kickin' on sashes now an' that's all right 'cause what fer does a boy want a sash?"

Whereupon Trescott perceived that the old man wore his brains above his shoulders and Trescott departed from him, rejoicing greatly that it was only women who could not know that there was finality to most disasters and that when a thing was fully done, no amount of door-slamming, rushing up stairs and down stairs, calls, lamentations, tears could bring back a single hair to the heads of twins.

But the rains came and the winds blew in the most biblical way when a certain fact came to light in the Trescott household. Little Cora, corroborated by Jimmie, innocently remarked that five dollars had been given her by her father on her birthday and with this money the evil had been wrought. Trescott had known it but he—thoughtful man—had said nothing. For her part the mother of the angel-child had, up to that moment, never reflected that the consummation of the wickedness must have cost a small sum of money. But now it was all clear to her. He was the guilty one—he! "My angel-child!"

The scene which ensued was inspiriting. A few days later, loungers at the railway station saw a lady leading a shorn and still undaunted lamb. Attached to them was a husband and father who was plainly bewildered but still more plainly vexed, as if he would be saying: "Damn 'em! Why can't they leave me alone!"

II

LYNX-HUNTING

JIMMIE lounged about the dining room and watched his mother with large serious eyes. Suddenly he said: "Ma—now—can I borrow Pa's gun?"

She was overcome with the feminine horror which is able to mistake preliminary words for the full accomplishment of the dread thing. "Why, Jimmie!" she cried. "Of al-l wonders! Your father's gun! No indeed you can't!"

He was fairly well-crushed but he managed to mutter sullenly: "Well, Willie Dalzel, he's got a gun." In reality his heart had previously been beating with such tumult—he had himself been so impressed with the daring and sin of his request—that he was glad all was over now and his mother could do very little further harm to his sensibilities. He had been influenced into the venture by the larger boys.

"Huh," the Dalzel urchin had said, "your father's got a gun, hasn't he? Well why don't you bring that?"

Puffing himself, Jimmie had replied: "Well, I can if I want to." It was a black lie but really the Dalzel boy was too outrageous with his eternal bill-posting about the gun which a beaming uncle had entrusted to him. Its possession made him superior in manfulness to most boys in the neighborhood—or at least they enviously conceded him such position—but he was so over-bearing and stuffed the fact of his treasure so relentlessly down their throats that on this occasion the miserable Jimmie had lied as naturally as most animals swim.

Willie Dalzel had not been checkmated for he had instantly retorted: "Why don't you get it, then?"

"Well, I can if I want to."

"Well, get it then."

"Well, I can if I want to."

Thereupon Jimmie had paced away with great airs of surety as far as the door of his home where his manner changed to one of tremulous misgiving as it came upon him to address his mother in the dining room. There had happened that which had happened.

When Jimmie returned to his two distinguished companions he was blown out with a singular pomposity. He spoke these noble words: "Oh, well. I guess I don't want to take the gun out to-day."

They had been watching him with gleaming ferret eyes and they detected his falsity at once. They challenged him with shouted jibes but it was not in the rules for the conduct of boys that one should admit anything whatsoever and so Jimmie, backed into an ethical corner, lied as stupidly, as desperately, as hopelessly as ever lone savage fights when surrounded at last in his jungle.

Such accusations were never known to come to any point for the reason that the number and kind of denials always equaled or exceeded the number of accusations and no boy was ever brought really to book for these misdeeds.

In the end they went off together, Willie Dalzel with his gun being a trifle in advance and discoursing upon his various works. They passed along a maple-lined avenue, a highway common to boys bound for that freeland of hills and woods in which they lived in some part their romance of the moment—whether it was of Indians, miners, smugglers, soldiers or outlaws. The paths were their paths and much was known to them of the secrets of the dark-green hemlock thickets, the wastes of sweet-fern and huckleberry, the cliffs of gaunt blue-stone with the sumach burning red at their feet. Each boy had, I am sure, a conviction that some day the wilderness was to give forth to them a marvelous secret. They felt that the hills and the forest knew much and they heard a voice of it in the silence. It was vague, thrilling, fearful and altogether fabulous. The grown folk seemed to regard these wastes merely as so much distance between one place and another place or as rabbit cover, or as a district to be judged according to the value of the timber; but to the boys it spoke some great inspiriting word which they knew even as those who pace the shore know the enigmatic speech of the surf.

In the meantime, they lived there, in season, lives of ringing adventure—by dint of imagination.

The boys left the avenue, skirted hastily through some private grounds, climbed a fence and entered the thickets. It happened that at school the previous day Willie Dalzel had been forced to read and acquire in some part a solemn description of a lynx. The meagre information thrust upon him had caused him grimaces of suffering but now he said suddenly: "I'm goin' to shoot a lynx."

The other boys admired this statement but they were silent for a time. Finally Jimmie said meekly: "What's a lynx?" He had endured his ignorance as long as he was able.

The Dalzel boy mocked him. "Why, don't you know what a lynx is? A lynx? Why, a lynx is an animal somethin' like a cat, an' it's got great big green eyes and it sits on the limb of a tree an' jus' glares at you. It's a pretty bad animal, I tell you. Why, when I—"

"Huh," said the third boy; "where'd you ever see a lynx?"

"Oh, I've seen 'em. Plenty of 'em. I bet you'd be scared if you seen one once."

Jimmie and the other boy each demanded: "How do you know I would?"

They penetrated deeper into the woods. They climbed a rocky zig-zag path which led them at times where with their hands they could almost touch the tops of giant pines. The grey cliffs sprang sheer toward the sky. Willie Dalzel babbled about his impossible lynx and they stalked the mountain side like chamois-hunters although no noise of bird or beast broke the stillness of the hills. Below them, Whilomville was spread out somewhat like the cheap green and black lithograph of the time—"A Bird's Eye View of Whilomville, N.Y."

In the end, the boys reached the top of the mountain and scouted off among wild and desolate ridges. They were burning with the desire to slay large animals. They thought continually of elephants, lions, tigers, crocodiles. They discoursed upon their immaculate conduct in case such monsters confronted them and they all lied carefully about their courage.

The breeze was heavy with the smell of sweet-fern. The pines and hemlocks sighed as they waved their branches. In the hollows the leaves of the laurels were lacquered where the sun-light found them. No matter the weather, it would be impossible to long continue an expedition of this kind without a fire and

presently they built one, snapping down for fuel the brittle un-
der-branches of the pines. About this fire they were willed to
conduct a sort of a play, the Dalzel boy taking the part of a bandit
chief and the other boys being his trusty lieutenants. They
stalked to and fro, long-strided, stern yet devil-may-care, three
terrible little figures.

Jimmie had an uncle who made game of him whenever he
caught him in this kind of play and often quoted derisively the
following classic: "Once aboard the lugger, Bill, and the girl is
mine. Now to burn the chateau and destroy all evidence of our
crime. But, hark'e, Bill, no wiolence." Wheeling abruptly, he addressed these dramatic words to his comrades. They were impressed; they decided at once to be smugglers and in the most
ribald fashion they talked about carrying off young women.

At last they continued their march through the woods. The
smuggling motif was now grafted fantastically upon the original
lynx idea which Willie Dalzel refused to abandon at any price.

Once they came upon an innocent bird who happened to be
looking another way at the time. After a great deal of manoeu-
vring and big words, Willie Dalzel reared his fowling-piece and
blew this poor thing into a mere rag of wet feathers. Of which he
was proud.

Afterward the other big boy had a turn at another bird. Then it
was plainly Jimmie's chance. The two others had of course some
thought of cheating him out of this chance but, of a truth, he was
timid to explode such a thunderous weapon and, as soon as they
detected this fear, they simply over-bore him and made it clearly
understood that if he refused to shoot he would lose his caste, his
scalp-lock, his girdle, his honor.

They had reached the old death-colored snake-fence which
marked the limits of the upper pasture of the Fleming farm.
Under some hickory trees the path ran parallel to the fence.
Behold, a small priestly chip-munk came to a rail and folding his
hands on his abdomen addressed them in his own tongue. It was
Jimmie's shot. Adjured by the others, he took the gun. His face
was stiff with apprehension. The Dalzel boy was giving forth fine
words. "Go ahead. Aw, don't be afraid. It's nothin' to do. Why,
I've done it a million times. Don't shut both your eyes, now. Jus'
keep one open and shut the other one. He'll get away if you don't

watch out. Now you're all right. Why don't you let'er go? Go ahead."

Jimmie with his legs braced apart was in the centre of the path. His back was greatly bent owing to the mechanics of supporting the heavy gun. His companions were screeching in the rear. There was a wait.

Then he pulled trigger. To him, there was a frightful roar, his cheek and his shoulder took a stunning blow, his face felt a hot flush of fire and, opening his two eyes, he found that he was still alive. He was not too dazed to instantly adopt a becoming egotism. It had been the first shot of his life.

But directly after the well-mannered celebration of this victory, a certain cow which had been grazing in the line of fire was seen to break wildly across the pasture bellowing and bucking. The three smugglers and lynx-hunters looked at each other out of blanched faces. Jimmie had hit the cow. The first evidence of his comprehension of this fact was in the celerity with which he returned the discharged gun to Willie Dalzel.

They turned to flee; the land was black, as if it had been over-shadowed suddenly with thick storm-clouds; and even as they fled in their horror, a gigantic Swedish farm-hand came from the heavens and fell upon them, shrieking in eerie triumph. In a twinkle they were clouted prostrate. The Swede was elate and ferocious in a foreign and fulsome way. He continued to beat them and yell.

From the ground, they raised their dismal appeal. "Oh, please, mister, we didn't do it. He did it. I didn't do it. We didn't do it. We didn't mean to do it. Oh, please, mister."

In these moments of childish terror, little lads go half-blind and it is possible that few moments of their after-life made them suffer as they did when the Swede flung them over the fence and marched them toward the farm-house. They begged like cowards on the scaffold and each one was for himself. "Oh, please let me go, mister. I didn't do it, mister. He did it. Oh, p-l-ease let me go, mister."

The boyish view belongs to boys alone and if this tall and knotted laborer was needlessly without charity, none of the three lads questioned it. Usually when they were punished they decided that they deserved it and the more they were punished the more they were convinced that they were criminals of a most subterranean type. As to the hitting of the cow being a pure accident and therefore not of necessity a criminal matter, such reading never entered their heads. When things happened and they were caught, they commonly paid dire consequences and they were accustomed to measure the probabilities of woe utterly by the damage done and not in any way by the culpability. The shooting of a cow was plainly heinous and undoubtedly their dungeons would be knee-deep in water.

"He did it, mister!" This was a general outcry. Jimmie used it as often as did the others. As for them, it is certain that they had no direct thought of betraying their comrade for their own salvation. They thought themselves guilty because they were caught; when boys were not caught they might possibly be innocent. But captured boys were guilty. When they cried out that Jimmie was the culprit, it was, principally, a simple expression of terror.

Old Henry Fleming, the owner of the farm, strode across the pasture toward them. He had in his hand a most cruel whip. This whip he flourished. At his approach the boys suffered the agonies of the fire-regions. And yet anybody with half an eye could see that the whip in his hand was a mere accident and that he was a kind old man when he cared.

When he had come near he spoke crisply. "What you boys ben doin' to my cow?" The tone had deep threat in it. They all answered by saying that none of them had shot the cow. Their denials were tearful and clamorous and they crawled knee by knee. The vision of it was like three martyrs being dragged toward the stake. Old Fleming stood there, grim, tight-lipped. After a time, he said: "Which boy done it?"

There was some confusion and then Jimmie spake. "I done it, mister."

Fleming looked at him. Then he asked: "Well, what did you shoot 'er fer?"

Jimmie thought, hesitated, decided, faltered, and then formulated this: "I thought she was a lynx."

Old Fleming and his Swede at once lay down in the grass and laughed themselves helpless.

THE LOVER AND THE TELL-TALE

WHEN the angel-child returned with her parents to New York the fond heart of Jimmie Trescott felt its bruise greatly. For two days he simply moped, becoming a stranger to all former joys. When his old comrades yelled invitation as they swept off on some interesting quest, he replied with mournful gestures of disillusion.

He thought often of writing to her but of course the shame of it made him pause. Write a letter to a girl? The mere enormity of the idea caused him shudders. Persons of his quality never wrote letters to girls. Such was the occupation of mollycoddles and snivellers. He knew that if his acquaintances and friends found in him evidences of such weakness and general milkiness, they would fling themselves upon him like so many wolves and bait him beyond the borders of sanity.

However, one day at school in that time of the morning session when children of his age were allowed fifteen minutes of play in the school-grounds, he did not as usual rush forth ferociously to his games. Commonly he was of the worst hoodlums, preying upon his weaker brethren with all the cruel disregard of a grown man. On this particular morning he staid in the school-room and with his tongue stuck from the corner of his mouth, and his head twisting in a painful way, he wrote to little Cora, pouring out to her all the poetry of his hungry soul as follows: "My dear Cora I love thee with all my hart oh come bac again, bac, bac gain for I love thee best of all oh come bac again When the spring come again we'l fly and we'l fly like a brid."

As for the last word he knew under normal circumstances perfectly well how to spell "bird" but in this case he had transposed two of the letters through excitement, supreme agitation.

Nor had this letter been composed without fear and furtive

glancing. There was always a number of children who for the time cared more for the quiet of the school-room than for the tempest of the play-ground and there was always that dismal company who were being forcibly deprived of their recess—who were being "kept in." More than one curious eye was turned upon the desperate and lawless Jimmie Trescott suddenly taken to ways of peace and as he felt these eyes he flushed guiltily, with felonious glances from side to side.

It happened that a certain vigilant little girl had a seat directly across the aisle from Jimmie's seat and she had remained in the room during the intermission because of her interest in some absurd domestic details concerning her desk. Parenthetically it might be stated that she was in the habit of imagining this desk to be a house and at this time with an important little frown, indicative of a proper matron, she was engaged in dramatising her ideas of a household.

But this small Rose Goldege happened to be of a family which numbered few males. It was in fact one of those curious middle-class families that hold much of their ground, retain most of their position, after all their visible means of support have been dropped in the grave. It contained now only a collection of women who existed submissively, defiantly, securely, mysteri-ously, in a pretentious and often exasperating virtue. It was often too triumphantly clear that they were free of bad habits. However, bad habits is a term here used in a commoner meaning because it is certainly true that the principal and indeed solitary joy which entered their lonely lives was the joy of talking wickedly and busily about their neighbors. It was all done with-out dream of its being of the vulgarity of the alleys. Indeed it was simply a constitutional but not incredible chastity and honesty expressing itself in its ordinary superior way of the whirling circles of life and the vehemence of the criticism was not less-ened by a further infusion of an acid of worldly defeat, worldly suffering and worldly hopelessness.

Out of this family-circle had sprung the typical little girl who discovered Jimmie Trescott agonizingly writing a letter to his sweetheart. Of course all the children were the most abandoned gossips but she was peculiarly adapted to the purpose of making

Jimmie miserable over this particular point. It was her life to sit of evenings about the stove and hearken to her mother and a lot of spinsters talk of many things. During these evenings she was never licensed to utter an opinion either one way or the other way. She was then simply a very little girl sitting open-eyed in the gloom and listening to many things which she often interpreted wrongly. They on their part kept up a kind of a smug-faced pretense of concealing from her information in detail of the wide-spread crime, which in effect may have been more elaborately dangerous than no pretense at all. Thus all her home teaching fitted her to at once recognize in Jimmie Trescott's manner that he was concealing something that would properly interest the world. She set up a scream. "Oh! Oh! Oh! Jimmie Trescott's writing to his girl! Oh! Oh!"

Jimmie cast a miserable glance upon her—a glance in which hatred mingled with despair. Through the open window, he could hear the boisterous cries of his friends—his hoodlum friends—who would no more understand the utter poetry of his position than they would understand an ancient tribal sign language. His face was set in a truer expression of horror than any of the romances describe upon the features of a man flung into a moat, a man shot in the breast with an arrow, a man cleft in the neck with a battle axe. He was suppedaneous of the fullest power of childish pain. His one course was to rush upon her and attempt by an impossible means of strangulation to keep her important news from the public.

The teacher, a thoughtful young woman at her desk upon the platform, saw a little scuffle which informed her that two of her scholars were larking. She called out sharply. The command penetrated to the middle of an early world struggle. In Jimmie's age there was no particular scruple in the minds of the male sex against laying warrior hands upon their weaker sisters. But of course this voice from the throne hindered Jimmie in what might have been a berserk attack.

Even the little girl was retarded by the voice but without being unlawful, she managed to soon shy through the door and out upon the play-ground, yelling: "Oh! Jimmie Trescott's been writing to his girl!"

The unhappy Jimmie was following as closely as he was allowed by his knowledge of the decencies to be preserved under the eye of the teacher.

Jimmie himself was mainly responsible for the scene which ensued on the play-ground. It is possible that the little girl might have run shrieking his infamy without exciting more than a general but unmilitant interest. These barbarians were excited only by the actual appearance of human woe; in that event, they cheered and danced. Jimmie made the strategic mistake of pursuing little Rose and thus exposed his thin skin to the whole school. He had in his cowering mind a vision of a hundred children turning from their play under the maple trees and speeding toward him over the gravel with sudden wild taunts. Upon him drove a yelping demoniac mob to which his words were futile. He saw in this mob boys that he dimly knew and his deadly enemies, and his retainers and his most intimate friends. The virulence of his deadly enemy was no greater than the virulence of his intimate friend. From the outskirts the little informer could be heard still screaming the news like a toy parrot with clockwork inside of it. It broke up all sorts of games not so much because of the mere fact of the letter-writing as because the children knew that some sufferer was at the last point and like little blood-fanged wolves they thronged to the scene of his destruction. They galloped about him shrilly chanting insults. He turned from one to another only to meet with howls. He was baited.

Then, in one instant, he changed all this with a blow. Bang! The most pitiless of the boys near him received a punch fairly and skilfully which made him bellow out like a walrus, and then Jimmie laid desperately into the whole world, striking out frenziedly in all directions. Boys who could handily whip him and knew it backed away from this onslaught. Here was intention—serious intention. They themselves were not in frenzy and their cooler judgment respected Jimmie's efforts when he ran amok. They saw that it really was none of their affair. In the meantime the wretched little girl who had caused the bloody riot was away by the fence weeping because boys were fighting.

Jimmie several times hit the wrong boy. That is to say, he several times hit a wrong boy hard enough to arouse also in him a spirit of wrath. Jimmie wore a little shirt-waist. It was passing now rapidly into oblivion. He was sobbing and there was one blood-stain upon his cheek. The school-ground sounded like a pine tree when a hundred crows roost in it at night.

Then upon the situation there pealed a brazen bell. It was a bell that these children obeyed even as older nations obey the formal law which is printed in calf-skin. It smote them into some sort of inaction; even Jimmie was influenced by its potency although as a finale he kicked out lustily into the legs of an intimate friend who had been one of the foremost in the torture.

When they came to form into line for the march into the school-room it was curious that Jimmie had many admirers. It was not his prowess; it was the soul he had infused into his gymnastics; and he, still panting, looked about him with a stern and challenging glare.

And yet when the long tramping line had entered the school-room his status had again changed. The other children then began to regard him as a boy in disrepair and boys in disrepair were always accosted ominously from the throne. Jimmie's march toward his seat was a feat. It was composed partly of a most slinking attempt to dodge the perception of the teacher and partly of pure braggadocio erected for the benefit of his observant fellow-men.

The teacher looked carefully down at him. "Jimmie Trescott," she said.

"Yes'm," he answered with a business-like briskness which really spelled out falsity in all its letters.

"Come up to the desk."

He arose mid the awe of the entire school-room. When he arrived, she said: "Jimmie, you've been fighting."

"Yes'm," he answered. This was not so much an admission of the fact as it was a concessional answer to anything she might say.

"Who have you been fighting?" she asked.

"I dunno, 'm."

Whereupon the empress blazed out in wrath. "You don't know who you've been fighting?"

Jimmie looked at her gloomily. "No, 'm."

She seemed about to disintegrate to mere flaming faggots of anger. "You don't know who you've been fighting?" she dehis plans for escape blended into a mere panic fear.

The maples outside were defeating the weakening rays of the afternoon sun and in the shadowed school-room had come a stillness in which nevertheless one could feel the complacence of the little pupils who had already passed through the flames. They were prepared to recognize as a spectacle the torture of others.

Little Johnnie Tanner opened the ceremony. He stamped heavily up to the platform and bowed in such a manner that he almost fell down. He blurted out that it would ill befit him to sit silent while the name of his fair Ireland was being reproached, and appealed to the gallant soldier before him if every British battle-field was not sown with the bones of sons of the emerald isle. He was also heard to say that he had listened with deepening surprise and scorn to the insinuation of the honorable member from North Glenmorganshire that the loyalty of the Irish regiments in His Majesty's service could be questioned. To what purpose, then, he asked, had the blood of Irishmen flowed on a hundred fields? To what purpose had Irishmen gone to their death with bravery and devotion in every part of the world where the victorious flag of England had been carried. If the honorable member for North Glenmorganshire insisted upon construing a mere pot-house row between soldiers in Dublin into a grand treachery to the colors and to Her Majesty's uniform, then it was time for Ireland to think bitterly of her dead sons whose graves now marked every step of England's progress and yet who could have their honors stripped from

Fourth page of the manuscript of "Making an Orator," showing Cora's and Stephen's handwriting

" 'JIMMY TRESCOTT'S GOT HIS PICNIC IN A PAIL!' "

One of Peter Newell's illustrations for the *Whilomville Stories*

manded, blazing. "Well—you stay in after school until you find out."

As he returned to his place all the children knew by his vanquished air that sorrow had fallen upon the house of Trescott. When he took his seat he saw gloating upon him the satanic black eyes of the little Goldege girl.

IV

"SHOWIN' OFF"

JIMMIE TRESCOTT'S new velocipede had the largest front wheel of any velocipede in Whilomville. When it first arrived from New York, he wished to sacrifice school, food and sleep to it. Evidently he wished to become a sort of a perpetual velocipede-rider. But the powers of the family laid a number of judicious embargoes upon him and he was prevented from becoming a fanatic. Of course this caused him to retain a fondness for the three-wheeled thing much longer than if he had been allowed to debauch himself for a span of days. But in the end, it was an immaterial machine to him. For long periods he left it idle in the stable.

One day he loitered from school toward home by a very circuitous route. He was accompanied by only one of his retainers. The object of this detour was the wooing of a little girl in a red hood. He had been in love with her for some three weeks. His desk was near her desk at school but he had never spoken to her. He had been afraid to take such a radical step. It was not customary to speak to girls. Even boys who had school-going sisters seldom addressed them during that part of a day which was devoted to education.

The reasons for this conduct were very plain. First, the more robust boys considered talking with girls an unmanly occupation; second, the greater part of the boys were afraid; third, they had no idea of what to say because they esteemed the proper sentences should be supernaturally incisive and eloquent. In consequence, a small contingent of blue-eyed weaklings were the sole intimates of the frail sex and for it they were boisterously and disdainfully called "girl-boys."

But this situation did not prevent serious and ardent wooing. For instance, Jimmie and the little girl who wore the red hood must have exchanged glances at least two hundred times in every school-hour and this exchange of glances accomplished everything. In them, the two children renewed their curious inarticulate vows.

Jimmie had developed a devotion to school which was the admiration of his father and mother. In the mornings he was so impatient to have it made known to him that no misfortune had befallen his romance during the night that he was actually detected at times feverishly listening for the "first bell." Doctor Trescott was exceedingly complacent of the change and, as for Mrs. Trescott, she had ecstatic visions of a white-haired Jimmie leading the nations in knowledge, comprehending all from bugs to comets. It was merely the doing of the little girl in the red hood.

When Jimmie made up his mind to follow his sweetheart home from school, the project seemed such an arbitrary and shameless innovation that he hastily lied to himself about it. No; he was not following Abbie. He was merely making his way homeward through the new and rather longer route of Bryant Street and Oakland Park. It had nothing at all to do with a girl. It was a mere eccentric notion.

"Come on," said Jimmie gruffly to his retainer. "Let's go home this way."

"What fer?" demanded the retainer.

"Oh, b'cause."

"Huh?"

"Oh, it's more fun—goin' this way."

The retainer was bored and loth but that mattered very little. He did not know how to disobey his chief. Together they followed the trail of red-hooded Abbie and another small girl. These latter at once understood the object of the chase and looking back giggling they pretended to quicken their pace. But they were always looking back. Jimmie now began his courtship in earnest. The first thing to do was to prove his strength in battle. This was transacted by means of the retainer. He took that devoted boy and flung him heavily to the ground, meanwhile mouthing a preposterous ferocity.

The retainer accepted this incomprehensible behavior with a

sort of bland resignation. After his over-throw, he raised himself, coolly brushed some dust and dead leaves from his clothes, and then seemed to forget the incident.

"I can jump further'n you can," said Jimmie in a loud voice.

"I know it," responded the retainer simply.

But this would not do. There must be a contest.

"Come on," shouted Jimmie imperiously. "Let's see you jump."

The retainer selected a footing on the kerb, balanced and calculated a moment, and jumped without enthusiasm. Jimmie's leap of course was longer.

"There!" he cried blowing out his lips. "I beat you, didn't I? Easy. I beat you." He made a great hub-bub as if the affair was unprecedented.

"Yes," admitted the retainer emotionless.

Later, Jimmie forced his retainer to run a race with him, held more jumping matches, flung him twice to earth and generally behaved as if a retainer was indestructible. If the retainer had been in the plot, it is conceivable that he would have endured this treatment with mere whispered half-laughing protests. But he was not in the plot at all and so he became enigmatic. One can not often sound the profound well in which lie the meanings of boyhood.

Following the two little girls, Jimmie eventually passed into that suburb of Whilomville which is called Oakland Park. At his heels came a badly-battered retainer. Oakland Park was a some-what strange country to the boys. They were dubious of the manners and customs and of course they would have to meet the local chieftains who might look askance upon this invasion.

Jimmie's girl departed into her home with a last backward glance that almost blinded the thrilling boy. On this pretext and that pretext, he kept his retainer in play before the house. He had hopes that she would emerge as soon as she had deposited her school-bag.

A boy came along the walk. Jimmie knew him at school. He was Tommie Semple, one of the weaklings who made friends with the fair sex. "Hello, Tom," said Jimmie. "You live 'round here?"

"Yeh," said Tom with composed pride. At school, he was afraid of Jimmie but he did not evince any of this fear as he strolled well inside his own frontiers. Jimmie and his retainer had not expected this boy to display the manners of a minor chief and they contemplated him attentively. There was a silence. Finally Jimmie said: "I can put you down." He moved forward briskly. "Can't I?" he demanded.

The challenged boy backed away. "I know you can," he declared frankly and promptly.

The little girl in the red hood had come out with a hoop. She looked at Jimmie with an air of insolent surprise in the fact that he still existed and began to trundle her hoop off toward some other little girls who were shrilly playing near a nurse-maid and a perambulator. Jimmie adroitly shifted his position until he too was playing near the perambulator, pretentiously making mince-meat out of his retainer and Tommie Semple.

Of course, little Abbie had defined the meaning of Jimmie's appearance in Oakland Park. Despite this nonchalance and grand air of accident, nothing could have been more plain. Whereupon she of course became insufferably vain in manner and whenever Jimmie came near her she tossed her head and turned away her face and daintily swished her skirts as if he were contagion itself. But Jimmie was happy. His soul was satisfied with the mere presence of the beloved object so long as he could feel that she furtively gazed upon him from time to time and noted his extraordinary prowess which he was proving upon the persons of his retainer and Tommie Semple. And he was making an impression. There could be no doubt of it. He had many times caught her eye fixed admiringly upon him as he mauled the retainer. Indeed all the little girls gave attention to his deeds and he was the hero of the hour.

Presently a boy on a velocipede was seen to be tooling down toward them. "Who's this comin'?" said Jimmie bluntly to the Semple boy.

"That's Horace Glenn," said Tommie, "an' he's got a new velocipede an' he can ride it like anything."

"Can you lick him?" asked Jimmie.

"I don't—I never fought with 'im," answered the other. He bravely tried to appear as a man of respectable achievement but with Horace coming toward them the risk was too great. However he brightly added: "*Maybe* I could."

The advent of Horace on his new velocipede created a sensation which he haughtily accepted as a familiar thing. Only Jimmie and his retainer remained silent and impassive. Horace eyed the two invaders.

"Hello, Jimmie."

"Hello, Horace."

After the typical silence, Jimmie said pompously: "I got a velocipede."

"Have you?" asked Horace anxiously. He did not wish anybody in the world but himself to possess a velocipede.

"Yes," sang Jimmie. "An' it's a bigger one than that, too! A good deal bigger! An' it's a better one, too!"

"Huh," retorted Horace sceptically.

"Ain't I, Clarence? Ain't I? Ain't I got one bigger'n that?"

The retainer answered with alacrity. "Yes, he has! A good deal bigger! An' it's a dindy, too!"

This corroboration rather disconcerted Horace but he continued to scoff at any statement that Jimmie also owned a velocipede. As for the contention that this supposed velocipede could be larger than his own, he simply wouldn't hear of it.

Jimmie had been a very gallant figure before the coming of Horace but the new velocipede had relegated him to a squalid secondary position. So he affected to look with contempt upon it. Voluminously he bragged of the velocipede in the stable at home. He painted its virtues and beauty in loud and extravagant words, flaming words. And the retainer stood by, glibly endorsing everything.

The little company heeded him and he passed on vociferously from extravagance to utter impossibility. Horace was very sick of it. His defense was reduced to a mere mechanical grumbling. "Don't believe you got one 't all. Don't believe you got one 't all."

Jimmie turned upon him suddenly. "How fast can you go? How fast can you go?" he demanded. "Let's see. I bet you can't go fast."

Horace lifted his spirits and answered with proper defiance. "Can't I?" he mocked. "Can't I?"

"No, you can't," said Jimmie. "You can't go fast."

Horace cried: "Well, you see me now! I'll show you! I'll show you if I can't go fast!" Taking a firm seat on his vermilion machine, he pedalled furiously up the walk, turned, and pedalled back again. "There, now!" he shouted triumphantly. "Ain't that fast? There, now!" There was a low murmur of appreciation from the little girls. Jimmie saw with pain that even his divinity was smiling upon his rival. "There! Ain't that fast? Ain't that fast?" He strove to pin Jimmie down to an admission. He was exuberant with victory.

Notwithstanding a feeling of discomfiture, Jimmie did not lose a moment of time. "Why," he yelled, "that ain't goin' fast 't all! That ain't goin' fast 't all! Why, I can go almost *twice* as fast as that! Almost *twice* as fast. Can't I, Clarence?"

The royal retainer nodded solemnly at the wide-eyed group. " 'Course he can!"

"Why," spouted Jimmie, "you just ought to see me ride once! You just ought to see me! Why, I can go like the wind! Can't I, Clarence? And I can ride far, too—oh, awful far! Can't I, Clarence? Why, I wouldn't have that one! 'Tain't any good! You just ought to see mine once!"

The overwhelmed Horace attempted to re-construct his battered glories. "I can ride right over the kerb-stone—at some of the crossin's," he announced brightly.

Jimmie's derision was a splendid sight. " '*Right over the kerb-stone*'! Why, that wouldn't be *nothin'* for me to do! I've rode mine down Bridge Street hill. Yessir! Ain't I, Clarence? Why, it ain't nothin' to ride over a kerb-stone—not for *me*! Is it, Clarence?"

"Down Bridge Street hill? You never!" said Horace hopelessly.

"Well, didn't I, Clarence? Didn't I, now?"

The faithful retainer again nodded solemnly at the assemblage.

At last Horace, having fallen as low as was possible, began to display a spirit for climbing up again. "Oh, you can do wonders," he said laughing. "You can do wonders. I s'pose you could ride down that bank there?" he asked with art. He had indicated a grassy terrace some six feet in height which bounded one side of the walk. At the bottom was a small ravine in which the reckless had flung ashes and tins. "I s'pose you could ride down that bank?"

All eyes now turned upon Jimmie to detect a sign of his weakening but he instantly and sublimely arose to the occasion.

"That bank?" he asked scornfully. "Why, I've ridden down banks like that many a time. Ain't I, Clarence?"

This was too much for the company. A sound like the wind in the leaves arose; it was the song of incredulity and ridicule. "O—o—o—o—o!" And on the outskirts, a little girl suddenly shrieked out: "Story-teller!"

Horace had certainly won a skirmish. He was gleeful. "Oh, you can do wonders!" he gurgled. "You can do wonders!" The neighborhood's superficial hostility to foreigners arose like magic under the influence of his sudden success and Horace had the delight of seeing Jimmie persecuted in that manner known only to children and insects.

Jimmie called angrily to the boy on the velocipede: "If you'll lend me yours, I'll show you whether I can or not."

Horace turned his superior nose in the air. "Oh, no, I don't ever lend it." Then he thought of a blow which would make Jimmie's humiliation complete. "Besides," he said airily, " 'tain't really anythin' hard to do. I could do it—easy—if I wanted to."

But his supposed adherents, instead of receiving this boast with cheers, looked upon him in a sudden blank silence. Jimmie and his retainer pounced like cats upon their advantage.

"Oh," they yelled, "you *could*, eh? Well, let's see you do it, then! Let's see you do it! Let's see you do it! Now!" In a moment the crew of little spectators were jibing at Horace.

The blow that would make Jimmie's humiliation complete! Instead, it had boomeranged Horace into the mud. He kept up a sullen muttering. " 'Tain't really anythin'! I could if I wanted to."

"Dare you to!" screeched Jimmie and his partisans. "Dare you to! Dare you to! Dare you to!"

There were two things to be done—to make gallant effort or to retreat. Somewhat to their amazement, the children at last found Horace moving through their clamor to the edge of the bank. Sitting on the velocipede he looked at the ravine and then with gloomy pride at the other children. A hush came upon them for it was seen that he was intending to make some kind of an ante-mortem statement.

"I—" he began. Then he vanished from the edge of the walk. The start had been unintentional—an accident.

The stupefied Jimmie saw the calamity through a haze. His

first clear vision was when Horace with a face as red as a red flag arose bawling from his tangled velocipede. He and his retainer exchanged a glance of horror and fled the neighborhood. They did not look back until they had reached the top of the hill near the lake. They could see Horace walking slowly under the maples toward his home, pushing his shattered velocipede before him. His chin was thrown high and the breeze bore them the sound of his howls.

V

MAKING AN ORATOR

IN THE school at Whilomville it was the habit when children had progressed to a certain class, to have them devote Friday afternoon to what was called elocution. This was in the piteously ignorant belief that orators were thus made. By process of school law unfortunate boys and girls were dragged up to address their fellow-scholars in the literature of the mid-century. Probably the children who were most capable of expressing themselves, the children who were most sensitive to the power of speech, suffered the most wrong. Little block-heads who could learn eight lines of conventional poetry and could get up and spin it rapidly at their class-mates did not undergo a single pang. The plan operated mainly to agonize many children permanently against arising to speak their thought to fellow-creatures.

Jimmie Trescott had an idea that by exhibition of undue ignorance he could escape from being promoted into the first class-room which exacted such penalty from its inmates. He preferred to dwell in a less classic shade rather than venture into a domain where he was obliged to perform a certain duty which struck him as being worse than death. However, willy-nilly he was somehow sent ahead into the place of torture.

Every Friday at least ten of the little children had to mount the stage beside the teacher's desk and babble something which none of them understood. This was to make them orators. If it had been ordered that they should croak like frogs it would have advanced most of them just as far toward oratory.

Alphabetically Jimmie Trescott was near the end of the list of victims but his time was none the less inevitable. "Tanner, Timmens, Trass, Trescott—" He saw his downfall approaching.

He was passive to the teacher while she drove into his mind the incomprehensible lines of "The Charge of the Light Brigade":

Half a league, half a league,
Half a league onward—

He had no conception of a league. If in the ordinary course of
life somebody had told him that he was half a league from home
he might have been frightened that half a league was fifty miles;
but he struggled manfully with the valley of death and a mystic
six hundred who were performing something there which was
very fine, he had been told. He learned all the verses. But as his
own Friday afternoon approached, he was moved to make known
to his family that a dreadful disease was upon him and was
likely at any time to prevent him from going to his beloved
school.

On the great Friday when the children of his initials were to
speak their pieces, Doctor Trescott was away from home and the
mother of the boy was alarmed beyond measure at Jimmie's
curious illness which caused him to lie on the rug in front of the
fire and groan cavernously. She bathed his feet in hot mustard
water until they were lobster red. She also placed a mustard
plaster on his chest. He announced that these remedies did him
no good at all—no good at all. With an air of martyrdom, he
endured a perfect downpour of motherly attention all that day.
Thus the first Friday was passed in safety. With singular patience he sat before the fire in the dining room and looked at
picture books, only complaining of pain when he suspected his
mother of thinking that he was getting better.

The next day being Saturday and a holiday he was miraculously delivered from the arms of disease and went forth to play,
a blatantly healthy boy.

He had no further attack until Thursday night of the next
week, when he announced that he felt very, very poorly. The
mother was already chronically alarmed over the condition of
her son but Doctor Trescott asked him questions which denoted
some incredulity. On the third Friday Jimmie was dropped at the
door of the school from the doctor's buggy. The other children,
notably those who had already passed over the mountain of
distress, looked at him with glee seeing in him another lamb
brought to butchery. Seated at his desk in the school-room, Jimmie sometimes remembered with dreadful distinctness every line

of "The Charge of the Light Brigade" and at other times his mind was utterly empty of it. Geography, arithmetic and spelling—usually great tasks—quite rolled off him. His mind was dwelling with terror upon the time when his name should be called and he was obliged to go up to the platform, turn, bow, and recite his message to his fellow-men. Desperate expedients for delay came to him. If he could have engaged the services of a real pain he would have been glad. But steadily, inexorably, the minutes marched on toward his great crisis and all his plans for escape blended into a mere panic fear.

The maples outside were defeating the weakening rays of the afternoon sun and in the shadowed school-room had come a stillness in which nevertheless one could feel the complacence of the little pupils who had already passed through the flames. They were calmly prepared to recognize as a spectacle the torture of others.

Little Johnnie Tanner opened the ceremony. He stamped heavily up to the platform and bowed in such a manner that he almost fell down. He blurted out that it would ill befit him to sit silent while the name of his fair Ireland was being reproached and he appealed to the gallant soldier before him if every British battle-field was not sown with the bones of sons of the Emerald Isle. He was also heard to say that he had listened with deepening surprise and scorn to the insinuation of the honorable member from North Glenmorganshire that the loyalty of the Irish regiments in Her Majesty's service could be questioned. To what purpose, then, he asked, had the blood of Irishmen flowed on a hundred fields? To what purpose had Irishmen gone to their death with bravery and devotion in every part of the world where the victorious flag of England had been carried? If the honorable member for North Glenmorganshire insisted upon construing a mere pot-house row between soldiers in Dublin into a grand treachery to the colors and to Her Majesty's uniform, then it was time for Ireland to think bitterly of her dead sons whose graves now marked every step of England's progress and yet who could have their honors stripped from them so easily by the honorable member for North Glenmorganshire. Furthermore the honorable member for North Glenmorganshire—

It is needless to say that little Johnnie Tanner's language

made it exceedingly hot for the honorable member for North Glenmorganshire. But Johnnie was not angry. He was only in haste. He finished the honorable member for North Glenmorganshire in what might be called a gallop.

Susie Timmens then went to the platform and with a face as pale as death whisperingly reiterated that she would be Queen of the May. The child represented there a perfect picture of unnecessary suffering. Her small lips were quite blue and her eyes, opened wide, stared with a look of horror at nothing.

The phlegmatic Trass boy with his moon-face only expressing peasant parentage calmly spoke some undeniably true words concerning destiny.

In his seat Jimmie Trescott was going half-blind with fear of his approaching doom. He wished that the Trass boy would talk forever about destiny. If the school-house had taken fire he thought that he would have felt simply relief. Anything was better. Death amid the flames was preferable to a recital of "The Charge of the Light Brigade." But the Trass boy finished his remarks about destiny in a very short time. Jimmie heard the teacher call his name and he felt the whole world look at him. He did not know how he made his way to the stage. Parts of him seemed to be of lead and at the same time parts of him seemed to be light as air, detached. His face had gone as pale as had been the face of Susie Timmens. He was simply a child in torment; that is all there is to be said specifically about it; and to intelligent people the exhibition would have been not more edifying than a dog fight.

He bowed precariously, choked, made an inarticulate sound, and then he suddenly said:

"Half a leg—"

"*League*," said the teacher coolly.

"Half a leg—"

"*League*," said the teacher.

"*League*," repeated Jimmie wildly.

"Half a league, half a league, half a league onward."

He paused here and looked wretchedly at the teacher.

"Half a league," he muttered—"half a league—"

He seemed likely to keep continuing this phrase indefinitely so after a time the teacher said: "Well, go on."

"Half a league," responded Jimmie.

The teacher had the opened book before her and she read from it:

> "All in the valley of Death
> Rode the—

Go on," she concluded.

Jimmie said:

> "All in the valley of Death
> Rode the—the—the—"

He cast a glance of supreme appeal upon the teacher and breathlessly whispered: "Rode the what?"

The young woman flushed with indignation to the roots of her hair.

> "Rode the six hundred,"

she snapped at him. The class was a-rustle with delight at this cruel display. They were no better than a Roman populace in Nero's time.

Jimmie started off again:

> "Half a leg—league, half a league, half a league onward,
> All in the valley of Death rode the six hundred.
> Forward—forward—forward—"

"The Light Brigade," suggested the teacher sharply.

"The Light Brigade," said Jimmie. He was about to die of the ignoble pain of his position. As for Tennyson's lines they had all gone grandly out of his mind leaving it a whited-wall.

The teacher's indignation was still rampant. She looked at the miserable wretch before her with an angry stare. "You stay in after school and learn that all over again," she commanded. "And be prepared to speak it next Friday. I am astonished at you, Jimmie. Go to your seat."

If she had suddenly and magically made a spirit of him and left him free to soar high above all the travail of our earthly lives she could not have over-joyed him more. He fled back to his seat without hearing the low-toned jibes of his school-mates. He gave no thought to the terrors of the next Friday. The evils of the day had been sufficient and to a childish mind a week is a great space of time.

With the delightful inconsistency of his age he sat in blissful calm and watched the sufferings of an unfortunate boy named Zimmerman who was the next victim of education. Jimmie of course did not know that on this day there had been laid for him the foundation of a finished incapacity for public speaking which would be his until he died.

VI

SHAME

DON'T come in here botherin' me," said the cook, intolerantly. "What with your mother bein' away on a visit, an' your father comin' home soon to lunch, I have enough on my mind—and that without bein' bothered with *you*. The kitchen is no place for little boys, anyhow. Run away, and don't be interferin' with my work." She frowned and made a grand pretence of being deep in herculean labors; but Jimmie did not run away.

"Now—they're goin' to have a picnic," he said, half audibly.

"What?"

"Now—they're goin' to have a picnic."

"Who's goin' to have a picnic?" demanded the cook, loudly. Her accent could have led one to suppose that if the projectors did not turn out to be the proper parties, she immediately would forbid this picnic.

Jimmie looked at her with more hopefulness. After twenty minutes of futile skirmishing, he had at least succeeded in introducing the subject. To her question he answered, eagerly:

"Oh, everybody! Lots and lots of boys and girls. Everybody."

"Who's everybody?"

According to custom, Jimmie began to singsong through his nose in a quite indescribable fashion an enumeration of the prospective picnickers: "Willie Dalzel an' Dan Earl an' Ella Earl an' Wolcott Margate an' Reeves Margate an' Walter Phelps an' Homer Phelps an' Minnie Phelps an'—oh—lots more girls an'—everybody. An' their mothers an' big sisters too." Then he announced a new bit of information: "They're goin' to have a picnic."

"Well, let them," said the cook, blandly.

Jimmie fidgeted for a time in silence. At last he murmured, "I—now—I thought maybe you'd let me go."

The cook turned from her work with an air of irritation and amazement that Jimmie should still be in the kitchen. "Who's stoppin' you?" she asked, sharply. "I ain't stoppin' you, am I?"

"No," admitted Jimmie, in a low voice.

"Well, why don't you go, then? Nobody's stoppin' you."

"But," said Jimmie, "I—you—now—each feller has got to take somethin' to eat with 'm."

"Oh ho!" cried the cook, triumphantly. "So that's it, is it? So that's what you've been shyin' round here fer, eh? Well, you may as well take yourself off without more words. What with your mother bein' away on a visit, an' your father comin' home soon to his lunch, I have enough on my mind—an' that without bein' bothered with *you*."

Jimmie made no reply, but moved in grief toward the door. The cook continued: "Some people in this house seem to think there's 'bout a thousand cooks in this kitchen. Where I used to work b'fore, there was some reason in 'em. I ain't a horse. A picnic!"

Jimmie said nothing, but he loitered.

"Seems as if I had enough to do, without havin' *you* come round talkin' about picnics. Nobody ever seems to think of the work I have to do. Nobody ever seems to think of it. Then they come and talk to me about picnics! What do I care about picnics?"

Jimmie loitered.

"Where I used to work b'fore, there was some reason in 'em. I never heard tell of no picnics right on top of your mother bein' away on a visit an' your father comin' home soon to his lunch. It's all foolishness."

Little Jimmie leaned his head flat against the wall and began to weep. She stared at him scornfully. "Cryin', eh? Cryin'? What are you cryin' fer?"

"N-n-nothin'," sobbed Jimmie.

There was a silence, save for Jimmie's convulsive breathing. At length the cook said: "Stop that blubberin', now. Stop it! This kitchen ain't no place fer it. Stop it! . . . Very well! If you don't stop, I won't give you nothin' to go to the picnic with—there!"

For the moment he could not end his tears. "You never said," he sputtered—"you never said you'd give me anything."

"An' why would I?" she cried, angrily. "Why would I—with you in here a-cryin' an' a-blubberin' an' a-bleatin' round? Enough to drive a woman crazy! I don't see how you could expect me to! The idea!"

Suddenly Jimmie announced: "I've stopped cryin'. I ain't goin' to cry no more 't all."

"Well, then," grumbled the cook—"well, then, stop it. I've got enough on my mind." It chanced that she was making for luncheon some salmon croquettes. A tin still half full of pinky prepared fish was beside her on the table. Still grumbling, she seized a loaf of bread and, wielding a knife, she cut from this loaf four slices, each of which was as big as a six-shilling novel. She profligately spread them with butter, and jabbing the point of her knife into the salmon-tin, she brought up bits of salmon, which she flung and flattened upon the bread. Then she crashed the pieces of bread together in pairs, much as one would clash cymbals. There was no doubt in her own mind but that she had created two sandwiches.

"There," she cried. "That'll do you all right. Lemme see. What 'll I put 'em in? There—I've got it." She thrust the sandwiches into a small pail and jammed on the lid. Jimmie was ready for the picnic. "Oh, thank you, Mary!" he cried, joyfully, and in a moment he was off, running swiftly.

The picnickers had started nearly half an hour earlier, owing to his inability to quickly attack and subdue the cook, but he knew that the rendezvous was in the grove of tall, pillar-like hemlocks and pines that grew on a rocky knoll at the lake shore. His heart was very light as he sped, swinging his pail. But a few minutes previously his soul had been gloomed in despair; now he was happy. He was going to the picnic, where privilege of participation was to be bought by the contents of the little tin pail.

When he arrived in the outskirts of the grove he heard a merry clamor, and when he reached the top of the knoll he looked down the slope upon a scene which almost made his little breast burst with joy. They actually had two camp fires! Two camp fires! At one of them Mrs. Earl was making something—chocolate, no doubt—and at the other a young lady in white duck and a sailor hat was dropping eggs into boiling water. Other grown-up people had spread a white cloth and were laying upon it things from baskets. In the deep cool shadow of the trees the children scurried, laughing. Jimmie hastened forward to join his friends.

Homer Phelps caught first sight of him. "Ho!" he shouted; "here comes Jimmie Trescott! Come on, Jimmie; you be on our side!" The children had divided themselves into two bands for some purpose of play. The others of Homer Phelps's party loudly endorsed his plan. "Yes, Jimmie, you be on *our* side." Then arose the usual dispute. "Well, we got the weakest side."

" 'Tain't any weaker'n ours."

Homer Phelps suddenly started, and looking hard, said, "What you got in the pail, Jim?"

Jimmie answered, somewhat uneasily, "Got m' lunch in it."

Instantly that brat of a Minnie Phelps simply tore down the sky with her shrieks of derision. "Got his *lunch* in it! In a *pail!*" She ran screaming to her mother. "Oh, mamma! Oh, mamma! Jimmie Trescott's got his picnic in a pail!"

Now there was nothing in the nature of this fact to particularly move the others—notably the boys, who were not competent to care if he had brought his luncheon in a coal-bin; but such is the instinct of childish society that they all immediately moved away from him. In a moment he had been made a social leper. All old intimacies were flung into the lake, so to speak. They dared not compromise themselves. At safe distances the boys shouted, scornfully: "Huh! Got his picnic in a pail!" Never again during that picnic did the little girls speak of him as Jimmie Trescott. His name now was Him.

His mind was dark with pain as he stood, the hang-dog, kicking the gravel, and muttering as defiantly as he was able, "Well, I can have it in a pail if I want to." This statement of freedom was of no importance, and he knew it, but it was the only idea in his head.

He had been baited at school for being detected in writing a letter to little Cora, the angel-child, and he had known how to defend himself, but this situation was in no way similar. This was a social affair, with grown people on all sides. It would be sweet to catch the Margate twins, for instance, and hammer them into a state of bleating respect for his pail; but that was a matter for the jungles of childhood, where grown folk seldom penetrated. He could only glower.

The amiable voice of Mrs. Earl suddenly called: "Come, children! Everything's ready!" They scampered away, glancing back for one last gloat at Jimmie standing there with his pail.

He did not know what to do. He knew that the grown folk expected him at the spread, but if he approached he would be greeted by a shameful chorus from the children—more especially from some of those damnable little girls. Still, luxuries beyond all dreaming were heaped on that cloth. One could not forget them. Perhaps if he crept up modestly, and was very gentle and very nice to the little girls, they would allow him peace. Of course it had been dreadful to come with a pail to such a grand picnic, but they might forgive him.

Oh no, they would not! He knew them better. And then suddenly he remembered with what delightful expectations he had raced to this grove, and self-pity overwhelmed him, and he thought he wanted to die and make every one feel sorry.

The young lady in white duck and a sailor hat looked at him, and then spoke to her sister, Mrs. Earl. "Who's that hovering in the distance, Emily?"

Mrs. Earl peered. "Why, it's Jimmie Trescott! Jimmie, come to the picnic! Why don't you come to the picnic, Jimmie?" He began to sidle toward the cloth.

But at Mrs. Earl's call there was another outburst from many of the children. "He's got his picnic in a pail! In a *pail*! Got it in a pail!"

Minnie Phelps was a shrill fiend. "Oh, mamma, he's got it in that pail! See! Isn't it funny? Isn't it dreadful funny?"

"What ghastly prigs children are, Emily!" said the young lady. "They are spoiling that boy's whole day, breaking his heart, the little cats! I think I'll go over and talk to him."

"Maybe you had better not," answered Mrs. Earl, dubiously. "Somehow these things arrange themselves. If you interfere, you are likely to prolong everything."

"Well, I'll try, at least," said the young lady.

At the second outburst against him Jimmie had crouched

down by a tree, half hiding behind it, half pretending that he was not hiding behind it. He turned his sad gaze toward the lake. The bit of water seen through the shadows seemed perpendicular, a slate-colored wall. He heard a noise near him, and turning, he perceived the young lady looking down at him. In her hand she held plates. "May I sit near you?" she asked, coolly.

Jimmie could hardly believe his ears. After disposing herself and the plates upon the pine-needles, she made brief explanation. "They're rather crowded, you see, over there. I don't like to be crowded at a picnic, so I thought I'd come here. I hope you don't mind."

Jimmie made haste to find his tongue. "Oh, I don't mind! I *like* to have you here." The ingenuous emphasis made it appear that the fact of his liking to have her there was in the nature of a law-dispelling phenomenon, but she did not smile.

"How large is that lake?" she asked.

Jimmie, falling into the snare, at once began to talk in the manner of a proprietor of the lake. "Oh, it's almost twenty miles long, an' in one place it's almost four miles wide! an' it's *deep*, too —awful deep—an' it's got real steamboats on it, an'—oh—lots of other boats, an'—an'—an'—"

"Do you go out on it sometimes?"

"Oh, lots of times! My father's got a boat," he said, eying her to note the effect of his words.

She was correctly pleased and struck with wonder. "Oh, has he?" she cried, as if she never before had heard of a man owning a boat.

Jimmie continued: "Yes, an' it's a grea' big boat, too, with sails, real sails; an' sometimes he takes me out in her, too; an' once he took me fishin', an' we had sandwiches, plenty of 'em, an' my father he drank beer right out of the bottle—*right out of the bottle!*"

The young lady was properly overwhelmed by this amazing intelligence. Jimmie saw the impression he had created, and he enthusiastically resumed his narrative: "An' after, he let me throw the bottles in the water, and I throwed 'em 'way, 'way, 'way out. An' they sank, an'—never comed up," he concluded, dramatically.

His face was glorified; he had forgotten all about the pail; he was absorbed in this communion with a beautiful lady who was so interested in what he had to say.

She indicated one of the plates, and said, indifferently: "Perhaps you would like some of those sandwiches. I made them. Do you like olives? And there's a deviled egg. I made that also."

"Did you really?" said Jimmie, politely. His face gloomed for a moment because the pail was recalled to his mind, but he timidly possessed himself of a sandwich.

"Hope you are not going to scorn my deviled egg," said his goddess. "I am very proud of it." He did not; he scorned little that was on the plate.

Their gentle intimacy was ineffable to the boy. He thought he had a friend, a beautiful lady, who liked him more than she did anybody at the picnic, to say the least. This was proved by the fact that she had flung aside the luxuries of the spread cloth to sit with him, the exile. Thus early did he fall a victim to woman's wiles.

"Where do you live?" he asked, suddenly.

"Oh, a long way from here! In New York."

His next question was put very bluntly. "Are you married?"

"Oh, no!" she answered, gravely.

Jimmie was silent for a time, during which he glanced shyly and furtively up at her face. It was evident that he was somewhat embarrassed. Finally he said, "When I grow up to be a man —"

"Oh, that is some time yet!" said the beautiful lady.

"But when I *do*, I—I should like to marry you."

"Well, I will remember it," she answered; "but don't talk of it now, because it's such a long time; and—I wouldn't wish you to consider yourself bound." She smiled at him.

He began to brag. "When I grow up to be a man, I'm goin' to have lots an' lots of money, an' I'm goin' to have a grea' big house, an' a horse an' a shot-gun, an' lots an' lots of books 'bout elephants an' tigers, an' lots an' lots of ice-cream an' pie an'—caramels." As before, she was impressed; he could see it. "An' I'm goin' to have lots an' lots of children—'bout three hundred, I guess—an' there won't none of 'em be girls. They'll all be boys—like me."

"Oh, my!" she said.

His garment of shame was gone from him. The pail was dead and well buried. It seemed to him that months elapsed as he dwelt in happiness near the beautiful lady and trumpeted his vanity.

At last there was a shout. "Come on! we're going home." The picnickers trooped out of the grove. The children wished to resume their jeering, for Jimmie still gripped his pail, but they were restrained by the circumstances. He was walking at the side of the beautiful lady.

During this journey he abandoned many of his habits. For instance, he never travelled without skipping gracefully from crack to crack between the stones, or without pretending that he was a train of cars, or without some mumming device of childhood. But now he behaved with dignity. He made no more noise than a little mouse. He escorted the beautiful lady to the gate of the Earl home, where he awkwardly, solemnly, and wistfully shook hands in good-by. He watched her go up the walk; the door clanged.

On his way home he dreamed. One of these dreams was fascinating. Supposing the beautiful lady was his teacher in school! Oh, my! wouldn't he be a good boy, sitting like a statuette all day long, and knowing every lesson to perfection, and—everything. And then supposing that a boy should sass her. Jimmie painted himself waylaying that boy on the homeward road, and the fate of the boy was a thing to make strong men cover their eyes with their hands. And she would like him more and more—more and more. And he—he would be a little god.

But as he was entering his father's grounds an appalling recollection came to him. He was returning with the bread-and-butter and the salmon untouched in the pail! He could imagine the cook, nine feet tall, waving her fist. "An' so that's what I took trouble for, is it? So's you could bring it back? So's you could bring it back?" He skulked toward the house like a marauding bush-ranger. When he neared the kitchen door he made a desperate rush past it, aiming to gain the stables and there secrete his guilt. He was nearing them, when a thunderous voice hailed him from the rear: "Jimmie Trescott, where you goin' with that pail?"

It was the cook. He made no reply, but plunged into the shelter of the stables. He whirled the lid from the pail and dashed its contents beneath a heap of blankets. Then he stood panting, his eyes on the door. The cook did not pursue, but she was bawling: "Jimmie Trescott, what you doin' with that pail?"

He came forth, swinging it. "Nothin'," he said, in virtuous protest.

"I know better," she said, sharply, as she relieved him of his curse.

In the morning Jimmie was playing near the stable, when he heard a shout from Peter Washington, who attended Doctor Trescott's horses: "Jim! Oh, Jim!"

"What?"

"Come yah."

Jimmie went reluctantly to the door of the stable, and Peter Washington asked: "Wut's dish yere fish an' brade doin' unner dese yer blankups?"

"I don't know. I didn't have nothin' to do with it," answered Jimmie, indignantly.

"Don' tell *me!*" cried Peter Washington, as he flung it all away —"don' tell *me!* When I fin' fish an' brade unner dese yer blankups, I don' go an' think dese yer ho'ses er yer pop's put 'em. I *know.* An' if I caitch enny more dish yer fish an' brade in dish yer stable, *I'll* tell yer pop."

VII

THE CARRIAGE-LAMPS

IT WAS the fault of a small nickel-plated revolver, a most incompetent weapon, which, wherever one aimed, would fling the bullet as the devil willed, and no man, when about to use it, could tell exactly what was in store for the surrounding country. This treasure had been acquired by Jimmie Trescott after arduous bargaining with another small boy. Jimmie wended homeward, patting his hip pocket at every three paces.

Peter Washington, working in the carriage-house, looked out upon him with a shrewd eye. "Oh, Jim," he called, "wut you got in yer hind pocket?"

"Nothin'," said Jimmie, feeling carefully under his jacket to make sure that the revolver wouldn't fall out.

Peter chuckled. "S'more foolishness, I raikon. You gwine be hung one day, Jim, you keep up all dish yer nonsense."

Jimmie made no reply, but went into the back garden, where he hid the revolver in a box under a lilac-bush. Then he returned to the vicinity of Peter, and began to cruise to and fro in the offing, showing all the signals of one wishing to open treaty. "Pete," he said, "how much does a box of cartridges cost?"

Peter raised himself violently, holding in one hand a piece of harness, and in the other an old rag. "Ca'tridgers! *Ca'tridgers!* Lan' sake! wut the kid want with ca'tridgers? Knew it! Knew it! Come home er-holdin' on to his hind pocket like he got money in it. An' now he want ca'tridgers."

Jimmie, after viewing with dismay the excitement caused by his question, began to move warily out of the reach of a possible hostile movement.

"Ca'tridgers!" continued Peter, in scorn and horror. "Kid like you! No bigger'n er minute! Look yah, Jim, you done been swappin' round, an' you done got hol' of er pistol!" The charge was dramatic.

The wind was almost knocked out of Jimmie by this display of Peter's terrible miraculous power, and as he backed away his feeble denials were more convincing than a confession.

"I'll tell yer pop!" cried Peter, in virtuous grandeur. "I'll tell yer pop!"

In the distance Jimmie stood appalled. He knew not what to do. The dread adult wisdom of Peter Washington had laid bare the sin, and disgrace stared at Jimmie.

There was a whirl of wheels, and a high lean trotting-mare spun Doctor Trescott's buggy toward Peter, who ran forward busily. As the doctor climbed out, Peter, holding the mare's head, began his denunciation:

"Docteh, I gwine tell on Jim. He come home er-holdin' on to his hind pocket, an' proud like he won a tuhkey-raffle; an' I sure know what he been up to, an' I done challenge him, an' he nev' say he didn't."

"Why, what do you mean?" said the doctor. "What's this, Jimmie?"

The boy came forward, glaring wrathfully at Peter. In fact, he suddenly was so filled with rage at Peter that he forgot all precautions. "It's about a pistol," he said, bluntly. "I've got a pistol. I swapped for it."

"I done tol' 'im his pop wouldn' stand no fiah-awms, an' him a kid like he is. I done tol' 'im. Lan' sake! he strut like he was a soldier! Come in yere proud, an' er-holdin' on to his hind pocket. He think he was Jesse James, I raikon. But I done tol' 'im his pop stan' no sech foolishness. First thing—*blam*—he shoot his haid off. No, seh, he too tinety t' come in yere er-struttin' like he jest bought Main Street. I tol' 'im. I done tol' 'im—shawp. I don' wanter be loafin' round dish yer stable if Jim he gwine go shootin' round an' shootin' round—*blim—blam—blim—blam!* No, seh. I retiahs. I retiahs. It's all right if er grown man got er gun, but ain't no kids come foolishin' round *me* with fiah-awms. No, seh. I retiahs."

"Oh, be quiet, Peter!" said the doctor. "Where is this thing, Jimmie?"

The boy went sulkily to the box under the lilac-bush and

returned with the revolver. "Here 'tis," he said, with a glare over his shoulder at Peter. The doctor looked at the silly weapon in critical contempt.

"It's not much of a thing, Jimmie, but I don't think you are quite old enough for it yet. I'll keep it for you in one of the drawers of my desk."

Peter Washington burst out proudly: "I done tol' 'im th' docteh wouldn' stan' no traffickin' round yere with fiah-awms. I done tol' 'im."

Jimmie and his father went together into the house, and as Peter unharnessed the mare he continued his comments on the boy and the revolver. He was not cast down by the absence of hearers. In fact, he usually talked better when there was no one to listen save the horses. But now his observations bore small resemblance to his earlier and public statements. Admiration and the keen family pride of a Southern negro who has been long in one place were now in his tone.

"That boy! He's er devil! When he get to be er man—wow! He'll jes take an' make things whirl round yere. Raikon we'll all take er back seat when he come erlong er-raisin' Cain."

He had unharnessed the mare, and with his back bent was pushing the buggy into the carriage-house.

"Er pistol! An' him no bigger than er minute!"

A small stone whizzed past Peter's head and clattered on the stable. He hastily dropped all occupation and struck a curious attitude. His right knee was almost up to his chin, and his arms were wreathed protectingly about his head. He had not looked in the direction from which the stone had come, but he had begun immediately to yell: "You Jim! Quit! Quit, I tell yer, Jim! Watch out! You gwine break somethin', Jim!"

"Yah!" taunted the boy, as with the speed and ease of a light-cavalryman he manoeuvred in the distance. "Yah! Told on me, did you! Told on me, hey! There! How do you like that?" The missiles resounded against the stable.

"Watch out, Jim! You gwine break somethin', Jim, I tell yer! Quit yer foolishness, Jim! Ow! Watch out, boy! I—"

There was a crash. With diabolic ingenuity, one of Jimmie's pebbles had entered the carriage-house and had landed among a row of carriage-lamps on a shelf, creating havoc which was apparently beyond all reason of physical law. It seemed to Jimmie that the racket of falling glass could have been heard in an adjacent county.

Peter was a prophet who after persecution was suffered to recall everything to the mind of the persecutor. *"There!* Knew it! Knew it! *Now* I raikon you'll quit. Hi! jes look ut dese yer lamps! Fer lan' sake! Oh, now yer pop jes break ev'ry bone in yer body!"

In the doorway of the kitchen the cook appeared with a startled face. Jimmie's father and mother came suddenly out on the front veranda. "What was that noise?" called the doctor.

Peter went forward to explain. "Jim he was er-heavin' rocks at me, docteh, an' erlong come one rock an' go *blam* inter all th' lamps an' jes skitter 'em t' bits. I declayah—"

Jimmie, half blinded with emotion, was nevertheless aware of a lightning glance from his father, a glance which cowed and frightened him to the ends of his toes. He heard the steady but deadly tones of his father in a fury: "Go into the house and wait until I come."

Bowed in anguish, the boy moved across the lawn and up the steps. His mother was standing on the veranda still gazing toward the stable. He loitered in the faint hope that she might take some small pity on his state. But she could have heeded him no less if he had been invisible. He entered the house.

When the doctor returned from his investigation of the harm done by Jimmie's hand, Mrs. Trescott looked at him anxiously, for she knew that he was concealing some volcanic impulses. "Well?" she asked.

"It isn't the lamps," he said at first. He seated himself on the rail. "I don't know what we are going to do with that boy. It isn't so much the lamps as it is the other thing. He was throwing stones at Peter because Peter told me about the revolver. What are we going to do with him?"

"I'm sure I don't know," replied the mother. "We've tried almost everything. Of course much of it is pure animal spirits. Jimmie is not naturally vicious—"

"Oh, I know," interrupted the doctor, impatiently. "Do you suppose, when the stones were singing about Peter's ears, he cared whether they were flung by a boy who was naturally vicious or a boy who was not? The question might interest him afterward, but at the time he was mainly occupied in dodging these effects of pure animal spirits."

"Don't be too hard on the boy, Ned. There's lots of time yet. He's so young yet, and— I believe he gets most of his naughtiness from that wretched Dalzel boy. That Dalzel boy—well, he's simply awful!" Then, with true motherly instinct to shift blame from her own boy's shoulders, she proceeded to sketch the character of the Dalzel boy in lines that would have made that talented young vagabond stare. It was not admittedly her feeling that the doctor's attention should be diverted from the main issue and his indignation divided among the camps, but presently the doctor felt himself burn with wrath for the Dalzel boy.

"Why don't you keep Jimmie away from him?" he demanded. "Jimmie has no business consorting with abandoned little predestined jail-birds like him. If I catch him on the place I'll box his ears."

"It is simply impossible, unless we kept Jimmie shut up all the time," said Mrs. Trescott. "I can't watch him every minute of the day, and the moment my back is turned, he's off."

"I should think those Dalzel people would hire somebody to bring up their child for them," said the doctor. "They don't seem to know how to do it themselves."

Presently you would have thought from the talk that one Willie Dalzel had been throwing stones at Peter Washington because Peter Washington had told Doctor Trescott that Willie Dalzel had come into possession of a revolver.

In the meantime Jimmie had gone into the house to await the coming of his father. He was in rebellious mood. He had not intended to destroy the carriage-lamps. He had been merely hurling stones at a creature whose perfidy deserved such action, and the hitting of the lamps had been merely another move of the great conspirator Fate to force one Jimmie Trescott into dark and troublous ways. The boy was beginning to find the world a bitter place. He couldn't win appreciation for a single virtue; he could only achieve quick rigorous punishment for his misdemeanors. Everything was an enemy. Now there were those silly old lamps—what were they doing up on that shelf, anyhow? It would have been just as easy for them at the time to have been in some other place. But no; there they had been, like the crowd that is passing under the wall when the mason for the first time in twenty years lets fall a brick. Furthermore, the flight of that stone had been perfectly unreasonable. It had been a sort of freak in physical law. Jimmie understood that he might have thrown stones from the same fatal spot for an hour without hurting a single lamp. He was a victim—that was it. Fate had conspired with the detail of his environment to simply hound him into a grave or into a cell.

But who would understand? Who would understand? And here the boy turned his mental glance in every direction, and found nothing but what was to him the black of cruel ignorance. Very well; some day they would—

From somewhere out in the street he heard a peculiar whistle of two notes. It was the common signal of the boys of the neighborhood, and judging from the direction of the sound, it was apparently intended to summon him. He moved immediately to one of the windows of the sitting-room. It opened upon a part of the grounds remote from the stables and cut off from the veranda by a wing. He perceived Willie Dalzel loitering in the street. Jimmie whistled the signal after having pushed up the window-sash some inches. He saw the Dalzel boy turn and regard him, and then call several other boys. They stood in a group and gestured. These gestures plainly said: "Come out. We've got something on hand." Jimmie sadly shook his head.

But they did not go away. They held a long consultation. Presently Jimmie saw the intrepid Dalzel boy climb the fence and begin to creep amongst the shrubbery, in elaborate imitation of an Indian scout. In time he arrived under Jimmie's window, and raised his face to whisper: "Come on out! We're going on a bear-hunt."

A bear-hunt! Of course Jimmie knew that it would not be a real bear-hunt, but would be a sort of carouse of pretension and big talking and preposterous lying and valor, wherein each boy would strive to have himself called Kit Carson by the others. He was profoundly affected. However, the parental word was upon him, and he could not move. "No," he answered, "I can't. I've got to stay in."

"Are you a prisoner?" demanded the Dalzel boy, eagerly.

"No-o—yes—I s'pose I am."

The other lad became much excited, but he did not lose his wariness. "Don't you want to be rescued?"

"Why—no—I dunno," replied Jimmie, dubiously.

Willie Dalzel was indignant. "Why, of course you want to be rescued! We'll rescue you. I'll go and get my men." And thinking this a good sentence, he repeated, pompously, "I'll go and get my men." He began to crawl away, but when he was distant some ten paces he turned to say: "Keep up a stout heart. Remember that you have friends who will be faithful unto death. The time is not now far off when you will again view the blessed sun-light."

The poetry of these remarks filled Jimmie with ecstasy, and he watched eagerly for the coming of the friends who would be faithful unto death. They delayed some time, for the reason that Willie Dalzel was making a speech.

"Now, men," he said, "our comrade is a prisoner in yon—in yond—in that there fortress. We must to the rescue. Who volunteers to go with me?" He fixed them with a stern eye.

There was a silence, and then one of the smaller boys remarked, "If Doc Trescott ketches us trackin' over his lawn—"

Willie Dalzel pounced upon the speaker and took him by the throat. The two presented a sort of a burlesque of the wood-cut on the cover of a dime novel which Willie had just been reading —*The Red Captain: A Tale of the Pirates of the Spanish Main.*

"You are a coward!" said Willie, through his clinched teeth.

"No, I ain't, Willie," piped the other, as best he could.

"I say you are," cried the great chieftain, indignantly. "Don't tell *me* I'm a liar." He relinquished his hold upon the coward and resumed his speech. "You know me, men. Many of you have been my followers for long years. You saw me slay Six-handed Dick with my own hand. You know I never falter. Our comrade is a prisoner in the cruel hands of our enemies. Aw, Pete Washington? He dassent. My pa says if Pete ever troubles me he'll brain 'im. Come on! To the rescue! Who will go with me to the rescue? Aw, come on! What are you afraid of?"

It was another instance of the power of eloquence upon the human mind. There was only one boy who was not thrilled by this oration, and he was a boy whose favorite reading had been of the road-agents and gun-fighters of the great West, and he thought the whole thing should be conducted in the Deadwood Dick manner. This talk of a "comrade" was silly; "pard" was the proper word. He resolved that he would make a show of being a pirate, and keep secret the fact that he really was Hold-up Harry, the Terror of the Sierras.

But the others were knit close in piratical bonds. One by one they climbed the fence at a point hidden from the house by tall shrubs. With many a low-breathed caution they went upon their perilous adventure.

Jimmie was grown tired of waiting for his friends who would be faithful unto death. Finally he decided that he would rescue himself. It would be a gross breach of rule, but he couldn't sit there all the rest of the day waiting for his faithful-unto-death friends. The window was only five feet from the ground. He softly raised the sash and threw one leg over the sill. But at the same time he perceived his friends snaking among the bushes. He withdrew his leg and waited, seeing that he was now to be rescued in an orthodox way. The brave pirates came nearer and nearer.

Jimmie heard a noise of a closing door, and turning, he saw his father in the room looking at him and the open window in angry surprise. Boys never faint, but Jimmie probably came as near to it as may the average boy.

"What's all this?" asked the doctor, staring. Involuntarily Jimmie glanced over his shoulder through the window. His father saw the creeping figures. "What are those boys doing?" he said, sharply, and he knit his brows.

"Nothin'."

"Nothing! Don't tell me that. Are they coming here to the window?"

"Y-e-s, sir."

"What for?"

"To—to see me."

"What about?"

"About—about nothin'."

"What about?"

Jimmie knew that he could conceal nothing. He said, "They're comin' to—to—to rescue me." He began to whimper.

The doctor sat down heavily.

"What? To rescue you?" he gasped.

"Y-yes, sir."

The doctor's eyes began to twinkle. "Very well," he said presently. "I will sit here and observe this rescue. And on no account
do you warn them that I am here. Understand?"

Of course Jimmie understood. He had been mad to warn his
friends, but his father's mere presence had frightened him from
doing it. He stood trembling at the window, while the doctor
stretched in an easy-chair near at hand. They waited. The doctor
could tell by his son's increasing agitation that the great moment
was near. Suddenly he heard Willie Dalzel's voice hiss out a
word: "S-s-silence!" Then the same voice addressed Jimmie at
the window: "Good cheer, my comrade. The time is now at hand.
I have come. Never did the Red Captain turn his back on a
friend. One minute more and you will be free. Once aboard my
gallant craft and you can bid defiance to your haughty enemies.
Why don't you hurry up? What are you standin' there lookin' like
a cow for?"

"I—er—now—you—" stammered Jimmie.

Here Hold-up Harry, the Terror of the Sierras, evidently concluded that Willie Dalzel had had enough of the premier part, so
he said: "Brace up, pard. Don't ye turn white-livered now, fer ye
know that Hold-up Harry, the Terrar of the Sarahs, ain't the man
ter—"

"Oh, stop it!" said Willie Dalzel. "He won't understand that,
you know. He's a pirate. Now, Jimmie, come on. Be of light
heart, my comrade. Soon you—"

"I 'low arter all this here long time in jail ye thought ye had no
friends mebbe, but I tell ye Hold-up Harry, the Terrar of the
Sarahs—"

"A boat is waitin'—"

"I have ready a trusty horse—"

Willie Dalzel could endure his rival no longer.

"Look here, Henry, you're spoilin' the whole thing. We're all
pirates, don't you see, and you're a pirate too."

"I ain't a pirate. I'm Hold-up Harry, the Terrar of the Sarahs."

"You ain't, I say," said Willie, in despair. "You're spoilin' everything, you are. All right, now. You wait. I'll fix you for this, see if
I don't! Oh, come on, Jimmie. A boat awaits us at the foot of the

rocks. In one short hour you'll be free forever from your ex—excwable enemies, and their vile plots. Hasten, for the dawn approaches."

The suffering Jimmie looked at his father, and was surprised at what he saw. The doctor was doubled up like a man with the colic. He was breathing heavily. The boy turned again to his friends. "I—now—look here," he began, stumbling among the words. "You—I—I don't think I'll be rescued to-day."

The pirates were scandalized. "What?" they whispered, angrily. "Ain't you goin' to be rescued? Well, all right for you, Jimmie Trescott. That's a nice way to act, that is!" Their up-turned eyes glowered at Jimmie.

Suddenly Doctor Trescott appeared at the window with Jimmie. "Oh, go home, boys!" he gasped, but they did not hear him. Upon the instant they had whirled and scampered away like deer. The first lad to reach the fence was the Red Captain, but Hold-up Harry, the Terror of the Sierras, was so close that there was little to choose between them.

Doctor Trescott lowered the window, and then spoke to his son in his usual quiet way. "Jimmie, I wish you would go and tell Peter to have the buggy ready at seven o'clock."

"Yes, sir," said Jimmie, and he swaggered out to the stables. "Pete, father wants the buggy ready at seven o'clock."

Peter paid no heed to this order, but with the tender sympathy of a true friend he inquired, "Hu't?"

"Hurt? Did what hurt?"

"Yer trouncin'."

"Trouncin'!" said Jimmie, contemptuously. "I didn't get any trouncin'."

"No?" said Peter. He gave Jimmie a quick shrewd glance, and saw that he was telling the truth. He began to mutter and mumble over his work. "Ump! Ump! Dese yer white folks act like they think er boy's made er glass. No trouncin'! Ump!" He was consumed with curiosity to learn why Jimmie had not felt a heavy parental hand, but he did not care to lower his dignity by asking questions about it. At last, however, he reached the limits of his endurance, and in a voice pretentiously careless he asked, "Didn' yer pop take on like mad erbout dese yer cay'ge-lamps?"

"Carriage-lamps?" inquired Jimmie.

"Ump."

"No, he didn't say anything about carriage-lamps—not that I remember. Maybe he did, though. Lemme see. . . . No, he never mentioned 'em."

VIII

THE KNIFE

I

SI BRYANT'S place was on the shore of the lake and his garden patch, shielded from the north by a bold little promontory and a higher ridge inland, was accounted the most successful and surprising in all Whilomville town-ship. One afternoon, Si was working in the garden patch when Doctor Trescott's man, Peter Washington, came trudging slowly along the road, observing nature. He scanned the white man's fine agricultural results. "Take your eye off them there melons, you rascal," said Si placidly.

The negro's face widened in a grin of delight. "Well, Mist' Bryant, I raikon I ain't on'y make m'se'f covertous er-lookin' at dem yere mellums, sure 'nough. Dey suhtainly is grand."

"That's all right," responded Si with affected bitterness of spirit. "That's all right. Just don't you admire 'm too much— that's all."

Peter chuckled and chuckled. "Ma Lode, Mist' Bryant, y-y-you don' think I'm gwine come prowlin' in dish yer gawden?"

"No, I know you hain't," said Si with solemnity. "B'cause if you did, I'd shoot you so full of holes you couldn't tell yourself from a sponge."

"Um—no seh! No seh! I don' raikon you'll git chance at Pete, Mist' Bryant. No seh. I'll take an' run 'long an' rob er bank 'fore I'll come foolishin' 'roun' *your* gawden, Mist' Bryant."

Bryant, gnarled and strong as an old tree, leaned on his hoe and laughed a Yankee laugh. His mouth remained tightly closed but the sinister lines which ran from the sides of his nose to the meetings of his lips developed to form a comic oval and he emitted a series of grunts while his eyes gleamed merrily and his shoulders shook. Peter, on the contrary, threw back his head and guffawed thunderously. The effete joke in regard to an American negro's fondness for water-melons was still an admirable pleasantry to them and this was not the first time they had engaged in badinage over it. In fact, this venerable survival had formed between them a friendship of casual roadside quality.

Afterward, Peter went on up the road. He continued to chuckle until he was far away. He was going to pay a visit to old Alek Williams, a negro who lived with a large family in a hut clinging to the side of a mountain. The scattered colony of negroes which hovered near Whilomville was of interesting origin being the result of some contrabands who had drifted as far north as Whilomville during the great civil war. The descendants of these adventurers were mainly conspicuous for their bewildering number and the facility which they possessed for adding even to this number. Speaking for example of the Jacksons—one couldn't hurl a stone into the hills about Whilomville without having it land on the roof of a hut full of Jacksons. The town reaped little in labor from these curious suburbs. There were a few men who came in regularly to work in gardens, to drive teams, to care for horses, and there were a few women who came in to cook or to wash. These latter had, usually, drunken husbands. In the main the colony loafed in high spirits and the industrious minority gained no direct honor from their fellows unless they spent their earnings on raiment—in which case, they were naturally treated with distinction. On the whole, the hardships of these people were the wind, the rain, the snow and any other physical difficulties which they could cultivate. About twice a year, the lady philanthropists of Whilomville went up against them, and came away poorer in goods but rich in complacence. After one of these attacks, the colony would preserve a comic air of rectitude for two days and then relapse again to the genial irresponsibility of a crew of monkeys.

Peter Washington was one of the industrious class who occupied a position of distinction for he surely spent his money on personal decoration. On occasion, he could dress better than the mayor of Whilomville himself, or at least in more colors, which was the main thing to the minds of his admirers. His ideal had been the late gallant Henry Johnson whose conquests in Watermelon Alley as well as in the hill shanties had proved him the equal if not the superior of any Pullman-car porter in the country. Perhaps Peter had too much Virginia laziness and humor in him to be a wholly adequate successor to the fastidious Henry Johnson but at any rate he admired his memory so attentively as to be openly termed a dude by envious people.

On this afternoon he was going to call on old Alek Williams because Alek's eldest girl was just turned seventeen and, to Peter's mind, was a triumph of beauty. He was not wearing his best clothes because on his last visit Alek's half-breed hound, Susie, had taken occasion to forcefully extract a quite large and valuable part of the visitor's trousers. When Peter arrived at the end of the rocky field which contained old Alek's shanty, he stooped and provided himself with several large stones, weighing them carefully in his hand and finally continuing his journey with three stones of about eight ounces each. When he was near the house, three gaunt hounds, Rover and Carlo and Susie, came sweeping down upon him. His impression was that they were going to climb him as if he were a tree but at the critical moment they swerved and went growling and snapping around him, their heads low, their eyes malignant. The afternoon caller waited until the Susie presented her side to him. Then he heaved one of his eight-ounce rocks. When it landed, her hollow ribs gave forth a drum-like sound and she was knocked sprawling, her legs in air. The other hounds at once fled in horror and she followed as soon as she was able, yelping at the top of her lungs. The afternoon caller resumed his march.

At the wild expressions of Susie's anguish, old Alek had flung open the door and come hastily into the sunshine. "Yah, you Suse, come erlong outa dat now. What fer you—oh, how'do, how'do, Mist' Wash'ton, how'do."

"How'do, Mist' Willums. I done foun' it necessa'y fer ter damnearkill dish yer dawg a' your'n, Mist' Willums."

"Come in, come in, Mist' Wash'ton. Dawg no 'count, Mist' Wash'ton." Then he turned to address the unfortunate animal. "Hu't, did it? Hu't? 'Pears like you gwine lun some saince by time somebody brek yer back. 'Pears like I gwine club yer inter er frazzle 'fore you fin' out some saince. Gw'on 'way f'm yah."

As the old man and his guest entered the shanty, a body of black children spread out in crescent-shaped formation and observed Peter with awe. Fat old Mrs. Williams greeted him turbulently while the oldest girl, Mollie, lurked in a corner and giggled with finished imbecility, gazing at the visitor with eyes that were shy and bold by turns. She seemed at times absurdly over-confident; at times, foolishly afraid; but her giggle consistently endured. It was a giggle on which an irascible but right-minded judge would have ordered her forthwith to be buried alive.

Amid a great deal of hospitable gabbling, Peter was conducted to the best chair out of the three the house contained. Enthroned therein, he made himself charming in talk to the old people who beamed upon him joyously. As for Mollie, he affected to be unaware of her existence. This may have been a method for entrapping the sentimental interest of that young gazelle or it may be that the giggle had worked upon him.

He was absolutely fascinating to the old people. They could talk like rotary snow-ploughs and he gave them every chance while his face was illumined with appreciation. They pressed him to stay to supper and he consented after a glance at the pot on the stove which was too furtive to be noted.

During the meal, old Alek recounted the high state of Judge Oglethorpe's kitchen garden which Alek said was due to his unremitting industry and fine intelligence. Alek was a gardener whenever impending starvation forced him to cease temporarily from being a lily of the field.

"Mist' Bryant he suhtainly got er grand gawden," observed Peter.

"Dat so, dat so, Mist' Wash'ton," assented Alek. "He got fine gawden."

"Seems like I nev' *did* see sech mellums; big as er bar'l, layin' dere. I don't raikon an'body in dish yer county kin hol' it with Mist' Bryant when comes ter mellums."

"Dat so, Mist' Wash'ton."

They did not talk of water-melons until their heads held nothing else, as the phrase goes. But they talked of water-melons until when Peter started for home that night over a lonely road, they held a certain dominant position in his mind. Alek had come with him as far as the fence in order to protect him from a possible attack by the mongrels. There they had cheerfully parted, two honest men.

The night was dark and heavy with moisture. Peter found it uncomfortable to walk rapidly. He merely loitered on the road.

When opposite Si Bryant's place, he paused and looked over the fence into the garden. He imagined he could see the form of a huge melon lying in dim stateliness, not ten yards away. He looked at the Bryant house. Two windows, down stairs, were lighted. The Bryants kept no dog, old Si's favorite child having once been bitten by a dog and having since died, within that year, of pneumonia.

Peering over the fence, Peter fancied that if any low-minded night-prowler should happen to note the melon, he would not find it difficult to possess himself of it. This person would merely wait until the lights were out in the house and the people presumably asleep. Then he would climb the fence, reach the melon in a few strides, sever the stem with his ready knife, and in a trice be back in the road with his prize. There need be no noise and, after all, the house was some distance.

Selecting a smooth bit of turf, Peter took seat by the roadside. From time to time he glanced at the lighted windows.

II

When Peter and Alek had said good-bye, the old man turned back in the rocky field and shaped a slow course toward that high dim light which marked the little window of his shanty. It would be incorrect to say that Alek could think of nothing but water-melons. But it was true that Si Bryant's water-melon patch occupied a certain conspicuous position in his thoughts.

He sighed; he almost wished that he was again a conscience-less pickaninny instead of being one of the most ornate, solemn and look-at-me-sinner deacons that ever graced the handle of a collection-basket. At this time, it made him quite sad to reflect upon his granite integrity. A weaker man might perhaps bow his moral head to the temptation but for him such a fall was impossible. He was a prince of the church and if he had been nine princes of the church, he could not have been more proud. In fact, religion was to the old man a sort of a personal dignity. And he was on Sundays so obtrusively good that you could see his sanctity through a door. He forced it on you until you would have felt its influence even in a fore-castle.

It was clear in his mind that he must put water-melon

thoughts from him and, after a moment, he told himself with much ostentation that he had done so. But it was cooler under the sky than in the shanty and as he was not sleepy he decided to take a stroll down to Si Bryant's place and look at the melons from a pinnacle of spotless innocence. Reaching the road he paused to listen. It would not do to let Peter hear him because that graceless rapscallion would probably misunderstand him. But assuring himself that Peter was well on his way, he set out walking briskly until he was within four hundred yards of Bryant's place. Here he went to the side of the road and walked thereafter on the damp yielding turf. He made no sound.

He did not go on to that point in the main road which was directly opposite the water-melon patch. He did not wish to have his ascetic contemplation disturbed by some chance way-farer. He turned off along a short lane which led to Si Bryant's barn. Here he reached a place where he could see, over the fence, the faint shapes of the melons.

Alek was affected. The house was some distance away, there was no dog and doubtless the Bryants would soon extinguish their lights and go to bed. Then some poor lost lamb of sin might come and scale the fence, reach a melon in a moment, sever the stem with his ready knife and in a trice be back in the road with his prize. And this poor lost lamb of sin might even be a bishop but no one would ever know it. Alek singled out with his eye a very large melon and thought that the lamb would prove his judgment if he took that one.

He found a soft place in the grass, and arranged himself comfortably. He watched the lights in the windows.

III

It seemed to Peter Washington that the Bryants absolutely consulted their own wishes in regard to the time for retiring; but at last he saw the lighted windows fade briskly from left to right and after a moment a window on the second floor blazed out against the darkness. Si was going to bed. In five minutes, this window abruptly vanished and all the world was night.

Peter spent the ensuing quarter-hour in no mental debate. His mind was fixed. He was here and the melon was there. He would have it. But an idea of being caught appalled him. He thought of his position. He was the beau of his community, honored right and left. He pictured the consternation of his friends and the cheers of his enemies if the hands of the redoubtable Si Bryant should grip him in his shame.

He arose and going to the fence, listened. No sound broke the stillness, save the rhythmical incessant clicking of myriad insects and the guttural chanting of the frogs in the reeds at the lakeside. Moved by sudden decision, he climbed the fence and crept silently and swiftly down upon the melon. His open knife was in his hand. There was the melon, cool, fair to see, as pompous in its fatness as the cook in a monastery.

Peter put out a hand to steady it while he cut the stem. But at the instant he was aware that a black form had dropped over the fence lining the lane in front of him and was coming stealthily toward him. In a palsy of terror he dropped flat upon the ground, not having strength enough to run away. The next moment he was looking into the amazed and agonized face of old Alek Williams.

There was a moment of loaded silence and then Peter was overcome by a mad inspiration. He suddenly dropped his knife and leaped upon Alek. "I got'che!" he hissed. "I got'che! I got'che!" The old man sank down as limp as rags.

"I got'che! I got'che! Steal Mist' Bryant's mellums, hey?"

Alek in a low voice began to beg. "Oh, Mist' Peteh Wash'ton, don' go fer ter be too ha'd on er ole man. I nev' come yere fer ter steal 'em. 'Deed, I didn't, Mist' Wash'ton. I come yere jes fer ter *feel* 'em. Oh, please, Mist' Wash'ton—"

"Come erlong outa yere, you ol' rip," said Peter. "An' don' trumple on dese yer baids. I gwine put you wah you won' ketch col'."

Without difficulty he tumbled the whining Alek over the fence to the road-way, and followed him with sheriff-like expedition. He took him by the scruff. "Come erlong, deacon. I raikon I gwine put you wah you kin pray, deacon. Come erlong, deacon."

The emphasis and reiteration of his layman's title in the church produced a deadly effect upon Alek. He felt to his marrow the heinous crime into which this treacherous night had betrayed him. As Peter marched his prisoner up the road toward the mouth of the lane, he continued his remarks. "Come erlong, deacon. Nev' see er man so anxious-like erbout er mellum-paitch, deacon. Seem like you jes' must see 'em er-growin' an' *feel* 'em, deacon. Mist' Bryant he'll be s'prised, deacon, findin' out you come fer ter *feel* his mellums. Come erlong, deacon. Mist' Bryant he expectin' some ole rip like you come soon."

They had almost reached the lane when Alek's cur Susie who had followed her master approached in the silence which attends dangerous dogs; and seeing indications of what she took to be war she appended herself swiftly but firmly to the calf of Peter's left leg. The melee was short but spirited. Alek had no wish to have his dog complicate his already serious misfortunes and went manfully to the defense of his captor. He procured a large stone and by beating this with both hands down upon the re-sounding skull of the animal, he induced her to quit her grip. Breathing heavily Peter dropped into the long grass at the road-side. He said nothing.

"Mist' Wash'ton," said Alek at last in a quavering voice, "I raikon I gwine wait yere see what you gwine do ter me."

Whereupon Peter passed into a spasmodic state in which he rolled to and fro and shook.

"Mist' Wash'ton, I hope dish yer dog ain't gone an' give you fitses?"

Peter sat up suddenly. "No, she ain't," he answered, "but she gin me er big skeer an' fer yer 'sistance with er cobble-stone, Mist' Willums, I tell you what I gwine do—I tell you what I gwine do." He waited an impressive moment. "I gwine 'lease you."

Old Alek trembled like a little bush in a wind. "Mist' Wash'ton?"

Quoth Peter deliberately: "I gwine 'lease you."

The old man was filled with a desire to negotiate this state-ment at once but he felt the necessity of carrying off the event without an appearance of haste. "Yes, seh; thank'e, seh; thank'e, Mist' Wash'ton. I raikon I ramble home pressenly." He waited an interval and then dubiously said: "Good evenin', Mist' Wash'ton?"

"Good evenin', deacon. Don' come foolin' roun' *feelin'* no mel-lums and I say troof. Good evenin', deacon."

Alek took off his hat and made three profound bows. "Thank'e, seh. Thank'e, seh. Thank'e, seh."

Peter underwent another severe spasm but the old man walked off toward his home with a humble and a contrite heart.

IV

The next morning, Alek proceeded from his shanty under the complete but customary illusion that he was going to work. He trudged manfully along until he reached the vicinity of Si Bryant's place. Then, by stages, he relapsed into a slink. He was passing the garden patch under full steam when, at some distance ahead of him he saw Si Bryant leaning casually on the garden fence.

"Good mornin', Alek."

"Good mawnin', Mist' Bryant," answered Alek with a new deference. He was marching on when he was halted by a word —"Alek."

He stopped. "Yes, seh."

"I found a knife this mornin' in th' road," drawled Si, "an' I thought maybe it was your'n."

Improved in mind by this divergence from the direct line of attack, Alek stepped up easily to look at the knife. "No, seh," he said scanning it as it lay in Si's palm while the cold steel-blue eyes of the white man looked down into his stomach, " 'tain't no knife er mine." But he knew the knife. He knew it as if it had been his mother. And at the same moment a spark flashed through his head and made wise his understanding. He knew everything. " 'Tain't much of er knife, Mist' Bryant," he said, deprecatingly.

" 'Tain't much of a knife, I know that," cried Si in sudden heat, "but I found it this mornin' in my water-melon patch—hear?"

"Watah-mellum paitch?" yelled Alek, not astounded.

"Yes, in my water-melon patch," sneered Si, "an' I think you know something about it, too!"

"Me?" cried Alek. "Me?"

"Yes—you," said Si with icy ferocity. "Yes—you!" He had become convinced that Alek was not in any way guilty but he was certain that the old man knew the owner of the knife and so he pressed him at first on criminal lines. "Alek, you might as well own up, now. You've been meddlin' with my water-melons!"

"Me?" cried Alek again. "Yah's *ma* knife. I done cah'e it foh yeahs."

Bryant changed his ways. "Look here, Alek," he said confidentially, "I know you and you know me and there ain't no use in any more skirmishin'. *I* know that *you* know whose knife that is. Now, whose is it?"

This challenge was so formidable in character that Alek temporarily quailed and began to stammer. "Er—now—Mist' Bryant —you—you—frien' er mine—"

"I know I'm a friend of yours, but," said Bryant inexorably, "who owns this knife?"

Alek gathered unto himself some remnants of dignity and spoke with reproach. "Mist' Bryant, dish yer knife ain' mine."

"No," said Bryant, "it ain't. But you know who it belongs to an' I want you to tell me—quick."

"Well, Mist' Bryant," answered Alek scratching his wool, "I won't say's I *do* know who b'longs ter dish yer knife an' I won't say's I *don't*."

Bryant again laughed his Yankee laugh but this time there was little humor in it. It was dangerous.

Alek seeing that he had gotten himself into hot water by the fine diplomacy of his last sentence, immediately began to flounder and totally submerge himself. "No, Mist' Bryant," he repeated, "I won't say's I *do* know who b'longs ter dish yer knife an' I won't say's I *don't*." And he began to parrot this fatal sentence again and again. It seemed wound about his tongue. He could not rid himself of it. Its very power to make trouble for him seemed to originate the mysterious Afric reason for its repetition.

"Is he a very close friend of your'n?" said Bryant softly.

"F-frien'?" stuttered Alek. He appeared to weigh this question with much care. "Well, seems like he *was* er frien' an', then agin, it seems like he—"

" 'It seems like he *wasn't*?" asked Bryant.

"Yes, seh, jest so, jest so," cried Alek. "Sometimes it seems like he *wasn't*. Then agin—" He stopped for profound meditation.

The patience of the white man seemed inexhaustible. At length his low and oily voice broke the stillness. "Oh, well, of course, if he's a friend of your'n, Alek! You know I wouldn't want to make no trouble for a friend of your'n."

"Yes, seh," cried the negro at once. "He's er frien' er mine. He is dat."

"Well, then, it seems as if about the only thing to do is for you to tell me his name so's I can send him his knife and that's all there is to it."

Alek took off his hat and in perplexity ran his hand over his wool. He studied the ground. But several times he raised his eyes to take a sly peep at the imperturbable visage of the white man. "Y-y-yes, Mist' Bryant. . . . I raikon dat's erbout all what kin be done. I gwine tell you who b'longs ter dish yer knife."

"Of course," said the smooth Bryant, "it ain't a very nice thing to have to do but—"

"No, seh," cried Alek brightly, "I'm gwine tell you, Mist' Bryant. I gwine tell you erbout dat knife. Mist' Bryant," he asked solemnly, "does you know who b'longs ter dat knife?"

"No. I—"

"Well, I gwine tell. I gwine tell who. Mist' Bryant—" The old man drew himself to a stately pose and held forth his arm. "I gwine tell who. Mist' Bryant, *dish yer knife b'longs ter Sam Jackson!*"

Bryant was startled into indignation. "Who in hell is Sam Jackson?" he growled.

"He's a nigger," said Alek impressively, "an' he wuks in er lumbeh-yawd up yere in Hoswego."

IX

THE STOVE

I

THEY'LL bring her," said Mrs. Trescott dubiously. Her cousin, the painter, the bewildered father of the angel-child, had written to say that if they were asked, he and his wife would come to the Trescotts for the Christmas holidays. But he had not officially stated that the angel-child would form part of the expedition. "But of course they'll bring her," said Mrs. Trescott to her husband.

The doctor assented. "Yes, they'll have to bring her. They wouldn't dare leave New York at her mercy."

"Well," sighed Mrs. Trescott after a pause, "the neighbors will be pleased. When they see her, they'll immediately lock up their children for safety."

"Anyhow," said Trescott, "the devastation of the Margate twins was complete. She can't do that particular thing again. I shall be interested to note what form her energy will take this time."

"Oh, yes, that's it!" cried the wife. "You'll be *interested*. You've hit it exactly. You'll be interested to note what form her energy will take this time! And then when the real crisis comes, you'll put on your hat and walk out of the house and leave *me* to straighten things out. This is not a scientific question; this is a practical matter."

"Well, as a practical man, I advocate chaining her out in the stable," answered the doctor.

When Jimmie Trescott was told that his old flame was again to appear, he remained calm. In fact time had so mended his youthful heart that it was a regular apple of oblivion and peace. Her image in his thought was as the track of a bird on deep snow —it was an impression but it did not concern the depths. However he did what befitted his state. He went out and bragged in

the street. "My cousin is comin' next week f'm New York.". . .
"My cousin is comin' tomorrow f'm New York."

"Girl or boy?" said the populace bluntly; but, when enlight-
ened, they speedily cried: "Oh, we remember *her!*" They were
charmed for they thought of her as an out-law and they surmised
that she could lead them into a very ecstasy of sin. They thought
of her as a brave bandit because they had been whipped for
various pranks into which she had led them. When Jimmie made
his declaration, they fell into a state of pleased and shuddering
expectancy.

Mrs. Trescott pronounced her point of view. "The child is a
nice child if only Caroline had some sense. But she hasn't. And
Willis is like a wax figure. I don't see what can be done unless—
unless you simply go to Willis and put the whole thing right at
him." Then for purposes of indication, she improvised a speech.
"Look here, Willis, you've got a little daughter, haven't you? But,
confound it, man, she is not the only girl-child ever brought into
the sun-light. There are a lot of children. Children are an ordinary phenomenon. In China, they drown girl-babies. If you wish
to submit to this frightful impostor and tyrant—that is all very
well, but why in the name of humanity do you make us submit to
it?"

Doctor Trescott laughed. "I wouldn't dare say it to him."

"Anyhow," said Mrs. Trescott determinedly, "that is what you
should say to him."

"It wouldn't do the slightest good. It would only make him very
angry and I would lay myself perfectly open to a suggestion that
I had better attend my own affairs with more rigor."

"Well, I suppose you are right," Mrs. Trescott again said.

"Why don't you speak to Caroline?" asked the doctor
humorously.

"Speak to Caroline! Why, I wouldn't for the *world!* She'd fly
through the roof! She'd snap my head off! Speak to Caroline! You
must be mad!"

One afternoon the doctor went to await his visitors on the
platform of the railway station. He was thoughtfully smiling. For
some quaint reason he was convinced that he was to be treated to
a quick manifestation of little Cora's peculiar and interesting
powers. And yet when the train paused at the station, there

appeared to him only a pretty little girl in a fur-lined hood and with her nose reddening from the sudden cold and—attended respectfully by parents. He smiled again, reflecting that he had comically exaggerated the dangers of dear little Cora. It amused his philosophy to note that he had really been perturbed.

As the big sleigh sped homeward, there was a sudden shrill out-cry from the angel-child: "Oh, mama! Mama! They've forgotten my stove!"

"Hush, dear, hush," said the mother. "It's all right."

"Oh but mama, they've forgotten my stove!"

The doctor thrust his chin suddenly out of his top-coat collar. "Stove?" he said. "Stove? What stove?"

"Oh, just a toy of the child's," explained the mother. "She's grown so fond of it—she loves it so—that if we didn't take it everywhere with her, she'd suffer dreadfully. So we always bring it."

"Oh," said the doctor. He pictured a little tin trinket. But when the stove was really unmasked, it turned out to be an affair of cast-iron, as big as a portmanteau, and, as the stage people say, practicable. There was some trouble that evening when came the hour of children's bed-time. Little Cora burst into a wild declaration that she could not retire for the night unless the stove was carried up stairs and placed at her bed-side. While the mother was trying to dissuade the child, the Trescotts held their peace and gazed with awe. The incident closed when the lamb-eyed father gathered the stove in his arms and preceded the angel-child to her chamber.

In the morning Trescott was standing with his back to the dining-room fire, awaiting breakfast, when he heard a noise of descending guests. Presently the door opened and the party entered in regular order. First came the angel-child; then the cooing mother; and, last, the great painter with his arms full of the stove. He deposited it gently in a corner and sighed. Trescott wore a wide grin. "What are you carting that thing all over the house for?" he said brutally. "Why don't you put it some place where she can play with it and leave it there?"

The mother rebuked him with a look. "Well, if it gives her pleasure, Ned?" she expostulated softly. "If it makes the child happy to have the stove with her, why shouldn't she have it?"

"Just so," said the doctor with calmness.

Jimmie's idea was the roaring fire-place in the cabin of the lone mountaineer. At first he was not able to admire a girl's stove, built on well-known domestic lines. He eyed it and thought it was very pretty but it did not move him immediately. But a certain respect grew to an interest and he became the angel-child's accomplice. And even if he had not had an interest grow upon him he was certain to have been implicated sooner or later because of the imperious way of little Cora who made a serf of him in a few swift sentences. Together they carried the stove out into the desolate garden and squatted it in the snow. Jimmie's snug little muscles had been pitted against the sheer nervous vigor of this little golden-haired girl and he had not won great honors. When the mind blazed inside the small body, the angel-child was pure force.

She began to speak. "Now, Jim, get some paper. Get some wood—little sticks, at first. Now we want a match. You got a match? Well, go get a match. Get some more wood. Hurry up, now! No. *No!* I'll light it my own self. You get some more wood. There! Isn't that splendid? You get a whole lot of wood an' pile it up here by the stove. An' now what'll we cook? We must have somethin' to cook, you know, else it ain't like the real."

"Potatoes," said Jimmie at once.

The day was clear, cold, bright. An icy wind sped from over the waters of the lake. A grown person would hardly have been abroad save on compulsion of a kind and yet when they were called to luncheon, the two little simpletons protested with great cries.

II

The ladies of Whilomville were somewhat given to the pagan habit of tea-parties. When a tea-party was to befall a certain house, one could read it in the manner of the prospective hostess who for some previous days would go about twitching this and twisting that and dusting here and polishing there; the ordinary habits of the household began then to disagree with her and her unfortunate husband and children fled to the lengths of their tethers. Then there was a hush. Then there was a tea-party. On the fatal afternoon, a small picked company of latent enemies would meet. There would be a fanfare of affectionate greetings during which everybody would measure to an inch the importance of what everybody else was wearing. Those who wore old dresses would wish then that they had not come and those who saw that, in the company, they were well-clad would be pleased or exalted or filled with the joys of cruelty. Then they had tea which was a habit and a delight with none of them, their usual beverage being coffee with milk.

Usually the party jerked horribly in the beginning while the hostess strove and pulled and pushed to make its progress smooth. Then suddenly it would be off like the wind, eight, fifteen or twenty-five tongues clattering with a noise like a cotton-mill combined with the noise of a few penny-whistles. Then the hostess had nothing to do but to look glad and see that everybody had enough tea and cake. When the door was closed behind the last guest, the hostess would usually drop into a chair and say: "Thank heaven! They're gone!" There would be no malice in this expression. It simply would be that, woman-like, she had flung herself head-long at the accomplishment of a pleasure which she could not even define and at the end she felt only weariness.

The value and beauty or oddity of the tea-cups was another element which entered largely into the spirit of these terrible enterprises. The quality of the tea was an element which did not enter at all. Uniformly, it was rather bad. But the cups! Some of the more ambitious people aspired to have cups each of a different pattern, possessing in fact the sole similarity that with their odd curves and dips of form they each resembled anything but a tea-cup. Others of the more ambitious aspired to a quite severe and godly "set" which, when viewed, appalled one with its austere and rigid family resemblances and made one desire to ask the hostess if the tea-pot was not the father of all the little cups and at the same time protesting gallantly that such a young and charming cream-jug surely could not be their mother.

But of course the serious part is that these collections so differed in style and the obvious amount paid for them that nobody could be happy. The poorer ones envied; the richer ones feared; the poorer ones continually striving to over-take the leaders; the leaders always with their heads turned back to hear over-taking foot-steps. And none of these things here written did they know. Instead of seeing that they were very stupid they thought they were very fine. And they gave and took heart bruises—fierce deep heart bruises—under the clear impression that of such kind of rubbish was the kingdom of nice people. The characteristics of outsiders of course emerged in shreds from these tea-parties and it is doubtful if the characteristics of insiders escaped entirely. In fact these tea-parties were in the large way the result of a conspiracy of certain unenlightened people to make life still more uncomfortable.

Mrs. Trescott was in the circle of tea-fighters largely through a sort of an artificial necessity—a necessity in short which she had herself created in a spirit of femininity.

When the painter and his family came for the holidays, Mrs. Trescott had for some time been feeling that it was her turn to give a tea-party and she was resolved upon it now that she was reinforced by the beautiful wife of the painter whose charms would make all the other women feel badly. And Mrs. Trescott further resolved that the affair should be notable in more than one way. The painter's wife suggested that as an innovation they give the people good tea but Mrs. Trescott shook her head; she was quite sure they would not like it.

It was an impressive gathering. A few came to see if they could not find out the faults of the painter's wife and these, added to those who would have attended even without that attractive prospect, swelled the company to a number quite large for Whilomville. There were the usual preliminary jolts and then suddenly the tea-party was in full swing and looked like an unprecedented success.

Mrs. Trescott exchanged a glance with the painter's wife. They felt proud and superior. This tea-party was almost perfection.

III

Jimmie and the angel-child, after being oppressed by innumerable admonitions to behave correctly during the afternoon, succeeded in reaching the garden where the stove awaited them.

They were enjoying themselves grandly when snow began to fall so heavily that it gradually dampened their ardor as well as extinguished the fire in the stove. They stood ruefully until the angel-child devised the plan of carrying the stove into the stable and there, safe from the storm, to continue the festivities. But they were met at the door of the stable by Peter Washington.

"What you 'bout, Jim?"

"Now—it's snowin' so hard we thought we'd take the stove into the stable."

"An' have er fiah in it! No, seh! G'w'on 'way f'm heh—g'w'on! Don' 'low no sech foolishin' round yer. No, seh!"

"Well, we ain't goin' to hurt your old stable, are we?" asked Jimmie, ironically.

"Dat you ain't, Jim. Not so long's I keep my two eyes right plumb squa-ah pinted at ol' Jim. No, seh!" Peter began to chuckle in derision.

The two vagabonds stood before him while he informed them of their iniquities as well as their absurdities and, further, made clear his own masterly grasp of the spirit of their devices. Nothing affects children so much as rhetoric. It may not involve any definite presentation of common-sense but if it is picturesque, they surrender decently to its influence. Peter was by all means a rhetorician and it was not long before the two children had dismally succumbed to him. They went away.

Depositing the stove in the snow, they straightened to look at each other. It did not enter either head to relinquish the idea of continuing the game. But the situation seemed invulnerable.

The angel-child went on a scouting tour. Presently she returned flying. "I know. Let's have it in the cellar! In the cellar! Oh, it'll be lovely."

The outer door of the cellar was open and they proceeded down some steps with their treasure. There was plenty of light; the cellar was high-walled, warm and dry. They named it an ideal place. Two huge cylindrical furnaces were humming away, one at either end. Over-head, the beams detonated with the different emotions which agitated the tea-party.

Jimmie worked like a stoker and soon there was a fine bright fire in the stove. The fuel was of small brittle sticks which did not make a great deal of smoke.

"Now what'll we cook?" cried little Cora. "What'll we cook, Jim? We must have somethin' to cook, you know."

"Potatoes?" said Jimmie.

But the angel-child made a scornful gesture. "No; I've cooked 'bout a millyon potatoes, I guess. Potatoes aren't nice, anymore."

Jimmie's mind was all said and done when the question of potatoes had been passed and he looked weakly at his companion.

"Haven't you got any turnips in your house?" she enquired contemptuously. "In *my* house, we have *turnips*."

"Oh, turnips!" exclaimed Jimmie, immensely relieved to find that the honor of his family was safe. "Turnips? Oh, bushels an' bushels an' bushels! Out in the shed."

"Well, go an' get a whole lot," commanded the angel-child. "Go an' get a whole lot. Grea' big ones. *We* always have grea' big ones."

Jimmie went to the shed and kicked gently at a company of turnips which the frost had amalgamated. He made three journeys to and from the cellar, carrying always the very largest types from his father's store. Four of them filled the oven of little Cora's stove. This fact did not please her so they placed three rows of turnips on the hot-top. Then the angel-child, profoundly moved by an inspiration, suddenly cried out.

"Oh, Jimmie, let's play we're keepin' a hotel an' have got to cook for 'bout a thousand people an' those two furnaces will be the ovens an' I'll be the chief-cook—"

"No; I want to be chief-cook some of the time," interrupted Jimmie.

"No; I'll be chief-cook my own self. You must be my 'sistant. Now, I'll prepare 'm—see? An' then you put 'em in the ovens. Get the shovel. We'll play that's the pan. I'll fix 'em an' then you put 'em in the oven. Hold it still now."

Jim held the coal-shovel while little Cora with a frown of importance arranged turnips in rows upon it. She patted each one daintily and then backed away to view it with her head critically side-ways.

"There!" she shouted at last. "That'll do, I guess. Put 'em in the oven."

Jimmie marched with his shovelful of turnips to one of the furnaces. The door was already open and he slid the shovel in upon the red coals.

"Come on," cried little Cora. "I've got another batch nearly ready."

"But what am I goin' to do with these?" asked Jimmie. "There ain't only one shovel."

"Leave 'm in there," retorted the girl, passionately. "Leave 'm in there an' then play you're comin' with another pan. 'Tain't right to stand there an' *hold* the pan, you goose."

So Jimmie expelled all his turnips from his shovel out upon the furnace-fire and returned obediently for another batch.

"These are puddings," yelled the angel-child gleefully. "Dozens an' dozens of puddings for the thousand people at our grea' big hotel."

IV

At the first alarm, the painter had fled to the doctor's office where he hid his face behind a book and pretended that he did not hear the noise of feminine revelling. When the doctor came from a round of calls, he too retreated upon the office and the men consoled each other as well as they were able. Once Mrs. Trescott dashed in to say delightedly that her tea-party was not only the success of the season but it was probably the very nicest tea-party that had ever been held in Whilomville. After vainly beseeching them to return with her, she dashed away again, her face bright with happiness.

The doctor and the painter remained for a long time in silence, Trescott tapping reflectively upon the window-pane. Finally he turned to the painter, and sniffing, said: "What is that, Willis? Don't you smell something?"

The painter also sniffed. "Why, yes. It's like—it's like turnips."

"Turnips? No; it can't be."

"Well, it's very much like it."

The puzzled doctor opened the door into the hall and at first it appeared that he was going to give back two paces. A result of frizzling turnips which was almost as tangible as mist had blown in upon his face and made him gasp. "Good god, Willis, what can this be?" he cried.

"Whee," said the painter, "it's awful, isn't it?"

The doctor made his way hurriedly to his wife but before he could speak with her, he had to endure the business of greeting a score of women. Then he whispered: "Out in the hall, there's an awful—"

But at that moment it came to them on the wings of a sudden draft. The solemn odor of burning turnips rolled in like a sea-fog and fell upon that dainty perfumed tea-party. It was almost a personality; if some unbidden and extremely odious guest had entered the room the effect would have been much the same. The sprightly talk stopped with a jolt and people looked at each other. Then a few brave and considerate persons made the usual attempt to talk away as if nothing had happened. They all looked at their hostess who wore an air of stupefaction.

The odor of burning turnips grew and grew. To Trescott, it seemed to make a noise. He thought he could hear the dull roar of this out-rage. Under some circumstances, he might have been able to take the situation from a point-of-view of comedy but the agony of his wife was too acute and, for him, too visible. She was saying: "Yes, we saw the play the last time we were in New York. I liked it very much. That scene in the second act—the gloomy church, you know, and all that—and the organ playing—and then when the four singing little girls come in—" But Trescott comprehended that she did not know if she was talking of a play or a parachute.

He had not been in the room twenty seconds before his brow suddenly flushed with an angry inspiration. He left the room hastily, leaving behind him an incoherent phrase of apology, and charged upon his office where he found the painter somnolent.

"Willis," he cried sternly, "come with me. It's that damn kid of yours!"

The painter was immediately agitated. He always seemed to feel more than any one else in the world the peculiar ability of his child to create resounding excitement but he seemed always to exhibit his feelings very late. He arose hastily and hurried after Trescott to the top of the inside cellar-stairway. Trescott motioned him to pause and for an instant they listened.

"Hurry up, Jim," cried the busy little Cora. "Here's another whole batch of lovely puddings. Hurry up now an' put 'em in the oven."

Trescott looked at the painter; the painter groaned. Then they appeared violently in the middle of the great kitchen of the hotel with a thousand people in it. "Jimmie, go up stairs," said Trescott and then he turned to watch the painter deal with the angel-child.

With some imitation of wrath, the painter stalked to his daughter's side and grasped her by the arm.

"Oh, papa, papa," she screamed. "You're pinching me! You're pinching me! You're pinching me, papa!"

At first the painter had seemed resolved to keep his grip but suddenly he let go her arm in a panic. "I've hurt her," he said, turning to Trescott.

Trescott had swiftly done much toward the obliteration of the hotel kitchen but he looked up now and spoke after a short period of reflection. "You've hurt her, have you? Well, hurt her, again. Spank her!" he cried enthusiastically. "Spank her, confound you, man! She needs it. Here's your chance. Spank her and spank her good. Spank her!"

The painter naturally wavered over this incendiary proposition but at last in one supreme burst of daring, he shut his eyes and again grabbed his precious off-spring.

The spanking was lamentably the work of a perfect bungler. It couldn't have hurt at all but the angel-child raised to Heaven a loud clear soprano howl that expressed the last word in even medieval anguish. Soon the painter was aghast. "Stop it, darling! I didn't mean—I didn't mean to—to hurt you so much, you know." He danced, nervously. Trescott sat on a box and devilishly smiled.

But the pasture-call of suffering motherhood came down to them and, a moment later, a splendid apparition appeared on the cellar-stairs. She understood the scene in a glance. "Willis! What have you been doing?"

Trescott sat on his box, the painter guiltily moved from foot to foot, and the angel-child advanced to her mother with arms outstretched, making a piteous wail of amazed and pained pride that would have moved Peter the Great. Regardless of her frock, the panting mother knelt on the stone-floor and took her child to her bosom and looked, then, bitterly, scornfully, at the cowering father and husband.

The painter, for his part, at once looked reproachfully at Trescott as if to say: "There! You see?"

Trescott arose and extended his hands in a quiet but magnificent gesture of despair and weariness. He seemed about to say something classic and, quite instinctively, they waited. The stillness was deep and the wait was longer than a moment. "Well," he said, "we can't live in the cellar. Let's go up stairs."

X

THE TRIAL, EXECUTION, AND BURIAL
OF HOMER PHELPS

FROM time to time, an enwearied pine-bough let fall to the earth its load of melting snow and the branch swung back glistening in the faint wintry sun-light. Down the gulch a brook clattered amid its ice with the sound of a perpetual breaking of glass. All the forest looked drenched and forlorn.

The sky-line was a ragged enclosure of grey cliffs and hemlocks and pines. If one had been miraculously set down in this gulch one could have imagined easily that the nearest human habitation was hundreds of miles away if it were not for an old half-discernible wood-road that led toward the brook.

"Halt! Who's there?"

This low and gruff cry suddenly dispelled the stillness which lay upon the lonely gulch but the hush which followed it seemed even more profound. The hush endured for some seconds and then the voice of the challenger was again raised, this time with a distinctly querulous note in it.

"Halt! Who's there? Why don't you answer when I holler? Don't you know you're likely to get shot?"

A second voice answered: "Oh, you knew who I was, easy enough."

"That don't make no diff'rence." One of the Margate twins stepped from a thicket and confronted Homer Phelps on the old wood-road. The majestic scowl of official wrath was upon the brow of Reeves Margate; a long stick was held in the hollow of his arm as one would hold a rifle and he strode grimly to the other boy. "That don't make no diff'rence. You've got to answer when I holler, anyhow. Willie says so."

At the mention of the dread chieftain's name, the Phelps boy daunted a trifle but he still sulkily murmured: "Well, you knew it was me."

He started on his way through the snow but the twin sturdily blocked the path. "You can't pass less'n you give the counter-sign."

"Huh?" said the Phelps boy. "Counter-sign?"

"Yes—counter-sign," sneered the twin, strong in his sense of virtue.

But the Phelps boy became very angry. "Can't I, hey? Can't I, hey? I'll show you whether I can or not. I'll show you, Reeves Margate."

There was a short scuffle and then arose the anguished clamor of the sentry: "Hey, fellers! Here's a man tryin' to run a-past the guard. Hey, fellers! Hey!"

There was a great noise in the adjacent under-brush. The voice of Willie could be heard exhorting his followers to charge swiftly and bravely. Then they appeared—Willie Dalzel, Jimmie Trescott, the other Margate twin, and Dan Earl. The chieftain's face was dark with wrath. "What's the matter? Can't you play it right? Ain't you got any sense?" he asked the Phelps boy.

The sentry was yelling out his grievance. "Now—he come along an' I hollered at 'im, an' he didn't pay no 'tention an' when I ast 'im for the counter-sign, he wouldn't say nothin'. That ain't no way."

"Can't you play it right?" asked the chief again with gloomy scorn.

"He knew it was me, easy enough," said the Phelps boy.

"That ain't got nothin' to do with it," cried the chief furiously. "That ain't got nothin' to do with it. If you're goin' to play, you've got to play it right. It ain't no fun if you go spoilin' the whole thing this way. Can't you play it right?"

"I forgot the counter-sign," lied the culprit weakly.

Whereupon the remainder of the band yelled out with one triumphant voice: "War to the knife! War to the knife! I remember it, Willie. Don't I, Willie?"

The leader was puzzled. Evidently he was trying to develop in his mind a plan for dealing correctly with this unusual incident. He felt, no doubt, that he must proceed according to the books but unfortunately the books did not cover the point precisely. However he finally said to Homer Phelps: "You are under arrest." Then with a stentorian voice he shouted: "Seize him!"

His loyal followers looked startled for a brief moment but

directly they began to move upon the Phelps boy. The latter clearly did not intend to be seized. He backed away, expostulating wildly. He even seemed somewhat frightened. "No; no; don't you touch me, I tell you; don't you dare touch me."

The others did not seem anxious to engage. They moved slowly watching the desperate light in his eyes. The chieftain stood with folded arms, his face growing darker and darker with impatience. At length, he burst out: "Oh, seize him, I tell you! Why don't you seize him! Grab him by the leg, Dannie! Hurry up, all of you. Seize him, I keep a-sayin'."

Thus adjured, the Margate twins and Dan Earl made another pained effort while Jimmie Trescott manoeuvred to cut off a retreat. But, to tell the truth, there was boyish law which held them back from laying hands of violence upon little Phelps under these conditions. Perhaps it was because they were only playing whereas he now was undeniably serious. At any rate they looked very sick of their occupation.

"Don't you dare," snarled the Phelps boy, facing first one and then the other; he was almost in tears—"don't you dare touch me."

The chieftain was now hopping with exasperation. "Oh, seize him, can't you! You're no good at all." Then he loosed his wrath upon the Phelps boy: "Stand still, Homer, can't you? You've got to be seized, you know. That ain't the way. It ain't any fun if you keep a-dodgin' that way. Stand still, can't you? You've got to be seized."

"I don't *want* to be seized," retorted the Phelps boy, obstinate and bitter.

"But you've *got* to be seized," yelled the maddened chief. "Don't you see? That's the way to play it."

The Phelps boy answered promptly: "But I don't want to play that way."

"But that's the *right* way to play it. Don't you see? You've got to play it the right way. You've got to be seized an' then we'll hold a trial on you an'—an' all sorts of things."

But this prospect held no illusions for the Phelps boy. He continued doggedly to repeat: "I don't want to play that way."

Of course in the end the chief stooped to beg and beseech this unreasonable lad. "Oh, come on, Homer. Don't be so mean.

You're a-spoilin' everything. We won't hurt you any. Not the tintiest bit. It's all just playin'. What's the matter with you?"

The different tone of the leader made an immediate impression upon the other. He showed some signs of the beginning of weakness. "Well," he asked, "what you goin' to do?"

"Why, first we're goin' to put you in a dungeon or tie you to a stake or something like that—just pertend, you know," added the chief hurriedly, "an' then we'll hold a trial, awful solemn, but there won't be anything what'll hurt you. Not a thing."

And so the game was re-adjusted. The Phelps boy was marched off between Dan Earl and a Margate twin. The party proceeded to their camp which was hidden some hundred of feet back in the thickets. There was a miserable little hut with a pine-bark roof which so frankly and constantly leaked that existence in the open air was always preferable. At present it was noisily dripping melted snow into the black mouldy interior. In front of this hut, a feeble fire was flickering through its unhappy career. Under-foot, the watery snow was of the color of lead.

The party having arrived at the camp, the chief leaned against a tree and, balancing on one foot, drew off a rubber boot. From this boot, he emptied about a quart of snow. He squeezed his stocking which had a hole from which protruded a lobster-red toe. He resumed his boot. "Bring up the prisoner," said he. They did it. "Guilty or not guilty?" he asked.

"Huh?" said the Phelps boy.

"Guilty or not guilty?" demanded the chief peremptorily. "Guilty or not guilty? Don't you understand?"

Homer Phelps looked profoundly puzzled. " 'Guilty or not guilty'?" he asked slowly and weakly.

The chief made a swift gesture and turned in despair to the others. "Oh, he don't do it right. He does it all wrong." He again faced the prisoner with an air of making a last attempt. "Now, lookahere, Homer, when I say, 'Guilty or not guilty,' you want to up an' say, 'Not guilty.' Don't you see?"

"Not guilty," said Homer at once.

"No—no—no. Wait 'til I ask you. Now wait." He called out, pompously: "Pards, if this prisoner before us is guilty, what shall be his fate?"

All those well-trained little infants with one voice sung out: "*Death!*"

"Prisoner," continued the chief, "are you guilty or not guilty?"

"But, lookahere," argued Homer, "you said it wouldn't be nothin' what would hurt. I—"

"Thunder an' lightnin'," roared the wretched chief. "Keep your mouth shut, can't ye? What in the mischief—"

But there was an interruption from Jimmie Trescott who shouldered a twin aside and stepped to the front. "Here," he said very contemptuously, "let *me* be the prisoner. I'll show 'im how to do it."

"All right, Jim," cried the chief delighted. "You be the prisoner then. Now all you fellers with guns stand there in a row. Get out of the way, Homer." He cleared his throat and addressed Jimmie. "Prisoner, are you guilty or not guilty?"

"Not guilty," answered Jimmie firmly. Standing there before his judge—unarmed, slim, quiet, modest—he was ideal.

The chief beamed upon him and looked aside to cast a triumphant and withering glance upon Homer Phelps. He said: "There! That's the way to do it."

The twins and Dan Earl also much admired Jimmie.

"That's all right so far, anyhow," said the satisfied chief. "An' now we'll—now we'll—we'll perceed with the execution."

"That ain't right," said the new prisoner suddenly. "That ain't the next thing. You've got to have a trial first. You've got to fetch up a lot of people first who'll say I done it."

"That's so," said the chief. "I didn't think. Here, Reeves, you be first witness. Did the prisoner do it?"

The twin gulped for a moment in his anxiety to make the proper reply. He was at the point where the roads forked. Finally he hazarded, "Yes."

"There," said the chief, "that's one of 'em. Now, Dan, you be a witness. Did he do it?"

Dan Earl having before him the twin's example did not hesitate. "Yes," he said.

"Well, then, pards, what shall be his fate?"

Again came the ringing answer, "*Death!*"

With Jimmie in the principal role, this drama hidden deep in the hemlock thicket neared a kind of perfection. "You must blindfold me," cried the condemned lad briskly, "an' then I'll go off an' stand an' you must all get in a row an' shoot me."

The chief gave this plan his urbane countenance and the twins and Dan Earl were greatly pleased. They blindfolded Jimmie under his careful directions. He waded a few paces into snow and then turned and stood with quiet dignity, awaiting his fate. The chief marshalled the twins and Dan Earl in line with their sticks. He gave the necessary commands: "Load! Ready! Aim! Fire!" At the last command the firing party all together yelled, "Bang!"

Jimmie threw his hands high, tottered in agony for a moment and then crashed full length into the snow—into, one would think, a serious case of pneumonia. It was beautiful.

He arose almost immediately and came back to them wondrously pleased with himself. They acclaimed him joyously.

The chief was particularly grateful. He was always trying to bring off these little romantic affairs and it seemed, after all, that the only boy who could ever really help him was Jimmie Trescott. "There," he said to the others, "that's the way it ought to be done."

They were touched to the heart by the whole thing and they looked at Jimmie with big smiling eyes. Jimmie, blown out like a balloon-fish with pride of his performance, swaggered to the fire and took seat on some wet hemlock-boughs. "Fetch some more wood, one of you kids," he murmured negligently. One of the twins came fortunately upon a small cedar tree the lower branches of which were dead and dry. An armful of these branches flung upon the sick fire soon made a high, ruddy, warm blaze which was like an illumination in honor of Jimmie's success.

The boys sprawled about the fire and talked the regular language of the game. "Waal, pards," remarked the chief, "it's many a night we've had together here in the Rockies among the b'ars an' the Indy-uns, hey?"

"Yes, pard," replied Jimmie Trescott, "I reckon you're right. Our wild free life is—there ain't nothin' to compare with our wild free life."

Whereupon the two lads arose and magnificently shook hands

while the others watched them in an ecstasy. "I'll allus stick by ye, pard," said Jimmie earnestly. "When yer in trouble, don't forgit that Lightnin' Lou is at yer back."

"Thanky, pard," quoth Willie Dalzel deeply affected. "I'll not forgit it, pard. An' don't you forgit, either, that Dead-shot Demon, the leader of the Red Raiders, never forgits a friend."

But Homer Phelps was having none of this great fun. Since his disgraceful refusal to be seized and executed he had been hovering unheeded on the outskirts of the band. He seemed very sorry; he cast a wistful eye at the romantic scene. He knew too well that if he went near at that particular time he would be certain to encounter a pitiless snubbing. So he vacillated modestly in the background.

At last the moment came when he dared venture near enough to the fire to gain some warmth for he was now bitterly suffering with the cold. He sidled close to Willie Dalzel. No one heeded him. Eventually, he looked at his chief and with a bright face said, "Now—if I was seized now to be executed, I could do it as well as Jimmie Trescott, I could."

The chief gave a crow of scorn in which he was followed by the other boys. "Ho!" he cried, "why didn't you do it then? Why didn't you do it?" Homer Phelps felt upon him many pairs of disdainful eyes. He wagged his shoulders in misery.

"You're dead," said the chief frankly. "That's what you are. We executed you, we did."

"When?" demanded the Phelps boy with some spirit.

"Just a little while ago. Didn't we, fellers? Hey, fellers, didn't we?"

The trained chorus cried: "Yes, of course we did. You're dead, Homer. You can't play any more. You're dead."

"That wasn't me. It was Jimmie Trescott," he said in a low and bitter voice, his eyes on the ground. He would have given the world if he could have retracted his mad refusals of the early part of the drama.

"No," said the chief, "it was you. We're playin' it was you, an' it *was* you. You're dead, you are." And seeing the cruel effect of his words he did not refrain from administering some advice: "The next time, don't be such a chuckle-head."

Presently the camp imagined that it was attacked by Indians

and the boys dodged behind trees with their stick-rifles shouting out, "Bang!" and encouraging each other to resist until the last. In the meantime the dead lad hovered near the fire looking moodily at the gay and exciting scene. After the fight the gallant defenders returned one by one to the fire where they grandly clasped hands, calling each other "old pard," and boasting of their deeds.

Parenthetically, one of the twins had an unfortunate inspiration. "I killed the Indy-un chief, fellers. Did you see me kill the Indy-un chief?"

But Willie Dalzel, his own chief, turned upon him wrathfully: "*You* didn't kill no chief. *I* killed 'im with me own hand."

"Oh!" said the twin, apologetically, at once. "It must have been some other Indy-un."

"Who's wounded?" cried Willie Dalzel. "Ain't anybody wounded?" The party professed themselves well and sound. The roving and inventive eye of the chief chanced upon Homer Phelps. "Ho! Here's a dead man! Come on, fellers, here's a dead man! We've got to bury him, you know." And at his bidding they pounced upon the dead Phelps lad. The unhappy boy saw clearly his road to rehabilitation but mind and body revolted at the idea of burial even as they had revolted at the thought of execution. "No!" he said stubbornly. "No! I don't want to be buried! I don't want to be buried!"

"You've *got* to be buried!" yelled the chief passionately. "'Tain' goin' to hurt ye, is it? Think you're made of glass? Come on, fellers, get the grave ready!"

They scattered hemlock-boughs upon the snow in the form of a rectangle and piled other boughs near at hand. The victim surveyed these preparations with a glassy eye. When all was ready, the chief turned determinedly to him: "Come on now, Homer. We've got to carry you to the grave. Get him by the legs, Jim!"

Little Phelps had now passed into that state which may be described as a curious and temporary childish fatalism. He still objected but it was only feeble muttering as if he did not know what he spoke. In some confusion they carried him to the rectangle of hemlock-boughs and dropped him. Then they piled other boughs upon him until he was not to be seen. The chief stepped forward to make a short address but before proceeding with it he thought it expedient, from certain indications, to speak to the grave itself. "Lie still, can't ye? Lie still until I get through." There was a faint movement of the boughs and then a perfect silence.

The chief took off his hat. Those who watched him could see that his face was harrowed with emotion. "Pards," he began brokenly—"pards, we've got one more debt to pay them murderin' red-skins. Bowie-knife Joe was a brave man an' a good pard but—he's gone now—gone." He paused for a moment, overcome, and the stillness was only broken by the deep manly grief of Jimmie Trescott.

XI

THE FIGHT

I

THE child life of the neighborhood was sometimes moved in its deeps at the sight of wagon-loads of furniture arriving in front of some house which with closed blinds and barred doors had been for a time a mystery or even a fear. The boys often expressed this fear by stamping bravely and noisily on the porch of the house and then suddenly darting away with screams of nervous laughter as if they expected to be pursued by something uncanny. There was a group who held that the cellar of a vacant house was certainly the abode of robbers, smugglers, assassins, mysterious masked men in council about the dim rays of a candle and possessing skulls, emblematic bloody daggers, and owls. Then, near the first of April, would come along a wagon-load of furniture and children would assemble on the walk by the gate and make serious examination of everything that passed into the house and taking no thought whatever of masked men.

One day, it was announced in the neighborhood that a family was actually moving into the Hannigan house, next door to Doctor Trescott's. Jimmie was one of the first to be informed and by the time some of his friends came dashing up, he was versed in much.

"Any boys?" they demanded eagerly.

"Yes," answered Jimmie proudly. "One's a little feller and one's 'most as big as me. I saw 'em, I did."

"Where are they?" asked Willie Dalzel as if under the circumstances he could not take Jimmie's word but must have the evidence of his senses.

"Oh, they're in there," said Jimmie carelessly. It was evident he owned these new boys.

Willie Dalzel resented Jimmie's proprietary way. "Ho," he

cried scornfully. "Why don't they come out then? Why don't they come out?"

"How'd I know?" said Jimmie.

"Well," retorted Willie Dalzel, "you seemed to know so thundering much about 'em."

At the moment, a boy came strolling down the gravel walk which led from the front door to the gate. He was about the height and age of Jimmie Trescott but he was thick through the chest and had fat legs. His face was round and rosy and plump but his hair was curly black and his brows were naturally darkling so that he resembled both a pudding and a young bull.

He approached slowly the group of older inhabitants and they had grown profoundly silent. They looked him over; he looked them over. They might have been savages observing the first white man or white men observing the first savage. The silence held steady.

As he neared the gate, the strange boy wandered off to the left in a definite way which proved his instinct to make a circular voyage when in doubt. The motionless group stared at him. In time, this unsmiling scrutiny worked upon him somewhat and he leaned against the fence and fastidiously examined one shoe.

In the end, Willie Dalzel authoritatively broke the stillness. "What's your name?" said he gruffly.

"Johnnie Hedge, 'tis," answered the new boy. Then came another great silence while Whilomville pondered this intelligence.

Again came the voice of authority—"Where'd you live b'fore?"

"Jersey City."

These two sentences completed the first section of the formal code. The second section concerned itself with the establishment of the newcomer's exact position in the neighborhood.

"I kin lick you," announced Willie Dalzel and awaited the answer.

The Hedge boy had stared at Willie Dalzel but he stared at him again. After a pause he said: "I know you kin."

"Well," demanded Willie, "kin *he* lick you?" And he indicated

Jimmie Trescott with a sweep which announced plainly that Jimmie was the next in prowess.

Whereupon the new boy looked at Jimmie respectfully but carefully and at length said: "I dunno."

This was the signal for an outburst of shrill screaming and everybody pushed Jimmie forward. He knew what he had to say and as befitted the occasion he said it fiercely. "Kin you lick me?"

The new boy also understood what he had to say and, despite his unhappy and lonely state, he said it bravely. "Yes."

"Well," retorted Jimmie bluntly, "come out and do it then! Jest come out and do it!" And these words were greeted with cheers. These little rascals yelled that there should be a fight at once. They were in bliss over the prospect. "Go on, Jim! Make 'im come out. He said he could lick you! Aw-aw-aw! He said he could lick you!" There probably never was a fight among this class in Whilomville which was not the result of the goading and guying of two proud lads by a populace of urchins who simply wished to see a show.

Willie Dalzel was very busy. He turned first to the one and then to the other. "You said you could lick him. Well, why don't you come out and do it then? You said you could lick him, didn't you?"

"Yes," answered the new boy, dogged and dubious.

Willie tried to drag Jimmie by the arm. "Aw, go on, Jimmie. You ain't afraid, are you?"

"No," said Jimmie.

The two victims opened wide eyes at each other. The fence separated them and so it was impossible for them to immediately engage but they seemed to understand that they were ultimately to be sacrificed to the ferocious aspirations of the other boys and each scanned the other to learn something of his spirit. They were not angry at all. They were merely two little gladiators who were being clamorously told to hurt each other. Each displayed hesitation and doubt without displaying fear. They did not exactly understand what were their feelings and they moodily kicked the ground and made low and sullen answers to Willie Dalzel who worked like a circus-manager.

"Aw, go on, Jim! What's the matter with you? You ain't afraid, are you? Well, then, say something." This sentiment received more cheering from the abandoned little wretches who wished to be entertained and in this cheering there could be heard notes of derision of Jimmie Trescott. The latter had a position to sustain; he was well-known; he often bragged of his willingness and ability to thrash other boys; well, then, here was a boy of his size who said that he could not thrash him. What was he going to do about it? The crowd made these arguments very clear and repeated them again and again.

Finally Jimmie, driven to aggression, walked close to the fence and said to the new boy, "The first time I catch you out of your own yard, I'll lam the head off'n you." This was received with wild plaudits by the Whilomville urchins.

But the new boy stepped back from the fence. He was awed by Jimmie's formidable mien. But he managed to get out a semi-defiant sentence. "Maybe you will and maybe you won't," said he.

However, his short retreat was taken as a practical victory for Jimmie and the boys hooted him bitterly. He remained inside the fence, swinging one foot and scowling while Jimmie was escorted off down the street amid acclamations. The new boy turned and walked back toward the house, his face gloomy, lined deep with discouragement, as if he felt that the new environment's antagonism and palpable cruelty were sure to prove too much for him.

II

The mother of Johnnie Hedge was a widow and the chief theory of her life was that her boy should be in school on the greatest possible number of days. He himself had no sympathy with this ambition but she detected the truth of his diseases with an unerring eye and he was required to be really ill before he could win the right to disregard the first bell, morning and noon. The chicken-pox and the mumps had given him vacations—vacations of misery, wherein he nearly died between pain and nursing. But bad colds in the head did nothing for him and he was not able to invent a satisfactory hacking cough. His mother was not consistently a tartar. In most things he swayed her to his will. He was allowed to have more jam, pickles and pie than most boys; she respected his profound loathing of Sunday-School; on summer evenings he could remain out of doors until 8.30; but in this matter of school she was inexorable. This single point in her character was of steel.

The Hedges arrived in Whilomville on a Saturday and on the following Monday Johnnie wended his way to school with a note to the principal and his Jersey City school-books. He knew perfectly well that he would be told to buy new and different books but in those days mothers always had an idea that old books would "do" and they invariably sent boys off to a new school with books which would not meet the selected and unchangeable views of the new administration. The old books never would "do." Then the boys brought them home to annoyed mothers and asked for ninety cents or sixty cents or eighty-five cents or some number of cents for another out-fit. In the garret of every house holding a large family there was a collection of effete school-books with Mother rebellious because James could not inherit his books from Paul who should properly be Peter's heir while Peter should be a beneficiary under Henry's will.

But the matter of the books was not the measure of Johnnie Hedge's unhappiness. This whole business of changing schools was a complete torture. Alone, he had to go among a new people, a new tribe, and he apprehended his serious time. There were only two fates for him. One meant victory. One meant a kind of serfdom in which he would subscribe to every word of some superior boy and support his every word. It was not anything like an English system of fagging because boys invariably drifted into the figurative service of other boys whom they devotedly admired and if they were obliged to subscribe to everything, it is true that they would have done so freely in any case. One means to suggest that Johnnie Hedge had to find his place. Willie Dalzel was a type of the little chieftain and Willie was a master but he was not a bully in a special physical sense. He did not drag little boys by the ears until they cried nor make them tearfully fetch and carry for him. They fetched and carried but it was because of their worship of his prowess and genius. And so all through the strata of boy life were chieftains and sub-chieftains and assistant-sub-chieftains. There was no question of little Hedge being towed about by the nose; it was, as one has said, that he had to find his place in a new school. And this in itself was a problem which awed his boyish heart. He was a stranger cast away upon the moon. None knew him, understood him, felt for him. He would be surrounded for this initiative time by a horde of jackal-creatures who might turn out in the end to be little boys like himself but this last point his philosophy could not understand in its fullness.

He came to a white meeting-house sort of a place in the squat tower of which a great bell was clanging impressively. He passed through an iron gate into a play-ground worn bare as the bed of a mountain brook by the endless runnings and scufflings of little children. There was still a half-hour before the final clangor in the squat tower but the play-ground held a number of frolicsome imps. A loitering boy espied Johnnie Hedge, and he howled: "Oh, oh! Here's a new feller! Here's a new feller!" He advanced upon the strange arrival. "What's your name?" he demanded belligerently, like a particularly offensive custom-house officer.

"Johnnie Hedge," responded the new-comer shyly.

This name struck the other boy as being very comic. All new names strike boys as being comic. He laughed noisily. "Oh, fellers, he says his name is Johnnie Hedge! Haw-haw-haw."

The new boy felt that his name was the most disgraceful thing which had ever been attached to a human being.

"Johnnie Hedge! Haw-haw! What room you in?" said the other lad.

"I dunno," said Johnnie. In the meantime a small flock of interested vultures had gathered about him. The main thing was his absolute strangeness. He even would have welcomed the sight of his tormentors of Saturday; he had seen them before at least. These creatures were only so many incomprehensible problems. He diffidently began to make his way toward the main door of the school and the other boys followed him. They demanded information.

"Are you through subtraction yet? We study jogerfre—did you, ever? You live here now? You goin' to school here now?"

To many questions he made answer as well as the clamor would permit and at length he reached the main door and went quaking unto his new kings. As befitted them, the rabble stopped at the door. A teacher strolling along a corridor found a small boy holding in his hand a note. The boy palpably did not know what to do with the note but the teacher knew and took it. Thereafter this little boy was in harness.

A splendid lady in gorgeous robes gave him a seat at a double desk in the end of which sat a hoodlum with grimy finger-nails who eyed the inauguration with an extreme and personal curiosity. The other desks were gradually occupied by children who first were told of the new boy and then turned upon him a speculative and somewhat derisive eye. The school opened; little classes went forward to a position in front of the teacher's platform and tried to explain that they knew something. The new boy was not requisitioned a great deal; he was allowed to lie dormant until he became used to the scenes and until the teacher found, approximately, his mental position. In the meantime, he suffered a shower of stares and whispers and giggles as if he were a man-ape, whereas he was precisely like other children. From time to time, he made funny and pathetic little overtures to other boys but these overtures could not yet be received; he was not known; he was a foreigner. The village school was like a nation. It was tight. Its amiability or friendship must be won in certain ways.

At recess he hovered in the school-room around the weak lights of society and around the teacher in the hope that somebody might be good to him but none considered him save as some sort of a specimen. The teacher of course had a secondary interest in the fact that he was an additional one to a class of sixty-three.

At twelve o'clock, when the ordered files of boys and girls marched toward the door, he exhibited—to no eye—the tremblings of a coward in a charge. He exaggerated the lawlessness of the play-ground and the street.

But the reality was hard enough. A shout greeted him. "Oh, here's the new feller! Here's the new feller!" Small and utterly obscure boys teased him. He had a hard time of it to get to the gate. There never was any actual hurt but everything was competent to smite the lad with shame; it was a curious, groundless shame but nevertheless it was shame. He was a newcomer and he definitely felt the disgrace of the fact.

In the street he was seen and recognized by some lads who had formed part of the group of Saturday. They shouted: "Oh, Jimmie! Jimmie! Here he is! Here's that new feller!"

Jimmie Trescott was going virtuously toward his luncheon when he heard these cries behind him. He pretended not to hear and in this deception he was assisted by the fact that he was engaged at the time in a furious argument with a friend over the relative merits of two Uncle Tom's Cabin companies. It appeared that one company had only two blood-hounds while the other had ten. On the other hand, the first company had two Topsys and two Uncle Toms while the second had only one Topsy and one Uncle Tom.

But the shouting little boys were hard after him. Finally they were even pulling at his arms.

"Jimmie—"

"What?" he demanded turning with a snarl. "What d'you want? Leggo my arm."

"Here he is! Here's the new feller! Here's the new feller! Now!"

"I don't care if he is," said Jimmie with grand impatience. He tilted his chin. "I don't care if he is."

Then they reviled him. "Thought you was goin' to lick him first time you caught him. Yah! You're a 'fraid-cat!" They began to sing: " 'Fraid-cat! 'Fraid-cat! 'Fraid-cat!" He expostulated hotly, turning from one to the other, but they would not listen. In the meantime the Hedge boy slunk on his way, looking with deep anxiety upon this attempt to send Jimmie against him. But Jimmie would have none of the plan.

III

When the children met again on the play-ground, Jimmie was openly challenged with cowardice. He had made a big threat in the hearing of comrades and when invited by them to take advantage of an opportunity, he had refused. They had been fairly sure of their amusement and they were indignant. Jimmie was finally driven to declare that as soon as school was out for the day, he would thrash the Hedge boy.

When finally the children came rushing out of the iron gate, filled with the delights of freedom, a hundred boys surrounded

Jimmie in high spirits for he had said that he was determined. They waited for the lone lad from Jersey City. When he appeared, Jimmie wasted no time. He walked straight to him and said: "Did you say you kin lick me?"

Johnnie Hedge was cowed, shrinking, affrighted, and the roars of a hundred boys thundered in his ears but again he knew what he had to say. "Yes," he gasped in anguish.

"Then," said Jimmie resolutely, "you've got to fight." There was a joyous clamor by the mob. The beleaguered lad looked this way and that way for succor as Willie Dalzel and other officious youngsters policed an irregular circle in the crowd. He saw Jimmie facing him; there was no help for it; he dropped his books— the old books which would not "do."

Now it was the fashion among tiny Whilomville belligerents to fight much in the manner of little bear-cubs. Two boys would rush upon each other, immediately grapple and—the best boy having probably succeeded in getting the coveted "under-hold" —there would presently be a crash to the earth of the inferior boy and he would be probably mopped around in the dust or the mud or the snow or whatever the material happened to be, until the engagement was over. Whatever havoc was dealt out to him was ordinarily the result of his wild endeavors to throw off his opponent and arise. Both infants wept during the fight, as a common thing, and if they wept very hard, the fight was a harder fight. The result was never very bloody but the complete dishevelment of both victor and vanquished was extraordinary. As for the spectacle, it more resembled a collision of boys in a fog than it did the manly art of hammering another human being into speechless inability.

The fight began when Jimmie made a mad bear-cub rush at the new boy amid savage cries of encouragement. Willie Dalzel, for instance, almost howled his head off. Very timid boys on the outskirts of the throng felt their hearts leap to their throats. It was a time when certain natures were impressed that only man is vile.

But it appeared that bear-cub rushing was no part of the instruction received by boys in Jersey City. Boys in Jersey City were apparently schooled curiously. Upon the onslaught of Jimmie, the stranger had gone wild with rage—boy-like. Some spark had touched his fighting blood and in a moment he was a cornered, desperate, fire-eyed little man. He began to swing his arms, to revolve them so swiftly that one might have considered him a small working model of an extra-fine patented wind-mill which was caught in a gale. For a moment, this defense surprised Jimmie more than it damaged him but, two moments later, a small knotty fist caught him squarely in the eye and with a shriek he went down in defeat. He lay on the ground so stunned that he could not even cry; but if he had been able to cry he would have cried over his prestige—or something—not over his eye.

There was a dreadful tumult. The boys cast glances of amazement and terror upon the victor and thronged upon the beaten Jimmie Trescott. It was a moment of excitement so intense that one cannot say what happened. Never before had Whilomville seen such a thing—not the little tots. They were aghast, dumbfounded, and they glanced often over their shoulders at the new boy who stood alone, his clenched fists at his side, his face crimson, his lips still working with the fury of battle.

But there was another surprise for Whilomville. It might have been seen that the little victor was silently debating against an impulse. But the impulse won, for the lone lad from Jersey City suddenly wheeled, sprang like a demon and struck another boy.

A curtain should be drawn before this deed. A knowledge of it is really too much for the heart to bear. The other boy was Willie Dalzel. The lone lad from Jersey City had smitten him full sore.

There is little to say of it. It must have been that a feeling worked gradually to the top of the little stranger's wrath that Jimmie Trescott had been a mere tool, that the front and centre of his persecutors had been Willie Dalzel, and being rendered temporarily lawless by his fighting blood, he raised his hand and smote for revenge.

Willie Dalzel had been in the middle of a vandal's cry which screeched out over the voices of everybody. The new boy's fist cut it in half, so to say. And then arose the howl of an amazed and terrorized walrus.

One wishes to draw a second curtain. Without discussion, or enquiry or brief retort, Willie Dalzel ran away. He ran like a hare, straight for home, this redoubtable chieftain. Following him at a heavy and slow pace, ran the impassioned new boy. The scene was long remembered.

Willie Dalzel was no coward; he had been panic-stricken into running away from a new thing. He ran as a man might run from the sudden appearance of a vampire or a ghoul or a gorilla. This was no time for academics—he ran.

Jimmie slowly gathered himself and came to his feet. "Where's Willie?" said he first of all. The crowd sniggered. "Where's Willie?" said Jimmie again.

"Why he licked him, *too*," answered a boy suddenly.

"He did?" said Jimmie. He sat weakly down on the road-way. "He did?" After allowing a moment for the fact to sink into him, he looked up at the crowd with his one good eye and his one bunged eye, and smiled cheerfully.

XII

THE CITY URCHIN AND THE CHASTE
VILLAGERS

AFTER the brief encounters between the Hedge boy and
Jimmie Trescott and the Hedge boy and Willie Dalzel,
the neighborhood which contained the homes of the boys
was, as far as child life is concerned, in a state resembling an-
archy. This was owing to the signal over-throw and shameful
retreat of the boy who had for several years led a certain little
clan by the nose. The adherence of the little community did not
go necessarily to the boy who could whip all the others but it
certainly could not go to a boy who had run away in a manner
that made his shame patent to the whole world. Willie Dalzel
found himself in a painful position. This tiny tribe which had
followed him with such unwavering faith, was now largely engaged in whistling and cat-calling and hooting. He chased a
number of them into the sanctity of their own yards but from
these coigns they continued to ridicule him.

But it must not be supposed that the fickle tribe went over in a
body to the new light. They did nothing of the sort. They occupied themselves with avenging all which they had endured—
gladly enough, too—for many months. As for the Hedge boy, he
maintained a curious timid reserve, minding his own business
with extreme care and going to school with that deadly punctu-
ality of which his mother was the genius. Jimmie Trescott suffered no adverse criticism from his fellows. He was entitled to be
beaten by a boy who had made Willie Dalzel bellow like a bull-
calf and run away. Indeed he received some honors. He had
confronted a very superior boy and received a bang in the eye
which for a time was the wonder of the children and he had not
bellowed like a bull-calf. As a matter of fact, he was often invited
to tell how it had felt and this he did with some pride, claiming
arrogantly that he had been superior to any particular pain.

Early in the episode he and the Hedge boy had patched up a

treaty. Living next door to each other, they could not fail to have each other often in sight. One afternoon they wandered together in the strange indefinite diplomacy of boy-hood. As they drew close the new boy suddenly said: "Napple?"

"Yes," said Jimmie and the new boy bestowed upon him an apple. It was one of those green-coated winter apples which lie for many months in safe and dry places and can at any time be brought forth for the persecution of the unwary and inexperienced. An older age would have fled from this apple but to the unguided youth of Jimmie Trescott it was a thing to be possessed and cherished. Wherefore this apple was the emblem of something more than a truce despite the fact that it tasted like wet Indian-meal. And Jimmie looked at the Hedge boy out of one good eye and one bunged eye. The long-drawn animosities of men have no place in the life of a boy. The boy's mind is flexible; he readjusts his position with an ease which is derived from the fact—simply—that he is not yet a man.

But there were other and more important matters. Johnnie Hedge's exploits had brought him into such prominence among the school-boys that it was necessary to settle a number of points once and for all. There was the usual number of boys in the school who were popularly known to be champions in their various classes. Among these Johnnie Hedge now had to thread his way, every boy taking it upon himself to feel anxious that Johnnie's exact position should be soon established. His fame as a fighter had gone forth to the world but there were other boys who had fame as fighters and the world was extremely anxious to know where to place the newcomer. Various heroes were urged to attempt this classification. Usually it is not accounted a matter of supreme importance but in this boy life it was essential.

In all cases the heroes were backward enough. It was their followings who agitated the question. And so Johnnie Hedge was more or less beset.

He maintained his bashfulness. He backed away from altercation. It was plain that to bring matters to a point he must be forced into a quarrel. It was also plain that the proper person for the business was some boy who could whip Willie Dalzel and these formidable warriors were distinctly averse to undertaking the new contract. It is a kind of a law in boy life that a quiet, decent, peace-loving lad is able to thrash a wide-mouthed talker. And so it had transpired that by a peculiar system of elimination most of the real chiefs were quiet, decent, peace-loving boys and they had no desire to engage in a fight with a boy on the sole grounds that it was not known who could whip. Johnnie Hedge attended his affairs; they attended their affairs; and around them waged this discussion of relative merit. Jimmie Trescott took a prominent part in these arguments. He contended that Johnnie Hedge could thrash any boy in the world. He was certain of it and to any one who opposed him he said: "You just get one of those smashes in the eye and then you'll see." In the meantime there was a grand and impressive silence in the direction of Willie Dalzel. He had gathered remnants of his clan but the main parts of his sovereignty were scattered to the winds. He was an enemy.

Owing to the circumspect behavior of the new boy, the commotions on the school-grounds came to nothing. He was often asked: "Kin you lick him?" And he invariably replied: "I dunno." This idea of waging battle with the entire world appalled him.

A war for complete supremacy of the tribe which had been headed by Willie Dalzel was fought out in the country of the tribe. It came to pass that a certain half-dime blood-and-thunder pamphlet had a great vogue in the tribe at this particular time. This story relates the experience of a lad who began his career as cabin-boy on a pirate-ship. Throughout the first fifteen chapters, he was rope's-ended from one end of the ship to the other end and very often he was felled to the deck by a heavy fist. He lived through enough hardships to have killed a battalion of Turkish soldiers, but in the end he rose upon them. Yes, he rose upon them. Hordes of pirates fell before his intrepid arm and in the last chapters of the book he is seen jauntily careering on his own hook as one of the most gallows pirate-captains that ever sailed the seas.

Naturally when this tale was thoroughly understood by the tribe, they had to dramatize it although it was a dramatization that would gain no royalties for the author. Now it was plain that the urchin who was cast for the cabin-boy's part would lead a life throughout the first fifteen chapters which would attract few actors. Willie Dalzel developed a scheme by which some small lad would play cabin-boy during this period of misfortune and abuse and then when the cabin-boy came to the part where he slew all his enemies and reached his zenith that he, Willie Dalzel, should take the part.

This fugitive and disconnected rendering of a great play opened in Jimmie Trescott's back garden. The path between the two lines of gooseberry-bushes was elected unanimously to be the ship. Then Willie Dalzel insisted that Homer Phelps should be the cabin-boy. Homer tried the position for a time and then elected that he would resign in favor of some other victim. There was no other applicant to succeed him. Whereupon it became necessary to press some boy. Jimmie Trescott was a great actor as is well known, but he steadfastly refused to engage for the part. Ultimately they seized upon little Dan Earl whose disposition was so milky and docile that he would do whatever anybody asked of him. But Dan Earl made the one firm revolt of his life after trying existence as cabin-boy for some ten minutes. Willie Dalzel was in despair. Then he suddenly sighted the little brother of Johnnie Hedge who had come into the garden and in a poor-little-stranger sort of a fashion was looking wistfully at the play. When he was invited to become the cabin-boy he accepted joyfully thinking that it was his initiation into the tribe. Then they proceeded to give him the rope's-end and to punch him with a realism which was not altogether painless. Directly he began to cry out. They exhorted him not to cry out, not to mind it, but still they continued to hurt him.

There was a commotion among the gooseberry-bushes, two branches were swept aside and Johnnie Hedge walked down upon them. Every boy stopped in his tracks. Johnnie was boiling with rage. "Who hurt him?" he said ferociously. "Did *you*?" He had looked at Willie Dalzel.

Willie Dalzel began to mumble. "We was on'y playin'. Wasn't nothin' fer him to cry fer."

The new boy had at his command some big phrases and he used them. "I am goin' to whip you within an inch of your life. I am goin' to tan the hide off'n you." And immediately there was a mixture—an infusion of two boys which looked as if it had been done by a chemist. The other children stood back, stricken with horror. But out of this whirl they presently perceived the figure of Willie Dalzel seated upon the chest of the Hedge boy.

"Got enough?" asked Willie hoarsely.

"No," choked out the Hedge boy. Then there was another flapping and floundering and finally another calm.

"Got enough?" asked Willie.

"No," said the Hedge boy. A sort of a war-cloud again puzzled the sight of the observers. Both combatants were breathless, bloodless in their faces, and very weak.

"Got enough?" said Willie.

"No," said the Hedge boy. The carnage was again renewed. All the spectators were silent but Johnnie Hedge's little brother who shrilly exhorted him to continue the struggle. But it was not plain that the Hedge boy needed any encouragement for he was crying bitterly and it has been explained that when a boy cried it was a bad time to hope for peace. He had managed to wriggle over upon his hands and knees. But Willie Dalzel was tenaciously gripping him from the back and it seemed that his strength would spend itself in futility. The bear-cub seemed to have the advantage of the working model of the wind-mill. They heaved; uttered strange words; wept; and the sun looked down upon them with steady, unwinking eye.

Peter Washington came out of the stable and observed this tragedy of the back garden. He stood transfixed for a moment and then ran toward it, shouting: "Hi! What's all dish yere? Hi! Stopper dat, stopper dat, you two! For lan' sake, what's all dish yere?" He grabbed the struggling boys and pulled them apart. He was stormy and fine in his indignation. "For lan' sake! You two kids act like you gwine mad-dogs. Stopper dat." The whitened, tearful, soiled combatants, their clothing all awry, glared fiercely at each other as Peter stood between them, lecturing. They made several futile attempts to circumvent him and again come to battle. As he fended them off with his open hands he delivered his reproaches at Jimmie. "I'se s'prised at *you!* I suhtainly is!"

"Why?" said Jimmie. "I ain't done nothin'. What have I done?"

"Y-y-you done 'courage dese yere kids ter scrap," said Peter virtuously.

"Me!" cried Jimmie. "I ain't had nothin' to do with it."

"I raikon you ain't," retorted Peter with heavy sarcasm. "I

raikon you been er-prayin', ain't you?" Turning to Willie Dalzel, he said: "You jest take an' run erlong outer dish yere or I'll jest nachually take an' damnearkill you." Willie Dalzel went. To the new boy, Peter said: "You look like you had some saince but I raikon you don't know no more'n er rabbit. You jest take an' trot erlong off home an' don' lemme caitch you round yere er-fightin' or I'll break yer back." The Hedge boy moved away with dignity followed by his little brother. The latter when he had placed a sufficient distance between himself and Peter, played his fingers at his nose and called out: "Nig-ger-r-r! Nig-ger-r-r!"

Peter Washington's resentment poured out upon Jimmie. " 'Pears like you never would unnerstan' you ain't reg'lar common trash. You take an' 'sociate with an'body what done come erlong."

"Aw, go on," retorted Jimmie profanely. "Go soak your head, Pete."

The remaining boys retired to the street whereupon they perceived Willie Dalzel in the distance. He ran to them. "I licked him!" he shouted exultantly, "I licked him! Didn't I, now?"

From the Whilomville point of view, he was entitled to a favorable answer. They made it. "Yes," they said, "you did."

"I run in," cried Willie, "an' I grabbed 'im an' afore he knew what it was, I throwed 'im. An' then it was easy." He puffed out his chest and smiled like an English recruiting serjeant. "An' now," said he, suddenly facing Jimmie Trescott, "whose side were you on?"

The question was direct and startling. Jimmie gave back two paces. "He licked you once," he explained haltingly.

"He never saw the day when he could lick one side of me. I could lick him with my left hand tied behind me. Why, I could lick him when I was asleep." Willie Dalzel was magnificent.

A gate clicked and Johnnie Hedge was seen to be strolling toward them.

"You said," he remarked coldly, "you licked me, didn't you?"

Willie Dalzel stood his ground. "Yes," he said stoutly.

"Well, you're a liar," said the Hedge boy.

"You're another," retorted Willie.

"No, I ain't, either, but *you're* a liar."

"You're another," retorted Willie.

"Don't you dare tell *me* I'm a liar or I'll smack your mouth for you," said the Hedge boy.

"Well, I did, didn't I?" barked Willie. "An' whatche goin' to do about it?"

"I'm goin' to lam you," said the Hedge boy.

He approached to attack warily and the other boys held their breaths. Willie Dalzel winced back a pace. "Hol' on a minute," he cried, raising his palm. "I'm not—"

But the comic wind-mill was again in motion and between gasps from his exertions, Johnnie Hedge remarked: "I'll show— you—whether—you kin—lick me—or not."

The first blows did not reach home on Willie for he backed away with expedition keeping up his futile cry: "Hol' on a minute." Soon enough, a swinging fist landed on his cheek. It did not knock him down but it hurt him a little and frightened him a great deal. He suddenly opened his mouth to an amazing and startling extent, tilted back his head, and howled, while his eyes, glittering with tears, were fixed upon this scowling butcher of a Johnnie Hedge. The latter was making slow and vicious circles evidently intending to renew the massacre.

But the spectators really had been desolated and shocked by the terrible thing which had happened to Willie Dalzel. They now cried out: "No, no, don't hit 'im anymore! Don't hit 'im anymore!"

Jimmie Trescott, in a panic of bravery, yelled: "We'll all jump on you if you do."

The Hedge boy paused, at bay. He breathed angrily and flashed his glance from lad to lad. They still protested: "No, no, don't hit 'im anymore! Don't hit 'im no more."

"I'll hammer him until he can't stand up," said Johnnie observing that they all feared him. "I'll fix him so he won't know hisself an' if any of you kids bother with *me*—"

Suddenly he ceased, he trembled, he collapsed. The hand of one approaching from behind had laid hold upon his ear and it was the hand of one whom he knew.

The other lads heard a loud iron-filing voice say: "Caught ye at it again, ye brat, ye!" They saw a dreadful woman with grey hair, with a sharp red nose, with bare arms, with spectacles of such magnifying quality that her eyes shone through them like two fierce white moons. She was Johnnie Hedge's mother. Still holding Johnnie by the ear, she swung out swiftly and dexterously and succeeded in boxing the ears of two boys before the crowd regained its presence of mind and stampeded. Yes; the war for supremacy was over and the question was never again disputed. The supreme power was Mrs. Hedge.

XIII

A LITTLE PILGRIM

ONE November it became clear to childish minds in certain parts of Whilomville that the Sunday-School of the Presbyterian Church would not have for the children the usual Tree on Christmas Eve. The funds free for that ancient festival would be used for the relief of suffering among the victims of the Charleston earth-quake.

The plan had been born in the generous head of the superintendent of the Sunday-School and during one session he had made a strong plea that the children should forego the vain pleasures of a Tree and, in a glorious application of the Golden Rule, refuse a local use of the fund and will that it be sent where dire distress might be alleviated. At the end of a tearfully eloquent speech the question was put fairly to a vote and the children in a burst of virtuous abandon carried the question for Charleston. Many of the teachers had been careful to preserve a finely neutral attitude but even if they had cautioned the children against being too impetuous they could not have checked the wild impulses.

But this was a long time before Christmas.

Very early, boys held important speech together. "Huh; you ain't goin' to have no Christmas tree at the Presperterian Sunday-School."

Sullenly the victims answered, "No, we ain't."

"Huh," scoffed the other denominations, "we are goin' to have the all-firedest biggest tree that ever you saw in the world."

The little Presbyterians were greatly down-cast.

It happened that Jimmie Trescott had regularly attended the Presbyterian Sunday-School. The Trescotts were consistently undenominational but they had sent their lad on Sundays to one of the places where they thought he would receive benefits. How-

ever, on one day in December, Jimmie appeared before his father
and made a strong spiritual appeal to be forthwith attached to
the Sunday-School of the Big Progressive Church. Doctor Trescott mused this question considerably. "Well, Jim," he said, "why
do you conclude that the Big Progressive Sunday-School is better
for you than the Presbyterian Sunday-School?"

"Now—it's nicer," answered Jimmie, looking at his father with
an anxious eye.

"How do you mean?"

"Why—now—some of the boys what go to the Presperterian
place, they ain't very nice," explained the flagrant Jimmie.

Trescott mused the question considerably once more. In the
end he said: "Well, you may change if you wish, this one time,
but you must not be changing to and fro. You decide now, and
then you must abide by your decision."

"Yessir," said Jimmie, brightly. "Big Progressive."

"All right," said the father. "But remember what I've told you."

On the following Sunday morning, Jimmie presented himself
at the door of the basement of the Big Progressive Church. He
was conspicuously washed, notably raimented, prominently polished. And, incidentally, he was very uncomfortable because of
all these virtues.

A number of acquaintances greeted him contemptuously.
"Hello, Jimmie! What you doin' here? Thought you was a Presperterian?"

Jimmie cast down his eyes and made no reply. He was too
cowed by the change. However, Homer Phelps, who was a regular patron of the Big Progressive Sunday-School, suddenly appeared and said: "Hello, Jim." Jimmie seized upon him. Homer
Phelps was amenable to Trescott laws, tribal if you like, but
iron-bound, almost compulsory.

"Hello, Homer," said Jimmie and his manner was so good that
Homer felt a great thrill in being able to show his superior a new
condition of life.

"You ain't never come here afore, have you?" he demanded,
with a new arrogance.

"No; I ain't," said Jimmie. Then they stared at each other and
manoeuvred.

"You don't know *my* teacher," said Homer.

"No; I don't know *her*," admitted Jimmie but in a way which contended, modestly, that he knew countless other Sunday-School teachers.

"Better join our class," said Homer sagely. "She wears spectacles; don't see very well; sometimes we do almost what we like."

"All right," said Jimmie, glad to place himself in the hands of his friend. In due time, they entered the Sunday-School room where a man with benevolent whiskers stood on a platform and said: "We will now sing Number 33—'Pull for the Shore, Sailor, Pull for the Shore.'" And as the obedient throng burst into melody the man on the platform indicated the time with a white and graceful hand. He was an ideal Sunday-School superintendent—one who had never felt hunger or thirst or the wound of the challenge of dishonor.

Jimmie, walking carefully on his toes, followed Homer Phelps. He felt that the kingly superintendent might cry out and blast him to ashes before he could reach a chair. It was a desperate journey. But at last he heard Homer muttering to a young lady who looked at him through glasses which greatly magnified her eyes. "A new boy," she said in a deeply religious voice.

"Yes'm," said Jimmie trembling. The five other boys of the class scanned him keenly and derided his condition.

"We will proceed to the lesson," said the young lady. Then she cried sternly like a serjeant, "The Seventh Chapter of Jeremiah!"

There was a swift fluttering of leaflets. Then the name of Jeremiah, a wise man, towered over the feelings of these boys. Homer Phelps was doomed to read the fourth verse. He took a deep breath, he puffed out his lips, he gathered his strength for a great effort. His beginning was childishly explosive. He hurriedly said:

"*Trust ye not in lying words, saying The temple of the Lord, The temple of the Lord, The temple of the Lord, are these.*"

"Now," said the teacher, "Johnnie Scanlan, tell us what these words mean." The Scanlan boy shame-facedly muttered that he did not know. The teacher's countenance saddened. Her heart was in the work; she wanted to make a success of this Sunday-School class. "Perhaps Homer Phelps can tell us," she remarked.

Homer gulped; he looked at Jimmie. Through the great room hummed a steady hum. A little circle, very near, was being told about Daniel in the lion's den. They were deeply moved at the story. At the moment they liked Sunday-School.

"Why—now—it means," said Homer with a grand pomposity born of a sense of hopeless ignorance—"it means—why it means that they were in the wrong place."

"No," said the teacher, profoundly, "it means that we should be good, very good indeed. That is what it means. It means that we should love the Lord and be good. Love the Lord and be good. That is what it means."

The little boys suddenly had a sense of black wickedness as their teacher looked austerely upon them. They gazed at her with the wide-open eyes of simplicity. They were stirred again. This thing of being good—this great business of life—apparently it was always successful. They knew from the Fairy-Tales. But it was difficult, wasn't it? It was said to be the most heart-breaking task to be generous, wasn't it? One had to pay the price of one's eyes in order to be pacific, didn't one? As for patience, it was tortured martyrdom to be patient, wasn't it? Sin was simple, wasn't it? But virtue was so difficult that it could only be practised by heavenly beings, wasn't it?

And the angels, the Sunday-School superintendent, and the teacher swam in the high visions of the little boys as beings so good that if a boy scratched his shin in the same room, he was a profane and sentenced devil.

"And," said the teacher, " 'The temple of the Lord'—what does that mean? I'll ask the new boy. What does that mean?"

"I dunno," said Jimmie blankly.

But here the professional bright boy of the class suddenly awoke to his obligations. "Teacher," he cried, "it means church, same as this."

"Exactly," said the teacher, deeply satisfied with this reply. "You know your lesson well, Clarence. I am much pleased."

The other boys, instead of being envious, looked with admiration upon Clarence while he adopted an air of being habituated to perform such feats every day of his life. Still, he was not much of a boy. He had the virtue of being able to walk on very high stilts but when the season of stilts had passed, he possessed no rank save this Sunday-School rank, this clever-little-Clarence business of knowing the Bible, and the lesson, better than the other boys. The other boys, sometimes looking at him meditatively, did not actually decide to thrash him as soon as he cleared the portals of the church but they certainly decided to molest him in such ways as would re-establish their self-respect. Back of the superintendent's chair hung a lithograph of the Martyrdom of St. Stephen.

Jimmie, feeling stiff and encased in his best clothes, waited for the ordeal to end. A bell pealed; the superintendent had tapped a bell. Slowly the rustling and murmuring dwindled to silence. The benevolent man faced the school. "I have to announce," he began, waving his body from side to side in the conventional bows of his kind, "that—" Bang went the bell. "Give me your attention, please, children. I have to announce that the Board has decided that this year there will be no Christmas tree, but the—"

Instantly the room buzzed with the subdued clamor of the children. Jimmie was speechless. He stood morosely during the singing of the closing hymn. He passed out into the street with the others, pushing no more than was required.

Speedily the whole idea left him. If he remembered Sunday-School at all, it was to remember that he did not like it.

Appendixes

THE ANGEL-CHILD

130.2 embraced; in] This is the reading of the manuscript, but in the first of six such alterations in pencil (see also 130.27, 133.6, 134.28, 135.32, 135.37) Cora has altered the text to read 'embraced. In'. For other examples of her interference with the manuscripts see "Lynx-Hunting," "The Lover and the Tell-Tale," and " 'Showin' Off.' " The changes in "The Angel-Child" are stylistic and at 130.27 and 134.28 are designed to prevent what she felt to be inadvisable repetition of words. It is possible that she consulted Crane and secured his approval before a typescript was made, but no evidence appears to suggest that she invariably did, and it is interesting to see that at 130.27 the printed texts preserve 'paid', which she had deleted in favor of her substitution, 'made'. On the whole, it seems better to ignore her editorial 'improvements' and always to revert to the original Crane holograph reading except in cases of positive error.

136.23 the position of buffer] The H reading *of a buffer* appears to be the same sort of sophistication found in the change in "Lynx-Hunting" of MS *as rabbit cover* to H *as a rabbit cover* (139.34), in "The Carriage-Lamps" of MS *in rebellious mood* to H *in a rebellious mood* (177.28), or in "The Knife" of "in air" to "in the air" (186.22).

LYNX-HUNTING

139.29 them] Crane's grammar was never very certain in references such as this, as witness the 1893 *Maggie*, "Wide dirty grins spread over each face" (38.20–21). The H reading *him* for MS *them* is very likely an editorial or compositorial 'correction' even though the manuscript might be defended if the sense were that each boy thought they all would some day, etc. However, the true sense is no doubt as H has it.

140.20 woods] This MS plural, as against the H singular *wood*, appears to be correct, and in accord with such phrases as "bound for that freeland of hills and woods" (139.22), and "The boys . . . entered the thickets" (139.40–140.1), but especially "At last they continued their march through the woods" (141.15). As indicated in the Historical Collations, the printers often had trouble with Crane's final 's', whether present or not.

141.8 often quoted] In pencil Cora interlined with a caret the words 'this uncle' (possibly 'Uncle'). Another alteration in this story came from her hand at 140.4 (see Editorial Emendations), which was accepted in altered form either in a typescript or a proof change as evidenced in the *Harper's* print. No evidence exists to suggest that Crane approved this stylistic change, which may have been made on Cora's own initiative. See also " 'Showin' Off,' " 152.14. Thus it is omitted from the present critical text.

143.22 man when he cared] In MS a double horizontal line (Crane's usual method of making a deletion) is drawn over a comma after *man*. It seems probable that the printer of H mistook this deletion mark as a dash, and so printed it. Although the dash has a superficial effectiveness, there seems little doubt that Crane's single intent was to delete the comma. One may grant that deletion of punctuation, like this, is very rare in his manuscripts (another example occurs at 231.9 after *bloodless*, however); on the other hand, the phrase does seem to have concerned him, and he apparently decided he wanted no pause at all after *man*. The deletion is so low, being over the comma, that there seems no chance that Crane intended it to serve simultaneously as a dash.

"Showin' Off"

152.14 retainer] This is the original reading of the MS, but Cora, possibly without authority, altered it in pencil by interlining the substitute *other*, which has stood in the text ever since. For a similar example of Cora's changes, see "Lynx-Hunting" 141.8 and its Textual Note.

155.13 he] The H compositor (or typist) seems to have misinterpreted the context in altering MS *he* to *you* so that in the prints Jimmie's retainer answers Jimmie directly instead of addressing the other children. That the MS is right may be shown by the retainer's answer at 154.15, "Yes, he has!" to Jimmie's direct question at 154.14, "Ain't I got one bigger'n that?" One may also consider 155.28, where the retainer "nodded solemnly at the assemblage" in answer to Jimmie's question, "Well, didn't I, Clarence? Didn't I, now?"

The Knife

188.17 windows] That Peter from time to time "glanced at the lighted windows", as in MS, as against H *window* may be shown by the statement at 188.4 that "Two windows, down stairs, were lighted" and by the fact that at 189.29 Alek "watched the lights in the windows."

The Stove

197.20 practicable] This H reading for MS *practical* appears to be an authentic typescript or proof correction, for *practicable* is indeed what stage people say. However, the line between *practical* and *practicable* was never quite clear in Crane's mind, as evidenced in *The Monster*, "In the sudden glance he threw from one to another he impressed them as being both leonine and impracticable" (30.1–2).

The Trial . . . of Homer Phelps

211.6 what] The H reading *that* would be automatically suspect as a 'correction', and fortunately evidence is at hand to show the authority of the MS. In "A Little Pilgrim" 236.10 MS and H agree in "some of the boys what go . . ." and in the manuscript *what* has been interlined above deleted *that*.

THE CITY URCHIN . . .

229.33 gallows] Because of the unfamiliarity of the usage, H and A1 seem to have accepted the MS spelling *gallous*. *Gallows* may be used as here, according to dictionaries, in the sense of *gallows bird*.

230.33 Wasn't] This H reading for MS *Warn't* may be a sophistication, since *warn't* is perfectly good dialect. On the other hand, this word occurs in Edith Richie's transcript of the manuscript and therefore may be a mistake on her part, especially since Crane nowhere else in the Whilomville series ever uses *warn't*.

A LITTLE PILGRIM

237.12 Sunday-School] MS is not consistent in capitalizing *School* although it does so the majority of times. The invariable lower-case *-school* in H and A (like their invariable *church* for MS *Church*) may represent only coincidental house styling in the two parts of the typesetting but possibly could derive from the forms of the typescript. Whichever the source, Crane's own intention to capitalize is demonstrated by his alteration in the MS at 237.3 of *-school* to *-School*.

237.36 the work] This crux appears in the second half of the story where A1 was set from the typescript and H from A1; both A1 and H read *her work*. The variant in the print from MS *the work* must represent either a typescript difference from MS or else an unauthoritative printer's corruption in A1 which Crane did not detect in the proof of H. Since *the work* is the less usual phrase, and *her work* the commonplace one, the odds favor inadvertent sophistication either in the typescript or in A1 instead of authorial change to a phrase that he would have been conscious of from the beginning.

EDITORIAL EMENDATIONS IN THE COPY-TEXT

[NOTE: Every editorial change from the copy-texts—whether the manuscripts or the *Harper's Magazine* printings—is recorded for the substantives, and every change in the accidentals, also, save for such silent typographical alterations as are remarked in "The Text of the Virginia Edition" prefixed to Vol. I of this collected edition when a print is the copy-text, and for the specific silent changes in the manuscripts that are listed in the Textual Introduction. Only the direct source of the emendation, with its antecedents, is noticed; the Historical Collation may be consulted for the complete history, within the texts collated, of any substantive readings that qualify for inclusion in that listing. An alteration assigned to the Virginia edition (V) is made for the first time in the present text if 'by the first time' is understood 'the first time in respect to the texts chosen for collation.' Asterisked readings are discussed in the Textual Notes. The wavy dash ~ represents the same word that appears before the bracket and is used in recording punctuation variants. An inferior caret ∧ indicates the absence of a punctuation mark. The following texts are referred to: MS (various), H (*Harper's Magazine*), A1 (Harper 1900).]

THE ANGEL-CHILD (MS)

129.0   I] A1; Part I MS; omit H
129.3–4   city— . . . confidence —] H; ~ , . . . ~ , MS
129.5   to do so] H; it MS
129.16   travail] H; travel MS
*130.2   embraced; in] V; embraced. In MS-A1 (*altered in* MS *by* Cora)
130.3   Begum] H; begum MS
130.8   ¶ On] H; *no* ¶ MS
130.13   through] H; through *deleted in* MS
130.15   temperamental] H; tempermental MS
130.18   five-dollar] H; ~ ∧ ~ MS
130.20   people—] H; ~ , MS
130.28   Bridge Street] V; ~ - ~ MS-A1
130.38   -School] V; -school MS-A1

131.5   villainy] H (villany); villiany MS
131.6   behavior] H; behaviour MS
131.15   fire),] H; ~) ∧ MS
131.20   inspiration] H; thought MS
131.29–30   happen to] H; aid MS
131.34   ¶ "Two] H; *no* ¶ MS
133.3   said] H; said that MS
133.6   want] V; wish MS-A1 ('wish' *interlined by* Cora *above deleted* 'want')
133.7   ¶ Neeltje] H; *no* ¶ MS
133.9   ¶ "Hurry] H; *no* ¶ MS
133.10   step, up] H; ~ ∧ ~ MS
133.15   She] H; she MS
133.17   back,] H; ~ ∧ MS
133.37   lady's-maid] H; ~ ∧ ~ MS
134.18+1   II] H; Part II MS

134.24 awaiting] H; waiting MS
134.24,34 angel-child] V; ~ ∧ ~ MS-A1
134.28 let fall] V; dropped MS-A1 ('dropped' *interlined by* Cora *above deleted* 'let fall')
134.31 Doctor] V; Docter MS; Dr. H, A1
135.6 ¶ He] H; *no* ¶ MS
135.12 ¶ The words] H; *no* ¶ MS
135.12,21 angel-child] V; ~ ∧ ~ MS-A1
135.14 Frock!] H; ~ , MS
135.24 tangled] H; shattered MS
135.29 back garden] H; ~ - ~ MS
135.32 And full] V; And then full MS-A1 ('then' *interlined by* Cora)

135.37 excitement] V; horror MS-A1 ('horror' *interlined by* Cora *above deleted* 'excitement')
136.9(*twice*),17,29; 137.22,25 angel-child] V; ~ ∧ ~ MS-A1
*136.23 of buffer] *stet* MS
136.26 position] H; positions MS
137.7 'cause] H; because MS
136.33 doctor's] H; docter's MS
137.12 finality] H; finalty MS
137.20 and with] H; and that with MS
137.21 he] H; Trescott MS
137.23 consummation] H; consumation MS

LYNX-HUNTING (MS)

138.2 said:] H (said,); said: "Ma." She turned and then with a gasp he blurted it all out. MS
138.5 preliminary] H; a few preliminary MS
138.6 al-l] H; all MS
138.9 Dalzel] H; Wallis MS
138.10–11 tumult— . . . request—] H; ~ , . . . ~ ∧ MS
138.15,18,26 Dalzel] Wallis MS
138.19 the] H; that MS
138.21–22 neighborhood— . . . position—] H; ~ ∧ . . . ~ ∧ MS
139.2 which had] H; which MS
139.6 the gun out] H; out the gun MS
139.17 exceeded] H; acceded MS
139.19 together,] H; ~ ∧ MS
139.24 miners, smugglers] H; smugglers, miners MS
*139.29 them] *stet* MS
140.4 The meagre] H; He had not known what was a lynx and the meagre MS ('the' *added by* Cora)
140.5 goin'] H; going MS
*140.20 woods] *stet* MS

140.23 toward] V; towards MS-A1
140.24–25 chamois-hunters] H; ~ ∧ ~ MS
140.28 Bird's Eye View] H (Bird's eye); bird's eye view MS
140.35 sweet-fern] H; ~ ∧ ~ MS
140.37 sun-light] V; sunlight MS-A1
*141.8 often quoted] V; often this uncle quoted MS-A1 ('this uncle' *interlined by* Cora)
141.11 Wheeling (*no* ¶)] H; ¶ MS
141.15 ¶ At] H; *no* ¶ MS
141.19–20 manoeuvring] H (manœuvring); manoevring MS
141.25 truth,] V; ~ ∧ MS-A1
141.35 Adjured] H; Abjured MS
142.16 The first] H; It might be noted that the first MS
142.18 discharged] H; *omit* MS
142.34 ²mister] H; *omit* MS
142.34 it.] H (it!); it. I didn't do it, mister. MS
143.7 way] H; measure MS
*143.22 man∧] *stet* MS

143.24 cow] H; cows MS
143.28 Old] H (*no* ¶); ¶ *and omit* 'Old' MS
143.32 Fleming] H; Old Fleming MS

143.34 faltered] H; faltered again MS

THE LOVER AND THE TELL-TALE (MS)

144.1 angel-child] V; ~ ∧ ~ MS-A1
144.3 moped,] H; ~ ∧ MS
144.15 However,] H; ~ ∧ MS
144.17 school-grounds] H; ~ ∧ ~ MS
144.19 brethren] H; brethern MS
145.8 felonious] H; felonous MS
145.19–20 hold . . . their . . . retain . . . their . . . their . . . have] H; holds . . . it's . . . retains . . . it's . . . it's . . . has MS
145.22–23 mysteriously,] H; ~ ∧ MS
145.26 principal] H; principle MS
145.35 the] H; this MS
145.38 adapted] H; adopted MS

146.9 crime,] H; ~ ∧ MS
146.9 in effect] V; pretense MS-A1 ('pretense' *interlined in pencil by* Cora, *with a caret, above deleted* 'in effect')
146.15 her—] H; ~ , MS
146.17–18 friends— . . . friends—] H; ~ , . . . ~ , MS
146.34 berserk] H; bersark MS
147.5 run] H; ran MS
147.31 intention—] H; ~ , MS
147.39 wrath] V; strife MS-A1 ('strife' *interlined in pencil by* Cora *above deleted* 'wrath')
148.37 ¶Jimmie] H; no ¶ MS
148.38 ¶ She] H; no ¶ MS
148.39 anger] H; wrath MS
149.1 blazing.] H; ~ ∧ MS
149.1 Well—] V; ~ + + + MS; ~ , H, A1

"SHOWIN' OFF"

150.9 But (*no* ¶)] H; ¶ MS
150.12 ¶ One] H; no ¶ MS
150.21 ¶ The] no ¶ MS
150.21 were] H; are MS
151.9 Doctor] V; Docter MS; Dr. H, A1
151.16 an] H; a MS
151.22 ¶ "Come] H; no ¶ MS
151.38 ¶ The] H; no ¶ MS
151.38 incomprehensible] V; *omit* MS-A1 (*deleted in pencil by* Cora)
152.6 ¶ But] H; no ¶ MS
152.7 ¶ "Come] H; no ¶ MS
152.8 ¶ The] H; no ¶ MS
152.11 ¶ "There!] H; no ¶ "There, MS
*152.14 retainer] V; other MS-A1 ('other' *interlined by* Cora *above deleted* 'retainer')

152.18 conceivable] H; concievable MS
152.20 became] H; becomes MS
153.6 ¶ The] A1; no ¶ MS, H
153.13 perambulator] H; perambulater MS
153.16 nonchalance] H; nonchalence MS
153.36 'im] H; 'em MS
153.39 brightly] V; *omit* MS-A1 (*deleted in pencil by* Cora)
154.15 ¶ The] no ¶ MS
154.31; 155.9–10 't all . . . 't all] V; 't'all . . . 't'all MS; 'tall . . . 'tall H, A1
154.38 me] H; *omit* MS
155.2 now!] H; ~ , MS
155.3 There,] H; ~ ∧ MS
*155.13 he] *stet* MS
155.23 -stone'!] V; - ~ !' MS-A1

156.5 outskirts] H; ~ - ~ MS
156.8 wonders!] H; ~ , MS
156.13 velocipede:] V; ~ . MS; ~ , H, A1
156.17 'tain't] H; Taint MS
156.19 receiving] H; recieving MS

156.22 ¶ "Oh] H; no ¶ MS
156.22 eh? Well] H; eh? You could? Well MS
156.24 jibing] V; jibeing MS; gibing H, A1
156.27 'Tain't] H; Tain't MS
156.35 an] H; a MS

MAKING AN ORATOR (MS)

[Cora's *hand*]
158.4 piteously] H; pitiously MS
158.6 fellow-scholars] H; ~ ∧ ~ MS
158.13 fellow-creatures] H; ~ ∧ ~ MS
158.16 preferred] H; prefered MS
158.19 However,] H; ~ ∧ MS
158.22 beside] H; besides MS
158.22 teacher's] H; teachers MS
158.25 toward] V; towards MS-A1
158.28 He] H; he MS
158.28 approaching] H; approching MS
158.30–31 "The . . . Brigade":] H; ∧ ~ . . . ~ . ∧ MS
159.1–2 ∧ Half . . . onward—∧] H; "~ . . . ~ —" MS
159.5 fifty] H; a hundred MS
159.13 ¶ On] no ¶ MS
159.13 great] H; first MS
159.16 lie] H; lay MS
159.20 all—] H; ~ , MS
159.21 downpour] H; down pour MS
159.22 Friday] H; friday MS
159.23 dining room] V; diningroom MS; ~ - ~ H, A1
159.29 Thursday] H; thursday MS
159.34 doctor's] H; Doctor's MS
159.37 school-room] A1; schoolroom MS; ~ ∧ ~ H
160.1 "The . . . Brigade"] H; ∧ ~ . . . ~ ∧ MS
160.2 arithmetic] H; arithmatic MS

160.2–3 spelling— . . . tasks—] H; ~ , . . . ~ , MS
160.5 bow,] H; ~ ∧ MS
160.5–6 his message] H; this cryptic message MS
160.6 fellow-men] H; ~ ∧ ~ MS
160.6 expedients] H; expediants MS
160.7 him. If] H; him. He had some dream of inducing a frothy convulsion to attack him. If MS
160.9 toward] V; towards MS-A1
160.11 weakening] H; weakning MS
160.12 school-room] A1; ~ ∧ ~ MS, H
160.15 calmly] H; omit MS
160.15 recognize] H; recognise MS

[Stephen's *hand*]
160.21 he] H; omit MS
160.22–23 Emerald Isle] H; emerald isle MS
160.30 carried?] H; ~ . MS
160.35 England's] H; Englands MS
160.36 honorable] Honorable MS
161.2 Glenmorganshire. But] H; Glenmorganshire but MS
161.3 honorable] H; Honorable MS
161.8–9 eyes, . . . wide,] H; ~ ∧ . . . ~ ∧ MS
161.15 school-house] H; school MS
161.30 "Half . . .] H *sets as verse throughout;* MS *treats as ordinary dialogue*

161.31,33,34 *League*] H; League MS
161.37 league . . . muttered— "half a league—"] H; League . . . muttered. "Half a League." MS

162.3 league] H; League MS
162.5 it:] H; ~ . MS
162.6–7,10–11,16,21–23 *set as verse* H; *as prose* MS
162.22 Death] V; death MS-A1

SHAME (H)

165.12 bein'] V; being H, A1
166.6 't all] V; 'tall H, A1
166.26 pillar-like] V; pillarlike H, A1
167.1 grown-up] A1; ~ ∧ ~ H
167.16; 168.27 *pail!*] V; *pail!* H, A1
167.35 angel-child] V; ~ ∧ ~ H, A1

169.8 pine-needles] V; ~ ∧ ~ H, A1
171.37; 172.3 "Jimmie (*no* ¶)] V; ¶ H, A1
172.2 bawling:] A1; ~ , H
172.10 "Jim (*no* ¶)] V; ¶ H, A1
172.14 "Wut's (*no* ¶)] V; ¶ H, A1
172.18,19 *me!*] V; *me!* H, A1

THE CARRIAGE-LAMPS (H)

174.11 high∧] V; ~ , H, A1
174.32 dish] V; dis' H; dis A1
175.29 ¶ "You] V; *no* ¶ H, A1
175.32 manoeuvred] V; manœuvred H, A1
175.35 somethin'] V; something H, A1
177.27 meantime] V; ~ ∧ ~ H, A1

177.35 quick∧] V; ~ , H, A1
179.3 dunno] V; dun'no' H, A1
179.11 sun-light] V; sunlight H, A1 (~ - | ~)
179.20 "If (*no* ¶)] V; ¶ H, A1
181.22 "Brace (*no* ¶)] V; ¶ H, A1

THE KNIFE (MS)

184.0 I] H; Part I MS
184.5 Doctor] H; Docter MS
184.11 on'y] H; o'ny MS
184.11 m'se'f] H; m'sef MS
184.11 covertous] H; covetous MS
185.25 any] H; *omit* MS
185.27 against] H; again MS
186.14 Susie,] H; ~ ∧ MS
*186.22 in air] *stet* MS
186.29 necessa'y] H; neccessa'y MS
188.3 stateliness] H; statliness MS
188.4 looked] H; look MS
188.5 lighted] H; alight MS
188.6 since] H; *omit* MS
188.7 pneumonia] H; pnuemonia MS

*188.17 windows] *stet* MS
188.17+1 II] H; Part II MS
188.21–22 water-melons] V; watermelons MS-A1
188.22 was] H; is MS
188.29 for] H; as for MS
188.36 water-melon] H (watermelon); watermelons MS
189.6 paused] H; paused a moment MS
189.21 come and scale] H; come, scale MS
189.30 retiring;] H; ~ ∧ MS
190.1 appalled] H; apalled MS
190.2 community] H; cummunity MS
190.4 cheers of his enemies] H; jeers of his friends MS

190.7   rhythmical] H; rythmical MS
190.22   ¹got'che!"] H; ~ ," MS
190.25   Wash'ton,] H; ~ ∧ MS
190.30   wah] H; where MS
190.32   whining] H; whineing MS
190.34   deacon.] H; deacon. Seem like you aint'n no hurry, deacon? MS
191.9   dogs;] H; ~ ∧ MS
191.18   voice,] V; ~ , MS-A1
191.22   I] H; omit MS
191.23   fitses?"] H; ~ " ∧ | MS
191.26   ²I tell you] H; omit MS
192.7   garden patch] V; garden-patch MS-A1

192.7–8   distance] H; distances MS
192.9   garden-fence] V; ~ - ~ MS -A1
192.12–13   word—] H; ~ . MS
192.24,26   'Tain't] H; ∧ Taint MS
193.12   gathered] H; laboriously gathered MS
193.28   Afric] H; afric MS
193.34   wasn't?"] V; ~ ?' " MS; " ∧ It . . . wasn't?" H, A1
193.35   Alek.] H; Alek, encouraged by Bryant's manner. MS
194.11   Bryant. . . .]   H;   ~ * * * MS
194.13   it] H; it's MS

THE STOVE (MS)

195.5   angel-child] V; ~ ∧ ~ MS-A1
195.8,24; 196.23,30,35; 197.11,17; 198.1; 203.16,18,26,34 doctor] H; docter MS
195.17   it!] H; ~ , MS
195.24   answered the doctor.] H; answered the docter. Mrs Trescott made no reply; she held the letter in her hand and stared at it as if the key to a feminine perplexity was concealed somewhere in it's brief and innocent lines. Finally, she read it again carefully from end to end, her brows contracted in a scholastic frown. "Well," she murmured at last, "I suppose—I suppose" —¶ "oh, it will be all right," said the docter. "She is original enough to turn up here and simply stupify us with her decorous behavior. Still—I'd like to know what she'll do first." MS
195.27   peace.] H; peace. He had had two or three crucial affairs since the time he had given his love to his cousin. MS
195.28–29   snow—] H; ~ ; MS

196.1   York.". . .] H; ~ !" ∧ MS
196.16   daughter] H; daugther MS
196.19   phenomenon] H; phenomena MS
196.29   right,] H; ~ . MS
*197.20   practicable] H; practical MS
197.23   up stairs] V; ~ - ~ MS-A1
197.24   Trescotts] V; Trescott's MS-A1
198.14–15   angel-child] V; ~ ∧ ~ MS-A1
198.19   No!] H; ~ ! MS
199.31   appalled] H; apalled MS
200.5   bruises—. . . bruises—] H; ~ , . . . ~ , MS
200.13   necessity—] H; ~ ; MS
200.20   should] H; would MS
201.10   g'w'on!] H; ~ . MS
201.11,15   seh!] H; ~ . MS
201.25   snow,] H; ~ ; MS
202.12   turnips!] H; ~ , MS
202.23   angel-child]   V; ~ ∧ ~ MS-A1
202.31   'm—] H('em); ~ , MS
202.38   There!] H; ~ , MS
203.9   'Tain't] H; ∧ Taint MS
203.34   ¶ The] no ¶ MS
204.3   it?] H; ~ . MS

204.33   yours!] H; ~ . MS
205.6   up stairs] V; ~ - ~ MS-A1
205.12   papa!] H; ~ . MS
205.13   ¶ At] H; no ¶ MS
205.14   go her] H; go of the MS
205.19   her!] H; ~ , MS

205.26   angel-child]   V; ~ ∧ ~ MS-A1
205.28   darling!] H; ~ . MS
206.10   up   stairs] V; ~ - ~ MS-A1

THE TRIAL, EXECUTION, AND BURIAL OF HOMER PHELPS (MS, H)

207.11,17 Halt! Who's] H; Halt; who's MS
207.12   low and gruff cry] H; cry, low, gruff, menacing, MS
207.18   shot?"] H; shot? Why dont you do things right?" MS
207.26   diff'rence] H; difference MS
208.10   sentry:] H; ~ . MS
208.14   appeared—] H; ~ , MS
208.31   voice:] H; ~ . MS
208.33   develop] H; develope MS
208.38; 209.8,9,10,21 Seize] H; Sieze MS
209.2,24,26,27,29,34 seized] H; siezed MS
209.8   out:] H; ~ . MS
209.11   adjured] H; abjured MS
209.12   manoeuvred] H (manœuvred); manoevred MS
209.19   tears—"don't] H; tears. "Dont MS
209.27   boy,] H; omit MS
209.31   promptly:] V; ~ . MS; ~ , H, A1
210.8   trial] H; trail MS
210.9   you] H; omit MS
210.9   thing."] H; thing." ¶ Then in an abused, almost martyred, tone, the Phelps boy cried: "Well, why cant one of the other fellers be siezed." ¶ "No," explained the chief with new patience. "No, Homer, you're the right one. Yes you are." All the band began to urge him. "Oh, go on, Homer. Let us sieze you. It wont hurt." ¶ "Well," he wavered. "Well"— ¶ "Oh, go on. Come ahead." ¶ "Well," he said ultimately, "if it **hurts**

now!" ¶ "Oh, it wont hurt. Come ahead. Take him by the arms, two of you." MS
210.15   preferable] H; preferably MS
210.19   lead.] H; lead. The camp in fact suggested Valley Forge to one's mind. It was not to be imagined that rational beings would wilfully endure such environment even for a short time and it was far beyond all human reckoning to concieve a number of creatures who would consider everything delightful. MS
210.20   arrived] H; arriving MS
210.23   which had a hole from which] H; from a hole in which MS
210.25   he asked.] H; omit MS
210.27   peremptorily] H; peremporily MS
210.33   Now] H; No, now MS
210.38   pompously:]   V; ~ . MS; ~ , H, A1
211.2,38 Death!] H; ~ ! MS
211.3   chief] H; stern chief MS
211.4   guilty?] H; ~ . MS
*211.6   what] stet MS
211.11   very] H; omit MS
211.11   contemptuously, "let] H; contemptuously. "Let MS
211.11   me] V; Me MS; me H, A1
211.18   judge— . . . modest—] H; ~ , . . . ~ , MS
211.19,22 ¶ The] H; no ¶ MS

Manuscript wanting

211.25 prisoner∧] V; ~ , H, A1
211.35 Earl∧ . . . example∧]
    V; ~ , . . . ~ , H, A1
211.39 role] V; rôle H, A1
211.39–212.1 drama∧ . . . thick-
    et∧] V; ~ , . . . ~, H, A1
212.2 lad∧] V; ~ , H, A1
212.3 stand∧] V; ~ , H, A1
212.4 countenance∧] V; ~ , H,
    A1
212.7 snow∧] V; ~ , H, A1
212.12 moment∧] V; ~ , H, A1
212.15 them∧] V; ~ , H, A1
212.18 affairs∧] V; ~ , H, A1
212.22 thing∧] V; ~ , H, A1
212.25 hemlock-boughs] V; ~ ∧
    ~ H, A1
212.26 murmured∧] V; ~ , H, A1
212.27 cedar∧tree] V; ~ - ~ H,
    A1
212.30 blaze∧] V; ~ , H, A1
212.39 hands∧] V; ~ , H, A1
213.2 Jimmie∧] V; ~ , H, A1
213.4 Dalzel∧] V; ~ , H, A1
213.15 warmth∧] V; ~ , H, A1

213.17 Eventually,] V; ~ ∧ H, A1
213.17 chief∧] V; ~ , H, A1
213.18 "Now (*no* ¶)] V; ¶ H, A1
213.20 scorn∧] V; ~ , H, A1
213.21 it∧] V; ~ , H, A1
213.24 chief∧] V; ~ , H, A1
213.31 said∧] V; ~ , H, A1
213.37 words∧] V; ~ , H, A1
213.39 Indians∧] V; ~ , H, A1
214.1 -rifles∧] V; ~ , H, A1
214.3 meantime] V; mean time
    H, A1
214.3 fire∧] V; ~ , H, A1
214.21 rehabilitation∧] V; ~ , H,
    A1
214.22 burial∧] V; ~ , H, A1
214.23 said∧] V; ~ , H, A1
214.28,38 hemlock-boughs] V;
    ~ ∧ ~ H, A1
214.29 rectangle∧] V; ~ , H, A1
214.36 muttering∧] V; ~ , H, A1
215.1 address∧] V; ~ , H, A1
215.4 boughs∧] V; ~, H, A1
215.7 began∧] V; ~ , H, A1
215.10 pard∧] V; ~ , H, A1

The Fight (MS)

216.0 I] H; *omit* MS
216.2 wagon-loads] H; ~ ∧ ~ MS
216.7 screams] H; skreams MS
216.12 near] H; about MS
216.22 ¶ Any] H; *no* ¶ MS
217.28 authority—] H; ~ . MS
217.34 ¶ I] H; *no* ¶ MS
218.14 Jim!] H; ~ . MS
219.1 received] H; recieved MS
219.7 him. What] H; him; what
    MS
219.25 II] H; Chapter II MS
219.32 vacations—] H; ~ , MS
220.2 -School] V; -school MS-A1
220.6 and] H; but MS
220.7 Monday∧] H; ~ , MS
220.20 beneficiary] H; benefi-
    cary MS
220.24 tribe,] H; ~ ∧ MS
221.3–4 cast away] H; castaway
    MS
221.9 sort] H; sorts MS

221.15 howled:] H; ~ . MS
221.23 ¶ The] H; *no* ¶ MS
221.25 ¶ "Johnnie] H; *no* ¶ MS
221.27 ¶ "I] H; *no* ¶ MS
221.35 ¶ "Are] H; *no* ¶ MS
221.38 main door] H; ~ - ~ MS
222.15 approximately,] H; ~ ∧
    MS
222.19 received] H; recieved MS
223.2 shouted:] H; ~ . MS
223.3 feller!"] H; feller! Jimmie,
    here he is!" MS
223.10 ten. On] H; ten; on MS
223.11 Topsys] H; Topseys MS
223.12 Topsy] H; Topsey MS
223.15 ¶ "Jimmie] H; *no* ¶ MS
223.23 sing:] H; ~ . MS
223.24 other,] H; ~ ∧ MS
223.27+1 III] H; Chapter III MS
223.28 play-ground] H;
    playground MS
223.32 of] H; for MS

224.10   succor] H; succour MS
224.12   books—] H; ~ , MS
224.39   rage—] H; ~ , MS
225.5   defense]   V;   defence MS-A1

225.9   could not] H; couldn't MS
225.9   cry;] H; ~ ₐ MS
225.16–17   -founded,] H; ~ ₐ MS
226.6   academics—he] H; academics. He MS

THE CITY URCHIN AND THE CHASTE VILLAGERS (MS)

[Edith Richie's *hand*]
227.4   child life] H; ~ - ~ MS
228.6   those] H; these MS
228.6   green-coated] H; ~ ₐ ~ MS
228.28   newcomer] V; ~ - ~ MS-A1
228.30   boy life] H; ~ - ~ MS
228.32   ¶ In] H; *no* ¶ MS
228.35   He] H; Johnnie Hedge MS
228.38–39   Dalzel and these] H (Dalzel,); Dalzel. There were not many boys in the school who could whip Willie Dalzell and these MS
229.1   boy life] H; ~ - ~ MS
229.1–2   quiet, decent, peace-] H; ~ ₐ ~ ₐ ~ MS
229.2   wide-mouthed]   H; ~ - ~ MS
229.3   transpired₀] H; ~ , MS
229.3–4   elimination₀ most] H; elimination, that most MS
229.5   desire] H; desires MS
229.6   not known] H; unknown MS
229.6   could] H; would MS
229.18   school-grounds] V; ~ ₐ ~ MS-A1
229.19   And] H; *omit* MS
229.21   A] H; The MS
229.21–23   supremacy   . . . tribe.] H;   supremacy   was fought out in the country of the tribe which had been headed by Willie Dalzell, MS
229.27   was] H; is MS

229.32   jauntily careering] H; officiating MS
*229.33   gallows]   V;   gallous MS-A1
229.37   that] H; which MS
229.37   was] H; is MS
230.3   part] H; place MS
230.12   was no other applicant] H; were no applicants MS
*230.33   Wasn't] H; Warn't MS
230.34   ¹fer] H; for MS
230.37   off'n] H; offn MS
230.38   mixture—] H; ~ , MS
231.3,6   ¶ "Got] H; *no* ¶ MS
231.15   ¹it] H; as MS
231.15   that] *omit* MS
231.25   shouting:] H; ~ . MS
[Stephen Crane's *hand*]
231.29   whitened] H; reddened MS
231.34   s'prised] H; 'sprised MS
232.13   erlong] H; er-long MS
232.16   ¶ The] H; *no* ¶ MS
232.18   ¹him!] H; ~ , MS
232.21   'im] H; 'em MS
232.37   either,] H; ~ ₐ MS
233.1   *me*] H; ME MS
233.6   the] H; *omit* MS
233.13   cry:] V; ~ . MS; ~ , H, A1
233.15   down] H; *omit* MS
233.17   howled,] H; ~ ₐ MS
233.23   out:] H; ~ . MS
233.28   protested:] H; ~ . MS
233.32   if] H; *omit* MS
233.32   *me*] H; ME MS
234.2   Hedge's] H; Hedges' MS

A Little Pilgrim (MS)

[NOTE: In this story 235.0–237.9 (Number 33—|) was set in H from copy derived from MS and A1 was set from proof of H. On the other hand, 237.9(|'Pull)–239.21 was set in A1 from copy derived from MS and H was set from a proof of A1. Before printing, H was revised throughout in proof, probably by Crane.]

235.0 PILGRIM] H; PILGRIM-AGE MS, A1

235.12 distress] H; pain MS, A1

235.28; 236.3,5,6 -School] V; -school MS-A1

235.30 receive] H, A1; recieve MS

236.3,5 Big Progressive] H, A1; Dutch Reformed MS

236.3 Doctor] H, A1; Docter MS

236.12 Trescott] H, A1; Again Trescott MS

236.12 once more] H, A1; *omit* MS

236.13 time,] H, A1; ~ ∧ MS

236.16,19,28 Big Progressive] H, A1; Dutch Reformed MS

236.29 seized] H, A1; siezed MS

236.35 ¶ "You] H, A1; *no* ¶ MS

236.35 you?] H, A1; ~ , MS

236.38 manoeuvred] H, A1 (manœuvred); manoevred MS

237.6 Jimmie,] H, A1; ~ ∧ MS

237.9 33—] H, A1; ~ ; MS

237.9–10 'Pull . . . Shore.'] A1, H; ∧ ~ . . . ~ ∧ MS

237.11 white] H; fat white MS, A1

*237.12 -School] V; -school MS-H

237.12–13 superintendent—] A1, H; superintendant, MS

237.14 dishonor.] H; dishonor, a man indeed with beautiful fat hands who waved them in greasy victorious beneficence over a crowd of children MS, A1

237.16 superintendent] A1, H; superintendant MS

237.20 a deeply] H; an oily and deeply MS, A1

*237.36 the work] *stet* MS

238.1–2 at the story] H; *omit* MS, A1

238.21 Sunday-School superintendent] A1, H; Sunday School superintendant MS

238.25 Lord'—what] A1, H; Lord?' What MS

238.38 -School] V; -school MS-H

239.5 superintendent's] A1, H; superintendant's MS

239.8 the superintendent] H; the fat hand of the superintendant MS, A1 (A1, superintendent)

239.20–21 Sunday-School] A1, H (-school); ~ ∧ ~ MS

WORD-DIVISION

1. *End-of-the-Line Hyphenation in the Virginia Edition*

[NOTE: No hyphenation of a possible compound at the end of a line in the Virginia text is present in the copy-text except for the following readings, which are hyphenated within the line in MS (or in H when that is the copy-text). Hyphenated compounds in which both elements are capitalized are not included.]

144.20	school-|-room	203.22	tea-|party
145.18	middle-|class	205.7	angel-|child
146.7	smug-|faced	208.1	counter-|sign
155.22	*kerb-|stone*	220.17	school-|books
191.2	mellum-|patch	225.16	dumb-|founded
195.2, 197.26, 198.6	angel-|child	227.24	bull-|calf
198.14	angel-|child [~ ∧ ~ MS]	230.20	poor-|little

2. *End-of-the-Line Hyphenation in the Copy-Text*

[NOTE: The following compounds, or possible compounds, are hyphenated at the end of the line in the copy-text. The form in which they have been transcribed in the Virginia text, listed below, represents the practice of MS as ascertained by other appearances or by parallels.]

132.19	eye-corner	174.16	turkey-raffle
138.22	over-bearing	175.31	light-cavalryman
139.26	dark-green	180.8	low-breathed
142.29	half-blind	181.22	white-livered
152.25	badly-battered	182.38	erbout
158.11	class-mates	188.16	roadside
161.10	moon-face	202.15	angel-child
162.36	low-toned	212.35	Indy-uns
170.33	shot-gun	213.5	Dead-shot
170.34	ice-cream	214.1	stick-rifles
171.34	bush-ranger	223.9	blood-hounds

HISTORICAL COLLATION

[NOTE: Only substantive variants from the Virginia text are listed here, together with their appearances in the manuscripts, the *Harper's Magazine* texts (H), and the 1900 New York Harper edition (A1). The 1900 Harper London edition (E1) appears to consist of the New York A1 sheets with a press-variant title-page and is thus without textual variation. The 1902 and the undated Harper New York editions (A2, A3) represent second and third printings from the same plates and are without textual variation. Thus neither A2–3 nor E1 are separately recorded here since in all respects their texts agree with A1. Collated texts not noted for any reading agree with the Virginia Edition.]

THE ANGEL-CHILD (MS)

129.0   I] Part I MS; *omit* H
129.5   to do so] it MS
129.16   travail] travel MS
130.13   through] *deleted* MS
130.27   paid] Cora *in pencil deleted and substituted* 'made' *in* MS
131.20   inspiration] thought MS
131.29   happen to] aid MS
132.12   Reifsnyder] Riefsnyder H, A1
132.23   anyone] any H, A1
132.37; 133.16   toward] towards A1
133.3   said] said that MS
133.6   want] wish MS-A1 (Cora's *alteration of SC* 'want')
134.18+1   II] Part II MS
134.24   awaiting] waiting MS
134.28   let fall] dropped MS-A1 (Cora *in pencil deleted and substituted* 'dropped')
135.2   ma-ma! Ma-ma! Ma-ma!] mamma! mamma! mamma! H, A1

135.4   of a] of H, A1
135.6   Yessir] Yes sir H, A1
135.24   tangled] shattered MS
135.32   And full] And then full MS-A1 ('then' *interlined by* Cora)
135.34   toward] towards A1
135.37   excitement] horror MS-A1 ('excitement' *substituted by* Cora *for* 'horror')
136.23   of] of a H, A1
136.26   position] positions MS
136.34   said he] he said H, A1
136.38   'emselves] themselves H, A1
137.2   was] were A1
137.7   kickin'] kicking H, A1
137.7   an'] and A1
137.7   'cause] because MS
137.13   -slamming] -slammings H, A1
137.19-20   and with] and that with MS
137.21   he] Trescott MS

257

Lynx-Hunting (MS)

138.2 said:] said: "Ma." She turned and then with a gasp he [he *interlined with a caret in black ink*] blurted it all out. MS
138.5 preliminary] a few preliminary MS
138.9,15,18,26 Dalzel] Wallis MS
138.12 glad] glad that H, A1
138.19 the] that MS
139.2 which had] which MS
139.6 the gun out] out the gun MS
139.17 exceeded] acceded MS
139.24 miners, smugglers] smugglers, miners MS
139.29 them] him H, A1
139.34 as rabbit] as a rabbit H, A1
139.36 inspiriting] inspiring H, A1
140.4 The meagre] He had ['kno' *deleted*] not known what was a lynx and the ['the' *added by* Cora *at end of page*] meagre MS
140.5 goin'] going MS

140.11 an] a H, A1
140.20 woods] wood H, A1
140.23 toward] towards MS-A1
141.3 of a] of H, A1
141.8 often quoted] often this uncle quoted MS-A1 ('this uncle' *interlined by* Cora)
141.23 Afterward] Afterwards A1
141.35 Adjured] Abjured MS
142.16 The first] It might be noted that the first MS
142.18 discharged] *omit* MS
142.32 toward] towards A1
142.34 mister] *omit* MS
142.34 it.] it. I didnt do it, mister. MS
143.7 way] measure MS
143.8 a cow] the cow H, A1
143.18,28 toward] towards A1
143.24 cow] cows MS
143.28 Old] *omit* MS
143.32 Fleming] Old Fleming MS
143.34 faltered] faltered again MS

The Lover and the Tell-Tale (MS)

145.19–20 hold . . . their . . . retain . . . their . . . their . . . have] holds . . . it's . . . retains . . . it's . . . it's . . . has MS
145.35 the] this MS
145.38 adapted] adopted MS
146.9 in effect] pretense MS-A1 ('pretense' *interlined by* Cora *above deleted* 'in effect')
146.11 at once recognize] recognize at once H, A1

146.36 to soon] soon to H, A1
147.5 run] ran MS
147.12; 148.19 toward] towards A1
147.39 wrath] strife MS-A1 ('strife' *interlined by* Cora *above deleted* 'wrath')
148.25 with a] with H, A1
148.28 arose mid] rose amid H, A1
148.39 anger] wrath MS

"Showin' Off" (MS)

150.12 toward] towards A1
150.16 at] in A1
150.21 were] are MS
151.16 an] a MS
151.38 incomprehensible] *omit* MS-A1 (*deleted by* Cora *in* MS)
152.4 further'n] farther'n H, A1
152.14 retainer] other MS-A1 ('other' *interlined by* Cora *in* MS *above deleted* 'retainer')

152.20 became] becomes MS
153.4 "I (*no* ¶)] ¶ H, A1
153.10,31,38 toward] towards A1
153.12 Jimmie (*no* ¶)] ¶ H, A1
153.36 'im] 'em MS
153.39 brightly] *omit* MS-A1 (*deleted by* Cora *in* MS)
154.15 "Yes (*no* ¶)] ¶ H, A1
154.38 me] *omit* MS
155.2 back] furiously back MS

155.13   he] you H, A1
156.18,27   anythin'] anything H,
   A1
156.22   eh? Well] eh? You could?
   Well MS

156.27   " 'Tain't (*no* ¶)] ¶ H, A1
156.35   an] a MS
157.6   toward] towards A1

MAKING AN ORATOR

[Cora's *hand*]
158.22   beside] besides MS
158.25   toward] towards MS-A1
159.5   fifty] a hundred MS
159.8   But (*no* ¶)] ¶ H, A1
159.13   great] first MS
159.16   lie] lay MS
159.17   She (*no* ¶)] ¶ H, A1
159.19   He (*no* ¶)] ¶ H, A1
159.22   With (*no* ¶)] ¶ H, A1
160.5–6   his message] this cryptic
   message ['cryptic' *interlined by*
   SC *above deleted* 'cryptic'] MS

160.6   Desperate (*no* ¶)] ¶ H, A1
160.7   him. If] him. He had some
   dream of inducing a frothy convulsion to attack him. If MS
160.9   toward] towards MS-A1
160.15   calmly] *omit* MS
[Stephen's *hand*]
160.21   he] *omit* MS
161.15   school-house] school MS
161.18   But (*no* ¶)] ¶ H, A1
162.17   The (*no* ¶)] ¶ H, A1
162.26   As (*no* ¶)] ¶ H, A1
162.29   "You (*no* ¶)] ¶ H, A1

SHAME (no MS)

165.6   feller] fellow A1
165.12   bein'] being H, A1

165.14; 169.2; 171.33   toward] towards A1
172.10   horses] horse A1

THE CARRIAGE-LAMPS (no MS)

174.12;   176.20–21   toward]   towards A1
174.32   dish] dis' H; dis A1
175.35   somethin'] something H,
   A1

176.10   the] the | the A1
177.28   in] in a A1
178.14   boys of] boys in A1
178.27   amongst] among A1

THE KNIFE (MS)

184.0   I] Part I MS
184.11   covertous] covetous MS
184.14   'm] 'em H, A1
184.21   git] get H, A1
184.23   'roun'] 'round H, A1
184.29   Peter] Pete A1
185.4   Afterward] Afterwards A1
185.25   any] *omit* MS
185.27   against] again MS
186.19   the Susie. Susie H, A1
186.19   him. Then] him, then H,
   A1
186.22   in air] in the air H, A1

186.27–28   how'do, how'do   . . .
   how'do. How'do] how do, how do
   . . . how do? How do H, A1
186.37   -shaped] -shape H, A1
186.39   oldest] eldest H, A1
187.7   three the] three that the H,
   A1
187.16   to supper] for supper A1
188.5   lighted] alight MS
188.6   since] *omit* MS
188.16   took seat] took a seat H,
   A1
188.17   windows] window A1

188.17+1   II] Part II MS
188.19   toward] towards A1
188.22   was] is MS
188.29   for] as for MS
188.32   of a] of H, A1
188.36   water-melon] water-melons MS
189.6   paused] paused a moment MS
189.21   come and scale] come, scale MS
190.4   cheers of his enemies] jeers of his friends MS
190.16   toward] towards A1
190.22   got'che . . .] got che . . . A1

190.25   Peteh] Peter H, A1
190.30   wah] where MS
190.34   deacon.] deacon. Seem like you aint'n no hurry, deacon? MS
190.39; 192.2   toward] towards A1
191.22   I] omit MS
191.26   ²I tell you] omit MS
192.2   a contrite] contrite A1
192.7–8   distance] distances MS
193.12   gathered] laboriously gathered MS
193.35   Alek.] Alek, encouraged by Bryant's manner. MS
194.13   it] it's MS
194.25   an'] and A1
194.26   lumbeh-] lumber- A1

THE STOVE (MS)

195.24   doctor.] docter. Mrs Trescott made no reply; she held the letter in her hand and stared at it as if the key to a feminine perplexity was concealed somewhere in it's brief and innocent lines. Finally, she read it again carefully from end to end, her brows contracted in a scholastic frown. "Well," she murmured at last, "I suppose—I suppose"— ¶ "oh, it will be all right," said the docter. "She is original enough to turn up here and simply stupify us with her decorous behavior. Still—I'd like to know what she'll do first." MS
195.27   peace.] peace. He had had two or three crucial affairs since

the time he had given his love to his cousin. MS
196.1,2   f'm] f'om H, A1
196.19   phenomenon] phenomena MS
196.28   attend] attend to H, A1
197.3   parents] her parents H, A1
197.20   practicable, practical MS
197.32   arms] arm A1
197.34   "What (no ¶)] ¶ H, A1
198.16   ¶ She] no ¶ H, A1
200.13   of an] of H, A1
200.20   should] would MS
202.2   somethin'] something H, A1
202.31   'm] 'em H, A1
204.25   come] came H1, A1
205.14   go her] go of the MS
205.16   toward] towards A1
205.34   in] at H, A1

THE TRIAL, EXECUTION, AND BURIAL OF HOMER PHELPS (MS in part)

207.10   toward] towards A1
207.12   low and gruff cry] cry, low, gruff, menacing, MS
207.18   shot?"] shot? Why dont you do things right?" [question mark altered from period] MS
207.26   diff'rence] difference MS
208.11   fellers! Hey!] ~ ? ~ ? H
208.18   come] came H, A1
209.11   adjured] abjured MS
209.13   boyish] a boyish H, A1

209.16   now was] was now H, A1
209.27   boy,] omit MS
210.8   trial] trail MS
210.9   you] omit MS
210.9   thing."] thing." ¶ Then in an abused, almost martyred, tone, the Phelps boy ['boy' interlined with a caret] cried: "Well, why cant one of the other [final 's' deleted] fellers be siezed." ¶ "No," explained the chief with

new ['new' *interlined above deleted* 'no'] patience. "No, Homer, you're the right one. Yes you are." All the band began to urge him. "Oh, go on, ['on' *interlined above deleted* 'on,'] Homer. Let us sieze you. It wont hurt." ¶ "Well," he wavered. "Well"— ¶ "Oh, go on. Come ahead." ¶ "Well," he said ultimately, "if it hurts now!" [*exclamation substituted for period*] ¶ "Oh, it wont hurt. Come ahead. Take him by the arms, two of you." MS

210.12 of] *omit* H, A1
210.15 preferable] preferably MS
210.19 lead.] lead. The camp in fact suggested Valley Forge to one's mind. It was not to be im-

agined that rational beings would wilfully endure such environment even for a short time and it was far beyond all human reckoning to concieve a number of creatures who would consider everything delightful. MS

210.20 arrived] arriving MS
210.23 which had a hole from] from a hole in MS
210.25 he asked.] *omit* MS
210.27 peremptorily] peremporily MS
210.33 Now] No, now MS
211.3   chief] stern chief MS
211.6   what] that H, A1
211.11 very] *omit* MS
211.11 *me*] Me MS; me H, A1
Manuscript wanting

THE FIGHT (MS)

216.0   I] *omit* MS
216.12 near] about MS
217.3   How'd] How d' H, A1
219.21; 221.32 toward] towards A1
219.25 II] Chapter II MS
220.6   and] but MS
221.3–4 cast away] castaway MS
221.9   sort] sorts MS
222.6   in] at H, A1
222.30; 223.4 toward] towards A1

222.33 "Oh (*no* ¶)] ¶ H, A1
222.34 Small (*no* ¶)] ¶ H, A1
223.2   "Oh (*no* ¶)] ¶ H, A1
223.3   feller!"] feller! Jimmie, here he is!" MS
223.27+1 III] Chapter III MS
223.32 of] for MS
224.19 be probably] probably be H, A1
225.9   could not] couldn't MS
225.22 But (*no* ¶)] ¶ H, A1

THE CITY URCHIN AND THE CHASTE VILLAGERS (MS)

[Edith Richie's *hand*]
228.6   those] these MS
228.29 is] was A1
228.35 He] Johnnie Hedge MS
228.38–39 Dalzel and these] Dalzel. There were not many boys in the school who could whip Willie Dalzell and these MS
229.4   most] that most MS
229.5   desire] desires MS
229.6   not known] unknown MS
229.6   could] would MS
229.19 And] *omit* MS
229.21 A] The MS
229.21–23 supremacy . . . tribe.]

supremacy was fought out in the country of the tribe which had been headed by Willie Dalzell. MS
229.27 was] is MS
229.32 jauntily careering] officiating MS
229.33 gallows] gallous MS-A1
229.37 that] which MS
229.37 was] is MS
230.3   part] place MS
230.12 was . . . applicant] were no applicants MS
230.21 of a fashion] of fashion H, A1

230.31   "Who (*no* ¶)] ¶ H, A1
230.33   Wasn't] Warn't MS
231.7   of a] of MS
231.15   ¹it] as MS
231.15   that] *omit* MS
231.25   toward] towards H, A1
[Stephen Crane's *hand*]
231.29   whitened] reddened MS
232.10   "Nig-ger-r-r (*no* ¶)] ¶ H,
A1

232.12   "'Pears (*no* ¶)] ¶ H, A1
232.12   unnerstan'] understan' H,
A1
232.18   "I (*no* ¶)] ¶ H, A1
232.21   'im] 'em MS
232.32   toward] towards A1
233.1,32   *me*] ME MS
233.6   the] *omit* MS
233.15   down] *omit* MS
233.32   if] *omit* MS

A Little Pilgrim (MS)

235.0   PILGRIM]   PILGRIMAGE
MS, A1
235.10   in a] in A1
235.12   distress] pain MS, A1
235.21;   236.10   Prespterterian]
Presbyterian A1
235.23   victims] victim A1
235.24   denominations] denomina-
tion A1
235.25   ever you] you ever A1
236.3,5   Big Progressive] Dutch
Reformed MS
236.12   Trescott] Again Trescott
MS
236.12   once more] *omit* MS
236.16,19,28   Big   Progressive]
Dutch Reformed MS
236.24–25   Prespterterian] Presbyterian A1

237.7   friend] friends A1
237.11   white] fat white MS, A1
237.14   dishonor.] dishonor, a man
indeed with beautiful fat [flat
A1] hands who waved them in
greasy victorious beneficence
over a crowd of children. MS,
A1
237.20   a deeply]   an oily   and
deeply MS, A1
237.21   The (*no* ¶)] ¶ H
237.36   the work] her work A1, H
238.1–2   at the story] *omit* MS, A1
238.14   knew] know H
239.8   the superintendent] the fat
hand of the superintendant MS,
A1 [superintendent]

ALTERATIONS IN THE MANUSCRIPTS

[NOTE: With the exceptions noted below, all alterations made in the manuscripts during their inscription or review are described here. The exceptions are as follows: (1) letters or words that have been mended or traced over for clarity without alteration of the original; (2) interlineations that repeat in a more clearly written form the identical original; and (3) deletions, mendings, or readings under alterations that could not be read. In this last connection, empty square brackets signify one or more illegible letters. Letters within square brackets are conjectural on some evidence and hence not wholly certain. In the descriptions of manuscript alterations, *above* means 'interlined' and *over* means 'in the same space.' The presence of a caret is always noticed.]

THE ANGEL-CHILD

129.2 warm] *interlined above deleted* 'summer'

129.5 citizens] *interlined above deleted* 'people'

129.7 through] *followed by deleted* 'which'

129.9 at blinding noon] *interlined with a caret before deleted interlined* 'at noon'

129.13 painter] *interlined above deleted* 'artist'; *the 'n' of 'an' has been deleted*

129.13 high degree.] *interlined above deleted* 'reputation.'

129.13 almost] *preceded by deleted* 'everybody'

129.17 looking] *followed by deleted* 'one'

129.18 he] *interlined with a caret*

129.23 They] *preceded by deleted* 'They'

129.24 confounded] *preceded by deleted* 'con-' |

129.27 It] *preceded by deleted* 'She'

130.2 embraced; in] *altered by* Cora *to* 'embraced. In'

130.5 for] *followed by deleted comma*

130.13 broke] *followed by deleted* 'f through'

130.20 Dan] *preceded by deleted* 'Sidney'

130.26–27 these children] *interlined with a caret above deleted* 'they', *later followed by* 'made' *added in pencil by* Cora *above deleted* 'paid'

130.28 small] *interlined above deleted* 'little'

130.32 for] *followed by deleted* 'the ex'

130.33 children] *followed by deleted* 'much'

130.39 about] *preceded by deleted* 'upon'

131.9 resembled] *followed by deleted* 'dr'

131.15 the] *interlined*

131.17 A cent] *preceded by deleted* 'Most of these wo | won-ders'

131.20 first] *preceded by deleted* 'thou'

131.20 inspiration] *interlined above deleted* 'thought'

131.20 to satisfy] *preceded by deleted* 'get the'

131.23 somebody] *preceded by deleted* 'one'

131.29 solemn] *preceded by deleted* 'mi'

131.29 something] *interlined with a caret*

131.31 belief] *interlined above deleted* 'creed'

131.31 in] *interlined above deleted* 'of'

131.31 capacity] *followed by deleted period*

131.34 -seven] *followed by deleted quote marks*

131.37 the] *interlined with a caret*

132.4 she] *interlined with a caret*

132.6 had] *interlined with a caret*

132.7 Neeltje,] *original period deleted and comma added*

132.9 new] 'n' *written over* 'a'

132.9 opened] *interlined*

132.19 ¹the] *altered from* 'they'

132.20 lazily] *interlined with a caret above deleted* 'vaguely'

132.27 wrecking] *altered from* 'wreckage'

132.28 Syriac] *interlined above deleted* 'Hebrew'

132.31 the name] *interlined with a caret above deleted* 'it'

132.35 nickname] 'nick-' *interlined with a caret*

132.38 our] *interlined with a caret above deleted* 'her'

133.3 their] *preceded by deleted* 'there' *altered from* 'they'

133.3 small] *followed by deleted* 'little'

133.3 leader] *followed by deleted* 'wo'

133.6 want] 'wish' *interlined with a caret by* Cora *in pencil above deleted* 'want'

133.9 horse] *interlined with a caret*

133.9–10 toiled step by] *hyphen after* 'step' *deleted*

133.11 arose;] *interlined above deleted* 'could be heard;'

133.21 third] *interlined with a caret above deleted* 'other'

133.31 to them] *interlined with a caret*

133.36 ordered] *followed by deleted* 'as'

133.37 lady's-maid] *preceded by deleted* 'maid-servant'

134.1 ²girl;] *semicolon added before deleted period*

134.2 on] *followed by deleted* 'through'

134.2 ceremony] *preceded by deleted* 'ex' *and then deleted* 'plan'

134.18 grin] *preceded by deleted* 'silly' *and followed by deleted period*

134.28 let fall] 'dropped' *interlined in pencil with a caret by* Cora *above undeleted* 'let fall'

134.28 lady's-journal] *preceded by deleted* 'woman's-jou'

134.29 gripped the] *interlined with carets at different times above deleted* 'clutched both'

134.32 was] *interlined with a caret*

134.35 understand] *followed by deleted* 'at all'

134.35 of it] *interlined with a caret*

135.4 and] *interlined above deleted* 'which'

135.9 which] *interlined with a caret above deleted* 'that'

135.11 look] *final* 'ed' *deleted*

135.14 do] *interlined with a caret*

135.15 arose] *interlined with a caret*

135.23 meantime] *final* 's' *deleted*

135.29 was] *followed by deleted* 'out'

135.32 And] *followed by interlined pencil* 'then' *in* Cora's *hand*

135.35 was] *interlined with a caret*

135.37 excitement] 'horror' *written in pencil by* Cora *below deleted* 'excitement'

135.38 he] *preceding 's' deleted*

136.1 gasped] *interlined above deleted* 'cried'

136.7,8 what] *interlined with a caret*

136.8 mother of] *followed by deleted* 'the angel'

136.9 -child?] *question mark altered from period*

136.9 herself?] *question mark altered from period*

136.10 With] *preceded by deleted* 'Of course'

136.14 Earl] *interlined above deleted* 'Phelps'

136.17 mother] *followed by deleted* 'over th'

136.18 But the] *originally* 'they' *but* 'y' *deleted and followed by* 'main', *also deleted*

136.22 ²was] *interlined with a caret*

136.24 the one] *interlined with a caret*

136.28 Neeltje.] *period altered from exclamation point*

136.29 He] *preceded by deleted* 'he'

137.1 washin'] *interlined above deleted* 'watchin' '

137.1 church] *preceded by deleted* 'short'

137.4 the] *interlined*

137.6 wouldn't] *followed by deleted* 'do'

137.6 kids.] *preceded by deleted* 'h' *and followed by deleted* 'heads'

137.7 kickin'] *altered from* 'kicking'

137.10 above] *interlined above deleted* 'upon'

137.12 ¹that] *followed by deleted* 'to disaster'

137.12 finality] *followed by deleted* 'an'

137.16 the rains] 'the' *interlined with a caret*

137.19 five] *preceded by deleted* 'th'

137.19 ¹her] *followed by deleted* 'that'

137.20 with] *preceded in MS by* 'that' *interlined with a caret*

137.22 that] *followed by deleted* 'neve'

137.24 all] *interlined with a caret*

137.25 "My] *altered from* 'Her' *and quote added*

LYNX-HUNTING

(All alterations are in the blue ink of the text unless otherwise specified.)

138.2 with large] *interlined above deleted* 'in a way the'

138.3 borrow] *followed by deleted* 's'

138.5 preliminary] *interlined with a caret*

138.5 accomplishment] 'ment' *interlined above deleted* 'ed'

138.6 wonders] *interlined above deleted* 'things'

138.12 ¹was] *interlined with a caret*

138.16 you] *interlined with a caret*

138.17 to] 't' *altered from original* 'i'

138.22 but] *followed by deleted* 'when'

138.24 that] *followed by deleted* 'when'

139.15 Such] *preceded by deleted* 'These'

139.25 their] *altered from* 'there'

139.30 forest] *final 's' deleted*

139.31 silence] *final 's' deleted in pencil*

139.33 wastes] *preceded by deleted* 'hills'

139.34 judged] *interlined with a caret*

139.36 they] *interlined with a caret*

140.1 thickets.] *followed by deleted* 'Willie Dalzel had been forced to read at school on the previous'

140.20 woods.] *period added and following* 'which' *deleted*

140.24 lynx] *followed by deleted period*

140.28 Eye] *followed by deleted* 'of'

140.32 They] *interlined with a caret above deleted* 'and'; *preceding period added*

141.8 often] 'this uncle' *interlined with a caret in pencil by* Cora

141.31 limits] *interlined above deleted* 'boundaries'

141.31 upper] *followed by deleted* 'limits'

142.9 two] *interlined with a caret*

142.11 It] *interlined above deleted* 'He'

142.17 with] *followed by deleted* 'he'

142.36 view] *preceded by deleted* 'idea'

142.36 boys] *interlined above deleted* 'them'

142.39 it] *interlined with a caret*

143.2 subterranean] *first* 'a' *altered from* 'e'

143.3 not] *followed by deleted* 'being'

143.6 woe] *preceded by deleted* 'hurt'

143.7 not] *interlined with a caret*

143.10 it,] *followed by deleted quote marks*

143.18 pasture] *interlined with a caret above deleted* 'farm'

143.22 man] *following comma deleted by two parallel lines*

143.34 then] *followed by deleted* 'said: "I thought she was a'

143.34 faltered] *interlined in* MS *as* 'faltered again'

THE LOVER AND THE TELL-TALE

144.4 old] *interlined with a caret above deleted* 'former'

144.6 disillusion] *final* 'ment' *deleted*

144.9 caused] *interlined above deleted* 'made'

144.9 shudders] *final* 's' *added*

144.9 Persons] *preceded by deleted* 'If an'

144.10 occupation] *final* 's' *deleted*

144.11 if] *followed by deleted* 'any of'

144.11–12 found in him] *interlined*

144.15 time] *interlined above deleted* 'hour'

144.19 his weaker] 'his' *interlined above deleted* 'their'

144.19–20 of a] 'a' *interlined with a caret*

144.21 and] *interlined with a caret*

144.22 head] *interlined with a caret*

144.23 hungry] *followed by deleted* 'little'

144.24 with] *interlined with a caret*

144.29 agitation.] *followed by deleted* 'Nor'

145.1 who] *interlined with a caret*

145.2 quiet] *interlined with a caret above deleted* 'seclusion'

145.7 with] *followed by deleted* 'a'

145.10 aisle] *preceded by deleted* 'isle f'

145.12 desk] *preceded by deleted* 'house'

145.23 pretentious] *preceded by deleted* 'luminous'

145.26 it is] *interlined with a caret*

145.35 family-circle] *hyphen added and* 'circle' *interlined*

146.4 never] *interlined with a caret*

146.4 utter] *preceded by deleted* 'speak'

146.9 pretense] *interlined in* Cora's *hand above deleted* 'in effect'

146.22 breast] *preceded by deleted* 'face'

146.23 of] *altered from* 'to'

146.31 no] *interlined with a caret*

147.1 decencies] *final* 'ies' *altered from* 'y'

147.5 shrieking] *followed by deleted* 'there'

147.14 knew] *interlined with a caret*

147.17 friend] *final* 's' *deleted*

147.20 the letter-] 'the' *interlined with a caret*

147.35 wretched] *interlined above deleted* 'poor'

147.35 bloody] *preceded by deleted* 'boys'

147.39 wrath] 'strife' *interlined by* Cora *above deleted* 'wrath'

148.2 cheek.] *preceded by deleted* 'brow.'

148.2 like] *followed by deleted* 'an [ ]'

148.7 by] *followed by deleted* 'h'

148.12 ²was] *followed by deleted* 'his'

148.20 perception] *preceded by deleted* 'perfections'

148.28 of the] *followed by deleted* 'awe of the'

149.3 the] *interlined above deleted* 'his'

149.3 knew] *interlined with a caret above deleted* 'saw'

"Showin' Off"

(*All alterations are in the blue ink of the text unless otherwise specified.*)

150.3 from] *interlined with a caret above deleted* 'in'

150.5 family] *preceded by deleted* 'tow'

150.6 upon] 'u' *altered from an undecipherable letter*

150.16 desk] *interlined with a caret*

151.8 during the night] *interlined with a caret*

151.18 not] *interlined*

151.18 Abbie] *followed by inserted period and deleted* 'at all'

151.21 notion.] *preceded by deleted* 'nothing.'

151.38 behavior] *preceded by* 'incomprehensible' *deleted by* Cora *in pencil*

152.2 dust] *preceded by deleted* 'mos'

152.4 you can] 'can' *interlined with a caret*

152.8–9 and calculated] *interlined with a caret*

152.14 retainer] 'other' *interlined by* Cora *in pencil with a caret above deleted* 'retainer'

152.19 But] 'B' *altered from* 'b'

152.30 blinded] 'ed' *interlined above deleted* 'ing'

152.34 walk.] *followed by deleted* 'It was Tommie'

152.38 Yeh] 'h' *altered from* 's'

153.1 well inside] *interlined above deleted* 'along'

153.2 display] *preceded by deleted* 'exp'

153.7 promptly] *interlined above deleted* 'simply'

153.11 nurse-] *preceded by deleted* 'nur'

153.16 appearance] *followed by deleted* 'of course'

153.20 face] *interlined above deleted* 'head'

153.22 object] *followed by deleted period*

153.23 him] *interlined with a caret*

153.24 noted] *preceded by pencil-deleted doubtful* 'd' *and followed by deleted* 'the proofs of'

153.25 And] *preceded by deleted* 'B'

153.27 eye] *interlined with a caret*
153.28 gave] *followed by deleted* 'him'
153.30 a boy] *interlined with a caret*
153.36 He] *followed by deleted* 'had'
153.39 brightly] *deleted by* Cora *in pencil*
154.2 as] *followed by deleted* 'his'
154.9 wish] *interlined above deleted* 'want'
154.14 that?] *question mark altered from period*
154.22 but] *followed by deleted* 'he'
154.28 little] *followed by deleted* 'J'
154.32 Jimmie] *interlined above deleted* 'Horace'
154.39 fast!] *exclamation point altered from period*
155.2 Ain't] 'A' *altered from* 'W'
155.9 't all] 'at' *deleted and* 't' *prefixed to* 'all'
155.10 ¹fast] *followed by deleted* 'at'
155.11 Clarence?] *question mark altered from period*
155.12 nodded] *interlined*

155.23 that] *added in left margin*
155.32 s'pose] *preceded by deleted* 'suppose'
155.36 you] *added later in left margin*
156.4 ridicule] *preceded by deleted* 'derision'
156.8 The] *followed by deleted* 'real but heretofore'
156.9 neighborhood's] *second* 'h' *altered from* 's'
156.9 superficial] *interlined with a caret above deleted* 'ho'
156.13 Jimmie] *preceded by deleted* 'The latter called'
156.15 nose] *final* 's' *deleted*
156.28 Jimmie] *final* 's' *deleted*
156.30 gallant] *interlined above deleted* 'daring'
156.38 The start . . . accident.] *interlined*
156.39 calamity] *interlined with a caret above deleted* 'precipitated accident' *in which* 'it' *is interlined with a caret after the second* 'p'
157.1 Horace] *interlined with a caret*
157.5 Horace] *followed by deleted* 'pus'

Making an Orator

(*In* Cora's *section the corrections are in blue ink but with a different pen from the initial inscription; in* Stephen's *section the corrections are in black and with the same pen unless otherwise specified.*)

[Cora's *inscription*]
158.4 orators] 'a' *altered from* 'o'
158.5 boys] *interlined by* SC *above deleted* 'lads'
158.5 girls] *interlined by* SC *above deleted* 'lassies'
158.6 literature] *preceded by deleted* 'stock'
158.6 mid-century.] *interlined by* SC *above deleted* 'time.'
158.7 who] *interlined with a caret*
158.8–9 the power of speech] *interlined by* SC *above deleted* 'impression'

158.12 many] *interlined by* SC *with a caret*
158.15 promoted] *interlined by* SC *above deleted* 'permoted' *which had been preceded by deleted* 'pro' *altered from* 'per'
158.17 classic] *interlined by* SC *above deleted* 'classical' *altered by* Cora *from* 'classicle'
158.20 torture] *interlined by* SC *above deleted* 'danger'
158.29 passive] *first* 's' *interlined by* SC *with a caret*

158.30 Charge] 'C' *altered from* 'c'

158.30–31 Brigade:] *following quotes deleted*

159.5 might] *interlined by* SC *above deleted* 'would', *after which he deleted* 'probably' *following* 'have'

159.6 he] *followed by a deleted word not to be read*

159.7 were] *followed by* SC *deleted* 'apparently'

159.9 Friday] 'F' *altered from* 'f' *by* SC

159.13 initials] *altered from* "innitals' *by deleting second* 'n' *in pencil and adding second* 'i'

159.16 caused] *interlined by* SC *above deleted* 'moved'

159.22 the first] *interlined with a caret by* Cora

159.26–27 miraculously] 'i' *altered from* 'a'

159.29 Thursday] *preceded by deleted* 'the'

160.1 The] 'T' *altered from* 't'

160.2 arithmetic] 'a' *altered from* 'A'

160.6 message] *preceding* 'cryptic' *interlined for clarity by* SC *above mended* 'criptic'

160.7 him.] *in the following excision in* H *from MS,* SC *interlined* 'dream' *above deleted* 'thought', 'convulsion' *above deleted* 'convultion', *and* 'attack' *above deleted* 'come to';* Cora *followed deleted* 'forthy' *with* 'frothy'

160.8 inexorably] *interlined by* SC *above deleted* 'inevitably'

160.11 maples] *preceded by deleted* 'M'

160.15 to] *followed by deleted* 'take'

[Stephen's *inscription*]

160.23 that] *preceded by deleted* 'with'

160.26 Her] *altered from* 'His'

160.27 of Irishmen] *interlined with a caret*

160.28 hundred] *interlined above deleted* 'thousand'

160.28 their] *added later in left margin*

160.33 Her] *altered from* 'her'

160.37 Glenmorganshire] 'o' *after* 'Glen' *deleted*

161.6 whisperingly] *final* 'ed' *deleted and* 'ingly' *added*

161.6 reiterated] *altered from* 'reieterated'

161.10 only] *interlined in blue ink with a caret*

161.11 peasant parentage] *interlined in blue ink above deleted* 'nothing at all'

161.11 undeniably] *interlined in blue ink above deleted* 'undenyably'

161.16 thought] *preceded by deleted* 'wou'

161.18 Light] *preceded by deleted* 'L' *altered from* 'B'

161.24 He] *interlined in black with a caret above* 'He' *written over* 'It'

161.25 specifically] *interlined in blue ink above deleted* 'pacifically'

161.26 edifying] 'y' *written over second* 'f'

161.29 said] *interlined above deleted* 'siad'

161.35 ¹half] *first* 'half' *preceded by deleted* 'Hal' *and a preceding deleted quote after* 'league'

162.1 indefinitely] *altered from* 'indefinitly'

162.7 Rode] MS 'rode' *altered from* 'rowed'

162.21 league . . . league] 'L' *altered from* 'l' *in each*

162.21 leg—league,] *after* 'league' *is a deleted dash*

162.24 the] *followed by deleted* 'the'

162.33 spirit] *preceded by deleted* 'free'

163.5 boy] 'o' *interlined with a caret*

THE KNIFE

184.27 meetings] *interlined above deleted* 'corne'

184.28–29 and his shoulders shook.] *interlined with a caret above deleted period after* 'merrily'

184.30 thunderously] *interlined with a caret above deleted* 'loudly'

185.2 had] *followed by deleted doubtful* 'a'

185.3 friendship] *preceded by deleted* 'casual'

185.3 casual] *interlined with a caret above deleted* 'a'

185.6 family] *followed by deleted* 'clinging'

185.10 descendants] *followed by deleted* 'of'

185.13 even] *interlined with a caret*

185.20 spirits] *followed by deleted* 'gaine'

185.27 them,] *interlined with a caret*

185.28 After] 'A' *written over* 'T'

185.28 would] *interlined with a caret above deleted* 'who'

185.29 rectitude] *interlined with a caret above deleted* 'virtue'

185.39 too] *followed by deleted* 'many'

186.10 the] *written over* 'a'

186.10 rocky] *interlined above deleted* 'stoney'

186.10 contained] *interlined with a caret*

186.12 finally] *followed by deleted* 'containin'

186.22 air] 'ai' *written over* 'ea'

186.22 at once] *interlined with a caret*

186.22 horror] *followed by deleted* 'at once'

186.25 the] *interlined with a caret*

186.26 open] *preceded at end of previous line by deleted* 'open'

186.28 Wash'ton] *preceded by deleted* 'Washin'

186.29 fer] *preceded by deleted* 'ter'

186.33 some] *preceded by deleted* 'somethin'

187.5 judge] *interlined with a caret*

187.9 him] *interlined with a caret*

187.11 sentimental] *interlined with a caret after the deletion of interlined* 'keen' *with a caret*

187.20 unremitting] *preceded by deleted* 'unwearied'

187.20 a] *interlined with a caret*

187.21 him] *interlined with a caret*

187.28 an'body] *altered from* 'anybody'

187.31 talk] *followed by deleted* 'melons'

187.34 they] *followed by deleted* 'f'

187.39 uncomfortable] 'e' *written over* 'y'

188.1 When opposite] "When' *added in margin and* 'o' *written over* 'O'

188.5 dog,] *preceded by deleted* 'bo [ ]' *and followed by deleted* 'th'

188.10 This] *preceded by deleted* 'He'

188.18 man] *followed by deleted* 'had'

188.20 would] *followed by deleted* 'not'

188.21 incorrect] 'in' *added later*

188.21 Alek] *preceded by deleted* 'Peter'

188.22 patch] *interlined with a caret*

188.25 pickaninny] 'a' *interlined above deleted* 'in'

188.27 him] *interlined with a caret*

188.35 fore-castle] *interlined above deleted* 'foc'sele'

189.8 himself] *interlined*

189.12 point] *preceded by deleted* 'portion'

189.19 extinguish] *preceded by deleted* 'put'

189.27 arranged] *preceded by deleted* 'lay'

189.31 fade] *followed by deleted* 'out'

190.7 myriad] *preceded by deleted* 'a thousand'

190.9 climbed] *preceded by deleted* 'advanced'

190.12 the] *preceded by deleted* 'th'

190.15 fence] *followed by deleted* 'from the lane in'

190.22 Alek] *preceded by deleted* 'old'

190.26 be] *interlined with a caret*

190.26 I] *preceded by deleted* 'O'

190.29 Peter.] *period added before deleted* 'bruttally.', *the second* 't' *having earlier been deleted*

190.36 his] *preceded by deleted* 'th'

190.38 into] 'in' *added later*

191.1 mouth] *interlined above deleted* 'head'

191.3 deacon] *preceded by deleted* 'as you be' *in which* 'be' *had earlier been deleted*

191.6 soon.] *interlined above deleted* 'erlong.'

191.18–21 "Mist' . . . shook.] *horizontal lines above and below mark off this passage*

191.18 "I] *preceded by deleted* 'whereupon'

191.25 me er] *interlined with a caret above deleted* 'be'

191.32 at once] *interlined above deleted* 'at once'

191.36 roun'] 'r' *written over* 'a'

191.37 troof] *preceded by deleted* 'truf', *itself preceded by earlier deleted* 'd' '

192.2 walked] *interlined with a caret above deleted* 'went'

192.6 slink] *preceded by deleted* 'slik'

192.11 Bryant,] *comma written over a period*

192.12 marching] 'ing' *added later*

192.12 when] *preceded by deleted* 'wen'

192.15 th'] *altered from* 'the'

192.18 seh] *preceded by deleted* 'sh'

192.19 Si's] *preceded by deleted* 'the white man'

192.20 eyes] *preceded by deleted* 'white'

192.29 you] *preceded by deleted* 'I'

192.32 said] *preceded by deleted doubtful* 'a'

192.32 icy] *preceded by deleted* 'sudden'

193.1 Me?] *question mark written over exclamation point*

193.5 whose] *altered from* 'who's'

193.7 challenge] 'n' *interlined with a caret*

193.17 know] *interlined with a caret*

193.32 er] *written over* 'a'

193.39 voice] *followed by deleted* 'aga'

194.8 in perplexity] *preceded by deleted* 'perplexedly'

194.13 ain't] *preceded by deleted* 'rath'

194.15 gwine] *interlined with a caret*

THE STOVE

195.3 written] *followed by deleted* 'that'

195.3 were] *interlined with a caret*

195.18 energy] 'rg' *written over* 'n'

195.21 straighten] 'r' *interlined*

195.28 image] *followed by deleted* 'was'

196.7 a] *altered from* 'as'

196.12 And] *inserted*

196.18–19 ordinary] *followed by deleted* 'phenomenon'

196.39 station,] *followed by deleted* 'he saw'

197.4 of] *followed by deleted* 'th'

197.4 It] *preceded by deleted* 'On'

197.11 chin] *interlined with a caret above deleted* 'head'

197.17 trinket.] *preceded by deleted* 'toy.'

197.34 What] *followed by deleted* 'in'

197.35 brutally] *altered from* 'bruttaly'

198.10 the stove] *interlined with a caret above deleted* 'it'

198.11 it] *interlined with a caret*

198.18 wood.] *preceded by deleted* 'match.'

198.22 you know] *interlined above deleted* 'you | cook'

198.31 it] *interlined with a caret*

198.33 that] *interlined with a caret*

198.33 there] *followed by deleted period; then semicolon added*

198.34 and her] 'her' *preceded by deleted* 'the'

198.35 lengths] 's' *deleted and then restored*

199.4 everybody] 'body' *interlined above deleted* 'one'

199.5 wish] *preceded by deleted* 'th'

199.7 the] *interlined with a caret*

199.13 like a] *followed by deleted* 'sil'

199.19 It] *followed by deleted* 'would'

199.22 only] *interlined with a caret above deleted* 'nothing but'

199.23 the] *interlined above deleted* 'tea-'

199.29 odd] *final* 's' *deleted*

199.30 a] *interlined with a caret*

199.31 viewed,] *followed by deleted* 'quite'

200.7 in shreds] *interlined with a caret*

200.8 these] *preceded by deleted* 'these te'

200.10 the result] *preceded by deleted* 'a consp'

200.28 then] *interlined with a caret*

200.29 swing] *followed by deleted period*

201.3 extinguished] *preceded by deleted* 'put'

201.3 They] *preceded by deleted* 'Then'

201.4 carrying] *followed by deleted* 'into'

201.14 long's] *followed by deleted* 'as'

201.20 rhetoric] *period added and following* 'elocution' *deleted*

201.23 the two children] *final* 'y' *of* 'they' *deleted and* 'two children' *interlined with a caret with* 'be' *deleted before* 'children'

201.27 the game] 'the' *altered from* 'their'

201.27 the situation] 'the' *interlined with a caret*

201.28 she] *interlined above deleted* 'they'

201.31 was open] *interlined with a caret*

201.38 of] *interlined*

202.2 somethin'] *altered from* 'something'

202.5 guess.] *following quotes deleted*

202.13 the] *interlined with a caret*

202.13 Oh, bushels an'] *followed by deleted* 'busels'

202.18–19 of turnips] *interlined*

202.20 always] *followed by deleted* 'in'

202.31 ovens.] *following quotes deleted*

202.32 pan] *preceded by deleted* 'plan'

202.32 an'] *altered from* 'and'

202.36 backed] 'ed' *added*

203.1 one of] *interlined with a caret*

203.12 obediently] *preceded by deleted* 'imme'

203.21 in] *altered from* 'into'

203.36–204.1 blown in] *interlined above deleted* 'fallen'

204.4 way] *interlined with a caret*

204.8 came] *followed by deleted* 'in'

204.22 saw *altered from* 'say'

204.22 we] *interlined with a caret*

204.26 comprehended] *interlined above deleted* 'knew'

204.26 know] *interlined with a caret*

204.30 leaving] *followed by deleted* 'up'

204.31 his] *interlined above deleted* 'the'

204.35 else] *interlined with a caret*

204.37 and] *followed by deleted* 'the'

205.23 last] *followed by deleted* 'he'

205.25 perfect] *preceded by deleted* 'pure'

205.32 pasture] *interlined above deleted* 'forest'

205.32 motherhood] *followed by deleted* 'suddenly'

205.37 -child] *followed by deleted* 'with'

205.38 and pained] *interlined*

206.4 his] *followed by deleted* 'painter, lo' [*possibly* 'bo']

206.6 and] *followed by deleted* 'she'

The Trial, Execution, and Burial of Homer Phelps

207.2 the branch] *interlined with a caret above deleted* 'bough'

207.4 ice] *followed by deleted* 'like'

207.6 a] *preceded by deleted* 'an'

207.6 enclosure] *interlined above deleted* 'enclouse'

207.8 could] *followed by deleted* 'easily'

207.9 old] *followed by deleted* 'faint'

207.12 This] *preceded by deleted* quote

207.14 The hush] *interlined with a caret above deleted* 'It la'

207.16 querulous] *first* 'u' *altered in pencil from* 'e'

207.17 holler?] *question mark altered from period*

207.19–20 easy enough] *interlined above deleted* 'all right'

207.21 diff'rence] *altered during inscription from* 'difference', *the* 'r' *being drawn over* 'e'

208.9 arose] *interlined with a caret*

208.9 clamor] *preceded by deleted* 'wail'

208.10 a man] *interlined with a caret above deleted* 'Homer Phelps'

209.1 The] *preceded by deleted* 'th'

209.16 whereas] *interlined above deleted* 'while'

209.22 loosed] *preceded by deleted* 'let'; *final* 'd' *was added later*

209.31 play] *followed by interlined deleted* 'it'

209.33 You've] 'Y' *altered from doubtful* 'D'

209.34 play it] *interlined with a caret*

209.39 lad] *interlined with a caret*

210.8 awful] *preceded by deleted* 'af'

210.18 watery] *preceded by deleted* 'wa snow'

210.21 drew] *altered from* 'withdraw'

210.21 boot] *second* 'o' *altered from* 'a'

210.27 not guilty] 'guilty' *altered from* 'guiltily'

210.31 made] *followed by deleted* 'his'

210.32 wrong] *preceded by deleted* 'rig'

210.37 wait."] *interlined above a deleted quote and dash*

210.38 "Pards] *preceded by deleted* ' "Prisoner'

211.5 said] *followed by deleted* 'that there'

211.9 there] *preceded by deleted* 't'

211.9 interruption] *altered from* 'interrupted'

211.16   Prisoner,] *followed by deleted* 'at the bar'

211.16   guilty?] *question mark altered from period*

211.19   chief] *interlined above deleted* 'judge'

211.20   glance] *added in left margin*

The Fight

216.1   the   neighborhood] *interlined with a caret above deleted* 'Whilomville'

216.4   time] *followed by deleted* 'or even'

216.8   cellar] *final* 's' *deleted in black ink*

216.9   of] *followed by deleted* 'th an'

216.10   men] *followed by deleted* 'deep'

216.10   dim] *interlined with a caret*

216.20   time] *followed by a comma deleted in black ink*

216.20   his] *interlined with a caret*

216.25   asked] *preceded by deleted* 'demande' *and followed by deleted* 'Jim'

216.30   proprietary] *preceded by deleted* 'way.'

217.16   steady] *preceded by deleted* 'study.'

217.18   circular] *preceded by deleted* 'circle'

217.32   second section] *followed by deleted* 'did not co[mst]' OR 'co[nist]'

217.37   pause] *preceded by deleted* 'period of hesit'

217.38   lick] *interlined above deleted* 'like'

218.1   Trescott] *followed by deleted* 'whi'

218.13   yelled] *interlined with a caret*

218.15   you! . . . aw!] *exclamations altered from periods*

218.18   simply] *interlined*

218.28   victims] *preceded by deleted* 'boys'

218.31   ferocious] *interlined above deleted* 'bloody-minded'

218.32   learn] *final* 'ed' *deleted*

218.34   displayed] 'di' *written over doubtful* 'es' *or* 'ex'

219.3   there] *followed by deleted* 'appeared'

219.6   thrash] *followed by deleted* 'his equals'

219.13   Whilomville] *preceded by deleted* 'crowd.' *The* 'W' *written over doubtful* 'B'

219.22   gloomy] *preceded by deleted* 'glooml' *and the start of* 'y'

219.23–24   environment's] *followed by deleted* 'palpable'

219.26   Hedge] *interlined with a caret*

219.27   school] *preceded by deleted* 'public'

220.2   respected] *preceded by deleted* 'requested'

220.11   sent] *followed by deleted* 'a'

220.12   books] *interlined with a caret*

220.12   selected] *preceded by deleted* 'approval'

220.18   Mother] 'M' *altered from* 'm'

220.19   properly] *followed by deleted* 'succeed'

220.20   should] *altered from* 'would'

220.20   Henry's] *interlined above deleted* 'John's'

220.23   Alone] *preceded by deleted* 'He had to'

220.27   support] *interlined above deleted* 'admire'

220.31   in any case.] *interlined with a caret that deleted period after* 'freely'

220.34   a special] *interlined above deleted* 'any'

220.38   were] *followed by deleted* 'these strata of'

221.1 nose] *interlined above deleted* 'ear'

221.15 espied] *followed by deleted* 'the strange'

221.35 jogerfre] 'j' *altered from* 'g'

221.39 unto] *interlined above deleted* 'in to' *with* 'u' *altered from* 'i' *in pencil*

221.39 As] *followed by deleted* 'bett'

222.8 by] *followed by* 'other' *deleted in pencil*

222.23 around] *followed by deleted* 'w'

222.24 teacher] *followed by deleted* 'must'

222.36 ²was] *preceded by deleted* 'ev'

222.39 disgrace] *interlined above deleted* 'shame'

223.35 finally] *followed by deleted* 'came out'

224.13 not] *followed by deleted* 'to'

224.19 probably] *followed by deleted* 'be'

224.19 mopped] *first* 'p' *added in pencil, and the* 'o' *strengthened*

224.25 bloody] *followed by deleted* '; if'

225.4 small] *interlined with a caret*

225.4 an] *interlined with a caret*

225.5 was] *preceded by deleted* 'had'

225.10 have] *followed by deleted* 'been'

225.13 ²the] *altered from* 'their'

225.25 too] *final* 'o' *added in pencil*

225.35 it] 't' *altered from* 'n'

226.3 he] *preceded by deleted* 'but'

The City Urchin and the Chaste Villagers

[Edith Richie's *hand, including alterations*]

227.7 adherence] *altered from* 'adherents'

227.15 coigns] 'gn' *altered from one or more illegible letters*

227.29 pride,] *comma inserted before deleted period*

228.2 together] *interlined above deleted* 'toward each other'

228.24 way,] *comma inserted before deleted period*

229.14 remnants] *preceded by deleted* 'the'

229.27 of the] *followed by deleted* 'oth'; 'of' *written over* 'to'

230.7 opened] *interlined above deleted* 'took place'

230.24 a] *inserted before deleted* 'the'

230.33 Wasn't] 's' *just possibly altered from* 'r'

230.36 goin'] *altered from* 'going'

230.39 stricken] *preceded by deleted* 'horr'

231.3 Got] *preceded by deleted* 'I've'; 'G' *altered from* 'g'

231.9 bloodless] *following comma deleted*

231.19 in] *followed by deleted* 'a'

231.19 bear-cub] *followed by deleted* 'method'

231.22 eye.] *followed by deleted* 'Pete'

[Stephen Crane's *hand*]

231.25 yere?] *question mark altered from period*

231.30 fiercely] *first* 'e' *written over* 'r'

231.32 him] *interlined with a caret*

231.33 fended] *altered from* 'fending'

231.34 "I'se] *preceded by altered* ' "Why?" sa'

232.1 you?] *question mark altered from period*

232.3 nachually] *preceded by deleted* 'nachur-'|

232.3 damnearkill] 'n' *deleted between* 'm' *and* 'n'

232.4 like] *interlined with a caret*
232.5 know] *interlined with a caret*
232.6 round] *preceded by deleted* 'a'
232.6 er-] *interlined*
232.7 or] *altered from* 'er'
232.8 placed] *preceded by deleted* 'reach'
232.10 at] *altered in pencil from* 'to'
232.24 whose] *altered from* 'who'se'
232.28 could] *interlined with a caret*
232.33 he] *interlined with a caret*
233.5 I'm] ''m' *inserted*
233.6 warily] *followed by deleted period*
233.9 motion] *followed by pencil-deleted final* 's'
233.10 I'll] *preceded by deleted* 'We'
233.12 not] *interlined with a caret but in black ink*

233.12 Willie] *preceded by deleted* 'Jimmie'
233.13 away] *followed by deleted doubtful* 'k'
233.13 up] *interlined with a caret*
233.17 startling] *altered from* 'startled'
233.17 extent,] *followed by deleted* 'while his'
233.21 really] *interlined with a caret;* 'really' *is deleted after* 'been'
233.25 yelled] *preceded by deleted* 'crie'
233.29 don't] *interlined with a caret*
233.32 any] *interlined above deleted* 'even' *or* 'ever'
233.36 say:] *colon inserted before deleted final* 's'
234.2 mother] *preceded by deleted* 'g'
234.2 Still] 'S' *altered from* 'H'
234.4 succeeded] *followed by pencil-deleted* 'two'

A LITTLE PILGRIM

235.1 minds] *interlined above deleted* 'intellects'
235.5 used] *followed by deleted* 'to'
235.11 use] *interlined with a caret above deleted* 'application'
235.25 you] *interlined above deleted* 'the world'
235.25 saw] *followed by deleted period and quote*
235.26 greatly] *interlined above deleted* 'much'
236.10 what] *interlined above deleted* 'that'
236.19 Big Progressive] MS *reading* 'Dutch Reformed' *is preceded by deleted* 'Presbyterian'
236.23 greeted] *preceded by deleted* 'gre'
236.32 good] *interlined above deleted* 'changed' *which is interlined above deleted* 'good'

236.33 show] *followed by deleted very doubtful* 'a'
237.1 but] *interlined with a caret*
237.3 -School] 'S' *altered from* 's'
237.8 with] *interlined with a caret*
237.16 superintendent] *first* 't' *altered from* 'd'
237.16 might] *followed by deleted* 'the'
237.21 trembling] *preceded by deleted* 'ter'
237.27 fourth] *interlined above deleted* 'third'
238.3 a] *interlined with a caret*
238.11 gazed] *interlined above deleted* 'looked'
238.12 stirred] *followed by deleted doubtful period*
238.17 patience] *interlined above deleted* 'charity'
238.18 patient] *interlined with a caret above deleted* 'charitable'

238.18 Sin] *preceded by deleted* 'Crime'

238.20 it?] *question mark followed by deleted quote*

238.25 temple] 't' *altered from* 'T'

238.28 of the class] *interlined with a caret*

238.32 much] *preceded by deleted* 'greatly'

238.33 looked] 'ed' *inserted*

238.36 virtue] *preceded by deleted* 'one'

238.38 rank] *followed by deleted* 'this'

238.39 Bible] 'B' *altered from* 'b'

239.8 end] *preceded by deleted* 'hav'

239.9 Slowly] *followed by deleted* 'and'

239.12 Give] *preceded by deleted* 'I hav'

The University of Virginia Edition of The Works of Stephen Crane

was composed, printed, and bound by Kingsport Press, Inc., Kingsport, Tennessee. The paper is Mohawk Superfine, and the types are Primer and Chisel. Design is by Edward G. Foss.